the

POSER

a dance with time

CAS RAGUEL

The Poser
a dance with time

"What matters it how far we go,
there is another shore you know upon the other side.
… Then turn not pale but come and join the dance."

—Lewis Carroll
The Lobster Quadrille
Alice's Adventures in Wonderland

Lines of a nonsense poem launch this strange tale. Those invited to join the dance are assured there is nothing to fear because a safe shore awaits them. But—as in another child's verse, The Spider and the Fly—is the true intent of the invitation hidden? What lies in wait for those who choose to dance the dance?

A mystifying loner, Quil Doolin, travels the southwest's high desert, drawn there by a puzzling urgency. As Quil contends with a multitude of adversities, she senses strange, unnatural powers advancing, coupled with a pressing need to uncloak the mastermind behind a progression of planet shattering catastrophes. Thrust into time-bending, mythical, and out-of-this-world gambles, she runs headlong into strange beings, some allies, some foes, as she searches for *the poser*, one pretending to be someone they're not.

Much like Alice in the wonderland stories, Quil wends her way through one after another challenge in an attempt to decipher clues, find the villain, and halt the devastation. An Alice parable maybe, but be forewarned, this is *not* a child's fairytale.

*There is a moment in every dawn
when light floats,
there is the possibility of magic.
Creation holds its breath.*

−Douglas Adams
Hitchhikers Guide to the Galaxy

tick the 1st

What matters it how far we go, there is
another shore you know upon the other side.
Then turn not pale but come and join the dance.

— Lewis Carroll
Alice's Adventure in Wonderland

one

I stand in dream light, an uncertain, perhaps vulnerable space between sleep and wake. A soft gray to the east hints coming of day. The air is brittle crisp, and cold wraps a chilling arm around my shoulders. Exhaling, breath leaves my mouth like a cloud of fog. Shivering, I walk to keep from stiffening.

The sky is stunning. Nothing blocks its splendor. A mist draping the moon softens its edges, making it appear more cryptic than usual. Why is it planet Earth has the largest, most perfectly placed moon in the solar system?

The above world. My eyes roam heaven's horizons; endless diamonds pirouette on a black velvet coverlet. Trying to make out constellations, I look for my sign, Aries the Ram. There's a pattern to everything I've heard said, but the night sky seems without a plan, more a crazy quilt stitching of mismatched shapes. Where's the Ram? Unimpressive compared to other signs, Aries has only three notable stars. Why would a goat be the lead sign of the astrological calendar? Ah, there it is. Considering it from different angles, I try to make out horns, torso, legs. I don't' see a goat.

Movement draws my eyes to the far side of the creek. A rustling follows. Slipping the sidearm from its worn leather holster, I ease toward the sound, staying in shadows, waiting for the predator to reveal itself—a coyote. The devious beast glares at me with pinched eyes then slinks away. A rush of air overhead reveals another predator, a hawk, its sharp vision and talons a deadly combination. The world is made up of hunter and hunted. At times, those roles reverse.

Facing east, I welcome the sun. The orange globe changes the first gray light to persimmon and stretches slender fingers to the heavens. It's time to toss back Earth's quilt and rise. There's work to be done.

An olden mesa, the eastern sentinel, has stood watch at the morning gate since time was but a whisper. Eons of weathering show on the loyal old guard, and much of its form lay crumbled at its feet. As the sun rises, it places a haloed crown on the sentinel's head. Recognition for long years of dedication, I decide. It's a good sign.

Life returns to the high desert with the coming light. Lop-eared jackrabbits scurry about, their rapid, jerky movements catching the corners of my eyes. Like a gentle sigh, a desert wind brushes my face. The earth breathes. As the morning warms, sagebrush gifts the air with a pleasing spice. The muted green shrub is plentiful here and wraps its perfume around me. I believe it's my favorite scent.

The high desert is just that, arid land at tall elevation, seven thousand feet or thereabout. There's minimal rain and snow, but the sun does not hide here. It's present in all seasons. A challenging country, many consider it too empty and tedious to bother with. I see it differently.

I'm Quil Doolin. My proper name is Quilty Doubleheader Doolin. That's a mouthful and seldom used. The middle name draws questions. Mr. Doublehead was a Cherokee war chief and distant kin, as I was told. Thought a fierce fighter and an able leader, he was assassinated by younger leaders of his tribe. No one questions the last name, which I find curious. A Doolin relative was an outlaw, a leader of a band of thieves who robbed banks, trains, and such. At a young age, he was gunned down by a posse. A chief and a thief. I know little else about my people, and no family is left to ask. No matter. Those in the past had their day. This is my time.

I've journeyed most of my time on this earth. Not overthinking current situations, I climb in my old plane, tuck my dog in the back seat, and go in search of new places. Most recently, I landed here, the Four Corners region, so labeled as it's where four states conjoin. I never know what I'll encounter with each move and play the cards as they're dealt.

Someone comes—headlights bounce along the rutted trail that leads to me. Ejecting the magazine from the Glock, my fingers slip over each cartridge to ensure a full load. I'm a shooter, here to undergo testing. Periodically, a shooter desiring a conceal-and-carry permit must go through recertification under the judicious eye of an examiner. I'm accustomed to being tested; it doesn't bother me much. Life overall seems a test. Handed my first gun at age seven, I pretty much know how this will go. I've carried a weapon everywhere I've traveled, and that's a lot of country. As it happens, I'm on a hunt and racing the clock. Who I hunt is unclear now, but my dreams are becoming sharper, and I know I'm getting closer with every tick of time.

The examiner arrives with the sun. The day begins.

two

Quil checked her watch. She'd finished a series of shooting drills with examiner Ned Nelson and now awaited his decision. The test consisted of the standard target shooting at varying distances. Could she hit what she aimed at determined a pass or a fail. While Ned examined the target, she reloaded magazines for a 15-round .40 caliber Glock, carefully inserting cartridges to avoid a future jam. Glancing up, she saw Ned placing a finger over each hole of the target. His lips moved as he counted.

"Not bad, Quil. Twenty-three out of twenty-five in the kill zone. That passes you."

"Where was I off? I can do better. I know I can." She looked over the target, her mind replaying each shot taken. "I was a hair off the line on these two. Okay, I'll not let my concentration slip next time."

"This is a good score, and it gets you renewed. But now, I wanna try a new drill. I've drawn a vertical line from the neck down to the groin on the fella pictured on the target. You can start either at the top and move down or from the bottom and move up. It's your choice but put as many as you can on the line. And to make it more interesting, I want you to shoot from the hip. I recall you saying you'd had some training in that sometime back. Let's see what you remember."

He carried the targeted stand back to a bluff that served as catcher for spent lead. Quil pushed loose hair under her hat, tugging it down tight, and adjusted her sun shades. The wind eternally blew here, and an unexpected gust could take a hat and glasses right off a body.

Watching the young woman set up started Ned wondering on why she was so hard on herself. She was one of the best shooters he'd ever worked with, but she seemed to need perfection, hating to be out of the zone. Not a competition shooter as many women were these days, and while she said she did some game hunting, that didn't seem to be a major interest. Didn't blink an eye when he asked her to shoot from the hip, which raised a question about her intentions. Yet, he understood the need for women to feel confident in knowing they could take care of themselves, especially those who traveled alone.

"Remember, Quil. This could save your life. Focus. Squeeze easy. Don't hesitate. Don't miss. Understood?" He moved about a yard away and slightly behind her.

"Got it." Caj shoved her left foot in the sand a couple of times to stabilize her stance, blanked out everything but the thin vertical line, and fired.

Quickly retrieving the target, Ned was chuckling as he walked back. "You were on the line all the way. Good shooting. And I see you started at the groin and went up." Exhaling loudly, he muttered, "Women always start with the balls."

Laughing, they let their dogs out for a quick run as they picked up brass from the morning's shoot. Ned's yellow lab, Sadie, immediately put her nose to the ground checking for scents. Her pug, Blackbird, ran over to check on Quil's wellbeing before trailing after Sadie. She and Ned worked fast as they needed to make another appointment.

"I told Seribeth we'd meet her at the bookstore. I'll see you there."

three

Quil headed for The Poet's Corner Bookstore in Durango's old town. Passing a bank, the clock in its tower reminded her she was running late. She increased speed, passing several cars while keeping an eye out for the law. She didn't need another ticket.

She looked forward to seeing bookstore owners Inger Karlsen and Gretchen Andrews, both well-known in the poetry genre and most often referred to as *the poets* rather than by given names. She and Seribeth had joined the book study group they hosted and had become close friends with them.

Luckily, she found a parking space near the front of the store and was surprised to see all members of the study group there, some inside, some out. Taking a few seconds, she let her eyes drift one to another. She had become acquainted with most through the bookstore. Except for Seribeth Cloud of the Southern Ute Nation, they had been pulled here from other areas. She didn't believe in coincidence, at least not much, and wondered what the significance of that could be.

Ned talked with Cedric O'Malley, just inside the door. An unusual pair. Both retired law enforcement officers, the two seemed exact opposites. Ned reminded her of a good Father Christmas figure, minus the beard and round belly. Maybe it was the snow-white hair and round-framed glasses riding his ruddy cheeks. Amiable and outgoing, it was easy to see him in his role as a lay minister in his church, although his other role wasn't so easy to see. A former Marine firearms instructor, he demanded near perfection on the firing range. A pastor who taught killing. Odd.

On the other hand, Cedric reminded her of a Hell's Angels' biker who'd lost one too many bar fights. He was another whose interests didn't fit his looks. Resembling a pot-smoking relic from the hippy era, he seemed more a cerebral type who spoke little about his interests other than writing protest articles on perceived injustices. She knew little about their newest member, and wondered if he was letting them see only a veneered layer of his real self. However, she could say the same for the rest of them. Who didn't have a secret or two tucked in a back pocket?

Seribeth's laughter drew her attention to the checkout counter where Inger, waving her hands wildly about her head, held Seri's full attention. Probably telling some outlandish story as only Inger could tell. They were another contradiction. Seri's hair was so black it looks blue in a particular light, indigo blue. Her strong Native American features contrasted sharply with Inger's delicate ice-princess look.

A pack of teenage bikers arrived, surrounding Jon and Gretchen, who waited on the front sidewalk. Jon Capshaw, a tall, dark-skinned man, was a surgeon specializing in sports injuries who relocated here to be close to his chosen pastimes of skiing and biking. He often sponsored excursions for teen members of a local youth organization. His sweetheart, Gretchen, a former teacher, now tutored students in English and math in off time. The kids all accounted for, Jon rode away with his gang of rowdies. Gretchen waved them off then stopped to check her reflection in the front window before entering the store.

The dog's whine brought Quil back. Bird wanted out. She had people to charm. The personable little pup loved attention. Opening the car door, the pug charged through the front entrance, heading straight for Inger, a favorite human.

"Hi, everyone. Sorry I'm late. Had to stop to pick up a package I'm delivering. Looks like you're both ready to go."

"Ready and waiting," said Ned. "I was telling them you're legal again."

"Well, maybe I shouldn't be glad to hear that, but when we travel, I think it's good someone is armed." Seribeth wore the customary jeans, dark shirt, and clerical collar.

"Couldn't agree more," Ned replied as he and Seri headed outside.

Quil tossed Bird's travel pouch on the counter. "Food, leash, and a sleep mat, but I doubt she'll slow down enough to nap."

"That's a given as I have a youth poetry session later, but she'll be worn out and ready to sleep when you pick her up. Don't worry about her; she'll be fine. But before you go, I'd like you to spend some time with this Lewis Carroll poem. I've never covered it with my students and would like your ideas on using it in class." She laid the book on the counter.

Quil leaned over and read the title, *The Hunting of the Snark*. "That's quite a deviation from the poems you generally favor. It might be difficult for the kids you mentor, based on their age, I mean, but I'll have a look. It's been a while since I read it."

"While you're at it, I have something else for you to think on."

Quil studied her friend, wearing a bright pink t-shirt bearing the words, *Don't judge me. I was born to be AWESOME, not perfect.* The shirt suited her to a *T*. Her ability to think playfully pulled kids to her like a magnet, but she was no stranger to the dark side. A *receiver* of cosmic warnings, she experienced cryptic alerts that came either as a flash of intuition or a gripping nightmare. She'd likened it to a needle pricking the reptilian brain that monitored the flight or fight response. Either type of premonition signaled something far from pleasant was about to happen. Studying Inger's face, it was clear that she needed to talk, and Quil needed to listen.

"You know I work with fantasy, children's fairytales. Fantasy's often written in a way that masks its real purpose, such as a truth or moral lesson, and children are expected to figure that out, but I don't think they do. Are we losing the ability to discern the real from the unreal?" Not waiting for a response, Inger rattled on nonstop.

Quil wondered what had brought this on. Never surprised at curious and sometimes outrageous words leaving her mouth, it was the eyes that revealed the seriousness of those words. "Do you want me to come by later to talk about this in-depth?"

"Maybe, maybe, but for now, think about how much of today's fantasy is truly fantasy and how much is purposely spun in a fantastical fashion to bury subliminal messages. Hidden communications that readers don't consciously detect. Why would they be doing that to us? Why? Why?"

There it was. Uncontrollable trembling, unflinching eyes fixed on some unearthly demon in a bizarre universe. Inger tangled her fingers in her long hair, torturing every strand she touched, pulling it out by fistfuls. *Time to intervene.*

"What was it, a passing feeling or the other?" carefully freeing Inger's fingers from hair to stop the shredding. Instantly, fingernails dug into her palms, and she struggled not to look down to see if she was bleeding.

"The other."

"About?"

"Chickens."

"Did you say chickens?"

"Yes, chickens. Maybe it was a play on the Henny Penny story about the sky falling, but it came to me several times, and that means— You probably want details now?" She paused to take a breath, her eyes darting back-and-forth, hunting for the dementor.

"No probably about it—unless you're putting me on. Are you putting me on, Inger?" Quil asked the question, though she knew the answer. She wanted to draw Ingrid's attention away from the demonic that had a hold of her.

"Of course, I'm not putting you on. See—see, there were lots of chickens, hens, and roosters but also ducks, pheasants, geese, many different feathered fowl. And we all banded together, staring at the sky. All the feathered folk ran around in a frenzy, trying to get away from a hand holding an ax above our heads. I'm trying to get away from it too, but the others—they all, they all run away. I can't keep up. They're leaving me behind!" Inger gasped, choking breaths rattling in her throat.

"Inger, it's me, Quil. You're with me. I'll never leave you behind. Never." She shook Inger's hands, trying to bring her back. "Can you see me? Inger? Look at me."

"Wh, what! Oh, Quil, it's you." Slowly, her breathing steadied, the trembling ceased, and her hands relaxed.

"Are you okay?"

"Okay? Well, you know that's always unsettled with me. But now that I've told another *receiver*, I won't feel solely responsible for the fate of the entire fowl population. That made no sense, did it?" She laughed, trying to sluff it off, then cleared her throat. "Have you had inklings lately about something *menacing* hovering over us?"

"You took a long way around to ask your question, sugar, but you finally did ask it. My answer … well, it's impossible to miss, wouldn't you say? Is there anything else?" Inger shook her head, seeming embarrassed by the effect the foreboding had on her, or maybe she felt overly fragile in needing to tell someone about them. But she was selective in who she shared her anguish.

"You did right in telling me. I need to know these things. Why don't I stay a while, and we can talk more." Inger shook her head. "Or if you think you're okay, I can go on now so you can get back to bookstore business."

"You need to go. Ned and Seri didn't say much, but it seemed this trip you're taking is important. I'm okay. I am, and right now, I think a cup of tea would be nice." She headed for the kitchen, removing shredded hair from her shirt.

Quil noticed Inger's limp was worse today. Wrestling with the demon had put unneeded pressure on her physically. Inger was born with a damaged spine but, possessing the will of a lioness, fought against being thought disabled. Suddenly, she turned back, a question poised on her lips but said nothing.

"This stays between us. I won't' tell anyone, and I'll pick up the book when I return." She rounded the counter, following Inger to the kitchen intending to watch over her for a while, but Gretchen appeared at the doorway, gave a quick wave, and took Inger's arm. The two looked out for each other, and Quil was glad for that.

Leaving the store, Seri and Ned, with his dog, quickly got in her SUV. It was only a twenty-minute drive to the Animas Airpark, but still, she had to pull the plane out, load up, and do a pre-flight check, all of which ate time.

While driving, Qu's thoughts remained of Inger. She hated that her friend suffered so from the hauntings cast upon her. The first time she'd met the petite, blonde poet, Inger pulled Quil aside, saying, *so you're one too,* recognizing her as a *receiver*, a label for those sent information through enigmatic channels. Numerous talks followed that one as Inger wanted to assign meaning to her mental strangeness. Both declined to assign a messianic connection as to do so was not their way. Instead, Inger leaned toward being a dupe of some demented jester in a distant realm or possibly cursed for reasons not yet discovered. But Inger lived and breathed fantasy worlds, always looking for fanciful explanations for day-to-day happenings. Contrarily, Quil had lived with her strangeness since childhood and accepted it as her reality. However, Inger's vision was more than a little troubling.

Chickens? No, I don't think so.

four

As she drove into the airport, Quil saw Gene and his partner, Jessie, pulling her Cherokee 180 out of the hangar. A small airfield, it hangared only forty planes and on average saw thirty flights a day. She felt fortunate to have a hangar close to Simpson's Flying Service as the Simpsons' were the best mechanics in the region.

"Good day, pilgrims," called Gene, watching the troupe exit the car. "Glad you let me know your flight plans, Quil so we could get the bird ready."

"Thanks, appreciate the help." Retrieving a pre-flight checklist and fuel tester from the baggage hold, she started the walkaround. Gene strolled alongside her.

"Is there anything I should know about this trip? Understand you're landing at the Jim Nighthawk ranch? Be there long?"

"I don't know. Jim called Seri, asking her to get Ned and me over as early as we could get there."

"Well, you have a cell phone. Call if you need help."

"I will. Thanks, Gene."

Loaded up, the Cherokee started smoothly, and she radioed her intentions. "Cherokee 8828 Whiskey at the north hangars, taxiing to runway 19."

Quil held short on the taxiway to perform a standard engine run-up. Everything checking out okay, she gave Ned and Seri a thumbs up, and took the runway. "Cherokee 8828 Whiskey rolling on one-nine, departing to the west."

When flight was straight and level, Ned looked over his shoulder at Seri. "Still no idea what might be happening with Nighthawk?"

"Nothing. I'm as in the dark as you are. Jim said to get there quick. It sounded urgent."

About ten miles out, Quil let Jim know of their approach. "Cherokee landing Nighthawk. Circling for a windsock check."

Jim responded immediately. "Good to hear you, Cherokee. Wind is light, ten to fifteen from the southwest."

Quil set up for a landing into the wind, touched down on grass, eased back the throttle, and taxied to a metal barn serving as a hangar.

She was expecting a long stay and parked near the hangar, but Jim insisted on pulling the plane inside under cover alongside his Cessna. Often looking up at the sky, he seemed uncharacteristically nervous as he boarded them in his pickup, asking Ned to ride shotgun and pointing Seri and her to the extended cab seat. As she got in, Quil saw a rifle leaning against the front seat. After Ned secured his dog in the pickup bed, they set off cross country.

In the back, Quil quietly removed her handgun from a backpack and strapped it on, noticing Ned glancing over the seat. He nodded. Ned always wore his sidearm, a habit from law enforcement days. Moving as quietly, Seri removed two blades from her satchel and slid them into the sides of her boots. It had become clear, they had not been invited to a leisurely picnic in the country.

"We're stopping at my grandfather's place first," said Jim, without explaining why. On any other day, Jim would have been considered rude. No usual polite conversation, no customary invitation into his home, or offer of coffee. Offering guests something in the way of friendship was standard, even if it was a cup of week-old coffee or a glass of water with rust settling at the bottom.

It didn't take long to reach his grandfather Albert's home. Knowing the practice of waiting to be acknowledged and invited inside, they stood beside the truck. No courteous invitation came from Albert either. He came out of the house and immediately started conversation.

"Preacher woman, good to see you. Have you prayed to the Great One for me lately?" Seri assured him she had and gave him a quick hug.

"And you, preacher man, have you been praying too?"

"Without question, Albert. You've been in my prayers."

"Flying woman, when are you going to take me upstairs in your bird? You keep promising."

"And every time I offer, you seem to have something else to do. I'm thinking it's because you don't trust a woman behind the wheel, especially one ten thousand feet up." That brought a chuckle from the elder Ute, and the group breathed a bit easier.

No one talked as Jim drove into high desert country. If you could call it that, the road followed a creek bed with water in a few spots, typical for this time of year. The windows were open, and a slight breeze brushed Quil's face. She inhaled deeply, savoring the hint of sweet acacia growing along the creek bed. Out the window, dust devils bounce around, looking like little paintbrushes dabbing color here and there. Above, circling hawks rode air currents in a clear, cerulean sky.

"This is good country for raising stock if people limit the numbers," said Albert, at last breaking the silence. "The water goes away too fast. My neighbors run about five hundred head of Dorper, but they have problems." Quil strained her neck to see ahead, knowing the reason for this trip was about to be made known. Jim drove toward a pickup near a bend in the creek where two men waited.

Albert introduced Samuel and Lucas Yellowhand, brothers who ran the ranch they were on. Somber faced, they nodded but spoke not at all. Both carried hunting rifles and wore sidearms. Standing on top of a high berm, the brothers pointed at something below. They all hurried down the gully.

Suddenly, Sadie dropped to the ground, hackles up. Instinctively, Quil fell to a knee, a hand on her gun, her heart rate doubling.

"The dog knows this is now a place of evil," said Albert.

A woman, standing nearby, turned to face them. "I'm the local vet, Gail Wheeler. I've seen nothing like this, ever.

Lucas told me of a similar thing in Utah. I'm waiting for a callback from a vet I know up there to see if he can shed light on it. Have any of you seen the likes of this before?" She pointed to sheep in a corral as well as those in a field.

No one responded. It was too bizarre. Instead, they hung back, knowing better than to rush in right away. A wrongdoing scene was like a written page. This one was a story written by animals themselves. Retrieving her camera, Quil first took several shots capturing the broader scene, then narrowed on a corral with a fence extending across the creek, allowing penned animals to get to water. Beyond the corral was open pasture for free grazing.

After several minutes of silence, they got back to the question the vet had asked. The answer was *no;* none of them had seen anything like this. It was unnatural. The pastured sheep were fixed in place, forelegs on the ground, hind legs standing, their heads tilted back on their shoulders, looking up at the sky—hundreds of sheep, all the same.

"They look to be praying," said Ned. "Of course, that can't be."

"Or wonder-fixed," said Quil.

Three sheep in the corral were in the exact, uncanny pose. The thing that set them apart was a stripe of red paint between their ears. Quil looked around, seeing Seri close to Albert and Ned hunkered down, studying the sheep. Jim and the brothers stood back as they'd already had a good look at this.

"Strangest thing I've ever seen," said Ned. "Are they dead or frozen stiff?"

"Neither one," said the vet. "I haven't done a complete examination, but they're alive and in a trance of some kind. It's a new one for me."

"Unearthly," Quil said, walking over to Albert and Seri.

"There's more," said Albert. Thinking he meant more to the scene, Quil turned around to take a closer look.

"No sign of struggle. No tracks of predator animals coming or going. Nothing to indicate they even tried to run.

Albert, why are these three sheep separate from those in the field?”

"Let's get down what they know first," said Ned, pulling a notebook from his pocket. "When did this happen?" The brothers and Jim stood beside Ned as he wrote down their remarks.

"We found them early this morning right at dawn," said Lucas, "but we saw things last night that … well, I'll explain. Shortly before midnight, we saw a white light above this place. A green ray of some type shot down, but in a second, it was gone. The white light stayed for maybe twenty to thirty minutes. We got in a pickup and were on the way here when we saw 'em." He stopped there. The rest kept quiet, giving him time to finish what he was going to say. But he didn't.

"Saw what," Ned finally asked.

"Flying sheep," said Lucas.

Surprised, they laughed, or Ned and Quil laughed. The others stayed silent.

"You can't mean they sprouted wings and flew," said Ned.

"Let me tell it, Lucas," said Samuel. "We were on our way with every firearm we owned but braked when we saw sheep in the sky. They were flying. The other side of the berm is lower than this side. You can't see our headquarters from here because of the rise, and from the other side, we couldn't see what was happening here."

"And the light was blinding. That didn't help," said Lucas.

"That's so," agreed Samuel. "Ned, the sheep didn't sprout wings. They looked frozen—contorted! Contorted is what I meant to say. But sheep were leaving the ground and flying into the light. We're grounded in today's world, not followers of the old ways, believing in demons—"

"Might be better if you did." Albert's voice was testy.

"Anyhow," continued Samuel, "we knew we weren't prepared to deal with whatever was going on, so we went back to the house. We saw the white light go out like it was just

18

switched off, but we waited until almost dawn before coming back over here.”

“You were smart to stay away,” said Ned. “Well, uh, what agency’s conducting the official inquiry into this?”

“We called Indian Affairs. They said they’d get an agent here as soon as they could, but no one’s shown yet. Jim called the FBI.” Lucas nodded at Jim, passing the question to him.

“I tried to get the FBI out. The government men don’t show interest in investigating on reservations. That’s why we’re asking you to get involved, Ned. The people need help in figuring out who’s doing this and why. You worked a long time in law enforcement around here and helped people when they needed it. We’re hoping you’ll help now.”

Furrows lined Ned’s brow. “The FBI rarely gets involved until the local law comes up with a suspect. I’ll see what I can do, but I don’t have high expectations. Quil, loan me your camera so I can get close-ups of these sheep.” Jim and the brothers went to the open field.

Quil crossed the fencing into the corral and knelt beside one of the sheep with a painted head. Albert and Seri moved to the fence, leaning on the top rail.

“Albert, why did the penned sheep have their heads painted. And why were they kept apart from those in the field?”

“To allow breeding to firm. Rough handling can cause ewes to abort. Only bred ewes were taken. We don’t think these three took breeding, and that’s why they were left behind. The vet can tell if they took or not.”

“The flying sheep came from this pen and none from the field?”

“Fifteen ewes were taken from the corral. None from the field.”

“How far along were the ewes?” asked Seri.

“About a month, maybe some less. A full carry is five months.”

“And all the brothers saw were lights above here, no aircraft landing or taking off?” Quil climbed out of the pen, walking a short span of fencing on both sides of the gate to check for signs of ground vehicles. Hearing whining, she saw Sadie flat to the ground, her muzzle between her paws. In front of her was something hidden in deep grass. Moving closer, she saw why Sadie cried. Three dead dogs, all three decapitated. Their heads laid right in front of their shoulders like they simply fell off.

"Oh, no. I'm sorry, girl." The dog growled then whined as a traveling shadow moved toward them. Quil felt hair raise on the back of her neck.

Overhead flew a raven, its shadow slipping across the dead as if granting a final rite of passage to the small spirits. Albert began a low chant, sounding like a mournful desert wind. Seri joined him, moving from one foot to the other in pace with the lilt.

Unexpectedly, Sadie raised her nose and moved away. Quil followed to see what she was onto. The dog sniffed an area where the ground and native grasses had been disturbed. Crouching, it suddenly dawned on Quil what she was seeing.

"Ned, bring the camera! The rest of you keep your distance for now." Ned moved beside her.

"Look here. I'm pretty sure these are skid tracks of a helicopter. It must have been a heavy as the tracks are several inches deep. A strong downdraft disturbed the surrounding terrain. Rotor downwash. Let's get measurements and photos before the wind erases the tracks."

"Skids? I think you're right. Let's look around. I'll go this way." Moving cautiously, they went separate ways looking for traces of anything that could be evidence, bending over occasionally to blow grass out of crevices to see if something recognizable appeared.

"Here's something," she called. "A shoe print."

Ned continued looking while Quil took photos. "Here's another print, though it's smaller."

"Okay. I'll get pictures of all of it. Did you see any tracks around the sheep in the field?" He shook his head. Removing a tape measure from her backpack, she laid it beside the tracks to gauge size.

Ned turned his attention back to the ranchers. "Have any of you been in this area?" None had.

Quil studied the placement of the footprints beside the rotorcraft tracks. "I'm thinking two aircraft were here. Two people stood beside the craft here and watched whatever was happening to the sheep in the corral. Do any locals have helicopters, Jim? And were aircraft seen when this happened?"

"No one around here has a helicopter that I know of, but I'll ask around to be sure." The brothers said they kept watch all night and saw no aircraft of any kind.

"What about sounds? Did you hear noise like an engine, a whirring, or maybe a whistling of wind?" Again, nothing.

The screel of a hawk, flying at some distance away, reverberated through the canyons. "Aircraft make noise, especially helicopters." Stepping off the approximate diameter where the rotorcraft landed, Quil suddenly shuddered. *What am I not seeing?* Sensing eyes on her, she spun around. Albert returned her gaze and pointed to the sky. Turning a full circle, she saw nothing above them. Still, she was unnerved and rejoined the others.

"Ned, the ranchers' dogs were killed," pointing toward the deep grass. "You need to take a close look."

"All three of them," said Lucas. "We'll show you."

"Tell me about these animals, Albert. I know little about sheep."

"I'll do that," said Jim, speaking fast, his eyes on Ned and the brothers. "Dorper are raised for meat and do well in arid country. They're easier to keep than other breeds and are good producers, seldom having lambing problems. They can be bred year-round." He stopped talking, seeing Ned walking back.

"That's a shame," said Ned. "No blood. Heads severed clean as a whistle. Maybe with a laser tool? This is the dangdest thing I've ever run across."

"There may be more than this going on," said Lucas. "When I talked to the tribal police, they said they'd had an increase in missing person reports. Most young females."

"What?" said Ned. "Give me the names of those you spoke with. We need to get on this right away. I'll get in touch with agencies to see what's been reported over the past year. Contact me immediately if others like this are found. Dr. Wheeler, call me if you hear from the Utah vet or anyone else who might shed light on this." The vet took Ned's card and returned to the corral.

Back at the vehicles, Ned and the brothers exchanged contact information. Having done what could be done, Jim drove away, leaving Samuel and Lucas to watch over their stock.

Quil glanced back at the brothers standing on the rise. Heatwaves coming off the desert floor gave a distorted, ghostly appearance to the image. Two shimmering specters wanting release from earth's hold so they could rise to the heavens. The mirage traveled with her.

At Albert's home, Jim tried to convince his grandfather to go with him as he didn't want him alone. Albert stubbornly refused. "Okay, I'll get my things and come back here." Jim was noticeably irritated as he helped Albert out of the truck, the rest following to say proper goodbyes. Albert walked directly to Quil, his eyes fixed to hers.

"Star people have returned. A dark watcher hunts." He again pointed to the sky.

Icy chills moved up her spine. "Grandfather, you should stay with Jim now."

"It does not hunt me, granddaughter." He turned and walked to the house.

On the return trip to Durango, Quil's thoughts moved, not to the tranced sheep or the decapitated dogs, but the image of the two shimmering men.

A mirage ... that was not.

five

Inger's poetry class was still underway. The children sat in a semi-circle singing along with a music video of *The Lobster Quadrille* from the *Alice in Wonderland* tale. Quil waited at the doorway for the chorus to end so she could lasso Bird away from the kids.

> *Will you, won't you,*
> *will you, won't you,*
> *won't you join the dance?*

Class over and children gone, Quil retrieved the dog paraphernalia, leaning in close to hug Inger. "If you *receive* anything else, let me know right away."

"You, too, huh? Then I'm not totally mad?"

Quil grinned. "No, sugar, like the Mad Hatter, you completely bonkers. But, haven't you heard? All of the best people are." Inger threw a book at her.

"Just for that, schizoid, you have to help clean up the Nook."

Quil ran a couple of laps on the running path around her housing addition. The dark events out west dominated her ponderings.

What caused the sheep to *contort*, to borrow Samuel's word? The vet said they had been tranced. It certainly felt supernatural. But why steal pregnant sheep? And why were the dogs beheaded rather than stunned like the sheep?

The stars were coming out as she turned toward the house. The crickets' night singing brought a steadiness to the evening, yet she glanced up several times, checking what might be in the sky. Sweating and out of breath, she closed the

23

back door and kicked off her shoes. Twilight was usually a favorite time of day for her; day was done, and she was inside her haven.

"I wonder how long this *in-between* will last?" She spoke out loud to hear a voice, even her own, or to any misplaced phantoms listening from the shadows. Chuckling, she quickly glanced into dark corners, glad nothing materialized.

Her life was a series of starts and stops. It was the in-betweens that could prove interesting. She wouldn't mind staying here a while longer. She like this place, thus far at least. But she did sense a high point coming, and that meant she'd be uprooted again. But for now, she'd check things out here and deal with the stop when it came.

She poured a glass of burgundy, set it on the hearth, and started logs burning. Of a sudden, the wine gleamed like a ruby jewel on a glass pedestal.

"A sign?" She gazed into the claret. "Ruby-red. Fear is blood red." Fear was evident at the ranch out west, although no one outright spoke the word. Flying sheep and a bloodless decapitation of dogs? She understood none of it.

But fear, that she understood. In her early years, she woke afraid every day. Children don't know they're different; it takes adults to explain it to them. There were certain things that made her uncommon, things that caused problems. She wasn't quite seven when she was taken from her parents. One day, an old woman, a stranger, came into the house and said, *Don't cry no more, sugar. We'll play in the snow today, and your eyes will cool down.* When the woman carried her out, she wiped her feet on the porch. *Remember to wipe your feet when you walk away from pain, and don't ever look back.* After that, she lived in the far-back hill country with Aunt Rhody and Uncle Will, and fear did not live with them.

Bird joined her in front of the fire, as was her habit, resting her head on Quil's knee. This spirit animal was smaller than any she'd had before and not what she was expecting to get when she went to the shelter. A small black lump nestled in a flat cardboard box surrounded by five other pups, all shades of grays and browns. A blackbird in a nest of wrens.

When she stopped at the pen, the black puppy waddled over and started woofing. Every time she woofed, she jumped backward. Laughing, she'd opened the gate, and the dog crawled into her hands. She knew she need look no more—the blackbird left with her.

Her first gift was a dog—that and a rifle from Uncle Will right after she moved in with him and Aunt Rho. She remembered his words when he handed them over. *This dog is a spirit animal that knows things we don't. They're put here to help. And it's time you have a weapon. You're bound to run across meanness in the outland. We don't abide meanness.* She had traveled with a gun and a spirit companion ever since.

"Enough of this, It's time to work." Questions aplenty. Silent aircraft, one a helicopter. She knew someone at Sikorsky who might be willing to talk to her.

Who would rustle pregnant sheep? That one was beyond her. Ned was following up on the theft, so she'd leave that one for later.

Why was she requested at the Nighthawk ranch? Jim could have flown Ned to his place. She had investigative training in her field, but this was in Ned's bailiwick. He didn't need her—unless it was for aircraft information.

No, Albert was the reason for her being there. The *dark watcher* comment was for her. And why the chill, rippling her spine, when she heard his words. *Was that cold fear or an intuitive reaction?* Did Albert see the dread that swirled around her at times? He said *it* did not hunt him. Did *it* hunt her?

Her eyes moved to the stone etching on the hearth. Strange, otherworldly star people gazed back with a round object floating overhead. Some said the disk was the sun or moon; others said a UFO. The indigenous people memorialized sky visitors through their petroglyphs. Now, she doubted there were few, if any, who hadn't heard of the star people's arrival. Those who came to watch. If Albert was right and they were back, why had they returned? She would bet not purely to watch this time. Inger was right. Something menacing was looming over them, and she had a gut-wrenching feeling they were not prepared to deal with it.

"So many pieces of a puzzle. I'm tired, Bird. Let's go to bed." But that idea was erased by wind rattling the windows—a whispering wind.

"Trust your intuition, it will protect you. Fear will not. Can you tell the difference between the two? In time, the pieces of the puzzle will fit together. Perhaps you would better understand how the parts fit one to another if involved in the dance. Remain in readiness and expect others now. I'll be watching. Listen for me."

Blackbird sat staring at her face. The dog heard what she heard. And what she hear was only one of many reasons she stayed alone most of the time. She wasn't like other people and finally gave up trying to get others to understand that and accept her.

When the voice first came, it said it was there as her guide and would stay near like a tiny Gnat fly riding on her shoulder that no one else could see. As a child, she talked to it daily but seldom did now. She called it Gnat as it said it didn't have a name. She didn't know who it was she talked to. Gnat has been with her for all her remembering years, and when all was said and done, she didn't care who the voice belonged to.

"Remain in readiness. We're not going to bed just yet, Bird. I'd better take care of this now." Removing handguns and long barrels from a gun safe, she arranged them in an order she'd used for years. Handguns on one side, rifles on the other, she laid them on a soft cloth on the dining table with bore cleaners, oils, patches, and rods. Disassembling them one at a time, she started at the chamber and worked in the direction projectiles traveled. A mental checklist quickly moved her through each weapon. It wouldn't take long. She did this with regularity.

six

Having finished raking the backyard, Quil sat on the deck steps watching Bird sniffing out a trail of an unknown varmint, probably a bug. The dog knelt on her front legs, her head sideways on the grass, and hind legs standing, reminding Quil of the sheep at the Yellowhand ranch. But Blackbird wasn't tranced. Pugs were bred to be cute, and she was certainly that, but specialized breeding had caused nasal problems. She'd once measured Bird's snout, less than an inch. She had to turn her head sideways and get down close to sniff out a trail of anything. Yet, she made life work for her. Hearing her phone, she ran to get it before the caller hung up.

"Hey, Seribeth. What's up? Is that right? Now, that is interesting, and we need to follow up. To do that, we'll need a backcountry vehicle; ours might not be a good choice. Inger drives one that'll go anywhere. Sure, let's meet with them. What time? Okay, see you at the bookstore."

A few early customers had started the day well at the bookstore, meaning money was coming in. Inger and Gretchen had received an early call from Seribeth asking if she and Quil could come by to discuss something important. Of course, they agreed.

"I'm thinking of writing a poem about creation. I haven't written a poem about that or even written one having the word creation in it. Have you, Gretchen?"

Gretchen stopped unpacking boxes of books and looked at Inger; her long ashen hair draping about her shoulders resembled an ermine stole. With eyes so pale they were almost translucent, Inger gazed into far-away space none other could see. So beautiful, so talented, so deserving of good things, but fate had played a bum trick on her. Perhaps she had been granted so much, she needed something to tether her to the earth, else she'd float away with the angels, wouldn't she?

"No, I haven't. What brings *creation* to the forefront of your poetic meanderings this morning?"

"I'm not sure. It just popped into my head as things seem to do with me."

Hearing the bell jingle on the front door, they smiled as Seribeth entered with Quil and Blackbird close behind.

"Hey, you two, "said Gretchen. "You're in time for tea. Let's go to the kitchen. Your call this morning has us curious. What's the topic?"

"Having babies," said Quil.

"Well, forget the tea. This calls for alcohol," laughed Inger as they gathered around the kitchen table.

"Hang on. I mean sheep having babies, specifically bred ewes stolen from the ranchers we met with yesterday. Here's the question. Of all things to rustle, why would anyone steal fifteen pregnant sheep out of hundreds? And all of that happened in thirty minutes."

"A mystery to solve," said Gretchen. "Give us the details."

"That's just it; there are no details," said Quil. "Well, other than the beheadings. Oh, and all five hundred sheep were frozen in a praying position with heads raised as if giving reverence to a higher power."

"Praying sheep?" said Inger. "And did you say heads were chopped off?"

"Yeah, I'm afraid so. But sliced off not chopped off. Those losing heads were herd dogs there to protect the sheep. What's odd, too, is three ewes were left behind as breeding didn't take with them. But you haven't heard all of the strangeness to this. Seri, were you puzzled by what the ranchers said?"

"Puzzled, yeah. And it's scary. That's the reason we wanted to talk with you two. After I got back to Ignacio yesterday, I made several calls as I had heard rumors of bright lights being spotted in out-of-the-way places. The strangeness yesterday might fit right in."

"What strangeness?" asked Inger.

"Flying sheep," said Quil, looking at Seri as Inger and Gretchen broke into laughter.

"Oh, for Pete's sake," said Gretchen. "You had us going with that one." Quil and Seri remained quiet, their faces serious. "You mean sheep flew?"

"We didn't see it," said Seri, 'but two ranchers witnessed it, and I believed them. Didn't you, Quil?"

"Yes, I did. Seeing sheep in the air, they went back to the house and waited for daybreak."

"They were frightened, and nothing's wrong with that," said Seri. "Anyway, I have locations of places where strange lights have been seen. One is in mountainous terrain south of Pagosa Springs and Bayfield, although it might or might not involve flying sheep."

"Perhaps this need not be as confounding as it appears," said Quil. "Seri, you heard Jim talking about the Dorper sheep being good producers and able to be bred year-round. That could play a part in this. Why? Because there's no earthly reason to steal pregnant sheep when they can be raised or bought. But what about an unearthly reason? What if the sheep were taken for some kind of secret genetic experiment—"

"Unearthly? Experiments?" interrupted Gretchen. "As in that ancient alien nonsense. Of course, you had to go there, Quil."

"Wait, Gretchen," said Seri. "Albert said star people had returned. Star people refer to stellar travelers."

"Star people, stellar travelers, ancient aliens, it doesn't matter what you call it. It's all rubbish, and it will not be discussed here."

"Now, hold on," said Quil. "Historical writings support gene-altering of humans by star beings, though, initially, it was only because they needed a worker race."

"Don't you know that's purposeful deception on the part of non-believers intent on undermining the foundation of religion?" Gretchen's fingernails nervously tapped the table.

"No, I don't know that," said Quil, her voice tense. "And I'm not solely referring to the ancient alien *rubbish*, as you called it. As we know them today, humans could have been bio-engineered by scientists from another planet. Humans are conducting genetic experiments now, including cloning. That doesn't take away from the existence of a supreme being. Eventually, there has to be a coming together of science and faith. Can't you see that?"

"And I've told you before, Gretchen," said Seri, "my people believe we *were* brought here from somewhere else. Just because we were created elsewhere and brought in doesn't make us rubbish. I'm insulted."

"Well, you can believe that if you wish, but we won't talk about it here. We're not a bunch of cooked-up lab freaks or an alien worker race bussed in from somewhere else in the universe!"

"What's happening here!" Inger slammed both palms on the table. "Why are you being such a turd today, Gretchen? You're taking this personally, and you shouldn't. As open-minded individuals, we welcome opinions—without condemnation—just as we encourage thinking outside the box. And I must ask you, my friend, could it be you've boxed yourself? Now, listen, all of you. We've hashed this through many, many times. We simply have to accept that our beliefs differ." The room became ultra-quiet.

"I agree with you, Inger," said Quil. "Seri and I will leave if you want. Although, I'd like to know how sheep can fly—if they do. Many governments are involved in impulse forms of power that could provide an answer. And Seri did put some effort into this matter and wanted you included in whatever we might choose to do."

"We can do it on our own," said Seri, abruptly standing.

"No, wait," said Gretchen, "wait a minute, please. I shouldn't have gotten bent out of shape the way I did. And I think I do feel boxed. It's not that I don't love our bookstore, Inger, I do. But our routine is the same day in day out. I unbox books, shelve books, order, purchase, and account for books. I need a change, and frankly, I wouldn't mind seeing a sheep fly." The room grew quiet again.

"Seri, where were those lights spotted?" Inger said, squeezing Gretchen's hand.

"Give me a minute." Seri ran out of the store, quickly returning with a map.

Smiles reappeared and excitement grew as weekend plans progressed. *Okay, Gnat, I call this acting on intuition. Let's see about joining that dance.*

Hearing the doorbell jingle, Gretchen rushed to the front to attend to customers but instead found Jon and Cedric. As they walked back to the kitchen, both were listening to Gretchen's excited jabbering when, suddenly, Cedric turned and went back to the front, holding his cell phone. In mere minutes, Ned showed up, and the questioning commenced.

"Quil, am I understanding this right?" said Ned. "You're going the top of an isolated mountain, searching for bright lights and anything else that might wander into view—including aliens?"

"Yeah, aliens," snorted Cedric. "Obviously, this was not well thought through. I expected more professionalism from you, Quil," jabbing a finger at her face. "You could jeopardize lives with a move like that. You don't know what's out there, and neither do you, Seribeth." He jabbed the same finger at Seri.

"I was raised here, Ned," said Seri, ignoring Cedric, "and an alien base near Dulce has been talked about for decades. Yesterday, Albert said the star people had returned. The two could be connected."

"Not that Dulce crap again." Ned shook his head, a look of disbelief on his face.

"You bet it's crap," snarled Cedric. "Aliens? Come on, Seri, you can't be serious. This whole idea is laughable, and so are all of you."

"Hold on!" Inger shouted. "You're trying to strong-arm us into doing things your way. We don't buy into that macho male *crap*, so stop dangling your dicks in front of us. We resent being treated like helpless females. Or worse, like hapless twits who never had an intelligent thought between the four of us."

"Okay, cool the tempers," said Jon, "and think about what you're proposing." Parading before the women, he looked to be presenting a final argument to a jury, "From what I've heard, you're thinking of this as merely a *fun* getaway without considering the negatives. Those negatives include, but may not be limited to, strange green beams, mysterious aircraft, hypnotized livestock, and decapitated dogs. Now, I ask you, why would you want to wade into the middle of something like that? The intelligent answer, of course, is you wouldn't. So after listening to all we've said, we're sure you'll come to the correct decision and cancel the proposed trip."

"Well, think again, you prancing prick!" Inger barked. "It'll take more than braying jackasses to change our minds!"

"You've all gone nuts," said Cedric, "and I say you're not going."

"What makes you think you're calling the shots, sphincter face!" Inger jabbed a finger at his face.

"I've got this, Inger," said Quil, speaking calmly.

"She's got this." Inger motioned to Quil.

Quil had worked hard to tame her prominent twang and lazy speech. But today, she ushered it all through the front door.

"What say we take a deep breath. It may not show, but we do appreciate the concern you spoke. And we can agree that perhaps, and I say *perhaps,* there might be a thing or two we didn't cover in our plannin'. But don't think just 'cause we're females, we can't handle ourselves. And we still have a day or so to go over this ag'in if we think it needs doin'. What rilin' us is you've judged us wrong without knowing the plannin' we've done." Quil leaned back in her chair, letting her eyes rest on Ned. "Plus, you inasmuch *ordered* us not to go, and as *you* know, Ned, that won't fly with me. We're goin'."

Ned opened his mouth to speak but abruptly snapped it shut. Taking a deep breath, he tried again. "Okay, I can agree with that. Why don't you tell me your plan—and I'll listen without interrupting. I'm only asking because I'm concerned for your safety. And *you* know that, Quil."

"I expect we can do that."

Seri was quick to open a map with a terrain layout. "A paved farm road off Highway 160 leads to a hunting trail across from this ranch." She tapped a finger on the map. "The trail was dragged recently to level out ruts. It is steep terrain, but the road has switchbacks to help in maneuvering the grade. It's between five to six miles to the observation site from the turnoff. An open meadow is easily seen from the selected lookout point. Elk or deer could be grazing there, but it's primarily a sheep pasture."

Gretchen took it from there. "We'll be on-site about ten. According to a meteorologist, there could be clouds but no rain's anticipated to cause a muddy trail up and back. We'll be in dark clothing for concealment, remain at a distance, and retreat at the first sign of discovery."

"I'll park on a downhill trajectory," said Inger, "and remain at the wheel on alert in case a quick getaway is needed. Gretchen will be in the car, serving as navigator."

"Quil and I'll be on the ground concealed by brush cover," added Seri. "The passenger doors will be left ajar to allow quick entry as needed."

"And we considered interior lights," said Inger. "A previous owner modified the Hummer, and I can switch those off." She looked pleased that she had thought of that.

"Who'll run the store?" asked Jon.

"We're going Sunday night. Our store's closed Sundays and Mondays. Gretchen and I can rest Monday if we're out overly late."

A sudden quiet was deafening. The women's remarks concluded, the men lowered their heads, mulling over the situation.

"And I'm bringing' all the guns I can tote," Quil said, her eyes still on Ned.

"Okay," said Ned. "It's clear you put thought into this, and it sounds … doable."

"They did do fairly good work in planning it," added Cedric.

"I agree. But I don't feel okay with you going without me. I'm a skilled shooter with firepower. I'm asking you to let me go with you."

"And me." Cedric quickly added. "I worked in undercover and stakeouts. I'm out of practice, but I have a forty-five for added firepower."

"And it'd be smart to have a doctor along just in case," said Jon.

Quil looked around the table, seeing the beginnings of smiles on the women's faces. "Inger, sugar, can you find room for these three in your Hummer?"

"Why, sho 'nuff, honey chil'. I 'spect I can—if we'uns think they'd be of some hep." The others laughed at her exaggerated mimicry of Quil.

"You talk like you got a mouth full of bees," said Quil, smiling. "And it seems we're all goin'."

seven

The day of the outing arrived. Church bells were calling as Quil drove down a street, commonly called worship drive. She was on her way to a small chapel where Seri waited. She slowed, seeing a police officer with a black armband directing cars to the curb. A double burial, two black hearses sat side-by-side in the parking lot of a large church.

As the cars carrying mourners passed, she glanced into a black limo bearing flags denoting family. Two skeletons stared back at he, their skulls draped with shrouds. Both raised bony hands, giving her the thumbs-up sign. Startled, Quil returned the thumbs up. Jerking her hand down, she shook her head and looked again. Pale faces of two elderly women bowed their heads under black mantillas. Watching the limo over her shoulder, Quil jumped when the officer tapped on the window, urging her forward.

Inside the chapel, she moved quickly to a small side pew. Seri was down front, chatting with parishioners, and waved when she saw Quil enter. Seri was often asked to be a guest pastor at regional churches. Today was the first time she'd been invited here and, as she sometimes did, asked Quil to attend with her. Quil glanced around the room. Not a large congregation, mostly Anglos. Letting go a long exhale as she sat down, she wouldn't mention the foreboding to Seri or anyone else. She never did. She filed the image away, hoping it would never find its way back to her.

Pulling a stool with her, Seri positioned it in front of the podium. "Hope you don't mind. I don't enjoy speaking from a dais." Seri was charismatic, just her presence brought smiles. Typically nervous the first time speaking at a church, she took the time to look at each person, letting them know she valued their presence. Her eyes traveled from one to the next, lastly resting it on Quil, who crossed her eyes, twitched her head like a dolt, and winked.

"I'd like to introduce the ugly, bat-faced woman in the second pew on my right. Most times, I call her my best friend and sister. Other times, I claim not to know her at all. Make welcome Quil Doolin." There was laughter as Quil stood and waved to those in the room.

"Okay. This morning, you have a choice. Some asked me to speak on the beliefs of my people. So you can hear the Ute story or a sermon titled: 'The Divisive Nature of Mankind and the Danger It Brings?' She listened to people's remarks and laughed. "It didn't take you long to make up your minds. Okay, the Ute story it is."

"In our culture, belief in a greater power rests with an individual and not so much with an organized group. In other words, church attendance isn't as relevant to us as to others. I don't believe we have to go to church to find God. The Creator is everywhere."

"The Ute, or the Nuche as we call ourselves, were the first people in these mountains. We've walked this land as far back as there is memory. We believe the Creator brought us here from somewhere else in the universe for a purpose. You may be taken aback by that comment, but the Ute are not the only indigenous people who believe they came from another place. Depending on who you talk to, you might get a slightly different version of the Ute story, but this is mine." As Seri talked, she walked back and forth before the group, at times adding animation to the telling.

"In the early days of the universe, only Sinawav, the Creator, and coyote walked the Earth. In that time, the coyote stood upright and sometimes took evening strolls with Sinawav. One day, Sinawav returned from elsewhere, carrying a bag. He told coyote to take the bag to a sacred valley and empty the bag's contents there. He cautioned coyote not to open the bag until he arrived at the destination. Coyote took the bag and while walking became curious, wanting to see what the bag held." Stopping before the congregation, Seri mimed holding a sack open and peeking inside. Unexpectedly, she leaped forward, randomly grabbing at people. Those on the front row dodged and laughed at themselves.

"To coyote's surprise, people jumped out of the sack running all directions. Coyote tried but couldn't catch any of them. Those that ran away became strangers to the Nuche, speaking different languages, and some became enemies. Coyote delivered only those left in the bag to the sacred valley. They are the Nuche people. Coyote returned the empty pouch to the Creator, saying he did as he had been told. But Sinawav knew what coyote had done and the trouble it would cause. 'No, coyote,' said Sinawav. 'you're a deceiver and have caused great problems for all the people of this land.' As punishment, from that day on the coyote has had to sneak around on all fours hiding from people and scavenging for food at night. The sneaky beast still causes trouble."

Quil grinned as hands raised. The questions were mostly the same wherever Seri spoke.

"Let me finish, please. I know many interpretations can be given that story. For me, the message is what's important. Sinawav brought us here to look after this world. It does not belong to us. We were told we could use what was here for our needs, but this planet was not to be owned. And I believe it was never intended that we be separate peoples, have different beliefs, or war against each other. People made many wrong turns in their time here by establishing conflicting political and religious paths that lead to war. There is only one God, and we should be only one people. We came together, and we must work together to heal this world. Maybe I'm too much of an idealist, but I believe we can make this a better place to live. Or maybe we need a do-over so we can try again to get things right. That's all I'll say now on our history. If you're interested, you can find out more at the cultural center in Ignacio."

Seri walked her own path, one foot on either side of an invisible line, her native culture on one side, the greater world on the other. Likewise, she found a middle path between the beliefs of her people and some of the beliefs in the larger world. Her way required strength and courage. It could work against her, but thus far, it hadn't. Seri was admired on both sides of the line. Although Quil worried for her. Messengers were not always well received.

On the way out, she asked Seri to come to her place whenever she could break free so they could go together to the bookstore, where the group was mustering.

Quil and Seri arrived at the bookstore after sunset and found the group loading the Hummer. Cedric had brought hooded binoculars he'd used on stakeouts and, as they came in, he handed them to Seri. Smiling, Seri hung them around her neck. A nice gesture, Quil thought. Looking at the activity around the room, she noticed Jon standing alone, hands shoved in his pockets, and a frown on his face. "Is something wrong, Jon?"

"I don't know, Quil. I think I feel left out. I don't have a gun and don't know what I'd do with one if I did, but still … you know."

"I brought a shotgun you can carry. It's easy to handle. I can give you a quick lesson now."

"Yeah, I'd like that."

"I'll get it." Returning, she talked while unzipping the case to remove the gun. "This is a Mossberg twenty-gauge pump-action shotgun that carries five shells. It's primarily used for bird hunting but can be effective as a defense weapon in close situations. Give me a minute while I check to see if the chamber is empty." Jon's mood, however, had done a reversal.

"I'm not carrying that." Jon crossed his arms and took a step back.

Quil wondered if he was intimidated by the weapon. "It's not difficult. Give me a few minutes to cover—"

"I said, I'm not carrying it." His attitude had turned sullen, and that confused her.

"Give me a chance—"

"Quil, look at me! I'm over six feet, and I'm black," loudly slapping his chest several times with the flat of his palms. "It's pink! P-I-N- K! Pink!"

All eyes were on her. "The stock is a rosy pink, yes, but the color isn't important—"

"Listen, you runty little she-hobbit! I'm not carrying a goddamn pink gun!" He stomped away.

Laughing, Cedric slapped his chest with both hands. "I hear ya, bro, I hear ya." If he intended humor, it fell flat, but it did start people talking.

Gretchen spoke quietly. "That was an insensitive, moronic thing to do, Jon."

"Asshole." Inger's glare was scalding.

"You are behaving like an ass." Seri gave him a chastising shake of her head.

"Oh, come on—" Jon jerked a black hooded sweater from his pack, quickly pulling it over his head.

"Well … well, those wanting a quick lesson on shotguns, come on over. And if the tall black man in the room chooses to observe, I won't object." The women huddled around Quil, following her hand movements. She looked up once, noticing Jon watching from a doorway.

"Let me try that." Inger reached for the gun. They each took turns handling the weapon, loading and racking shells into the chamber. Afterward, they broke off in twos and threes as they waited to leave. Ned and Cedric sat with Quil on the sofa.

"What're you doing with a pink shotgun?" asked Cedric.

"Short version. Several roughnecks were giving me trouble at a backcountry airstrip where I was based. I thought a shotgun might help send a message. I didn't want a pink gun. It was the only one the store had in stock, and I didn't want to wait for another to be ordered in."

"Time to roll." Inger wasn't hiding her excitement; a grin covered her entire face.

Loading the cased shotgun in the rear compartment, Ned's dog padded in, laying down beside it. Quil had left Blackbird home as she wasn't as easy-going as Sadie, plus the little dog had a problem with the concept of *quiet*. If she felt threatened, she intended for every person in the county to know it. Taking a seat, Quil listened as Cedric and Ned shared history.

"What branch were you in?"

"The Corp. I made gunnery sergeant but decided I wanted my family away from a military setting. I moved us to the Four Corners area and worked in both city and county law enforcement. But I still worked with guns as I was made a shooting instructor. I continued instructing after retiring. How about you?"

"Air Force but saw no action. They sent me to language school where I learned passable Russian and then stationed me on an island off Alaska. A cold, dismal place. Walked around the entire island the first day. I requested reassignment to anywhere there were people but was denied. I spent a year listening to Russian fishermen talking on short-wave radios with wives or other fishing boats. I didn't re-up after that and got into police work. Eventually, I was assigned to hostage negotiations and undercover work. I liked both."

"Undercover? Is that where you picked up that bushy beard and long-hair look?"

"Yeah, I liked the look and kept it after leaving undercover work. I stuck out at regional meetings; got lots of gawks."

"I have a feeling that didn't bother you at all." Ned laughed when Cedric shrugged.

eight

It was quiet at the observation site. So quiet, it was unnerving. Inger and Gretchen were inside the car parked near a downed tree that offered good cover. Both wore dark ski masks so the light wouldn't reflect off their faces. The rest were on the ground behind scrub and fallen tree limbs.

The minute they turned off the county road, the air felt oppressive, bearing down on Quil. She repeatedly scanned the sky, glancing at the others to see if they were experiencing the same edginess, but they seemed at ease. Perhaps they masked their apprehension. On the ground, she tried to relax, stretching out and leaning on her elbows.

A musky odor of damp soil rose from under the brush. Sometimes, the slightest thing could nudge a memory. Quil ran a finger through the loam, remembering tending garden with her Aunt. Their garden soil smelled rich like this. This would be just right for spring sowing. Long summers of weeding followed planting. Culling the tares, Aunt called it. Getting rid of what didn't belong. She had become good at culling tares.

Ned's dog nosed in beside her, pawing at the fresh-dug ground. Suddenly, Sadie raised her nose high, turning it one way and another. Quil hurriedly looked over the meadow but saw nothing that would cause alarm.

Then it happened. All night noises stopped. No bird calls. No insect buzzing. Nothing. Sadie whined and lowered to the ground. Quil knew what the dog smelled—fear. They all dropped low. Glancing over a shoulder, Quil saw Inger and Gretchen slide down in the seat.

The white light came in an instant. Wide-eyed, she looked at Seri. They moved their heads under branches, pulling limbs aside so they could see below.

Blinded by the light, Quil moved her eyes to the edge of the meadow—a small flock of sheep milled about there. A green flash came. The sheep dropped to their knees; their heads turned toward the light. Quil gasped, shocked at the suddenness.

No one moved. An outline of a second craft appeared silhouetted against the moonlit sky. Black and triangular, it hovered above the ground before it settled. No rotors. It wasn't a helicopter, but it had thrusters that battered the grass down in a circular pattern. No noise came from either ship. Deathly silent.

Quil saw movement in the white light above. Something was coming down. *What on earth is that! A Grey? No! It wasn't!* She had wondered if grey aliens would be a part of this and half-expected to see one. But this thing was spindly and incredibly tall, maybe eight or nine feet. A second floated down, same as the first. Pale, hairless, large eyes rimmed in black, they glided above the ground, moving directly to the sheep. *Is that music I hear?* Strange vibrating notes sounded as the aliens moved, like low registered strings, a cello or viola. The fingers! The long wispy fingers, moving like threads, created musical notes. One tall alien held a hand instrument that emitted yellow or green flickers when passed near the tranced animals. The second marked selected animals. The two worked quickly, knowing what they were after.

At the black craft, three people now stood beside it. A crimson robed figure towered over two others whose forms seemed to move in waves. A holographic image? Something felt wrong about those two. Quil sensed evil. One looked to be female with bright, orange-red hair. She couldn't see the details of the other. Leaving the red-cloaked figure at the ship, they joined the wispy ones huddled over sheep. They seemed to be arguing with the tall aliens.

Squinting, Quil forced her eyes to pierce the moving veil surrounding the shorter ones. *No! That's not possible! Green—snakes! Serpents people!* Both had serpent forms, yet not the same. The red-headed one had a wedge-shaped head; the other's head was long and slender.

Abruptly, the white light swept to the far side of the meadow. *Oh, no!* Two men climbed out of a brush hunting blind and ran. Caught in the light, they shimmered as they were lifted. The light released them to the ground near the black airship. Stunned, they struggled to get to their feet.

The red-haired serpent had a silver apparatus, holding it like a pistol. It tossed its head back and cackled, the sound booming through the valley. Running to one of the men, with a single swipe, she severed his arm. He fell, screaming. Insane laughter erupted from both serpents. Kneeling at his side, the second man pulled him into his arms. On knees, they begged to be let go. Still laughing, the serpent ran to the second man and made another slicing motion. The man's head bounced when it hit the ground. In a frenzy, the snakeheads kicked it around like a ball.

The man with the severed arm struggled to his feet, gazing down at his fallen comrade. He would not beg again. This was his dying day. He knew that. Facing the tall aliens, he yelled. "You bastards! Kill me! Make it quick! Kill me!" The tall ones backed away, pointing up to the hovering ship.

But it was the hunter's last act on this Earth that chilled Quil's blood. He looked straight up the mountain—at them. *He knows we're here!* A green beam hit him, and he stumbled, trying to keep his legs under him. Slowly, he swayed and dropped to his knees. Again, he looked up as if trying to find someone. *I swear he's looking straight at me!* Another beam hit him, and he crumpled to the grass. Never again would this man struggle to stand.

The figure in the crimson robe reentered to the aircraft. A fourth person, wearing a blue uniform, jumped out and, shouting, herded the serpents back inside the ship.

Then, sheep flew.

The sheep's' bodies, distorted as they were, gave an appearance of leaping from the ground with heads raised in reverence to a divine. But what spirited them away fell far short of divine. The wispy aliens followed the sheep, like shepherds tending a flock. Quil shivered as the shimmering bodies of the hunters left the earth to join the light, the severed arm and head eerily moving with them. In mere seconds, both ships were gone.

Forgive me; please forgive me. Grief flooded over her, wave on suffocating wave. She tried to draw air into her lungs but couldn't. Heart pumping against my ribs, she wanted to scream—to kill! *Remain calm,* an inner voice whispered. *But I failed them.*

An owl's screech shattered the silence. Still beside her, Sadie lifted her nose, testing the air, then skulked to the vehicle. *Get up! Get to the Hummer!* Quil struggled to get her legs under her. Grabbing a limb, she got turned around and standing. Seeing Seri trying to stand, she grabbed an arm and pulled her up. They stumbled toward the Hummer.

Quil saw the others staggering to the car. Jon got there first. The door ajar, he pulled it wide for the dog. With a backward glance to see if Ned was following, Sadie jumped inside and moved to the rear. Jon followed the dog and quickly pulled the shotgun from its case. On knees, he took rear guard.

At the door, Ned motioned them to passenger seats. Quil took the one behind Inger and Seri, the one behind her. Ned got in beside Quil, sitting on the seat's edge, while Cedric remained outside, his forty-five drawn. Using hand motions, Ned let Inger know she wasn't to start the car. He pointed to the emergency brake and then mouthed the word *neutral,* pointing to the gearshift. Nodding, Inger shifted into neutral and released the brake, but the Hummer didn't move. Inger turned questioning eyes to Ned.

Ned motioned to Cedric. Holstering his gun, Cedric drew in several breaths, placed his hands on the doorframe and lunged. Only slight movement. Jumping out of the car on her side, Quil placed hands on the door frame and nodded at Cedric. Together, they rocked the vehicle until it rolled. Back inside, she drew the Glock and took watch.

As they rolled away, some eyes searched the sky, some eyes searched for a way off the mountain of death.

Escape lay on Inger's shoulders. *I have to get off this godforsaken mountain.* Her hands gripped the steering wheel, and paralyzing fear struck, snatching her breath away. She heard a sharp intake of air. *Crap! That was me!*

A lifetime she'd fought being a cripple. But she was behind the wheel, and here she was no cripple. *I can do this.* The Hummer was rolling; she edged it onto the track.

Steering down the steep grade with no power, no lights, she stayed to the outside of the switchbacks to slow the vehicle while keeping it moving downward. Seeing the county road ahead, she turned the key. The engine growled, and she headed for the highway. The distance stretched forever. *Where is it—where, where?*

Quil wasn't looking for the highway. She was looking at the sky. She couldn't escape the hunter's eyes. The moon refused to let her out of its sight, scowling down, sending an accusing glare. Along the roadway, pine trees severed the moon's head with every passing. But it reappeared, again and again, wearing the dead man's eyes and screaming *coward! Coward!*

"They knew we were there. We did nothing, and they knew we were there."

"Oh, god, I know." Seri's voice was as somber as a grave.

"There!" Gretchen speared the air with a finger. "There it is!"

Inger switched on headlights, timed her entry, and as smooth as glass, maneuvered the Hummer between two semi-trucks. Exhaling softly, she whispered, "Elvis has left the building."

Quil leaned forward, touching Inger's arm. "How you holding up?"

"Approaching total shutdown, but okay for now. And the name's Henny Penny. You know the rest."

"Yeah, the sky has fallen."

"Stay close. I feel something's with us, and whatever it is, it's big and mean."

"I'm right here." But Quil felt it, too, a bloody ax floating overhead.

Silence ruled on the long drive back to Durango, each trying to make sense of the nightmarish scene they'd witnessed.

But the mountain rode with them, looming over their heads, turning surreal to real, confidence to paralyzing terror, bravery to Jell-O—shaking, quaking Jell-O—as demon dread descended, demanding its toll.

nine

"Close the door!" shouted Jon. "For God's sake, close the door!" Sirens of a fire engine screamed like a banshee, its rotating lights slinging red spikes across the vehicle. The Hummer sat in the garage with the engine running. Gretchen pressed the button, closing the door. Reaching over the center console, Ned turned off the ignition, handing the keys to Inger. But Inger sat unmoving, her eyes glazed, her hands clutching the steering wheel. Gretchen held out her hand; Ned dropped the keys in her palm.

"Inside. We need to go inside," said Jon.

Cedric was the first out of the car and opened the door for Gretchen. "Something's wrong with Inger," she said, stumbling as she got out. She placed a hand on the wall to steady her footing.

Jon jumped out of the back, rushing to the driver's door. "Okay, sweetheart. You got us here. Now, we need to get inside." Gently prying her hands off the wheel, he turned her in the seat, pulling her to him. Carrying Inger, he met Gretchen at the door and entered the house.

Quil seemed outside herself, watching everything in a slow-motion film. *I've never been so exhausted.* Ned was motioning for Seri to get out of the car. Seri, behind her, wasn't responding. "Go ahead, Ned. We'll follow." Slow getting out, they seemed to move in half-time.

Jon had Inger in a recliner, elevating her feet. Inger was shaking. Gretchen pulled an afghan off the sofa, handing it to Jon then moved away. "Inger, look at me. Move your eyes to my face. Can you hear me? Inger, look at me."

"She's coming out of an adrenaline surge," said Ned. As he spoke, Gretchen collapsed in a stuffed chair. "Others are too. Everyone sit down."

She and Seri were still at the doorway. Suddenly, Ned was there, holding Seribeth's arm, leading her to the sofa.

From out of nowhere, Cedric appeared, his hand on her arm. "Get away from me." Quil stumbled by him, a smell of sour sweat irritating her nose. Against a bookshelf, she felt her knees give way and slumped to the floor. Cedric walked past her, turned on the gas log in the fireplace, and sat, staring at the flames.

Seri was crying. "That's a good sign," said Ned. "She's coming out of it."

"Good, sweetheart," said Jon. "Take deep breaths now. Okay, Inger's back." Jon touched her ski mask, intending to remove it, but Inger shook her head. He left it on.

They sat, voiceless; Quil knew not how long. Hamstrung by the malicious cruelty, she could think of nothing but having forsaken the shimmering men.

"Listen, everyone." Cedric paced back and forth in the center of the room, lighting a cigarette as he moved. "I know what we just went through was traumatic, but we need to find out *if* what we saw was what others saw. What I'm about to say may sound callous, but we need to document what happened up there. If we don't, we'll start questioning ourselves. Our brains can trick us into disremembering the truth. If something's too difficult to accept, our minds will fill in with false perceptions. Isn't that right, Ned?"

"We do need to log what happened."

"Can we talk first?" Jon asked. "I need to hear people speaking to me."

"Talk?" barked Cedric, seeming irritated. "Okay, how do you want to do this? Who wants to start? Gretchen, you start."

"Oh, no! I'm gobsmacked. I can't—" With a hand covering her mouth, she ran out of the room. Hearing retching, Jon followed. The rest of them sat with heads down except for Cedric, who continued to pace. Gretchen returned, carrying a towel. "Someone else ...." Waving a hand seemed all she could manage.

"Not you? Okay, then you start this, Quil."

"Wait up!" Jon snapped. "When I said I wanted to hear people talking, I didn't mean being interrogated. You can't order Quil or any of us to talk."

"No, I'll talk," said Quil, feeling anger rising to her throat. "What d'you want to hear, Cedric. That we enjoyed our fun-filled evening and look forward to a replay soon? Those men begged for their lives, and that red-headed bitch laughed. She sliced off his head, with no more thought than if he was a …."

"A dog," said Ned. "Just like the herd dogs."

"She slaughtered those men, and we watched. We failed as human beings, Cedric. I know that. But I also know, as sure as I'm here now, that I'll kill that bitch. I'll see her dead."

A moan came from across the room. Eyes turned, seeing Seri unfasten her collar, crumple it in a wad, and toss it to the floor. "I'm helping you."

Quil nodded, just once. Seri returned the nod. A pact made and sealed.

"We have to tell some agency about this." Jon's voice rasped. "We can't let 'em get by with such brutality!"

"Okay, listen!" Cedric yelled. "First, who would we tell? The CIA, the FBI, the military. Hell! That miserable excuse for a human being was wearing an air force uniform! No! Bringing an agency into this—no! We'd be signing our death warrants. Local law isn't the answer either. They'd only take it to a higher level. Say something, Ned! You're a cop!"

"We, uh … we need to think about what we do. But let's hold off contacting any agency for now. Not until we find out more about what was going on up there. We need to do something, but right now, I don't know what that is. My god, that was … my god."

"Okay. For now, we carry on as normal as we can." Cedric marched back and forth, his voice rising. "We talk to each other and no one else. No one else!" He slapped a fist in the palm of the other hand. "There could be follow-up at the scene by those things or the military. If they find evidence of us being there, they'll come looking. We left footprints, tire tracks. We put in writing what we saw, maybe not right now, but sometime tonight. And we keep it locked away in a safe place." His eyes were wild, and he looked close to losing it altogether.

"We have a safe," Gretchen said quietly.

"Sit down, Cedric, and get back in control," said Ned. "Inger, don't drive the Hummer for a while. If you need to get somewhere, let one of us know. The bookstore should open the same as any Tuesday. Everything should go on as usual—no, one change to that. Except, one of us should be here and armed. You two shouldn't be alone. Most everyone knows that Hummer, and it leads directly to you. We can be here; we have the time."

"You're right," said Quil. "We need to be objective. But I must believe we can do something about this wrong. Doing nothing won't work, and hiding isn't the answer. Now, I need to get myself thinking straight. I'm going home. Too many cars are parked around the bookstore in the middle of the night. It's a sure giveaway if they do come looking."

"I'm staying with you, Quil," said Seri. "I don't want on the road driving to Ignacio."

"Wouldn't have it any other way. I have an alarm system. We'll feel somewhat protected." She said that to reassure herself as much as for Seri.

"I'm staying here with the poets," said Jon. "I walked here from my house."

"I should stay here, too," said Ned. "I'm armed and can provide protection. I'll move my car to your house, Jon."

"I feel better knowing the two of you are staying here," said Quil, getting up from the floor. "Our tire tracks could be a problem. Jon, the offer of the shotgun is still open."

"I'll sure enough take it."

"Quil, we both have units in the same subdivision," said Cedric, quieter now, having regained self-control. "How about me staying with you and Seri? That'd put two guns at each place. I'll park my car in the garage and walk over. No one would know I'm there who shouldn't know."

"Sounds okay. Tomorrow, our thinking will be clearer, and we can decide what to do."

"Well, I'm getting Inger to bed. She should rest." Jon walked to her chair.

"Inger, dear. Don't you think you should take off the ski mask?" said Gretchen.

"No, I'm sleeping in it. I like the feeling of being hidden." Intending to lift her, Inger slapped Jon's hands away. "What are you doing?"

"I'm trying to get you to bed. You need rest."

"I'll get there on my own." Putting the recliner in an up position, she struggled to stand.

"Inger, let one of us help," said Quil. "I'll walk with you." She knew Inger had to be physically drained; they all were.

"I'll do it myself. And count me in, Quil. I want that bitch dead too. Now, you can walk with me, Jon, but leave my mask alone." They slowly made their way out of the living room.

"And me. I'm in." Gretchen said, following them out.

Walking to Seri, Ned picked up her crumpled collar. Saying nothing, he handed it to her. Seri shoved it in a pocket.

ten

At her townhouse, Quil walked from window to window on both levels, peering through the blinds. Seeing no movement, she returned to the living room where Seri waited for Cedric. Her jaws ached from gritting her teeth. Pacing, she felt Bird's head bump the calf of her leg with each step she took. Giving in, she sat on the floor, petting the dog, to let her know she was alright. Seri hadn't moved away from the front door, eyes focused out the side glass.

"He's here." She opened the door, and Cedric rushed inside, carrying a duffel bag.

"I'm glad to be with people I know. I brought a change of clothes. If it's okay, I'd like to shower. This has been a long, rough day."

"Maybe it would be good to clean up first and talk afterward. We're all dirty and sweaty. Cedric, I put you in the guest room upstairs. Seri's sleeping in my room. I have twin beds in there."

"I planned on the couch down here."

"If you do that, none of us will get any sleep. The dog will think you an intruder and bark all night." Cedric shrugged.

"You know where the pajamas are, Seri. You take the upstairs shower, and Cedric, you the one down."

The living room quiet, Quil thought about the wretched incident. They could have been slaughtered with those hunters. She'd never been through anything so debilitating. If that's what *joining the dance* meant, she dreaded future invitations. Leaning back on the sofa, she let her eyes close. She didn't know what was coming, but it was coming. A door opened and closed. Cedric came out of the bathroom, tossing his duffle at the foot of the stairs. Rather than sitting, he nervously toured her bookshelves.

"You have a large collection of books. Mind if I browse? I need to stay busy." As he read titles, he mumbled to himself.

"Aviation reading. Expected those. Artbooks? Didn't expect those. Ancient history, Native American mythology, bibles of various faiths. An interesting mix. Why are some cabinets closed? Are you hiding secrets of Aztec treasure? I'm sorry, let that go. It's my nerves."

"That's okay. I disclose what's in there to a few who share my interest. I'm not opening them for you if that's where you're leading."

Seri descended the stairs ,looking clean, smelling of powders and sprays, and wearing Minnie Mouse pajamas. Her wet hair in plaits, the ends resembled small scrub brushes.

"I see you found the bath fragrances." Quil headed upstairs.

"Your turn, old woman, and go heavy on the soap. If we're spending the night in the same room, I expect a better smelling you."

"Ouch. I'll do what I can. I'm activating the alarm system. So you know, the windows are wired as well as the doors."

Seri studied the man at the bookshelves. A white man with an extreme amount of hair. Oddly, the frizzled hair and beard contradicted the neat, tailored clothes he wore. She wondered what he'd look like if he neatened his head. Cedric abruptly turned, staring at her. She felt uneasy, but such was the norm for her as she needed to become acquainted before being comfortable around another. Cedric seemed to be assessing her too. He spoke first.

"I like the easy manner between you and Quil. You know each other well. I'm being as direct as I can be in saying this. That vow to take vengeance on the red-haired serpent is troubling. You shouldn't go out on your own looking for those things. Don't do it."

Seri turned her back to him and walked to the windows, peering through the blinds.

"Have you ever seen those things before tonight?" he asked.

"No. Elders say the *star travelers* have been here since ancient days. Some are thought friendly, some not. Can you not see why we must find out what they're up to?" Her inquiry was meant with silence. Cedric wasn't listening to her. Instead, he was pulling books from shelves, flipping pages, as if searching for something, and hurriedly reshelving them. *He doesn't think I'm worthy of his ears.*

"You asked a question but ignored my response. That's demeaning. You white people think you know more than natives who've been here a long time. You don't."

"What?" He faced her. "I didn't intend to be demeaning. And I can somewhat agree with you. Some white people are pompous idiots professing to know everything, but other times it's to cover up a lack of knowledge. I apologize. And to your question, I admit I didn't believe your story about aliens until I saw them."

"Do you always have to learn by observation?"

"Not always. I admit I need to school myself in these matters. I don't know how to do that, not quickly, at least. Maybe we can figure that out together. I'm honestly concerned some in the group might go off alone to avenge the deaths of the hunters. That shouldn't happen."

"I heard you the first time."

"Seribeth, I'm only concerned for you. Don't take unnecessary risk." Seri said nothing.

"So, change of subject. What's Quil's lineage? Do you know?" Still, Seri didn't speak. He shrugged and sat in a side chair.

"A mix."

Leaning forward, he placed his elbows on his knees. "A mix of what?"

"Indigenous, of course."

"I hope you know I'd never intentionally offend you, but I don't understand. Are you saying she's part Ute?"

"No."

Nodding, Cedric leaned back, removed a band from a pocket, and secured his hair at the nape of his neck.

"Cherokee. As I said, she's a mix. Quil's different. She doesn't know how she's different. We do."

"We, who?"

"The indigenous, of course." *Seriously? How did the white man get to the top of the ladder? At times, they seem dumb as fence posts.*

"Look, I'm open to learning what I can so I can be of help. I'm educated, and I'm intelligent. What do you think … look, I'm stymied here? I don't know how to communicate with you about your people or aliens—or, frankly, anything when you're dressed up as Minnie Mouse."

"Oh," she murmured, looking at her nightclothes and smiling. "Okay, I'll start with the basics. After asking a question, wait to give the other person time to consider a response. Waiting shows respect, but that doesn't mean ignoring what they say, as you did with me. We measure our words carefully before speaking to avoid creating space between us and another. Indians are slow to speak because they're thinking. White people speak quickly but often without enough thought." She waited to give him time to respond. He just stared at her.

"You say you're intelligent; however, in my opinion, you struggle with cognitive deficiencies in many areas." She let that sink it. Suddenly, a small laugh came from Cedric.

"Now, that stung. You inasmuch said I'm about as smart as a box of rocks. But that was a good comeback. Now, give me a minute." He laughed again. "Okay. I once knew a very bright person who said the path to enlightenment involved the elimination of opinion. Although total elimination might be too extreme, one should temper opinion with a fair dose of open-mindedness." He folded his hands and waited.

"And now I admit you might be smarter than I thought."

Quil came down the stairs looking scrubbed, her short, wet hair in ringlets, and wearing pajamas with Donald Duck parading with his three duck nephews.

"What's with the cartoon fetish?" snorted Cedric. Pigtails and curly locks? Ducks and mice? And you two are going to take on aliens? We should be worried."

"What's wrong with ducks and mice?" asked Quil. "What did I miss?"

"We'll talk later." Seri quietly laughed.

"We'd better document the incident on the mountain. I agree that it should be done tonight." Quil handed pads and pens around, and they wrote for about thirty minutes. She slid the accounts in a manila envelope, placing it in a desk drawer. Again, she glanced through blind slats. "Everything looks okay. Let's hope it stays that way."

Upstairs, she and Seri turned down bed covers, knowing they would sleep little, if at all. "What's up with Cedric?"

"He wants to know more about us. Maybe we seem mysterious. We did some opinion swapping. I insulted him by saying I didn't think him overly smart, but, in his favor, he didn't take offense. He seems genuine in wanting to learn what he can to help."

Quil moved to the windows and opened the blinds , allowing moonlight to sift through. They sat cross-legged on the floor, facing each other. "The weight of this is on my shoulders. I put our friends in danger. It was me who pushed to go to that mountain."

"I'll tell you what I think, Quil. You were the catalyst getting us to a place we were supposed to be. But I'm also burdened. I'm a fool and a failure. I can't put the collar back on."

"What are you talking about?"

"Sunday morning, I told people we could heal this world by working together. I thought I was a messenger here to help in fixing what's wrong. Now, I know I'm just a ... a wannabe somebody. I must have looked ridiculous to people."

"No, that's not right. If humanity fails, it won't be because of people like you. Be the messenger you were sent to be, but do it another way."

"Right now, I can't think of how to do that?"

"Wear the collar, and perhaps the *how* will come to you."

Moonlight sifted through the blinds, the shadows of the slats marking their faces with dark stripes. Quil pointed to Seri's face. "You're wearing war paint, preacher woman. The face of a warrior. It's a good look for you. But something's missing." She pulled Seri's crumpled collar from her jacket and fastened it around her neck. "That's it. Now, you're ready to do battle." Seri laid her hand on the collar and nodded.

Lying in bed only provided what seemed to be endless minutes to agonize about what they didn't do. Unable to sleep, Quil quietly went to the window, and with the pinch of a finger, sent a dusting of moonbeams above Seri's head. *Rest now, sister.*

Downstairs, Quil sat on the floor before the closed cabinets. Beckoned files floated from shelves to her lap. Deep in concentration, she jumped when Blackbird pawed her knee. The dog eyed the staircase. Quil circled a hand above them.

Carrying a penlight, Cedric slipped down the stairs and walked toward the closed book cabinets.

"The cabinets are locked. You can't open them." Quil spoke in his mind, closely watching his face. Appearing puzzled, he turned and walked toward the desk. Halfway there, he turned, looking back at Quil, shook his head, and continued to the desk. He pulled at a drawer knob; it wouldn't budge. He tried the next—same thing.

"You don't want in the desk. Go back to bed and sleep now."

Frowning, Cedric slipped up the stairs.

How interesting, *Mr. Undercover Cop.* For what are you searching? She sent folders back to shelves, watching as the cabinet doors silently close. Of a sudden, the room vanished from around her. A small light appeared, no bigger than a glint from a match head, and she was beside a figure wearing a trailing crystal robe and a lampshade on its head. They seemed to be floating in a hallway of prisms, light casting soft pastel colors.

"Greetings, Quil."

"Who are you?" she asked, noticing the speaker's voice was female.

"I'm the one Gnat told you to expect."

"Oh, yes. Gnat said to expect others now. Do you know you have a lampshade on your head? I find that strange."

"Do I? Do you know you have one on your head?"

Quil reached up, feeling a covering. "Why is this on my head?"

"It could be for there any number of reasons."

"Are you a spirit? When you move, I can see right through you."

"That's because I'm transparent. Transparency is good; nothing to hide, you know."

"That's true about transparency. But your statement is flawed as I can't see your face. The lampshade conceals it."

"You'll get used to it. But you called me. Do you have matters to discuss?"

"I wasn't aware I'd called you, although I would like to talk to someone. But I need to know who you are first."

"I'm an intercessor, one who listens or serves as a sounding board. At times, I may provide gleanings from… um, let's call it 'elsewhere'."

"That's confusing, but I guess I'm to talk with you. It's the deaths I witnessed. I let fear paralyze me. I couldn't have fought or even run if I'd been given a chance."

"You were sent a message. There will be others. Emotions exist for reasons, but they shouldn't control. Fear is inside you; you cannot run from it. Recognize it as fear and set it aside. It's a matter of preparedness."

"But why did we have to go through that? Why couldn't we have received the message another way? You could have briefed us at a meeting."

"Why do you ask for an answer when you know the answer? Did you feel the pain of those dying so tragically? Did you see the fear on the faces around you? Did you sense a betrayal when you didn't act to halt an injustice? No briefing at a meeting could give you that. Being involved, even

only as a watcher, allows knowing. Knowing allows assessment, and that leads to solving the problem."

"Yes, I understand all that, but I still don't know what I'm to do. And you're tossing out philosophical precepts rather than giving solid answers. If I'm to solve this problem, I need to know options."

"I'm not here to do the work you're to do. There must be others who possess what's needed. Seek them out. To march forward requires resolve, readiness, and relentless reworking. Constantly observe, see where vulnerabilities exist, and correct. Good night, Quil."

eleven

Someone was shaking her. "Why did you sleep down here?" Seri sat on the ottoman with Blackbird at her feet.

"The windows. We need to check outside," said Quil.

"I've looked, and from what I could see, things seem okay. I was going to let Bird outside but want you to check before doing that. Come on." Quil cautiously cracked the back door an inch to check outside before opening the doggie door.

"Cedric's up, too. And the others are coming here about ten. Is that okay with you?"

"Of course. What time is it? We need to get ready." They met Cedric on the staircase.

"Did you get any sleep at all?" he asked. "I need coffee. Is it okay if I make some?" Cedric looked more tired than he did last night.

"Go ahead. The coffee's in a canister on the counter."

"We'll change and be right down," said Seribeth. Upstairs, they dressed in jeans and sweatshirts. "I need to find out the identity of those hunters so I can notify their families and spread the word about the danger. We can't keep quiet about this."

"Don't go alone to see the families. I'll arrange to go with you if you need to travel. And move in with me for a while."

"Maybe that's a good idea. I'll think about it and let you know."

"Good. Do you see my phone?" Seri pointed to Quil's rumpled bed. She hurriedly sent a text before they went downstairs.

"Have you considered what to do next?" Quil asked as Cedric poured a mug of coffee.

"Speaking as a cop, normally a follow-up at the scene would be in order. That's the worst thing to do in this case."

"Those hunters must have had a vehicle on a hunting trail or the county road. I can put out feelers in the Ute community to learn their names."

"We shouldn't be talking to anyone now. I told you that last night."

"Were they Ute?" Quil asked, ignoring Cedric's comment.

"I don't know. I was in shock watching the horrific murders. I think Ute or Apache. They only wanted to take elk meat to their families. I can ask our police department to comb hunting trails around there."

Cedric's phone rang. In a hurry to get it, he dropped his cup, sloshing coffee across the table. Quil dashed to the kitchen for paper towels.

"Yes, about ten is okay, Ned." He disconnected. "I'm sorry about the spill. The others are on the way."

"I'll be right back." Quil hurried to the garage, returning with a flip chart stand, and hastily outlined a grid with initials across the top and a listing of topics along the left side. She pulled a cover over the chart when she heard the doorbell.

"Glad to see y'all," She waved them to the living room. "Make yourselves as comfortable as you can, considering."

"I'll serve as a facilitator when you're ready." Quil saw Gretchen peeking under the chart cover. Ned talked as he moved toward the sofa.

"I'm starting shooting instruction for everyone except you, Quil. I'll test your proficiency, Cedric so you both can assist in training the rest. I have guns I can try people on to see what works best for each one."

"One with punch power for me," said Inger. "Will you help me get an Uzi machine gun? I want to be prepared if we run into those freaks."

"I want one that fires missiles." Jon scowled, seeing Cedric attempting to conceal a smirk. "I'm serious. We need weapons that'll bring those suckers down."

"I'll be glad to help on the range," Quil said, "but now, let's calendar when we can be on watch at the bookstore." They quickly did that and moved on.

"Where do we begin?" Cedric asked, removing a notepad from his satchel.

"Dulce." Seri looked at Ned to see if he'd object.

"No argument from me today. I've lived here a long time and heard the stories about Dulce and aliens but shrugged it off as tabloid trash. Will you kick this off, Quil?"

"Okay, but stay open to possibilities. What I can offer is general information and opinion. Don't expect fact-based answers. There are a number of topics. I'll touch on each one and note where relevant information is on the shelves. After that, the ball's in your court. Limit comments now so I can move quickly. Any questions?" Everyone sat waiting.

"To start, we reside on a paranormal highway, the 37th parallel." She unfolded an aeronautical chart with highlighted notations and ran a finger along a line. "Many consider this a flight path used by interstellar travelers. It isn't the only one, but it is a primary one, and it's in our backyard. Gretchen, tape this to a wall, please."

"I'm on it."

"Next item is UFO sightings around Dulce; dated information that most people never accepted as being valid. But we just witnessed aliens here, and those sheep are being taken some place, so Dulce can't be overlooked." She opened the first cabinet. "The Dulce information is on these shelves."

"As we know, Area 51 came into existence after the UFO crash at Roswell. Many believe it was to back-engineer alien aircraft. However, that was in the cold war era, and many thought it was to develop spy planes to keep an eye on Russia. Some went so far as to say the UFO phenomenon was a farce to detract from stealth efforts."

"This is old news, Quil," said Cedric.

"I'm getting to the point. Because of unidentified aircraft and strange lights around Dulce, rumors spread about Archuleta Mesa being the location of an alien base."

"Still old news," said Cedric. "I want in the files. The others agree with me, don't you?" Cedric sat on the edge of his chair, scanning faces to see if he had support.

"What you want doesn't matter squat, Cedric. Let me talk. There are three possible base locations close to us. One is Dulce; a second is the Sleeping Ute Mountain north of where the sheep theft just occurred; and a third is Archuleta Mountain, not to be confused with Archuleta Mesa. The Mountain is a possibility because a UFO or spy plane supposedly crashed there. A paved road was constructed to remove what did go down there." Seri had her hand up.

"Understand, the government cannot go on tribal land without the consent of the tribe, but that's what happened on Archuleta Mountain. Neither the Southern Ute nor the Jicarilla Apache constructed that road. Also, a ranch known as *the compound* north of the Mountain is believed to have a connection with the hidden base." As Seri talked, Quil moved to the chart taped to the wall.

"I noted the three base locations on this chart with a yellow marker. The files on underground bases are in the second cabinet. Now, this is where things get squirrelly. Tunnels. Note these red lines radiating away from Dulce. Tunnels and possibly an underground rail system are alleged to connect Dulce with military bases, laboratories, and who knows what else." Cedric walked to the chart, briefly studied it, and returned to his chair.

"I hesitate to turn you loose on this last cabinet. What's here describes a multi-level base and details of what it contains. It's grisly. Human experimentation, gene manipulation, cloning, and more. If true, they're using us as lab rats, purpose unknown. And underground bases around here is not the only concern. There are over a hundred underground military bases rumored to be joint projects between our government and extraterrestrials. So, Cedric, I'm not overly surprised we saw a human in a military uniform on the mountain. A lot of information is on these shelves. You select what you want to know more about."

"I have more information at my place I can bring over,' added Seri.

Cedric started toward the cabinets, carrying a dining chair.

"Hold off a minute. There's another item I want on the table that involves very unusual occurrences. Inger, I'd like your attention to this one." Inger nodded and leaned forward.

"Okay. There seem to exist—and I'm reaching for words here—target spots where paranormal hiccups occur—bizarre happenings. No one can figure out how or why it's happening or who's causing it. Those involved have come to believe they're part of a group hallucination project. Mind control efforts by the government. I've done limited reading on group control experiments and can see why people might think as they do."

"What do you mean by bizarre?" asked Inger.

"Tears in the sky, exposing other worlds, parallel universes. Some said they witnessed weird creatures crawl through sky holes."

"Now, this is too much," sneered Cedric. "Who would believe nonsense like that?"

"Me, that's who," snapped Inger. "I'll take those files, Quil."

"They're in red folders. That's it. I have no answers. The only way we can know what's real is to go find out for ourselves. Now, I want to go over our accounts. Inger, did you bring yours?"

"I did. Do I pass them to those authoring the reports?"

"Yes, please. Seri, you hand out ours. Gretchen, you said you would facilitate." Seri opened the desk drawer removing the envelope.

"Wait!" snapped Cedric. "Don't you keep the desk drawers locked?"

"No, I don't." Cedric hurriedly walked to the desk, trying drawers, each sliding open easily. Turning, he saw everyone staring.

"Well, you should. Someone could have broken in here and taken that envelope. We need to take precautions now. This is a serious situation." He returned to his chair, a scowl on his face.

"Eyes to the board," said Gretchen. "We have the beginning of a list. We'll add to it if need be. Description of aliens is first. When I call your name, give me your response."

When done, they noted sameness and variance. All noted two aerial vehicles, two floating aliens with stringy fingers, two types of serpent people, one with orangish-red hair, a red-cloaked being at a distance, and one human.

"I've looked through my files for possible alien types," said Quil. "The tall wispy ones could be *Mantians* from the Sombrero galaxy. The man in the robe remains a question mark. The reptilians, or at least the red-headed serpent, could be a member of the flying dragon species from Sirius in the Canis Major constellation. The other one seems to be a home-grown reptilian from right here on Mama Earth."

"We have snake people on Earth?" Gretchen raised her eyebrows.

"It's alleged they've been here as long or longer than our earliest hominids. Some even contend members of a serpent race did the initial DNA alteration of hominids in Africa."

"DNA manipulation on apes by snake people?" Cedric said. "You're becoming more ridiculous as you go."

"I said *allege*, and I'm responding to Gretchen's question. Others say reptilians were run off this planet because of a breach of an agreement between them and other astral travelers that journeyed here. If they were run off, it seems some were left behind, or they came back. Another species is given credit for gene splicing in Australia that played a role in achieving modern-day humans."

"You mean Africa, not Australia," said Cedric.

"No, I mean Australia. Australian Aboriginals are one of our oldest societies, and interestingly, their DNA indicates an unknown gene, one that many think could be non-human."

"I think you're wrong on that. The Sumerians are our oldest society."

"Sumer was one of our earliest known civilizations," said Quil. "There's a difference, and why are you so contentious? This isn't a chicken-or-egg debate."

"Retract the claws, Quil," said Seri. "Cedric, you can use Quil's computer to do a web search. It might help." Seri smiled at Cedric. "She wouldn't object."

"Thanks, Seri. I'll think about doing that later, but now we need to stay on mark."

"That we do," replied Quil. "Moving to aircraft. The black ship could be one of our own called a *delta* or a *triangle* engineered from pilfered alien technology. I couldn't see the one above us."

"We did," said Inger, "or at least, its outline."

"I'll show you what it looks like." Gretchen opened a large tote and removed a kitchen pan. "It looked like a tall rounded-top aspic mold."

"A bell ship like the vimana of Hindu epics," said Quil. "Huh, I wasn't expecting that."

"I thought a saucer, maybe," said Seri.

"Yeah, me, too. What about sounds? Did you hear strange music, vibrating tones? Inger, what about you?"

"No music or vibrating tones," said Inger. Nor did anyone else.

"Well, there's some variance," said Quil, "and as for me, I think what we saw was real and not a hallucination."

"No question in my mind," said Gretchen. "Return your narratives for safekeeping. And I'm taking this chart exercise." Gretchen removed the sheet, folding it into a size to fit in the manila envelope.

Cedric moved his chair before the cabinet, holding the Dulce files. Inger, Gretchen and Jon delved into red files. Quil moved to the sofa between Seri and Ned, concentrating on Cedric.

"Okay, Cedric, and you, too, Ned. As former military, what can you tell me about *deep black ops*?"

"Why don't you tell me what you know?" Cedric tossed files on the floor and spun his chair around.

"That's an interesting response. You start, Cedric. Tell us what you know."

"I know it isn't smart to be talking about it."

"Your continual questioning hasn't gone unnoticed, Cedric, however it doesn't seem to have gained you much.

Has your undercover training failed you now that you're old and out of practice?"

"Hoo-ha! I bet that burned," snickered Inger. Cedric glowered.

"But as you seem hesitant to talk, let me start. Deep black ops are joint military and alien bases that involve human experimentation. The funding comes from siphoned-off dollars from approved government programs." She paused a moment, checking Cedric's reaction. "They operate under a shadow government dedicated to managing extraterrestrial affairs. How am I doing, undercover cop?"

"You know more than most, and what you said is accurate—as far as I know. But understand this, I am not now, nor have I ever been involved with *deep black*. I found time on my hands while on an island and did some rumor checking."

"You hacked government records?" asked Seri.

"Let's say I was lucky enough to find interesting reading while fighting frostbite. When my tour was up, I told them to take their boy scout camp and shove it. My government had me listening to Russian fishermen while they played house with aliens. Pissed? Hell, yes. Where are the deep black files in these cabinets, Quil?"

"You won't find deep black records in this house." Cedric looked at the other three women.

"Keep your probing eyes away from us," said Gretchen. "We don't have them."

"Then I have another question. Who did the hunter look at when he knew he was going to be killed?" All eyes turned to Quil.

The question took Quil by surprise, but she wasn't going to argue the point. "He was targeting me."

"Come on, Quil, you need to say more than that. It seems you're somehow a key to understanding what's going on. How do you figure into this?" Cedric wasn't expecting to see the small smile that crinkled the corners of Quil's mouth. The tilt of her head didn't read as deference either.

"Perhaps it was a message I'm the one to pursue this—and not you, Cedric. So to be clear, I don't expect any of you to follow me down this rabbit hole."

"You say the most infuriating things at times, Quil," said Seri. "You're not doing this without me, sister."

"Ain't that the truth," said Inger. "I'm probably on a first-name basis with those weirdos from parallel universes. What about you, Gretchen?"

"What's the proper attire for rabbit holes this season?" said Gretchen as she smoothed her hair before the hall mirror.

"Good, that's decided." Inger pulled a bottle of bourbon from her bag. "Quil, I'd like a few cubes of ice in a glass, please. Anyone else? Gretchen?"

"Make mine a double, dear, and remind me to restock our liquor cabinet. My, my, things are getting interesting, aren't they?"

"Allow me to bartend." Jon took the bottle from Inger and walked to the kitchen. "What about the rest of us? You know, the men in the room?"

"That's up to you three," said Inger. "You've seen what tagging along with the gals gets you into."

"I'm not ready to drop this," growled Cedric. "I think you're with an organization that has their mitts in this up to their elbows. What agency are you with, Quil?"

"She's a fey, Cedric," snorted Inger. "A fey knows things—and it has nothing to do with agencies, organizations, or, frankly, anything you would know about."

"What's a fey?" Ned asked, looking at Jon, who shook his head.

"Have I said too much, Quil?"

"You're committed now, sugar. You owe 'em an answer. Make it a good one." Quil leaned back to watch, as did Seri and Gretchen.

"Come close, and I'll tell you," whispered Inger. Ned and Jon moved their chairs next to Inger. "Have you ever met someone who appears from a mist, carries a faraway look in her eyes, and speaks as if casting spells. Not like a witch, no, no, but one who seems unnatural, in an elusive sorta way, with a voice like a willow reed, low and haunting. She moves oh, so cautiously. With a watchful eye, she steps from a dream as the moon drips silver tears, rides pale beams at the tick of midnight, sees the moon at midday. Then poof … she's gone, leaving nothing more than a lingering sigh."

The room was so quiet, the tick-tock of the clock on the mantle was all that was heard. "Shh, shh, listen. Hear the wyvern's wings. A fey this way flies. Shh." Inger placed a finger over her lips and grinned.

"You either tweaked higher than a kite, or you know all that because you're one of 'em," said Jon. Applause and laughter erupted from the women.

"Can we get serious now?" Cedric said. "Last night, it was Loony Tune characters; today, it's fairies. They're not real, Jon."

"Fairies? You mean little people?" asked Jon.

"What do you mean little people aren't real? said Seribeth. "Little people have saved members of my tribe that were injured or caught in blizzards in the high mountains. They live in caves up there."

"Well, hell," said Cedric. "It isn't my preference, but could I have some bourbon, Inger?"

"What is your preference?" Inger pulled bottles of scotch and brandy from her tote.

"Scotch," pouring the liquor in with his coffee.

Quil studied Cedric. His long wiry hair and beard hung in tangles, cloaking his face, but it didn't hide his eyes narrowed in anger. Or was that anxiety?

"Cedric, you strike me as someone tossing pebbles in a pond to see what churns up from below. No more skipping stones. Tell us what you know."

Startled, he exhaled loudly and ran his hands over his face, disheveling his hair and beard more than they already were.

"What I know? I know we're in danger—that's what I know. There used to be six of us on this quest for truth. I'm alone now, the only one left. The others were murdered—or taken. But … okay, here's what I can tell you. Initially, our military agreed to the abduction of humans for study purposes.

69

That meant the humans taken would be revived and returned to normal lives when the study was completed. The aliens immediately broke the agreement, and the military terminated the program.”

“I'm sorry about your friends,” said Seri. “It pained you to tell us that.”

“Yes, it did,” said Ned, “and Cedric, you're not alone now.”

“You don't think the deep black ops ended?” Quil said. “Where's the funding coming from?”

“The same way as before. The program was only stamped *terminated*. There are many levels of black ops. The deep black budget is jammed in the middle of them all, making it impossible to locate the one we were after. It's completely cut off from oversight, no records to track, no contacts, nothing. I came here thinking Dulce might be a lead to finding out more about its operation.”

“Experimentation on humans hasn't stopped?” said Ned.

“I'd say that's correct,” replied Cedric.

“What do the Frankenstein doctors want from us?” asked Jon. “We're not a complex animal to figure out.”

“From human experimentation, I don't know. They're obviously after what this planet offers.”

“Humans as lab rats,” said Ned. “I can't accept that. We have to take action.”

“Start with Dulce,” said Seri. “A former law enforcement officer there could be of help. You might know him, Ned.”

“Yeah, I know who you're talking about. I'll contact him, and I wanna go to the Mesa and see for myself. What about the rest of you?”

“Only a small cotangent should go,” Quil said. “We'd create too much attention if we made it a group trip.”

“Right,” agreed Cedric. “Ned and I could go with a made-up story about me being new here and curious about UFO rumors. Quil, I don't want to leave you out if you want to go.”

"I don't need to go now. Moving on—Seri said she'd contact the Ute Police to see about identifying the hunters. What about that, Ned?"

"Not yet. I'll go to the Ute and Apache departments and look through missing person sheets. They all know me. I'll do that as quick as I can."

"That's it for now. Seribeth's staying with me for a while, and we're going to Ignacio for her things. If you all leave, be sure to lock up here."

"I'll go with you." Cedric started reshelving files.

"Not necessary. We won't be long."

"Okay, but no action on your own. This is well settled. Take no action on your own."

"Right." Quil pulled the door to.

twelve

They took Seribeth's car. Quil secured Bird in the back before jumping in the passenger seat. "We need to move this along. Wait a sec." She opened her backpack, checking the number of spare magazines for the Glock. "I'm good here. Let's go."

"I'm amazed. It took you, oh, a whole two minutes before you decided to take action on your own."

"Yeah, thanks. You know, Jon had a good idea about getting high-powered weapons. We need military involved. Let's talk to Wolf Severo. Hopefully, he'll be willin' to join us."

"I'm sure he will, and Josiah Lehi of Ute Mountain was in the Army, a sniper assigned to the Rangers. Wolf knows Josiah and others who might be interested in joining, especially when they learn the way the hunters died."

Arriving at the Peoples Church outside Ignacio, Seri drove to the back of the main building to a single-wide trailer, serving as a guest cottage. "It shouldn't take long to gather my clothes. Storage boxes are in the shed. Would you collect my files while I pack?"

Quil was on the way back with boxes but stopped hearing shouts from the church. Gracie Dove waved. She and her husband Adam pastored the church where Seri served as the youth minister. Gracie was an imposing six-foot Amazonian superwoman with a heart of solid platinum.

"Hey Quil, it's good to see you." Wrapped in a welcome hug, Quil's head disappeared in Gracie's ample bosom. "Why haven't we seen you lately? Consulting work still taking you to distant lands?"

"Afraid so. It's my destiny to wander, it seems."

"Hi, Gracie." The screen door slammed behind Seri. "I'll be staying with Quil for a little while. It'll be hard to get by without me, I know, and I only hope you can survive my absence."

Laughing, Gracie enveloped Seri in a greeting like the one given Quil. "Little cloud, my sky is always empty when you're not here." She studied the faces of the two women. "I see darkness troubling your souls. Let's go inside and talk about it?"

"Let's start now," said Seribeth. "Gracie can handle information better than anyone I know."

"Works for me."

Later, as they drove into Quil's addition, Seri said, "Are you still planning on going to Hazel Berry's art workshop?"

"We're supposed to stick to our usual schedules, so I guess we should attend. We'll go together. My car or yours, doesn't matter."

"Sounds good. The lights are on at your house."

Quil knocked on the door. "Hey, inside. Come help carry stuff."

"Certainly. Tell me what you need to be done." Cedric followed them to the car and grabbed a box of files. Quil and Seri maneuvered suitcases out of the back seat and followed him in.

"I'm ordering Chinese. I haven't eaten in several days."

"We haven't either, and Chinese would be great." They gave him their preferences.

"I'll make the call. Shouldn't take but about thirty minutes."

"Was the group able to make sense of the info on the shelves?" She looked at the cabinets as she walked by. Things looked in good order.

"We did, and good news. Ned arranged a trip to Dulce. That'll happen Friday if all goes as planned."

"I wasn't expecting such quick action. I can give you names of people to talk to down there." Seri pulled a file from a box on the floor.

"That's for later reading," said Cedric. "Quil, I'm here for another night. Ned and Jon are staying at the bookstore again. As a precaution."

"I don't know if that's necessary, but we'll work with it." She'd rather he not stay over again but could think of no reason to decline his offer.

"That's the doorbell. I'll get it," said Cedric. Opening the door with his wallet in hand, he was surprised to see someone other than a delivery person. From law enforcement habit, he made mental notes of the man's appearance: very tall and well built, a Native American male, long black hair pulled back and held with a leather strap, aviator glasses, and an olive-green t-shirt that said *Semper F,* the Marine Corps motto. *Nor* did he miss a Scout Sniper tattoo.

"Can I help you?"

"I'm looking for Quil Doolin. Does she still live here?"

"Yes, she does. I'll call her for you."

"No need to call me. Hey, Wolf. Please come in. It's great to see you." Seri hurried to hug Wolf.

"Hey, you two. I brought pizza. Thought we might have supper together and catch up on small talk. I haven't seen you in a long while." Handing the cartons to Seri, he turned back to Cedric, still at the door, holding his wallet. "I'm Standing Wolf Severo." Extending a hand, he waited while Cedric collected himself.

"Oh, right. I'm Cedric O'Malley. Good to meet you." Placing the wallet back in his pocket, he shook the big man's hand. "Did you say your name was *Standing Wolf?* That's unusual."

"Not for an Indian. Most call me Wolf."

"I meant no disrespect."

"None taken. On another point, that beautiful Ute lady you seem to have trouble keeping your eyes off of is family. Need I say more?"

"I'd never do Seribeth harm."

"Just what I wanted to hear." Wolf tossed his head back in an easy laugh. "Now that's out of the way, when do we eat? I find the sharing of a meal a civilized way to solidify an understanding.”

“That sounded scholarly; I mean educated,” said Cedric.

“I am educated and smart to boot.”

Responding to the doorbell, Cedric came face-to-face with another stranger. A husky Native American male, average height, muscular build, wearing a somber expression, western hat and boots, dark glasses, and long black hair in braids.

“Is that a bucket of chicken you’re carrying?”

“Yes. Does Quil Doolin live here?”

“She does. Come on in.” Remaining by the door, Cedric watched the second stranger being warmly greeted. “Huh. It seems we’re having a party. Wish I’d been invited.”

“Hey, Josiah,” said Wolf. “Glad you could drop by tonight.” After shaking hands with Josiah, Cedric moved to a chair beside the fireplace.

Five minutes later, the Chinese food arrived. At the dining table, the group chatted about the weather, an upcoming rodeo, and elk hunting, obviously avoiding the reason for their guests’ presence.

“Well, Seri, it appears you discussed the matter on the mountain with a few others.” Seri looked around the table before responding.

“I talked to a trustworthy person named Gracie Dove who knows how to move information quickly. These men can be trusted and have military backgrounds. You probably could tell that.”

Cedric’s eyes moved to the two men quietly observing him. “Yeah, the Semper Fi t-shirt and Scout tat on Wolf’s arm were good clues he was military.”

Rolling up his shirtsleeve, Josiah displayed a tattoo of the Ranger Regiment’s coat of arms. Josiah’s eyes never left Cedric’s face.

“Uh-hm. A Ranger. And a sniper, I’m guessing.”

“Special sniper training at Quantico.” Josiah rolled down his sleeve.

"Well hell, let's get to it. What do you guys want to know? We can tell you what we saw and provide info on aircraft. That said, we have no idea how to go up against these bastards. Where do you want to start?"

They spent the following hours going over accounts of the murders on the mountain. Seri and Quil sketched the ships and types of extraterrestrials. Cedric described the air force uniform in detail. The ray weapon garnered much interest. Listening to the description, the military men thought it a directed-energy weapon, one that either could paralyze for an extended period or stop the heart, resulting in a quick death.

"We have enough to start." Wolf gathered the drawings and copies of the accounts. "We'll keep in touch. Don't speak of us to anyone outside of your group. Just know we're standing with you."

Cedric stood back, watching the guests give parting hugs to Seri and Quil. He spoke as soon as the door closed.

"I need sleep. I have the morning shift at the bookstore. I think you two drew afternoon duty as Inger wants your help in a poetry class. This week's calendar assignments are on the desk." Starting upstairs, he turned back to the women. "When I saw your guests, I wasn't certain including others was a good idea. Now, I'm glad you brought them in."

"Thank you, Cedric," said Seri, patting his hand, resting on the railing. He responded by squeezing hers gently. Seri was smiling. Quil couldn't tell if Cedric was.

thirteen

The dog let out a sharp bark. Hearing light tapping at the door, Quil palmed her gun and waited.

"It's me, Cedric. I'm going downstairs. Go back to sleep."

Seri moved around restlessly. "Don't get up. I'm going down to talk to him before he leaves. We have plenty of time before we go to the bookstore." Grunting, Seri pulled the cover over her head.

Cedric's satchel was on the table. Quil glanced at the clock. He had hours before having to report for bookstore duty. "Have you heard from Ned?"

"Just now. He and Jon are returning to their places but can be available anytime."

"I need to tell him about Wolf and Josiah."

"Leave Ned to me. I can approach it from a military angle. I'm sure he'll recognize their names. He knows most everyone around here."

"I don't want you taking heat for something you didn't do."

"I don't think he'll be upset. I assure you I'm not. I never wanted to be a soldier, but I'll be on the front lines when the shooting starts. I'm glad for professional military help. Those two have experience we need."

"You're right about that."

"On a different note, something Seri said is bothering me. She said you're different, but you don't understand your difference, although indigenous people do. That's puzzling. What did she mean?"

"Seri said that? H'm? I can't say for sure, but I believe it has to do with indigenous peoples' ways of seeing inside a person. An ability others don't possess. They tell me I don't know my inner self yet. I lived with a full-blood Indian aunt from age seven who clung to her belief in nature spirits. Even with that upbringing, I have no explanation."

"Being indigenous could account for it, I guess. Here's the point. There are times when I feel you somehow invading my mind. Frankly, it's unsettling. Or am I totally off base?"

"I don't invade others' minds. At times, others' thoughts come to me. It doesn't happen often."

"Thoughts come to you? Are you a mentalist? A mind reader? Have you followed up with anyone on that ability?"

"There's no reason to follow up."

"Aren't you interested in knowing if you have superior abilities?"

"Look, we all filter noise through the brain's auditory cortex, letting only certain signals through. Otherwise, there'd be a discordant mess going on in our heads all the time, and we'd go insane. I seem to allow in more than most." Abruptly stopping, Quil realized she spoke sharper than intended.

"That's not an answer. You seem to have built a wall to keep people from knowing you."

"I was raised by hill people who preferred solitude, however they didn't entirely cut us off from community. They were selective in who they chose to be around. I haven't built a wall around myself. I just prefer privacy." She took his coffee mug and poured the remains in the sink. "You'd better get a move on. I wouldn't want you to be late getting to the bookstore." There was no missing the intended message. Cedric grabbed his valise and left.

Cedric's persistent probing was troubling. At least, she didn't tell him she could penetrate his mind if she chose to. She avoided mind delving as it seemed an unnecessary invasion of others' privacy. However, yesterday the *deep black ops* information came through from him as clear as a bell. But he'd felt her in his mind. Her abilities to mind probe had always caused questioning, especially as a child.

She recalled the day she brought her mind-reading into the light. She and Aunt Rho sat at the kitchen table, inserting cardboard strips into a slat bonnet that matched a flour sack smock. Aunt didn't have money to buy ready-made new things, so she made most of Quil's clothes out of flour sacks.

"Knowing what other people are thinking is easy. It's like snatching their thoughts out of the air." Aunt was quiet for a spell before she spoke. *"That sounds like stealing to me."* Quickly, I said, *"Not really. They were used thoughts like the barely-used clothes at the second-hand store. And since they were already used thoughts just flung in the air, and since I didn't take something unthought from their heads, nothing's wrong with it. 'Sides, the gnat fly on my shoulder said it was okay."*

Aunt knitted her eyebrows. *"Somehow, that seems to make sense, somehow."* Leaning close, Aunt scoured both my shoulders, hunting for the fly but didn't see anything. *"No matter. You tell that fly, you're to follow rules of this house now, and taking people's things is not allowed. You hear me, child'?* She said that a lot, and I always said: *"Yes, ma'am, I will."* Of course, I didn't have to tell the fly, as it was right there listening.

Later, Aunt changed her mind about me snatching thoughts. We were peddling flowers to town grocers. Aunt was good at growing things. One man was haggling over what he'd pay, and I could tell Aunt was wearing down. I tugged her skirt, motioning her close to whisper in her ear. *"He'll pay a dollar more each bunch than what he's saying. His barely-used thoughts floatin' free in the air told me so."* Aunt looked hard at me. *"Be that right?"* She asked a dollar more per bunch, and the grocer agreed.

She gave me two quarters to spend at the second-hand store. *"You can tell me other peoples' barely-used thoughts if you do it in a whisper. Just hold up a finger, hold it high like this, and I'll listen."* I spent twenty cents of the first quarter on the *Alice in Wonderland* books, leaving me a buffalo head nickel left over that I still have. With the second quarter, I bought a pair of yellow rubber boots to wear when scattering feed and grit in the chicken yard. Chickens are messy creatures and were never grateful for all I did for them, and they could be mean. I learned fast to dodge sharp beaks and tearing spurs.

"I'm dodging right now, Cedric, but I won't always be, and I've been known to wring a neck or two."

"What are you mumbling about?" asked Seri, stretching her arms as she walked into the kitchen. "Did Cedric already leave?"

"*Pfft*, you know me, always muttering as I'm thinking through things. Cedric left early for the bookstore."

"Guess we'd better get our act together too."

They arrived at the bookstore shortly before noon to give Inger time to prepare for class and Gretchen a chance to run to the post office. Still there, Cedric seemed engrossed in a computerized chess game while observing the coming and going of bookstore patrons. Cedric, however, was a changed man. He'd been to a barber and now sported a neat beard and trimmed hair pulled back in a man's ponytail. Seri glowingly praised his appearance, and Cedric reveled in her praise.

That afternoon, eight kids perched on floor cushions in the children's nook eager for their first poetry session. Inger introduced an icebreaker she employed to get children up, moving around, and having fun. The icebreaker involved a conga line dance done to the jingle of the Energizer Bunny commercial. The kids wore floppy bunny ears and made up their own dance steps to the music. Along with ears, Inger wore a jacket with a gargantuan-sized bunny tail tacked to her backside.

With a signal from Inger, Quil turned on the music. Holding a cowbell, Inger led the line, clomping her feet in a shuffle. *Clomp, clomp, clomp, clomp.* After the fourth shuffle, she rang the cowbell, and everyone shook their booties. With every bootie shake, the bell passed to another child. The room vibrated with laughter and the gonging of a cowbell.

Gretchen, working at the counter, often glancing at the children and tapping her foot to the music.

"Quil and Seri seem to enjoy children's play antics as much as the kids," said Cedric.

"They do. Especially Quil, as she, like Inger, has a fondness for fantasy tales. When possible, Inger includes them in children's activities."

"That could explain the cartoon characters on Quil's pajamas."

"Actually, it does. Inger gives Quil Disney sleepwear every Christmas. Inger may seem like a ding-dong, but she's extremely astute to needs of the heart."

"That's an interesting way of phrasing that."

"And don't think Quil's uneducated because she speaks hill vernacular at times. She made it through college at an accelerated speed and can be an intellect when she chooses. If you test her, you'll find that out. Seri, too, holds a degree and is as smart as they come."

"Whoa, pull back on the reins. Listen, I wasn't criticizing anyone. I consider all of you intelligent, engaged individuals, and I respect you. But can you tell me what Quil does? I know the rest of you better than I do her."

"Why do you ask?"

"Okay, I'm tired of being looked at like I'm a serial killer seeking a next victim. For a while, now, I've entertained the idea of writing novels. I need to think about things other than what I've dwelled on for the last many years. I'm looking for interesting characters, that's all."

"You want us in a book? My goodness, why didn't you say that? Quil's an independent consultant and conducts risk assessments and industrial accident investigations. She's known for taking the side of the working class in what she does—but don't get me wrong, she's fair in her determinations."

"Thanks, Gretchen. That would make for an intriguing character in a novel. All of you would. Please keep this to yourself as people act differently when they know they're being observed. You're solidly based, and I know you'll be yourself, regardless."

"Sure, and thank you."

Cedric glanced up from his chess game as two men entered and stood looking over the store. Those with the children did not overlook their entrance either. The cowbell's gong suddenly turned into an all points alert.

A large man, wearing dress slacks and a long-sleeved white shirt, walked beside a shorter one in similar clothing and dark glasses. Both had very short hair, possibly military cuts. The larger of the two walked to the entryway of the children's nook and stopped to read the *Lobster Quadrille* poem on a wall poster. Huffing, he turned to Gretchen. "This makes no sense. It's ridiculous."

"It's for children. It's not ridiculous to children."

The man watched as the children shook their backsides when the cowbell rang. Again, he turned to Gretchen. "What are those stupid people doing? They're teaching children inappropriate behavior. Stop that activity."

"The people are not stupid, and it's perfectly appropriate behavior for children. I will not stop the dancing."

The smaller man spoke to his companion in lowered tones. Pivoting sharply, both walked around the store, reading book titles. Occasionally, the shorter man stopped the larger one to confer in whispers. At a display stand of Durango area brochures, the large man selected several of everything available, tucking them under his left arm held at his chest.

In the nook, Quil pulled off her bunny ears, handing them to Inger. Retrieving her backpack, she unzipped the pocket housing the Glock and walked to the front. She glanced at Cedric as she walked toward the magazine racks. He responded with a slight nod. Seri moved to the Nook's doorway, slipped her cell from a pocket, and snapped a photo of the two.

The large stranger again strolled near the counter area. Abruptly, he jumped backward, startled by a Siamese cat crawling out of an oversized handbag. Yawning, it exposed every tooth in its feline head. The cat had one ear mostly gone, fur missing in splotches on its head, and a tail that bent several directions. Plus, the outlandish cat sported an expression that clearly said, *Don't mess with me, Bubba.*

The cat was precious to Gretchen. She'd nursed it back to good health after finding it in a muddy culvert badly mauled and near death. Because of its mangled appearance, she named it *Troll.*

Staring at Troll, the man shuddered. "What kind of beast is this? It's hideous."

"She's a waif."

Moving in front of Gretchen, the cat arched its back, hissing at the man menacing her owner.

"It's so ugly, it's hard to look at its face. You should kill it."

"Its face is not nearly as hard to look at as that dick growing out of your left ear." His left arm clutching brochures, the man raised his right hand to his ear—his right ear.

"Your other left, stupid." Gretchen's voice had achieved scream volume. "Get out! I'm calling the police!"

At that moment, Cedric's tapped a button on his computerized chess game. A mechanized voice loudly said: *ENTER YOUR NEXT MOVE.*

Spinning around, the men stared at Cedric. His hand inside his carry case, Cedric returned the stare. Neither could they miss Quil, who also had a hand inside a pack. That was enough to size up the situation. The shorter man grabbed the free arm of the other one, pulling him out the door.

"Send an officer here right away," said Gretchen on the phone. "Two men just left here created a disturbance and threatened to kill my cat."

Watching from the front window, Quil saw the men stop at a silver sedan, drop the brochures inside, and head toward the visitor's bureau. An officer reported within minutes, got a description of the men from Gretchen, and the car from Qui, and left to pursue the perps.

"I believe we are found," said Cedric.

"I believe you are correct," replied Gretchen.

Having received a text from Cedric, Ned and Jon charged in out of breath. "Bring us up to speed."

Quil stood at the Nook doorway as Inger brought the class to a close. "We'll start *Alice in Wonderland* next session, and after that, you write your own poems." Inger looked pleased as she watched the children chatting with newfound friends. Parents arrived, and the store soon emptied. Gretchen locked the door, and all of them moved to the living room.

"This is feeling like home." Jon sank into a chair beside the fireplace.

"Who were those sons of bitches!" Inger wasn't restraining her ire. "They were menacing, and I had a room full of children."

"I'm contacting law enforcement people to form a militia." Ned sat on the sofa studying his cell phone. "I know a number of former officers who can spread the word."

"Don't react too quick," said Cedric. "Let's talk this out first. We don't want to expose ourselves."

The discussion continued for hours. Hesitant to go separate ways, they didn't know what might be waiting outside.

Ending a phone call, Seri said, "Maybe we don't have to be as worried as we thought."

"What do you mean?" Quil had seen Seri texting right after the confrontation with the two strange men.

'I sent a message asking for help. I just received a response, saying the two men we were concerned about have been neutralized."

"Shit!" Cedric jumped up from his chair. "Shit! It's the military guys, isn't it? Thank you for bringing them in as fast as you did."

"Cedric, you really need to work on your language," said Seri, grinning.

Laughing, he hugged her close. "I'll start on that right away. Damn, but they acted fast, didn't they?"

"Damn, but they did." Seri blushed at his attention.

Buzz. Gretchen dashed to answer the phone. "That was the police. They received complaints about those men from other businesses. And this is interesting. The sheriff's department yellow-tagged an abandoned car on a side road to New Mexico. The description fits the one driven by the offenders."

"The SO needs to assign an officer to observe that car," said Ned, "and we don't know who those men might have contacted before they were stopped."

"We're being invaded," Quil said. "You're right, Ned. We need an army. But how can we form a militia or get help from the organized military if we're hiding?" Her remarks were for Cedric. Recognizing her intent, he bristled.

"You need to back off, Quil, and let those of us with military or law enforcement backgrounds handle this."

That evening, Quil studied road maps and aeronautical charts, attempting to make a connection between rustled sheep and the three possible alien base sites. Seri sat at the kitchen bar, drafting a sermon. Every few minutes, a wadded yellow ball whizzed by Quil's head en route to the floor.

"Redecorating my dining room?"

"I swing between a sermon on 'it's time to hide; seek shelter in the mountains, caves, and under rocks' to one that says, 'now's the time to take up arms and stand with your brethren, firm against wickedness at our door'. Whose that?"

The dog growled and ran to the door, her tail wagging. "It's a friend, whoever it is." Peering through the side glass, Quil opened the door, hurrying Wolf and Josiah inside.

"Do you have time to talk now?" Wolf looked like he'd run the gauntlet.

"Come in. We're glad you're safe. What do you need? I have chilled water and energy drinks."

"Water, but we need to wash up first," said Josiah.

"Call Cedric, Seribeth. We have things to show you," said Wolf. Cedric hurried over, and they gathered at the dining table.

"Okay, let's just say the excursion was interesting. We had no problem pulling the men to the side of the road, and they didn't put up much of a fight. To avoid gunfire, we used knives to silence them. They had no identification on them or in the car. We did find papers, a video recorder, and a couple of interesting-looking pieces; weapons, we think. We didn't bring any with us as they could have been fitted with tracker beacons."

"We can't read what's written on the papers," said Josiah. "It's hieroglyphs of some kind. But I uploaded it and what was on the recorder to my laptop."

"And this'll get your attention," said Wolf. "When they were no longer active, one of them turned into a green serpent man, and his eyes had slit pupils."

"A reptilian," whispered Quil.

"A shapeshifter." Seribeth's hand moved to her clerical collar.

"A problem," said Cedric. "They move among us, and we don't know they're aliens."

"Aliens posing as humans," Quil said. "Why would they be doing that? Josiah, show us what you recorded."

Josiah connected his laptop to the TV. On screen was the entrance of a cave. Parked in front was heavy equipment, including tunnel boring and dirt-moving machinery. As the cameraman moved around, reptilians and humans in varying military uniforms were plentiful, but they saw neither wispy aliens nor red-cloaked figures. Whoever handled the camera walked through the entrance into interconnecting tunnels. A large cavern revealed lines of delta aircraft. The camera then turned upward, revealing what appeared to be a sky opening, then the screen went dark.

Buzz. Quil grabbed her phone, listened, and motioned for Josiah to disconnect his computer. Flipping to a news channel, she upped the volume. Flames filled the screen. A reporter was speaking.

... two explosions in the mountains north of Durango, Colorado. Firefighters are being dropped in to contain the fires. No agency has information on what caused the explosions. Approximately twenty to thirty miles apart, the only access to either area is by unmaintained hunting trails.

Quil glanced at Wolf and Josiah. Both sat motionless, no facial expressions at all. No one would guess either knew anything about what they were viewing.

While listening, a bulletin skimmed across the screen announcing breaking news.

A third explosion has been reported on a side road near the Colorado and New Mexico state lines. It's believed a car exploded; however, no confirming information is available. Local law enforcement has blocked all access.

Again, an aerial shot showed flames shooting skywards. Quil muted the volume. "What did you do with the aliens' bodies and belongings?"

"We placed them in plastic bags and buried them in two separate locations," said Josiah.

"To answer your next question, the burial locations are where firestorms presently reach to the heavens. The third explosion is where we left the aliens' car."

"Thank goodness you had the insight to bury what you took. There must have been explosive mechanisms hidden somewhere."

"And thank God you both are alright," said Seri.

"Where's your vehicle, the one you came here in?" asked Cedric.

"Parked down the hill at the back of a dirt lot. We walked up here," said Josiah.

"Is there anything of the aliens in the car?"

"No, nothing," replied Wolf.

"Okay, I'm driving you to your car, and you're parking it in my garage. I leave my car outside occasionally, and no one will be suspicious seeing it parked in front of my place."

"That's unnecessary," argued Wolf. "We'll be okay out there."

"You're staying with us tonight," said Quil. "No arguing."

When everyone was back, they decided Wolf would stay in Quil's guest room, and Josiah would stay with Cedric. Both were ready for showers and a change of clothes.

Before leaving, Quil asked Josiah to copy the strange document and the video of the alien cave to several thumb drives. "Multiple copies will better assure one survives." When finished, Josiah provided each of them with a copy.

"Another stressful day ends," said Seri as she turned back bed covers. "I'm dreading what tomorrow might bring. I guess we take it as it comes."

"We did the right thing bringing in Wolf and Josiah. Let's hope we keep making right decisions."

fourteen

"Blackbird's gone. She must be downstairs with Wolf." Quil padded down the stairs, seeing Wolf studying the security system panel.

Barreling down the stairs, Seri plowed into her. "What's up?"

Wolf pointed to the window. "Company's here. Quil, disarm this thing, so we can let them in."

"What's going on?" Quil asked as the troop marched by.

"I called this session to update you before we leave," said Wolf. "We've considered what's priority now, and citizen safety tops the list. Spread the word to stay out of the mountains and other isolated areas. It's critical night hunters get the news. Do it through people you know and trust. We're setting up a communication center with Gracie Dove in Ignacio."

"I'll give you the contact number." Josiah took a pad from Quil's desk. "I know people with camera drones, thermal-energy type, that can spot people off body heat. With those, we'll have better luck getting night hunters to safety. It remains to be seen if the drones can spot UFOs."

"That leads to the next item," said Wolf. We need some idea of where the aliens will show up next. It does no good to go where they've been. With notice, we can be waiting, although without heavy artillery, all we can do is attempt to track them to their base. For now, all we can be is hunt dogs."

"The meadow we observed had lights spotted several times by locals," said Seri. "News travels quickly through the community."

88

"That might be the best way to determine if a location is being targeted," said Josiah. We don't know the extent of the enemy's activities. Maybe the sightings are heavier here because of Dulce, but we need to know any location they're occurring."

"I've lived here most of my life, and I can't place that cave location," said Wolf. "I'm contacting pilots I know to involve them in air search."

"I have something to add," said Ned. "These things must be all around us. We need to pay attention to the actions of people we come across. Don't approach anyone you suspect is an alien, as you could put yourself in danger. For now, get information for follow through."

"But why are they posing as humans? I haven't figured out the *why* of it yet," said Quil.

"Once we're able to spot them," said Jon, "maybe we'll learn what they're up to."

"I don't think they'll be difficult to spot." Gretchen looked at Inger, who nodded. "The actions and speech of the two yesterday were not what you would call normal. The large man spoke in choppy sentences, and frankly, wasn't burning high octane. We're not sure he was real."

"You mean he might be manufactured, a fabricant?" said Ned.

"Yeah, we think he was a fabricant and an idiot fabricant at that," said Inger. "The other one seemed to be schooling him."

"And the smaller one never took off his sun shades," said Quil. "Maybe they're light sensitive or concealing slit pupils."

"Let's get back to the question of why they pose as humans," said Ned. "Law enforcement agencies are concerned about indirect measures being taken to control people. As an example, illegal prescriptive drug use is turning people into mental zombies. Painkillers and anti-depressants are easy to get, and people hooked are easily controlled because of their need to get more. Could they be posing as humans to do that kind of thing? And I hear it's spreading through our military branches."

"I agree about the drug issue," said Cedric, "but what about other tactics to covertly undermine this planet? Problems talked about for decades have yet to be solved. I mean the ozone layer, air and water contamination, and more. The planet's becoming a scrap heap, and we don't seem to have the ability to correct it."

"Plus, the enemy has superior war machines," Wolf said, grinning. "That's a hell of a good military strategy. They help us dig the dirt out from under us so when the battle starts, all they need do is shove us in a hole we dug for ourselves."

"Have we already given them too great a lead in a war we didn't know we were in?" Quil looked at Wolf. "This is too big for just us. We need to find help."

"And fast," added Josiah. "Let's be on our way, Wolf."

"Before you go," said Ned, "I found out the identity of the hunters. Ramon and Roberto Torres of the Jicarilla Apache Nation. I believe they're the youngest sons of a widow living about ten miles outside Dulce."

"Oh, no." Seri moved beside Ned. "I know the family. Has anyone told the mother about the boys?"

"No. The Apache PD posted a missing person's bulletin. I knew the family years ago. I'm going down tomorrow. Seri, I'd like you to go with me."

"I'll clear my calendar. Quil, how about you?"

"If you and Ned are going, I'll stay with Inger and Gretchen."

"I'm attending an EPA meeting at the Double Down gold mine, or I'd go with you," said Cedric. "I'm checking on dumping in the rivers."

"Josiah and I'll go," said Wolf. "Dulce's in the Apache neighborhood, and we need their help."

fifteen

"It's not right sitting in an art class when the world is collapsing. Let's bow out."

"We're here, so let's stay awhile," said Seri. "Hazel will be hurt if we leave before it starts. Go find something to read on the bulletin board."

At the board, Quil listened to a conversation at a nearby table between Mary, a local art instructor, and a newcomer. The newcomer repeatedly touched Mary's arm as if to sympathize.

"Oh, I feel for you so much. Bless your heart. Friends of mine have had similar situations and had success with a product that can be gotten without a prescription."

"Oh, is that right?" Mary shifted in her chair, looking uncomfortable. "I put off taking anything, thinking I should be able to deal with the loss. But I might consider it, as I'm having trouble coping. How would I go about getting some?"

"No problem. I have it in the car. I picked up extra the last time I bought it. I'll get it for you now."

Quil asked an acquaintance nearby who the newcomer was. "Ramona Rand from Farmington. She moved in from somewhere south, maybe El Paso. She does oils or maybe acrylics."

Quil kept a watch on Ramona Rand. Occasionally, the newcomer rubbed at her eyes. *What's with the eye thing.* Quil moved closer to eavesdrop.

"Is your eye bothering you?" asked Mary. "You keep rubbing at it."

"It's nothing serious, merely a fleck of dust under a contact. You know how it is with contacts."

"I have a cleaning solution in my purse. Take your contact out, and I'll be right back."

"Oh, no, I can't do that. I'll take care of it later. Truly, it's okay. Thank you, though. You're so very kind." She rubbed Mary's forearm again.

Quil wasn't buying that bogus touchy-feely crap. Can't Mary see what's going on? Getting Seri's attention, they walked outside. "I believe we've got one." After listening, Seri nodded in agreement.

"What do we do about her?"

"Learn what we can. She's smooth though, non-threatening, sickeningly personable. I see how some might accept her without question—especially if they're knee-deep in depression."

As customary, participants chatted across tables while trying out new art techniques. Talk centered on several women who had dropped out of activities because of health reasons. Seeking more information, Seri received the expected answer. All had problems dealing with nerves, depression, stress, and all were on mood-altering drugs.

Quil watched the poser glide smoothly around the room, cooing and chatting with class attendees. At one point, Ramona interrupted the class, giving a drawn out explanation of a calendar change for a plain air art group, no members of which were present.

As the Rand woman talked, Quil overheard mutterings of a woman two chairs away and leaned closer. "Why does she do this every time a group meets?" said the muttering woman. "And the one she chums with does the same thing."

Quil asked her to explain. "Ramona and her red-headed friend are always placing themselves in front of groups even though they hold no formal office or have good reason to do so. The red-headed woman is more than a little disturbing. Some are afraid of her."

"I'm going to the car, Seri. See if you can get Mary and the poser to the other side of the room for about ten minutes. I'll explain later."

On return to the classroom, Quil walked by Mary's art portfolio, sliding an envelope inside. At the close of the workshop, she gathered materials while Seri went to the ladies' room. Unexpectedly, Mary sat down beside her.

"Thank you, Quilty, both for the words of caution and those of encouragement. Your idea is a good one, and I'll follow up, starting tomorrow. I felt something was wrong with the direction I was heading, but it's a confusing time now. You helped me do a course correction before it had a chance to do damage. Now, what do I do with this twenty dollar bottle of pills?"

"Slip it into my backpack? Maybe it's traceable to the drugmaker." As she stood, Mary shoved the vial into Quil's pack.

Seri rejoined her at the table. "Is everything okay with Mary?"

"She's not taking the drugs."

"What about the others who are?"

"Mary's seeing to it. I think the best solutions come from people involved in a problem. Mary's a good one to lead that movement here. Let's go. We'll wait in the car and follow the Rand woman to wherever she's going."

"First, let's snap a couple of selfies to include the poser." But while doing that, several acquaintances drew them into an art show discussion, resulting in their missing the snake's departure.

"We made a mistake, Seri. We should have been right behind that Rand woman when she left."

"I hate we missed her leaving too, but we're lucky to run across one so quickly. Look what we discovered. They're really working the drug angle in this community."

"Something's bothering me about this. I can see how undermining us at the ground level would hasten an enemy's takeover attempt—I get that. But I feel we're being distracted from focusing on a bigger problem. It's like they're purposely keeping things stirred up to hide what they're really up to."

"Possibly, but the drug distraction is serious. I'm concerned about what's happening to our people, and we need to deal with the here-and-now."

"We need to broaden our thinking. We're missing something."

sixteen

Today, Quil had watch duty at the bookstore while the rest were on the move. Seri and Ned were meeting with the Torres family in Dulce. Cedric was at the Double Down Mine meeting with the EPA, and Jon had doctor duties. They were keeping to planned activities, but Quil felt it still was the wrong thing to be doing. But she busied myself shelving magazines and books.

"Seri told us about the poser at the art workshop," said Inger. "Describe her so we'll recognize her if she comes in here."

"I'll send you photos. To describe her actions, think of the Duchess in the Alice tales. She's shifty. Always sidling up to others, unable to keep hands off people, playing at being nice. The kind that wraps insincerity in gooey words. Her close friend seems to be the red-haired slayer serpent.

"Ah, yes. The Red Queen always yelling 'off with their heads' and the Duchess displaying condescending affection at inappropriate times," said Inger. "Two bad bitches."

"Fitting, isn't it?"

"What can we do about 'em?"

"I sent texts to Ned and Cedric. Seri's giving details to Wolf and Josiah in Dulce. We'll stumble across their whereabouts one of these days and deal with them."

"Do you think the freaks will stay out of sight now that two of them were neutralized?" Gretchen asked Quil the question, although she was looking at Inger.

"Possibly, however they seem to be brazen about their activities."

"Go ahead, Inger," said Gretchen. "Let's talk about it so we can make a go or no go decision."

94

"What are you talking about?' asked Quil.

"Okay, Quil, but listen before you disagree with me. Ever since the incident on the mountain, I can't sleep, and I'm exhausted all the time. It's getting difficult to face the world. When I was a social worker, I encouraged people to address their fears and monsters, not speaking literally of green snake monsters, but you know what I mean. Bottom line, I have to go back to the mountain and see it again. First, to affirm I escaped a sure death, and second, I'm working to do something about the wrong committed there."

"Go back—up there?" Quil turned to Gretchen. "How do you feel about this?"

"I would like never to see *that* mountain again, but I am having problems letting it go. Perhaps if we could walk away, rather than sneak away like cowards, we could better accept things and leave it behind us."

"If the uglies are keeping a low profile, as we hope they are," added Inger, "this is the time to go back, even if only for a few minutes. I know Ned would stop us, but he'll be gone tomorrow, and tomorrow's the day to go."

"Well, *pfft!* From experience, Inger, I know getting you to change your mind is like buttin' a stump. Please give this greater consideration."

"My mind's made up. Ned told me not to drive my Hummer, but I will. It's that important to me."

"I'll go with them." Jon had entering through the back door and listened to the conversation. "I'll take my car. It's four-wheel, and I've had it on hunting trails."

"Tomorrow's a workday," Quil said, trying to think of an argument against the action they proposed. Although, she wasn't sure she wanted to argue against it, as she, too, was drowning in self-reproach.

"If we close two hours earlier than usual, we should have enough time to get there, satisfy our need to look, and leave the mountain before dark."

Quil's anxiety spiked thinking about returning to that cursed mountain, but she knew Inger, and Inger had decided she was going. "Jon, are you handling a weapon now?"

"I bought a forty-five and had two lessons with Ned. And I've practiced with your shotgun."

"Only two lessons?" Jon's face fell.

"They were long lessons. He made me practice for four hours each session. Ned's a good instructor. I learned a lot from him."

"He is a good instructor; it's the marine in him. Damnit, Inger, you know I'll go. You knew that all along, didn't you?"

"Yeah, I did."

That afternoon, Quil listened to Seri recount the meeting with Mrs. Torres. "She's strong, and the family is planning a grieving ceremony. Something's up. You're too quiet? What's going on?"

"Inger and Gretchen are going back to *that* mountain as they want to see it in daylight, hopin' it'll let them move on. Inger's having problems with sleep and day-to-day functioning."

"Guilt. I also carry shame from not raising a hand to stop those monsters. Are you going?"

"I can't let them go alone. Jon's takin' his car. Ned and Cedric won't be here tomorrow, so we're leaving two hours before closing with plans to drive there, look, and drive back."

"I'm going too."

seventeen

They were back on the mountain again, and Quil hated that they were. The others seemed just as edgy.

The drive took less time than planned. Jon parked at the same spot they were before but kept the vehicle idling while Quil and Seri did a quick look around. Giving Jon a wave, he switched off the engine and opened doors for Inger and Gretchen. They all huddled near the car, occasionally allowing their eyes to move down to the meadow.

It was nearing dusk, and already long fingers of evening crept through the trees. The sun was sinking to its knees in the western sky, and night would be on them when it slid behind distant peaks.

"I need to give Bird a quick walk before we go back." Seri went with her to a treed area where Bird nosed around searching for a spot. Suddenly Bird froze, the hair on her back standing straight up. Built like a pint-sized armored tank, the dog planted herself between Quil and whatever was in the scrub, growling a warning.

"Get behind me, Seri." Chills ran down both Quil's arms as she scoped the brushwood. From the corner of an eye, she saw Seri moving toward her. Bird stood her ground, her hind feet throwing grass and dirt backward, threatening whatever was—

A snakehead charged straight for them, pulling a silver device from a scabbard. Quil put two in its chest, saw it stagger, but it didn't go down. Raising the gun for a headshot, she heard the whistle of a blade as a knife enter the snake's eye. Its head jerked backward, and it dropped.

Jon was on the run, forty-five drawn. Quil held the serpent in her sights, watching Jon inch closer to the crumpled body.

"Wait, Jon. What if it's playing possum?" said Quil. Where's the weapon it was holding? I don't see it."

"What if it can do weird thing," said Seri, "like spray chemicals if we get too close."

"Yeah, I'll get a long stick." With a dead limb, Jon punched it in the legs, chest, and head. Moving closer, he kicked it repeatedly in the ribcage. "Well, it's not breathing."

Bird let go a low, rumbling growl and raced up the rise. Quil turned, seeing a man in uniform, trying to get a bead on the dog. Bird was spinning between Inger and the soldier, lunging at his legs, hitting him in the knees. Gretchen was running toward Inger; Jon and Seri were running uphill. *Blocked shot!*

"Get down!" screamed Quilt. Gunfire! Blackbird dropped.

A shotgun blast exploded, the sound ricocheting across the valley. The attacker stumbled backward, clutching his side. Quil heard the gun rack, and a second blast hit him dead square in the belly. He went down. Hands on his midsection, he screamed, rolling side to side.

Running toward Blackbird, Quil's eyes darted between Inger the man on the ground. The recoil had thrown Inger against a tree.

"Damnit! Help me, Gretchen! I'm going down!" Gretchen was already with her.

"Get Inger to the car," Jon shouted, cautiously moving toward the uniformed man, weapon raised.

"I have Inger," yelled Gretchen.

Quil held Blackbird's head off the ground. The dog struggled to get a breath through her mouth, her nose blocked with dirt. No whining, just pleading eyes asking for help. "Little girl, what have you done? Hold on, baby," wiping dirt from Bird's nose and mouth. Then Jon was there, kneeling beside them. "Can you help her?" Jon's hands quickly moved over the dog.

"Flesh wound, upper thigh. Bad gash, no bone broken that I can tell. I can save her. I brought a med kit." Removing his sweater, he wrapped the dog and carried her to the car.

Quil stayed on alert, watching the downed traitor. "Inger! Where did he come from?"

"That stand of pines," motioning to the left.

Quil scanned for movement. Beside her, Seri held a second knife, her eyes raking the thicket where the snakehead materialized. She quietly mumbled, shifting from one foot to the other.

"Help me. Stop bleeding. Stop—bleeding." Pleading for help, the injured man received compassion from no one.

"Seri, listen. Do you hear me?" Seri stopped swaying and nodded. "Get photos of his face, insignia, anything identifying."

Glancing down, Quil saw a gun within the man's reach and kicked it away. "Why are you helping these beasts?"

"Can't—beat 'em. Joined—winning side."

"Well, you're on the losing side today. You're a dead man. She took out your belly. Tell us where their base is? Is it Dulce?"

The turncoat struggled to breathe, red foam oozing from the sides of his mouth. His body was giving in to the inevitable. He whispered in jerks, spitting blood with each word. "Dulce, no, cold, ice, cold. Tracer. They—fix me. Uh, not dying."

Tracer! Quil's heart slammed against her ribs. "Why wait, Bucky? I can fix you right now." Raising the Glock, she put two to his chest and one in his head. "Everybody in the car!" Starting to walk away, Quil spun around and emptied the Glock in him. "See if they can fix that, you sniveling coward."

"I'm going for my knife," said Seri.

Quil raced after Seri, sliding a fresh magazine in the Glock. Seri was reaching for her knife as Jon skidded to a stop, grabbing her arm.

"Don't touch fluid from the body!" He yanked antiseptic wipes from a packet, handing them to her.

"Wh—what!" Quil dropped to a knee her eyes on the sky.

"What's wrong? What is it?" cried Seri.

"Oh, god, we have to go!" said Quil. "Did you see that? Did you see it?"

"I didn't see anything." Seri was running for the car. Jon wasn't moving.

"Jon, get to the car. I'll trail."

"Not before I do this!" He pulled a short machete from his belt, and with a single swing, severed the serpent's head. A swift kick sent it sailing between branches of a nearby tree. "That's for the men murdered here, you disgusting pile of heathen shit!" Quickly wiping his knife, he let the sheets drop to the ground.

"No, don't leave anything they can trace!"

"Damnit, Quil." Jon dug a hole with the machete, swept in the tell-tale wipes, and kicked dirt, covering the hole. Grabbing his arm, she pulled him toward the car.

They'd lost the sun. Darkness covered them. Outside the car, Quil shivered in the chilled night air staring at the sky. "We are leaving! Can't you see we're leaving!"

"Get in," shouted Jon.

Quil jumped in as he spun out. Grabbing binoculars, she searched above the mountaintop. Jon turned onto the county road and headed for the highway. But she had to know.

"Is Blackbird—"

"I think she'll be okay. She's heavily bandaged to slow the bleeding. I gave her something for pain. She's sleeping. I'll stitch the wound when we get to the house."

"Thank you, Jon." Exhaling, Quil leaned her head against the glass.

"What did you see?" Seri whispered, her hand on Quil's shoulder.

"I don't know. It couldn't be … I must be losing my mind."

"Look behind us! What's that!" Jon yelled. Their hearts stopped, expecting to see the enemy on their bumper. Instead, flames shooting skyward lit the darkness on the mountain where they'd escaped death—for a second time.

"Someone's destroying evidence," said Quil. "They're burning the remains of the dead." *Is that to help us or to help the enemy?*

"What the blue blazes happened back there?" asked Jon.

"It was chaos, loose and running wild," said Gretchen.

"Well, we're never going back! Never!"

As they approached Durango, cells ringing meant only one thing. Ned or Cedric was trying to reach them. No one answered.

"It's all my fault," said Inger.

"Facing them won't be easy." Gretchen's eyes were on Inger, who was getting antsier by the second.

"I can't face them," said Inger. "I don't know why, but I get so nervous around Ned I can't put two words together. I blather like an idiot when he's demanding an answer. It's like going through a police interrogation. And now, there are two cops."

"It's never easy with Ned," said Quil, "but given time, he'll calm down. Stand firm, maintain eye contact, and don't mince words."

"Eye contact, don't mince words," repeated Inger.

Jon drove by the front of the bookstore. Ned and Cedric sat on a park bench, a pile of overturned coffee cups a sure sign they'd been there a while. Focusing on papers, neither noticed the car passing. Jon drove down the alley and parked beside the poets' garage.

"I'll get Bird inside." Jon gave Quil a reassuring look. "She'll be okay. I'll come by your house later to check on her."

Gretchen cleared the table to give Jon space to work. "I'll let Ned ad Cedric in the front and delay as long as I can."

Seri carried Jon's medical bag, asking what he wanted first. "I've had training in emergency response care for accident victims. I can assist."

"Glad for the help."

Quil watched Jon skillfully address the wound. When finished, he laid medicinal items on the table. "Take these with you. I'll go over their use when I come by later." He constructed a splint made from items in the kitchen. "This is to keep her from putting weight on the leg. She'll need help to get outside."

"I can carry her." Quil glimpsed Gretchen near the front door with Ned and Cedric, listening to talk about the Dulce trip.

"Where are the others?" Cedric looked around the bookstore.

"In the kitchen. Blackbird's hurt."

Ned rushed beside Quil. "Is she going to be okay? What happened?" Before Quil could answer, Inger blurted a response.

"She was protecting me. I was the reason we went back there, and she got shot, Ned." Inger leaned against the table, bracing for what was coming next.

Ned stood stock-still a full minute before he huffed and shook his head. "Back on the mountain! What were you doing back *there*?" Both Ned and Cedric had eyes riveted on Inger's face.

"We were killing things. Quil and Seri killed a snake freak. I killed a military man. Then Quil killed him again. Jon hacked off the snake's head and kicked it in a tree."

"That sums it up nicely, Inger." Quil couldn't keep from grinning. Gretchen and Seri turned away, trying not to laugh. "Inger's not to blame for my dog being shot. Bird saved all of us tonight. She'll be okay. Jon's seeing to that. And you might want to turn on the news. Another fire burns on a mountain tonight. I'll let the others give details. I'm taking Bird home."

Gretchen found a box with handles to serve as a pet carrier. "Leave her in the box," said Jon. "If she wakes and needs to go outside, carry the box and lift her out carefully. The less handling, the better."

"Okay. I'm leaving now. Seri, would you come to the house with Jon later? That way, you can be here to assist Inger in explaining why we went back to the mountain." Seri walked outside with her.

"Do you want me to stay somewhere else tonight? Do you need alone time?"

"Oh, god no. I want you with me tonight, old woman."

"Good. Any ideas on how to help Inger with the tongue-tied issue. I ache for her."

"Ask Ned to deal with it. He'll find a way to tear down fences getting in the way of a connection there. I've seen him do it before."

Quil carried Bird inside, placing the box on her desk, then built a fire. It wasn't 't cold enough for a fire; she just wanted one. Looking into wax light brought calmness.

"What a mess, and we keep making it worse. We've twisted the tail of the tiger now, and they'll come looking for sure. Why are our military people bailing on us? The traitor's dying words … what was he trying to say?" She grabbed a journal from the desk and jotted down what she could recall. Maybe later, she could figure out what she was overlooking.

Walking to the desk, she gazed down at her dog. "Little Blackbird. You saved us. So small, but size didn't matter. You did what you were put here to do. All you ever asked was occasional recognition of your worth and tender handling. I hope I haven't failed you."

Walking window to window, she peeked out blinds, scanning around her townhouse. Hearing a car door slam, she rushed to the front door. Jon was carrying a medical case plus a duffle bag.

"I'll let Jon tell you why he's carrying a duffle," said Seribeth.

"I thought you could have trouble carrying the box up and down the stairs and decided to stay the night. Cedric told me you have a guest room, and Seri can sleep in your bedroom. That way, I'll be available if Bird wakes experiencing pain. Is it okay to put her box on the dining table for now?"

"Sure, that's fine." Quil watched as he checked the dog.

"Her breathing has stabilized. She'll experience pain for a long while and probably will have a limp after this, a war wound. I'll check on her off and on through the night and let you know if we need to get her to the vet hospital." He carried the box upstairs as Quil followed with his bags.

While dressing for bed, Quil sought information on what happened after she left the bookstore.

"Was Ned difficult? I hope he didn't lose his temper with Inger."

"He was surprisingly calm. I think that was due to no one being hurt, other than your dog, I mean. Plus, I think he and Cedric were shocked we women dropped a couple of the enemy."

"What about Dulce? What did they learn about an alien base?"

"A lot about Dulce, but not what we wanted to hear. They met with several people, but none they talked to could confirm an alien center. They still see lights and UFOs. Most think it's a government shim-sham to hide what's really going on.'

"Disappointing. What about military help?"

"None yet. Ned's contacted a lot of people, and former military and law enforcement are joining up in a citizen army. They're calling themselves the Shadow Squad, because they have to stay concealed for now."

"With what we're up against, that isn't enough. A militia might be all we can do for now, but we need military might with us."

"They know that, Quil. They're trying to come up with answers, but they're being cautious in advertising our presence. Cedric knows these people and how they work. They are trying."

"I'm not criticizing. I'm worried, is all, and tired. Let's get some rest." They went to bed, but as soon as Seri was asleep, Quil went downstairs, wanting to be alone.

She was glad the feverish demands of the day were over. Her eyelids heavy, she let them close. When she opened them, she was walking in the rain. Broad drops fell about her, yet she wasn't wet. Touching a crystal wall, she watched the droplets run down the glass. Up the passageway, she saw the shade lady coming toward her.

"Hello, Quil. Pressing matters disturb your spirit. Let us not waste time. It continuously runs, you know?"

"Yes, I do know that. Well, to begin, we're facing a powerful enemy. We're outmatched and without organized military help."

"That's one," said the lady.

"Yes, one. And an unknown creature—as black as the night in which it flew—spoke in my mind, saying danger was near and to leave. It brought a warning. Perhaps it can help us. How do I find it?"

"That's two."

"Two. And my spirit animal was badly wounded, saving our lives. She needs care, and I worry for her, as demands on me are multiplying."

"That's three." The lady waited, anticipating another one or two, but Quil offered no other.

"Let's start with two, the unknown bringing the warning. The question may not be how do you find it, especially if it's extraordinary. Perhaps you should allow the mysterious to find you. You'll know of what I speak in due time."

"Due time is fickle; it may forget to show. Why can't I know now?"

"The hands of the clock say you're not ready. Now for three. The clock does say it's time to remove your lampshade and enter an awareness shift, leading to self-discovery. As you do not need cover now, perhaps your spirit animal could wear it while healing, safe and concealed from danger."

"This comes off?" Quil lifted the covering off her head and saw that it was, indeed, a lampshade. She heard a small *yip* and saw Blackbird beside her. Lowering the shade, it fit perfectly on her small head. Then, the dog vanished. Hearing a chuckle, Quil tried to look under the lady's lampshade, but she walked on.

"Now, for number one. A particularly difficult one, it is too. Answers do exist, but it's for you to weed them out. You know how to weed, don't you? Why not test yourself? Where are you looking? Are you standing too near to see clearly?

Can gain be found in new eyes? Do you sense someone waiting for you? You have much to think about. Shouldn't you get to it? Good night Quil, and don't forget two."

Quil woke with a start. The phone blinked, a text from Inger: *Remember to bring Bird's medicinal when you drop her by tomorrow morning.*

Now, that was truly baffling. She laid back down ,thinking about the talk with *Shade*, the name she'd given the crystal lady, focusing on the second item on the list: *Allow the mysterious to find you.* Her eyes drifted shut again.

> "Just then flew down a monstrous crow
> as black as a tar barrel."
>
> —Lewis Carroll
> *Through the Looking Glass*

eighteen

"What time is it?" Quil threw off the afghan, seeing Seri on the ottoman, looking perplexed.

"Something's not right with me. How can I be sleeping as soundly as I do with so many problems going on? It's abnormal. Maybe I need to see a shrink, or a witch. I know a healing witch near the ridgeline south of the Wiminuche. Do you think I should give her a call?"

"You're okay. At least you're sleeping. I'm having strange dreams and wake up wondering who the heck is talking in the middle of the night ... who's that talking now?"

"Talking? It has to be Jon."

It was Jon, talking to her dog as he came downstairs. "Hi, you two. Look! I removed the splint, and Bird's able to stand on her own. The wound is still ugly, and it'll take time to heal, but she's going to be okay. Isn't that great!" Setting the box on the table, Blackbird peeked over the rim, looking spent and standing on three legs.

"It's more than great. It's a wonderment." Quil gently stroked Bird's ears. "Inger will watch over her for a while now, Jon. Since you live close to the bookstore, can you be available if help's needed?"

"Even better. I'm moving in with Gretchen and Inger. It just makes sense, doesn't it? I'm surprised we didn't think of it before. Gretchen and I decided this morning. I'll take Bird with me when I leave, which is right now as I want to get her settled."

As he was driving away, Quil ran to his window, motioning him to roll it down. "I almost forgot. Tell Inger to leave the lampshade on Bird's head. Never take it off."

"What lampshade?" He looked at Blackbird in the box next to him.

"Inger will understand. Will you tell her?"

"Uh-hm. Sure, I'll tell her." As he drove away, he looked over his shoulder and shook his head.

"Coincidence shows up at the oddest times," said Seri. "One of these days, I'd like you to explain that bygone-day language you sometimes speak. Start with *wonderment*. Who says that nowadays?"

"Who says nowadays, nowadays?"

"Yeah, back to the war. I forgot to mention that instruction on large-caliber weapons starts this weekend. Ned mentioned it last night. I told him we wanted in, but he said women weren't allowed. Do you think you could get him to change his mind?"

"Not even us? That doesn't sound like Ned. Why would he say that?"

"Because we have no experience using large-caliber weapons. How do we get experience if we're not allowed to handle them?"

"That still doesn't sound like Ned, but let's find someone who will give us training. What about Wolf or Josiah? Would one of them do it for us?"

"I'm already dialing." Seri was smiling when she disconnected. "Yes! Josiah said he'd be honored to provide training. We start today. And other women are wanting in. I told him to say nothing to Ned or Wolf about us being involved."

"Why Wolf?"

"He wouldn't want me exposed to danger. He's very shielding of family, expects women to stay home and out of harm's way. He's always been one to protect his own. And, on that note, Wolf will be teaching a class this weekend and could make a fuss if we run into each other. Maybe that won't happen."

"When he sees how good we are, he'll change his mind." In a roundabout way, Seri had answered her question. It wasn't Ned protesting women's involvement.

Quil's phone buzzed. It was Josiah. "Thanks for doing this. Sure, I can. Let me jot it down. Okay, I'll do my best."

"He's wasting no time. While you help Gracie at the communications center, I'm to go to the army surplus store and get materials for concealment training. Have you heard of Ghillie suits?" They studied web screens giving details of camouflage preparation for snipers. "Josiah said there'd be other costs as we go through training. Wait here a second." She ran upstairs, returning with an envelope. "Take this cash for Gracie and Adam."

"Wolf is providing money for supplies and equipment."

"I can help. This could get costly. What size boot do you wear? I can't get combat boots for the others, but I can get ours today."

"Size nine. I'll repay you for what you get me."

"Consider it an early birthday gift, preacher woman."

"Thanks, and I'll get this to Gracie."

Quil made a quick trip to the army surplus store for the requested items, enough for eight women. She felt excitement growing as she loaded boxes of camouflaged field uniforms, canvas, burlap, and netting. *Finally, we're doing something.* Picking Seri up at the church, they drove to a large field in nearby mesa country.

On arrival, they joined a half-dozen diverse women, all gun familiar, some hunters, some target shooters. Weapon familiarization was first on the roster followed by concealment tactics.

"Gather scraps of shrubbery, dried grass, leafy twigs, and such for your Ghillie suits to aid in concealment. Devising camouflage outfits can be fun but don't look at it that way. This is war, not a game. You're preparing to hunt and kill the enemy."

They rubbed sooty grease on our faces and dirt over the shredded burlap strips hanging from netting. When done, Seri jokingly said they resembled tattered goblins out of a fairytale. In reality, they looked good, real good.

"Okay, look away for ten minutes, and then locate me." Ten minutes passed. They scanned the terrain section by section but failed to detect Josiah's whereabouts.

"This is what I expect of you. I do not want you found!" Hearing Josiah's voice, they saw him materialize out of the landscape and walk in their direction. Understanding what they had to do, they got to work, staying at it for hours. Receiving a call on a two-way, Josiah barked orders.

"We have the okay to move to the firing range. It will be ours for the remainder of the day. There will be no talking. You will not acknowledge anyone speaking to you. When we arrive, take a position on the orange line. Get your weapon set and you into position. You'll see multiple targets in the field in front of you. Starting with the closest and, on my command, begin firing. Remember, focus, focus, focus. I'll be walking the line, observing your hits and ability to remain motionless. Do you understand?"

"Yes, sir," they shouted.

Shooting went remarkably well; this they knew how to do. Pleased with their performance, Josiah gave kudos up and down the line. Showing due diligence, each woman was on the orange line because she wanted in the fight. One day, lives could depend on skills learned today, and they well understood that.

A sudden commotion almost broke their focus—almost. Wolf's voice pierced the sound of gun reports. Quil heard Seribeth's name mentioned several times. She continued firing, but it was impossible not to listen.

"Seri, you shouldn't be here. You're jerking the gun when you pull the trigger, throwing off your aim. Anyway, you're needed back at the church. Let's go."

"I'm staying. I make my own decisions. Josiah's my instructor, not you. And you're the cause of me jerking the gun." Speaking Ute, she seemed to have gotten the message across as Wolf stomped away.

Quil concentrated on annihilating her share of targets, but it wasn't long before she felt a nudge on her boot. She didn't react, hoping Wolf would allow later discussion. But he wasn't waiting.

He knelt on a knee. "I don't want women in this, Quil. It's dangerous out in the field. I'm asking you to leave with me. If you go, Seri will too."

Quil came close to letting him disrupt her firing. But Josiah ended it for them all. "That's all for today. Good job! Be here tomorrow, same time. Don't be late."

"We're good at this," said Quill. "You know that, Wolf." She and Seri wasted no time in leaving.

Yelling was all they heard as they drove away. "Should we go back and stop that?" Quil pulled under a large cottonwood.

"No, they'd better work it out themselves." Seri lowered her window. Wolf was throwing equipment in his truck, and the noise blocked most of what he said, but they did hear: "No, not mine. Not in battle. Never." Josiah, also throwing equipment in the truck, was saying things like: 'New day. Women want in. Skilled shooters." Then Wolf walked away with a phone at his ear.

"Let's go," said Seri. "It's over."

After training, Quil and Seri went to her trailer to clean up. Gracie tapped on the screen door before coming in. "Josiah called. Ranchers north of Sleeping Ute Mountain spotted lights at the same site the last two nights. The men's squad has left, heading that way. They don't know when they'll be back."

"Should we get ready to go?" asked Quil.

"Not this time. Josiah said you need more practice. He wanted me to get the news to you right away."

Relaxing that evening was impossible. It was the abruptness of being involved in war preparation only to have it yanked away. Was there a reason for that? Quil tried to read but tossed the book aside. Suddenly, wind whistled around the corners of the house. Gnat was bringing a message.

"A shift begins. You possess a singular gift, and others seek your involvement. As in a mathematical game, choices may be added and subtracted. Consider the plus and minus. The end decision remains with you. Today will not be the same as yesterday. The mystery of you begins to unfold."

The mystery of me unfolds? *Good. Whatever it is, I'm ready for it.* Plus and minus? Simple math. Doesn't sound difficult.

nineteen

Quil hadn't rested well. The atmosphere, crackling with electricity, adding to her uneasiness. She didn't like a feeling she was having. Nerves, just jangled nerves. She called Gracie, who said she hadn't heard from the men in the field, but Seri needed to talk.

"When the other women heard Josiah would be gone for an unknown time, they decided to go ahead without him. If you're in, get a move on. Be here about nine."

"Did Josiah leave rifles and ammo?"

"No. Gracie expects a shipment today or tomorrow. We'll be working on concealment again. Josiah said we weren't ready, so we're getting ready. Are you in?"

"I'm in, and it sounds like we're stepping up the pace.

On the way to the range, Quil received a text and pulled to a curb, thinking it might be from Seri. Instead, it was Gene, telling her to be at his hangar mid-afternoon. "He must have found something on the plane that needs fixing. Great! Another repair cost I don't need."

She was last to arrive at the training site. The others were in field suits, sitting in a circle, Seri and Gracie included. Quil noticed a lot of hand gesturing and occasional yelling, and stayed in the car to listen. No question, all of them wanted to go forward, although their reasons why varied. A couple voiced a desire to join the men's squad. A tall woman, noticeably agitated, did most of the talking.

"Didn't you get the message? The men will never accept us as equals in their squad. They think we're weak, fragile as a spider's web they can brush aside. We're too frickin' easy to push out of the way." She flicked her wrist like brushing aside a bug.

113

"Then why are we bothering with training if we'
won't be accepted?" asked another.

"One day of training, one lousy day, and I used all my
money to buy these clodhopper boots," said another. "I won't
eat for a month."

The yelling grew louder. Seri and Gracie tried to quell
the storm of protests, but they weren't having a positive effect.
Getting out of the car, Quil strolled over, swinging her Ghillie
suit and whistling a tune.

"Dang, I'm glad that boot camp is done. Thought
we'd never get finished up. But it's by us, and now we can get
on with what we need to be doin'."

The group shut up, staring at Quil. "Get on with what?
There's nothing to get on with. Is there?" The tall woman
asking turned her gaze to Gracie.

"Sure there is," Quil said hurriedly. "Gracie, now that
the words out about reportin' of sightings, I just bet you're
flooded with calls, asking for help. Am I right in that?"

"Uhhh, hallelujah, praise be. We have been flooded
with calls. Flooded, I say. People are asking for help all over
the place. Isn't that right, Seri?"

"Praise be. The people are calling, and we are needed.
We must prepare to battle the demonic forces of evil.
Hallelujah! Praise be!"

Suddenly, squad members were laughing. The tall,
outspoken woman looked at Quil. "You're full of it, short
stuff, but you just might be the one to lead us against the
demonic forces of evil. Let's get on with this."

Quil caught Gracie's eye and rubbed her thumb
against a forefinger, hoping she'd read it correctly.

"Those needing monetary assistance for supplies see
me after today's training. We've had funding come in." A few
sighs of relief, and they were back on track.

"Now, let's talk," said Quil. "From what I've
gathered, no one of us has a military background. So we're
not military, but we need a military attitude. Josiah said this
isn't a game. We're in this to hunt and kill the enemy. If we
stay, we're willingly dedicating our lives to something other

than ourselves. What's so important that you're here? For country, for family, for self?"

"For me, it's family," said the tall woman. "My name is Gabby Torres, by the way. We do need a military attitude. And we need to hear criticism, honest criticism to improve. No hurt feelings allowed. We work hard." Quil studied the woman, an intense person, and wondered about her background.

"Good," said Seri. "Gracie told me earlier we received a shipment of earpieces, field communications equipment. We've set aside enough for us. Thinking about that, we might need to drop our real names and go with code assignments. Any ideas? Numbers? English? Spanish?" Everyone but Gabby wanted numbers in English. Argumentative, she stubbornly pushed for Spanish. She lost the vote.

"Seri, you start as this was your idea." Counting off, Quil was last, eighth of the eight. She wondered about the woman named Gabby, now with the code name of Three. With the last name, Torres, she was probably a relative of the Torres brothers who were murdered on the mountain. That being the case, would she be able to control her emotions? If she couldn't, she could put them all in danger. Still, the woman had a right to be here. Checking the time, the day was slipping by, and Quil needed to push the group forward. "I opt for a separate squad. Let the men come to us if they want us fighting at their side."

"Let's name the squad," said a soft-spoken African American with the code name of Four. "We need an identity." And another debate ensued.

"How about the Spider Squad," said Quil. Again, she pushed for a decision. "True, a spider web can be brushed aside, but a spider and its web cling to what's brushing it away. Spiders are stalkers. They move without noise, and with many eyes, they see what others cannot. And their bite … deadly."

As her gaze traveled from one to another, Quil saw nods of agreement. And on that day, the Spider Squad came into being. The eight became of one mind, one mission. A squad of unknowns, invisible to almost everyone. Even they didn't understand their place in what was to come. But they were fast learners, and they'd catch on quick. They had to. They had to, or they would die.

Okay, let's do this," said Seri. "Today, it's concealment. Someone volunteer. You have ten minutes to get set. After that, we're coming for you." Tough on themselves and each other, repeats were required until satisfaction was achieved. Like a gunshot ricocheting through their minds, Josiah's words resonated throughout the day.

This is what I expect of you. I do not want you found!
Word to live by, literally.

twenty

Tired, dirty, and out of sorts, Quil wondered why Gene hadn't told her what required repairing with an estimate of cost. She needed to keep the plane airworthy. She already felt negligent not being in the air, hunting for the enemy cave.

The hangar doors were closed on the Simpson's hangar, and Gene stood at the walk door motioning for her to come in that way. Leaving her jacket in the car, she slipped the sidearm in the backpack rather than wearing it exposed. Pushing her tiredness aside, she dug deep for a smile, and hurried to greet her mechanic.

"Hey, Gene. I hope what you're about to tell me doesn't wreck my bank account. What's the problem?"

"Let's talk over here." He sat in a plastic patio chair and motioned to one facing him.

"Is it that bad? She's flying okay. I've noticed nothing to cause concern." She took the chair offered and dropped her pack beside it.

"Your plane is in top-notch condition. It's you that looks worse for wear."

"If the plane's okay, why am I here?"

"What's going on with you, Quil? You more out-of-sorts recently than I've ever seen you?" Standing, he walked to a table where a teapot sat on a hot plate. "I'm having tea and think a cup would be good for you."

Quil fidgeted in the chair, jumpy as a set of bedsprings. But she'd been edgy all day. She sipped the tea and found it relaxing. Moving the chair next to a workbench, she set the cup beside a vat of water, leaned back, and gave Gene a nod, wanting to hurry this along.

117

"It's best to be straightforward. There are things you should know, starting with me." Standing, he set his cup on a table."

"What the—" Rearing backward sent the chair flying and her to the floor. Grabbing for anything to hold on to, she collided with the water vat, dumping its full contents on top of her. "Umph!" Her elbows cracked as they slammed against the slab floor. Stunned, she fought a torrent of water punching her in the chest.

GUN! Get gun! Frantically trying to stand, her shoes slipped in the water, and she hit the concrete again. She lunged for the backpack—and came up short.

"Don't go for it, Quil." A tall blue creature stood unruffled, watching the show.

Facedown on the floor, she snuck a look at him. *Weapon? No, don't see one. Get away! Get out of here!* On her knees, she scurried out of the water. Hands up as a shield, she slowly backed away and bumped into a large tool case.

"Are you going to kill me?"

"No."

"What are you?"

"I believe 'who are you' is the proper way to question my presence. Nonetheless, I'll respond. I'm an interstellar visitor from another planet."

"But—you're blue! Skin, eyes—now, those eyes are weird! This is bad, really bad! Keep away from me, you weird freak!"

"Weird freak! Me, a freak! Don't you think you're weird to me? I resent the crude, offensive language."

With a swing of an arm, he sent the table skidding across the room, sending hot plate and cups bouncing. Taking several steps toward Quil, he stopped and sharply reversed. Strange noises came from his head.

Damn, I'm in trouble! Quil looked for anything to use as a weapon. The eruption of wheezes suddenly stopped, and the big blue guy turned around. *Look calm and in control.* She quickly leaned against the toolbox, wringing water from her soaked shirttail. The blue man was tall, maybe seven feet, with a large head and almond-shaped eye, wrapping the sides of his head. In another setting, she'd probably think him quite striking, but at this particular moment, she found him as scary as the devil himself.

"Gene—no, that's wrong. You're not Gene. Look, whatev—whoever you are, I'm tired and—a lot has fallen on me of late. But I've upset you, and I stand corrected and apologize for the crudeness." *Breathe, just breathe.* "Okay, starting again, tell me *who* you are and *why* you're here?"

Hearing the door open, Quil saw Jessie enter. "Be careful, Jessie!"

"I see you started without me." In a ripple of light, Jessie vanished, and a second blue visitor entered the room.

"Aw, crap," was all Quil could muster.

The alien Jessie looked at the mess on the floor and at Quil backed against the tool case. "What happened here?"

"She did a drop and flop. I took her by surprise. And I thought I planned this rather well."

Entering a storage room, Jessie returned with towels and a mop. Heading toward Quil, he stopped, seeing a raised hand that made it clear he wasn't to come near her. He tossed her the towels and proceeded to … tidy up?

"You broke the hot plate. The cost of a replacement comes out of your pocket. If you're unable to restrain your bad humor, I'll take over here."

"I'm now in balance and will continue. Pick up another hot place when next out and charge it to my account."

"I'm not picking up another hot plate. You broke it; you pick one up."

Am I addled? Are they bickering over a hot plate while I stand here trying not to scream? Suddenly, attention returned to her.

"Why don't you sit on the tool case, Quil, and we'll talk." said the blue Gene. "We must convey a great deal of information in a short period. Listen without interruption. We'll respond to queries when finished." He pulled two chairs in front of the tool chest.

Quil needed time. No weapon, no immediate escape plan, the better move was to sit, listen, and recover. She climbed on top of the toolbox.

"Now I begin. You may refer to us by our assumed Earth names. We are Procyon, a species from the fourth planet of the Canis Minor constellation. We've come to help humanity. While we're not members of the Assembly, there are members of that body who seem trustworthy, keeping us informed."

"What's the Assembly?"

"You interrupted! And I just began! You're to listen; I'm to speak. The Assembly is an oversight group comprised of various species, some of whom now walk this planet. Its initial intent was to study the human species as it naturally moved through development. Earth's inhabitants have been studied for millennia. The end date of the study approaches. What's to happen after that is unspecified."

"It's up in the air, so to speak." Alien Jessie sat next to alien Gene.

"Yes. Now that the study is nearing completion, certain predator species have established a clandestine band, a rogue group. Nasty beings they are too. Infiltrating this planet, they stand ready to take over, to pounce at the study's end. We aim to stop them. We require your assistance in so doing."

Slowly, Quil raised a finger. Gene's eyes rolled outward. "What is it?"

"Why doesn't the Assembly stop the nasty rogue band? Are there any humans on that Assembly?"

"Again, reserve your questions. Now, I continue. Because this country entered into an agreement with a species represented on the Alliance, other Alliance members cannot interfere. We believe there are members would like to assist humans but they're rule-bound and cannot or will not. Human representatives do attend Assembly sessions, but being of low status, they have little influence and no vote."

"As the Assembly will not intervene to stop the rogue band," added Jessie, "a second clandestine group was formed, its purpose to help the people of Earth. Procyon's, or Cyons for short, established the second band comprised of upright citizens bent on halting the malevolent horde causing widespread destruction in the universe. However, with support of certain of your military, the rogue group on Earth has become a major threat. Quick action is required to contend with that threat.”

Quil opened my mouth to speak but snapped it shut. *Clandestine groups? Humans studied? Malevolent hoard? S*he needed answers.

“Okay, ask your question,” said Gene. “You’re short on patience this evening.”

“For good reason! Why don’t Earth’s representatives take action to stop the rogues? I think I know the answer to that.”

“What is your supposed answer?”

“Humans in uniform are being seen with aliens. I’m thinkin’ Earth’s representatives are military traitors. Who are they? I want names.”

“We’re unable to provide such information.”

Quil raised her hand again, bringing on another bout of wheezing from Gene. “It’s clear you’re not going to sit and quietly listen. Ask.”

“You said the outcome of the study is unknown. What does that mean? Will humans have a say in the final decision? Are the humans on the Assembly representing humanity as they should, or are they selling us out for—what? Power? Do Assembly members care what happens to us, or are we nothing more than specimens, like blobs of bacteria?”

“That’s a number of questions,” said Jessie. “In brief, some members seem to care. The Assembly is split on what happens at the study’s end. The human attendees are of questionable character. They may be putting forth an effort to intervene on behalf of humanity; however, our sources aren’t convinced of that.”

“What happens to humans at the end will be disturbing to hear, and we will not discuss it,” added Gene. “We must move on to why you’re here. We have need of your people. You now know we can project in human form. The Reptoids can also, and they move among you in community life. An extensive group exists in this area. We need you and your people to help in identifying them.”

“And we must locate their base of operations,” said Jessie.

"Are you saying you'll join with us to fight them? We need weapons, heavy weapons. We haven't anything to match what they have."

"That's not an option," said Gene. "Our race decided eons ago not to provide weapons to another species. Your government chose to cooperate with one or more Assembly members. The problems you're having on Earth are of your own making."

"I don't entirely agree with that. Some species entered into an agreement with a *few* members of our government. A covert undertaking. Are those aliens the *Wisps,* the willowy ones with long fingers that vibrate when they move?"

"The Wisps, to your terminology, are Mantians, an insectoid species," said Jessie. Wisps are exceptional in the field of bioengineering. Reptoids is another second species in the agreement with your government. Those here are but one group of a thirteen-member faction fighting under the banner of the XIII-POX, or POX for short. An extremely vicious coalition, they're the dregs of civilized societies and are intent on conquering Earth. We've yet to uncover why Earth was fingered as a prime goal of theirs. But if they succeed, humans will be enslaved, subjected to hard labor, tortured, and consume as food. Also, we don't understand why the Mantian scientists have taken the divergent course they have and joined the Reptoids. We believe an unknown is orchestrating the enemy POX force, that's gathering power as it moves through the universe."

"The Wisp scientists have something to gain, or they wouldn't be involved," said Quil. "Have you uncovered any clues as to who the orchestrator is? What about the one in a red cloak?"

"An unknown, but one not represented on the Assembly. And its appearance is too recent for it to be the maestro behind this. This war has been going on for decades. We don't know the role of the red-cloaked being."

"You said you have a counterforce. Is it sizeable?"

"It's building," said Jessie. "I believe it important you know why we're here. We came to assist your people in progressing as a species without harmful interference. We were the first to talk to your government, but your military wanted weapons. We refused, and because of that refusal, Procyon's were not welcome here. Now, we hide, but we're still here and still intent on assisting you."

"I doubt that would have happened if our people had had a say in things. Is your counterforce base located here?"

"Yes, but we won't divulge its location. The Assembly base is on the moon."

"The moon. Away from prying eyes. Can I have a few minutes to consider all you've told me?" Jessie and Gene politely folded their hands in their laps and waited.

Think, now. What's my aim here? *Plus and minus signs*. Plenty of the minus. Have there been any plus?

"Okay. Let me summarize what I understand thus far. You say you want to help. We welcome help. We need weapons. You won't provide weapons, and though not stated, I'm guessing you won't provide a fighting force either."

"That's correct," said Gene.

"No weapons, no fighting force, no inclusion in Assembly considerations. What kind of help are you willing to give?"

"We can provide knowledge," said Jessie, "and while we won't provide military support at this juncture, others might be willing to do so."

"Ah! Who are they, and when do I talk to them?"

"You're not allowed to talk to anyone else," said Gene.

"Why not? Is it me? Is it because I'm not military? I know military people and can bring them here to talk to you."

"It must be you," said Gene. "We believe you've been sent as an emissary. You're … uncommon. Surely, you've recognized you're not fully human."

Like a fish yanked from water, Quil sat glassy-eyed, mouth gaped, unable to speak.

"Apparently, she hadn't figured that out," said Jessie.

"Don't tell us you've never heard voices speaking to you when no one was present? Talking with people who weren't there? You're telepathic. You can converse mentally and, most importantly, with those of different species."

"Voices? Yes, I do hear voices. I've always had a lotta clutter in my head. Now, I'm not saying I believe you, but if I'm not fully human, what am I? I mean, where does the non-human part of me hail from?"

"That's a question we have of you," said Gene. "Observers have tried to ascertain that but failed. You don't exactly fit any species of which we know. Do you know where in the universe that would be?"

"I've just now learned I'm an alien! Hold on—are you saying the Assembly scientists tampered with me? Was I genetically altered?"

"We're not sure about you, but all humans are the product of bioengineering by one of numerous species from other worlds. Skin coloring, eye shape, and physical traits trace to the species responsible for experimentation."

"Race distinction? Was that the purpose of the gene manipulation?"

"No, not really," said Jessie. "A group of scientists decided to use you in a gene-refining project, a digression from the Assembly's purpose."

"And we're the result of that digression. Test-tube babies thrown down here to intermingle, boiled up like a pot of gumbo?"

"You oversimplify," said Gene. "The scientists went through the Alpha phase of testing in a controlled environment and moved to Beta testing, studying specimens in the field. Species found unfavorable were removed. Humans result from extensive experimentation and testing."

"So it's done; the experiment's successfully completed. Why are the scientists still around?"

"You were not a success. With many genetic components in play, the experiment got away from them, and things went wrong. A single ultra-dominant gene carrying the aggression factor took over. Your species continuously war with each other, and that has been deemed unacceptable."

"Okay, they're stirring the pot again. We're back in the hands of the gene-brilliant scientists for further refinement. Is this a never-ending game they play?"

"Most of the Assembly favor beginning again," said Jessie.

"Meaning?"

"You know what that means."

"Extermination! How? A mass extinction event? This planet has had five or more of those, already. Is the Assembly responsible for those, too?"

"You've become tedious," said Gene. "It's pointless to talk of the past."

"Tedious or not, I want to know why they don't leave, and let us work it out."

"They lack faith in your ability to do that," said Jessie.

"Too, there are the immigrants to consider," added Gene.

Quil didn't have the grit to pursue that and sat drumming a foot against the toolbox.

"Survivors from other planets who escaped death by the POX need a place to restart their societies," said Jessie.

"How did they find us? Do a fly-over, see the lady with the torch, and exclaim: 'Ah, why not here? No one would notice us in that pot of misfits.'"

"No, and that's a puerile remark. Of course, the divested sought approval of the Assembly." Gene was becoming irritable again.

"But they didn't ask us, the humans inhabiting this planet."

"The Assembly denied the immigrants' request, thus any further discussion is unnecessary."

"I want to talk to those on the Assembly. If the members are intelligent enough to manipulate life forms, they should be willing to discuss options for continuing what they've created."

"The Assembly showed no empathy for the wandering refugees, and they'd show even less with you," said Jessie. "After being denied, the immigrants came to us. We've helped some assimilate on the planet, and others work with our counterforce in varying capacities."

"We're wasting time," said Gene. "Let's move to the reason you're here. We believe you're meant to serve as a bridge between humans and those of other worlds."

"Oh, I see. My role would be to obtain information and convey it to the counterforce. That seems easy enough to do."

"No, you would convey any information you might obtain to the two of us. Only us. As I said before, you cannot speak to anyone else."

"I speak to you out loud and in English. I fail to see how that makes me a telepathic bridge!" Gene attempted a response, but Quil cut him off. "Being an emissary means interacting with everyone with no restrictions. Why can you not see that?"

"Because we're limiting those with knowledge of our hidden base to protect our people? Why cannot you see that?"

"Oh! Okay, I get that part. But we're the vulnerable ones here, and we'd remain vulnerable with the emissary setup you described. Why? Because we'd remain on the outside of a protective circle. I want inside the circle." Having gathered the plus and minus of the situation, Quil made her decision. "I thank you for the information, and again, I want you involved with our cause, but bottom line, we need more. I'm leaving."

"We're not ready for you to leave. Please sit."

"No. I'm tired and need rest." She headed for the door.

"Quil, you're forbidden to speak of this to anyone," said Gen. "This is an urgent matter and not to be taken lightly. I'll make inquiries. Possibly someone will come forward to address your issues. That's all I can do. This meeting stands adjourned."

tick the 2nd

The time has come ... to talk of many thing:
of shoes and ships and sealing-wax,
of cabbages and kings and why the sea
is boiling hot and whether pigs have wings.

— Lewis Carroll
Alice's Adventures in Wonderland

twenty-one

I ran to the car. My hands shook, giving me trouble fitting the key in the ignition. Did that happen? I pinched a nipple. *Uh! That hurt.* Well, it's not a waking nightmare.

At the end of Runway 01, I pulled the car over and walked into the desert. Standing on a crest, feather lights whirled about me.

"I know you're here. Of all I heard this evening, what bothers me most is I didn't figure this out for myself." A beam of moonlight appeared, and I stepped onto a glass pathway. Beside me was Gnat, who lit up like a fire in a bottle each time he spoke.

"It matters not if you were born of ancestral roots here or from cosmic stirrings elsewhere."

"I'm not concerned with that now. For the first time in my life, I feel threatened by what's *up there*. It's time to consider many things. Dealing with unknowns tops the list. Staying alive ranks right up there with it."

From behind a cluster of low-lying clouds, the moon tiptoed into the open as if to introduce herself. "I'm coming up there. Get used to the idea. You *will* answer to me."

"There may be a time for rebellious encounters, but you still have learning ahead. Control is key. Consider carefully words of others. Speaking softly can achieve more than the loudest of shouts. Wisdom is within. Use you wisely."

A sharp wind howled, and I was at my car. Opening the door, the glow of the interior light revealed a figure standing beside a gnarled juniper. A second figure stood in deep shadow.

"Are you alright?" Jessie stepped into the light.

"I'm working on it, Jessie. I'll get there." Slamming the car door, I sped away.

The answering machine light was blinking. I considered ignoring it but didn't. Seri updated me on several fronts. "The rifles came in, and the squad is eager to try them out. Seven at the firing range."

"Seven? Okay. I might be late."

"Josiah needs to talk to you. Here's his number. He'll tell you what it's about."

"Okay, anything else?"

"Inger called. They're seeing strange people roving the streets like the two in the bookstore. Gretchen tailed a couple to get car descriptions and photos."

"Oh, no. I don't want them hurt, though they could uncover useful information. Maybe they should go ahead but take serious precautions."

"I voiced concern for their safety, asking them to halt what they were doing, but Inger wouldn't hear arguments against it. What's going on with the plane? Will it be costly?"

"Not in dollars, in time maybe."

Next was Josiah. "Good to hear from you, Quil. I need to pass on information. We've encountered a problem. We've expanded the number of volunteers in the field. Word of mouth is bringing them in. Plus, increase sighting reports have us traveling all the time, and the sightings are taking the squad further away from home base." I heard a sharp intake of breath.

"Here's the problem. We're being set up. No matter what we do, we're being hit and losing men. Someone's passing our location to the enemy. We have a mole, and we haven't been able to identify him."

"Are there military people you trust to vet the men?"

"We did that. Nothing came from it. We've decided it's futile to continue the same strategy we've been using. If things don't turn around, we're disbanding the squad. We don't want to do that as we need to identify this guy before we come back. We're swapping turns going out alone to observe only. Wolf's out now. One of us has to watch the men. It's not good distrusting those who're supposed to be fighting alongside us."

"Will you two be okay alone out there?"

"Better than if we had a squad with us. Keep eyes and ears open, and let us know if you pick up clues about who this guy might be. Have to go now."

Not ready to attempt sleep, I sat on the deck steps considering the day's interactions. The Spider Squad, now a contrarian group, intended to fight the enemy under its own rule. The Shadow Squad, now an outlier, was in trouble, needing to eliminate a treacherous traitor. The blue people was a card not yet dealt. When they contact me—if they contact me—my options are to stay the hard line or give in. Did I make a mistake taking a firm stance against their directions? My intuition tells me passing on information only to those two won't help us.

A muffled sound came from the woods to my left. Glancing at the pine grove, I saw the black-winged creature rising from a stand of trees. The sound of rushing wind grew louder with its approach. As it glided overhead, I didn't turn away, and I didn't run.

I'm not afraid of you. I want you to know that.

twenty-two

Quil pulled into the training site, seeing Spiders setting up for long-distance shooting. Seri stood alone on top of a hill, looking out over broad canyon country. Quil walked to her side. "I'll listen."

"I'm not troubled, just watching the wind play in the valley. It's a sea of rippling grass. The wind's always moving from one place to another, always hunting for something. Like you. For what do you hunt, Quil?"

"I don't know myself." She gazed at the valley. "I sometimes think life is a series of things found, things lost. A repeating pattern, always ending with things lost rather than things found. Shouldn't that be the other way around?"

"Seems like it should. Can you see ahead?"

"No. Hopefully when this is finished, we'll stand here again, appreciating the beauty of this world. But now the squad's waiting."

"You go. I'd like to stand in this peace a while longer."

Sometimes sadness comes like drifting snow gently covering the soul with sorrow, a melancholy almost sweet. Taking a step back, Quil quietly slipped away, leaving Seri on the rise. She ached inside. She knew why.

Space, distance, separation, loss. It seemed the nature of things. It was coming; she knew that. At times, a person's absence weaves through the air, leaving a sadness, but with it came the sweetness of memory. Perhaps it was a gentle nudge to think of them at that moment as wherever they were, they were thinking of her too. That can bring a smile, but it doesn't always take away the ache. Sighing, she called the team in to start the practice.

"Hustle! Everybody gather 'round." Quiet fell as they sat on the ground. "I gave Gracie a call earlier today. She'll be by later to report on any sightings she may have received. Until then, we go over the types of alien life forms we've seen on our planet and the aircraft they use. We can't take action on aircraft or enemy on the ground if a ship is nearby."

"What do we do? Stand back and watch as they slowly take over?" Three seemed overly snarky this morning.

"We make like the spiders we are. We lie in wait, track, hunt, and when we get the chance—"

"We bite. Silent killers. I like it." Three pulled a knife from her belt and tested its edge.

"Here are photos of what the Reptoids look like, two types. Pass these around. The snake creatures are shapeshifters and can assume human form. Pay attention to the eyes. They shield them under contacts or behind dark glasses. In the next photo, the one appearing to be a human in military uniform is, in fact, a human—a traitor. We call them *traits* for short. They could be from any branch of service. We've killed both reptoids and *traits*."

"We're going to kill humans?" asked Six.

"They wouldn't hesitate to kill us. They've already tried. We're also responsible for finding the enemy base. Coming around is a photo of the outside entrance. It looks to be inside a mesa or mountain. If you recognize or run across it, tell us immediately. Good timing. Here comes Gracie now."

"The sighting reports coming in are local. The Shadow Squad is still north, and I don't know if I should let them know or not."

"The answer is *not*. The Shadow Squad has enough worries. So that everyone's on the same link, the men's squad has a mole they're trying to flush out. They're being set up, and they've lost men. What could happen if we called hem back here? Anybody?"

"They'd bring the mole here. He'd see our setup, the supply warehouse, the comm center, everything," said Two.

"That makes this an easy decision," said Three. "We go in."

"Not so easy. What if it's a con to draw us out?" No one responded. They had a problem. All eyes were on Three, repeatedly jabbing a combat knife in the ground.

"Never stick your blade in the ground," Seri snapped. "You chance breaking the tip or dulling the edge."

"What's the answer then?" Three jumped up, holding the knife and glaring down at Seri.

"Sheath that blade—and sit down!" Quil was on her knees, gun drawn. "Never threaten a teammate!" Gracie tossed a water bottle to Three, who caught it on the fly. Quickly securing her knife, she sat down, her head dropping to her chest.

"Okay. Now let's figure out an answer." Quil glanced at Seri, holding a throwing blade but nodding okay. "Tonight, we check out a reported sighting. A practice run—no engagement!" But the group seemed not to be listening, their eyes on Three.

"But I believe in choices. Are you in or out? Be honest with yourselves and us. Seri and I can go alone, but this is an opportunity for you to see the enemy firsthand. Don't go unless you're a hundred percent convinced you wanna be there. Speak up." No one responded. Quil exchanged looks with Seri and shrugged.

"You've got a *go* from me," said Three, and everyone quickly agreed.

"I'll have the location marked on a map by the time we get back to the church," said Gracie. Quil pulled Seri aside.

"Seri, take the squad to the firing range while I talk to Three."

"Walk with me, Gabby." Three fell in step beside Quil. They stopped under a tree and faced each other. "What's gnawing at you? Your hotheaded actions will get us all in trouble. I wear my temper close to the skin too, and so does Seri. Never think of taking either of us on. If you call preacher woman out, and she's holding a knife, you're looking at hellfire. She'll send you there." She pointed toward Seri, in the shadow of a tree with a knife in each hand.

"Yeah. Yeah, okay, I hear what you're saying. I am letting personal things bear on me. Of all the people here, I should be able to work my way through it. But I feel everyone's against me. I'm always outvoted. The others don't want me here, and I'm the one with the most reason to be in this fight."

"Explain that."

"My brothers. No one will tell me how they died on that mountain. My family thinks they're protecting me by keeping it from me, but it's constantly on my mind. I've tried to explain that it's the knowing that will allow release, but they don't agree. I know I have a temper, but I can control it. I just need to know how my brothers died."

"I didn't know they were your brothers, and I'm sorry. You're right. You deserve to know, but get a grip on yourself. This is going to hurt like fury." Quil went through the torture and murder of her brothers and their bravery in facing death. Gabby asked questions, and Quil responded truthfully. Tres voiced her need for retribution, and Quil told her of the pact she and Seri had made to avenge their deaths. At first, Gabby stood listening, but suddenly rage took over, and she closed on Quil.

"No! This is mine! Mine! Give me your word, Quil, Your word! Your word!"

Quil gripped Gabby's shoulders as she was shaking badly. "My word. I understand and give my word. And know the team accepts you. The others didn't agree to go on the excursion tonight until you said you were in. I noticed that, why didn't you? We're not always going to agree. Accept that. Now, *Tres*, take a walk before you rejoin your teammates." Gabby mouthed the name, *Tres*, nodded, and set off.

"Hey," Quil called out, seeing Tres turn back. "If I understood you correctly, there may come a day when members of this squad will need your training."

"And I'll be there."

Seri walked over, standing with Quil. "Will she be a problem?"

"I think she'll be okay. From now on, she's to be called *Tres* instead of Three. She needed a win, even if only a small win. Spread the code change to the others. And get knife training set up for everyone. How did we overlook that?"

"Tres? You're a marshmallow, but okay. I already have a lesson plan laid out for knife skills. I'll schedule it in."

"I thought of another thing. We can't go into backcountry in convoy. We need a vehicle that'll carry all of us. What about Inger's Hummer?"

"I'll go. I miss seeing the poets." Seri jogged to her car.

On her return, they loaded gear for an early start to the site. Then they waited. The tension was thick, and Quil decided to mosey to learn more about team members.

"Hey, number Six. I'm Quil. Tell me about yourself."

"Hi, Quil. Okay, the name is Emma Sparrow, and I'm Southern Ute. Until this came up, I was in college studying cultural history and anthropology. I intend to ensure the culture of my people continues. If all goes as it should, that is. You don't have to tell us about yourself. Seri's already filled us in on that."

"She did? That's scary. I'd like to talk more about your culture one day. When we're together like this, I'll call you Emma; otherwise, it'll be Six. Okay with you?" The young woman nodded. "Are you ready for tonight, Emma Six?"

"Ready here," she said, smiling.

Quil moved on, sitting beside a sweet-looking woman, on the shorter side, who wore a number Four on her left pocket. "So, Four, tell me about yourself. Where do you hail from?"

"Me, heck, I'm nobody special. The name's Tilde Lebeau from Baton Rouge in the great state of Louisiana. I was a political science teacher at a local college. That was okay, but I enjoyed my side job better."

"Did you have any success teaching people to be politically smart?"

"Not to brag about."

"You're from my part of the country, which is a distance from here. How did you find yourself out this way?"

"My grand-meré had a vision. We're witches. I went home after work one day and found my bags packed, and she'd sewn her secret cache of money in the lining of my favorite jacket. I had no choice. She told me I was destined to journey to this location to find a woman with eyes of blue crystal. That'd be you, I reckon."

"You're a witch?"

"I am, but my family doesn't practice dark sorcery. We sell potions and perform charms and spells to soothe a person's worry. Did you follow that?"

"Yeah, I did. My aunt had a special talent in wonder-working and was sometimes called a thaumaturgus."

"That's high-powered magic. So you're one, too?"

"I didn't say I was one. Tell me, Tilde. Do you ever … never mind."

"Dream? Were you going to say dream?"

"Yes, I was."

"I dream They're strange. My grand-meré told me to pay attention to the symbolism in dreams as it can help us prepare for the unexpected coming at us."

"I have strange dreams too. Aunt said we have to figure out what our subconscious is trying to tell us about our waking life." *This person is someone I know from another passage. I'm' sure of it. How interesting we meet up again now.* "What's the side business you mention?"

"Lingerie. Lingerie parties, to be exact. I provide only the finest, most current panty and bra wear, nighties, delicates in all shapes and forms. You name, I carry it." She grinned, displaying a noticeable gap in her front teeth which made her smile even more fetching.

"No lie? That's an interesting job. I'd like to see your line one day."

"Oh, for sure you will. I bet five bucks you're wearing granny panties. Let me show you what you should be wearing. Stand beside me." Before Quil could say *jackrabbit*, Tilde had their field pants at their knees.

"Okay, not grannies, but, really now, men's long-legged boxers? That's tragic. You should be in low-rise sheer lace boy shorts, and the color should be *blue serenity* to match your eyes. The matching bra has uplift cups. You could use a little help with the sag."

"I sag?"

Tilde cupped her hands under her breasts and lifted. Quil did the same.

"Not too bad. Definitely stay with *blue serenity*. My color is *blush pink,* as it goes with my Nubian skin. Here, you can feel the lace; it's delicate to the touch," pulling out a packet from her carryall.

"That's a fine made lace. The style you have on is nice, and I've always liked blue." There was a jerk on her elbow. "What!"

Seri held her arm, pointing over her shoulder. The squad sat big-eyed, watching as she and Four considered each other rears and handled their boobs.

"She specializes in lingerie," yelled Quil. "Only the very finest lingerie," Quil hurriedly pulled up her trousers as the other team members rushed over. Tilde gave them the lace samples to pass around.

"Can you tell us what color's best for each of us," as Suzie Two.

"Sure, I can. But let me start with one of you. I choose you, Seribeth."

"Me? No, choose someone else. I'm not into fancy underthings."

"Sure, you are," said Tilde. "We're today's women, proud of who we are and ready to strut our stuff. That's why each of us is in this military squad."

Before Seri could say more, Four had turned her turned around with trousers at the knees.

"See, Seri is tall, well-proportioned, and on the muscular side. She should be in a low hipster brief, lace-trimmed but modest in the front. Though, the back should have a beautiful lace butterfly. The color for her is definitely a soft, *moonglow yellow*." The squad had all eyes on Seri's posterior. Quil glanced at her face, noticing a rosy glow covering it. Four, meantime, continued to enlighten the group.

"I have sample swatches of fabric and brochures, showing the styles I can pass around you now. I'll hold a lingerie party when we can find the time."

"That sounds fun, and thanks for the info," said Quil. "Seeing that boom box in the back of your vehicle, it looks like you're into music too."

"I can play something now. It might ease the tension." Tilde gave Quil a mischievous grin.

"You saw right through that, huh? Then ramp it up, Four." Quil expected melodic tones to ease shredded nerves, but no. A raspy voice attacked the air, wailing incoherently.

"Play it again," shouted the squad, and Four laughingly obliged. Feeling the rhythm, they broke into dance, teasing teammates, laughing, working off nervousness. Standing to the side, Quil chuckled at how easily Tilde had charmed the group to cohesiveness using lingerie and dance. *Me, heck, I'm nobody special.* So very wrong.

"Was that planned?" asked Seri, joining Quil. "I can only make out words here and there, and they make no sense, but it is settling nerves. Who's that singing?"

"Dylan. Look at that. They're trying to do a country line dance to an old hippie song protesting government corruption."

"Seems fitting, but I don't think they have the beat."

"Maybe a bit out of step with each other is all."

"I don't' know how I got coaxed into displaying my rear. Humiliating, but the funny thing is, I don't feel embarrassed now. It reminds me of being in a college dorm again. Someone was always holding underwear parties."

"You were charmed into it. You know that dancing looks like fun. Let's show 'em how it's done." Laughing, they joined the line.

Things turned serious again. Little talk occurred on the road. Glancing at team members, Quil saw somber faces, furrowed brows, hands clasping and unclasping. *I hope they hold together if uglies do show.* "Pay attention. Take note of slide areas, fallen trees, and obstacles that could cause problems on the return."

"This is the location." Seri pulled into a stand of Ponderosa pines.

While applying face grease, Quil and Seri divided the squad into two units, the Brown Recluse and the Black Widow. Seri opted for Brown Recluse; Quil got Black Widow. Before separating, she placed a finger over her lips and whispered, "Are we together?"

The reply came back quietly but firmly. "Together."

"Let's do this," said Seri, speaking low. "Two, Five, Seven with me."

"Tres, Four, Six with me." As they slipped away, Quil said, "Remember why we're here."

"I know what I'm to do and not to do," murmured Tres. "I'd like you to trust me."

"The first time you see these freaks, unexpected things can happen. Fear clouds your brain, you freeze, and panic hits like nothing ever experienced. It isn't a matter of trust now. I want you prepared."

Taking an overwatch position, Quil wanted a clear view of anything that might threaten her unit and knew Seri was doing the same. They went to stealth mode, rifles ready and eyes on scopes.

A hushed stillness snaked around them like a dank fog off a chilling sea. The scream of a banshee drove icy fingers down spines; a night predator had sent an alarm. Quil whispered *set* into her earpiece and listened to heavy breathing shortly followed by silence.

The white light spread over the meadow, and a green beam dropped a herd of sheep. While Wisps descended, a black delta appeared, hovered, and landed. The Wisps labored over sheep as two reptoids watched. The red-haired snake and her partner were not present.

Quil had an optimal view of the triangle craft. A human pilot, sat sideways in an opened doorway, observing the Wisps. She centered the rifle's crosshairs on the pilot. *If I brought you down, what would the others do?*

In fifteen minutes or less, both crafts rose and were gone. In another ten, a prolonged howling echoed through the darkness. Slowly, night creatures ventured out and again foraged for food. It always had amazed Quil, how quickly animals adapted to whatever came their way.

Still, they waited. A half-hour passed before Quil said, *withdraw*. Focusing on where her comrades lay concealed, she watched three shapes slowly moving backward, staying low to the ground, slipping under pine boughs, moving from shadow to shadow. *Just like drill.*

The units joined up at the Hummer. On the drive down the twisting trail, all eyes watched for obstacles. The return trip went without incident, and Seri increased speed on the county road heading back to Gracie's place. There was little talk by squad members.

Arriving at the Dove's home, the garage door opened, and Seri pulled straight in. Gracie had been watching for them. Entering the house, the group removed field gear and followed Gracie to the living quarters.

"Well," said Gracie.

The six viewing alien invaders for the first time nodded. "We've been introduced," said Tres.

As unit leaders, Quil and Seri listened as the team talked, watching for emotional flags, early signs of potential problems.

"Good job. The prep work paid off." Quil quietly applauded.

"Congratulations, team. Get some rest," echoed Seri.

Gracie pointed to a stack of sleeping bags in a corner. "Welcome to our home. We're grateful you're safe and with us tonight. Sleep anywhere you find a floor that suits you. The bathroom is the second door on the left. We're up at six. Remember to pray."

Quil and Seri slipped outside to exchange views. "I'm impressed."

"Me too," said Seribeth. "Tres didn't give you any trouble. I admit to having concerns."

"Tres feels she's carrying the honor of her people on her shoulders. That's a lot to bear. I know the feeling. I'm sure you do too."

"It's a heaviness I've not felt before." Seri cleared her throat, which meant she had more to say. "I need to tell you something. There's been talk about you. Squad members ask about your abilities. They say you hardly talk, then sense you in their minds, followed by you bring them together on point."

"Okay. I'm sure you handled that appropriately."

Uh-huh, you know, I may have suggested, uh, perhaps you were an angel receiving guidance from the Creator." She spoke rapidly, slinging her words out.

"What! You didn't! Tell me you're kidding?"

"No, I said that."

"Well, assure them such is not the case. I honestly can say I have no idea what I am or what I'm doing."

"Something's troubling you. What is it is?"

"No, I mean yeah. First, I feel unprepared for what we're facing. I'm being pushed into unexpected situations and taking risks I may regret. Second, members of the squad are good people. I'm feeling attachment growing, and I'm not sure I should let that happen. I already worry for them.

"First, of anyone's able to handle trying situations, it's you. Trust yourself. Second, I share the attachment with the team. What's wrong with enlarging the family? Maybe it's time to grow it some. Worry will happen wherever we find ourselves in."

"You're the wise one here, Seri, and yeah, we can grow the clan if we want. And apparently, we want. But I have another thing bothering me. I just can't envision it."

"Can't envision what?"

"A big, yellow butterfly on your butt." Quil winked and ducked. Seri had a wicked left jab.

twenty-three

"Heads up, spiders. We go out again tonight. Be back here no later than six. Until then, take care of personal business, visit your folks, read a book, but don't spend all day on the firing range. We know you can shoot. Now take off." They scattered like chaff in the wind. "Seri, I'm going to check on mv dog. I'll be back in plenty of time."

At the bookstore, Inger listened to several women talking about her most recently published poetry book. From Inger's scowl, she wasn't liking what she was hearing. But Inger was a businesswoman and knew she had to bite her tongue at times to make sales.

"I must say," remarked one, "I believe you've over valued this latest book. I've read the first few poems and found them uninspiring. Shouldn't you consider lowering the cost?"

"I agree, Matilda," said another, "the ones I skimmed were filled with hard-to-comprehend gibberish while others reeked of platitudes. Nothing piqued my interest. I doubt you'll be moving these off your shelves anytime soon."

"Slashing the price might do the trick," said the third. "And, Inger, you really should consider another genre, or at least do your research as you've worn thin the whole mystical thing. It's coming across as … well, as tired. Of course, that's just my opinion."

"Oh, but I agree," said Matilda. "I'll buy one to support you, but only if you cut the price."

Quil loudly cleared her throat. "My deepest apologies, madams. I'm in town for a short period and must be at the regional airport in an hour to catch my plane. I've been sent by the South African Poetry League to speak to the

143

author of this book," holding up Inger's book for viewing. "The book won top honors in an award's program. The league wishes to buy several hundred for the Johannesburg university. It's received rave reviews. I have the address where you're to send the books, shipping at our cost, naturally."

"How marvelous," said Matilda. "But you'll need to wait your turn. I'm first in line. I'll take a dozen of these, Inger. Don't bother to wrap them individually. I plan on giving them as gifts and will do that myself." The other two hurriedly purchased a dozen each.

"Come now," said Matilda, "let's not keep the buyer waiting. She does have a plane to catch." The bell jingled as they rushed from the store, all speaking at the same time.

"South Africa?" said Inger. "Your Brit brogue was bloody awful, but I appreciate the rescue. And the sale of those books will help make overhead. Sit and nuss Blackbird while I make tea. She's doing just fine. No problems with her wound. Jon's good about caring for her."

Quil sat on a floor cushion with Blackbird in her lap. The dog's wound was tender, but she was on the way to recovery. But just as Inger was pouring tea, Quil's phone beeped. It was Jim Nighthawk.

"It's my grandfather. He said he must see you today. Can you come right away?"

"Is he ill?"

"No, he's in good health, and his mind seems clear. He won't tell me why he wants to see you, but he insists you come."

"Tell Albert I'm on my way."

Another on-the-spur trip out west without an explanation as to why. And Albert had asked for only her to come. Apprehension fell on her like a wet blanket.

"Sorry, Inger, but I have to go."

"Come by when you get back. We'll share information we've collected through our spying activities."

The plane was fueled and ready for flight. She looked toward the Simpson hangar but didn't see Gene or Jessie. Jogging over, she didn't think they would refuse to talk to her if she walked in and started a conversation, but a note on the door indicated they'd gone to Santa Fe to pick up a plane.

Jim was waiting for her at his hangar. Again, he insisted on pushing her plane undercover. "Grandfather's waiting at the old sheep shed. I still don't know why, but you're taking a ride in his old Jeep. There's a full tank of gas, and I loaded a flare pistol and a case of bottled water in the back. Call if you get into trouble."

Albert sat on the gate to a stock pen. "It's a good day for a ride, Quil." He climbed into the Jeep and waved for her to get behind the wheel. "Go northwest," he said, pointing a direction. Driving away, Quil was glad to find the remnant of a road to follow. Concentrating on chugholes, she listened as Albert reminisced about places they passed that held meaning in his life. Each had stories, many about his wife, Annie, who he'd lost long ago.

"Pay attention now. This can be tricky," motioning her off the dirt road toward a distant red mesa. The sketchy trail worsened, at times disappearing altogether.

"Why are we traveling today, Albert?"

"I had a vision."

Quil had heard of native people professing to enter a higher state of consciousness to converse with spirits and was curious to know more. "Was it a sweat lodge vision?"

"Ye." He hesitated before he said more. "And peyote."

"Albert? We're out in the middle of nowhere because you got stoned on peyote? A vision? You had a drug-induced delirium, that's all. We're going back."

"Pull over here." Thinking he wanted to argue about returning, she pulled alongside scraggy piñons.

"We walk now." He pointed to a mesa.

"Up there? That's a long hike. I'm not sure you can walk that far."

"Bring water. I'm too old to carry much of anything."

Removing his walking stick from behind the seat, he set off. She had no choice but to follow. Placing with water and the flare pistol in her backpack, she trotted after him. They steadily climbed, at last reaching the face of the mesa.

"We go to the right here."

"We can't go to the right. The trail bends to the left."

"Watch." Walking to a stand of wind-swept trees, he pushed aside branches and disappeared. "Why aren't you behind me? Weren't you watching?" Hustling to catch up, Quil shoved her way through branches, emerging smelling of juniper berries.

"Pay attention; more turns ahead. I'll show things to remember so we can find out way back down from here."

Close on his heels, she noted markers he pointed out, sometimes stacking stones to serve as guideposts. *For whatever reason, this is important to him.*

"We're here."

Rounding a corner at a sharp angle, Quil stopped cold. The pool was unlike anything imaginable. Dazzling turquoise water shimmered like a jewel-studded mirage. Desert foliage and cactus flowers were in bloom, some completely out of season.

"This is astonishing. How do you know of this place?"

"I need to sit." He picked his way over rough ground to the other side of the pool where a pathway opened wider, and sat on a boulder at the edge of a rock slide.

"Water. Did you bring any?"

"Oh, yes," handing him a bottle and taking one for herself.

"This is a sacred place. My great grandfather brought me here when I was small. He told me the story over there," waving a hand toward a mesa wall. "He said there was a sanctuary up here too, but I haven't found it yet."

Moving to the wall, Quil saw petroglyphs of star people, strangely shaped beings, wearing head ornaments and holding unusual apparatus, possibly weapons. Other figures were stick people who faced each other in a circle.

"What does this one portray? Does it have special meaning?"

"It's the dance of the star people. Go that way," pointing a finger down the mesa.

"Okay, but stay right where you are. More water's in the pack next to you. Don't wander away and call if you need me."

"Nowhere to go. We're where we need to be. Quil, nature is stronger than man, but man is a part of nature. The might of nature's spirit is in all things. It's a strength we should remember and call on when we face big forces."

"Big forces? Okay." She understood not a word of that but nodded and continued to the next wall of glyphs. "This one's confusing," she whispered. "I said this one is confusing," speaking louder so Albert could hear. She studied the figures. "It looks like stick people are being flung into the air? And some figures have long sticks, or maybe they're lances. Wait! Are those flying machines? That can't be right, not in that period of time. What does this wall depict?"

"A battle."

It wasn't Albert! She spun around. The water bottle flew from her hand, landing at the feet of a formidable figure. The black-winged creature! Instinct hit, and she went for the Glock.

"You need no weapon."

She froze. *What do I do?* Combing her memory, she tried to recall what Gnat had told her. Something about control being key and speaking softly and … what else? Oh yeah, no rebellious encounters. *Stay in control and don't give lip.*

"Albert, can you come over here, please?" She tried to keep her voice pleasant to mask her anxiousness. But that didn't last.

"Albert, come over here!" She spoke almost at a shout but still got no response from Albert.

"Okay, no weapon." Removing her hand from the gun, she faced the *big force* in front of her. Tall, seven feet or more, black plated armor and a head covering resembling a menacing bird of prey. Black wings folded behind lay so flat, she hardly noticed them. And it had no face. *Is it a robot or a cyborg? It did sound mechanized.* She looked head to feet and up again, arriving back at its head. Without warning, the head covering vanished. Jumping backward, she slammed against the mesa wall. *Wow! That cannot be a robot.* His facial features were without flaw; dark brown skin matched the color of his hair that fell to his shoulders. Simply put, he was perfection. And she was glad to see he was human. Winged and oversized, but some variety of human.

"Tell me, Earthling called Quil, do I meet with your approval?" The alien stormed back and forth; his eyes, coldly appraising her, made her uncomfortable. There was no hint of friendliness about him.

"The Procyon said you called him a weird freak. Did you refer to him as that, and did you intend insult?"

"Oh, uh, yes, I did, but I was startled. I didn't mean to be insulting." She studied his manner of speaking, thinking it very like a Scottish burr with trilled *r*'s and soft vowels. But her gawking seemed to annoy him. *I don't seem to be making a favorable impression. Now's the time to keep my mouth shut.*

"If you wish to voice your perceptions, then proceed?"

"I have no perceptions to voice. I do have a question. I'm told I'm only part human, and I'm curious about the other part of me. Are you part human? And the wings—are those a part of the armor or a part of you?"

"You wish species history? Now? That's the first thing you ask?"

"Well, you know, the species question can wait." *What happened to keep the mouth shut?* "You talk, and I'll listen." She clenched her jaws. He said noting. Minutes passed. He seemed to be considering his next move. Her best move was to say nothing.

"The *Provenance,* an elder race, seeded many planets to ensure a continuance of their civilization. Citizens of many worlds, including those of Earth, arose from the Provenance foundation. They vary in physical appearance. The Circle of Twelve maintains a watch over Provenance planets, though some worlds are unaware of that oversight. Citizens distinguish regions by providing a resident planet, galaxy, or constellation. Other than Earth, I don't know your origin. We're similar but differ in detail. To appease your curiosity,

I'll show you my form." A mechanism silently engaged, and his plated armor fell away, exposing his body—in its entirety.

What the—! She rapidly blinked as he turned a circle, displaying his full physique. And as hard as she tried, she couldn't not look.

"Okey-doke. Yes, I see. The wings are a part of you and not the armor. Thank you. That was very considerate."

I'm an idiot! I just thanked this guy for flashing me. What now? Did she stand there pretending she was worldly? Maybe that would work. So she did that. She stood with an absurd grin smeared across her face and pretended—whatever it was she was pretending. *Nope, he's laughing and looking at me like I'm an idiot.*

His armor reappeared. "Let's talk. Sit."

Sit? She sat down where she was, her back against the mesa wall, watching as he walked to a boulder a short distance away, where he sat with elbows on his knees, wings resting behind.

"Perhaps you would consider moving closer?" he said, without looking at her.

Closer? Hurrying to a pile of fallen rocks, she pointed to a boulder, looking at him for approval. He nodded. She climbed to the top, bringing her almost to eye level with him.

"I'm told you're strong-willed, obstinate, and argumentative. Is it true you gave the Cyon a directive?"

"A directive? I wouldn't say it was precisely a directive. I requested to speak to someone else who could answer questions and provide help. Is that what you mean?"

"Possibly, however, the Cyon said you were more forceful, to the point of turning aggressive."

"Assertive."

He rubbed his chin, one eyebrow hiked. "I appreciate frankness—to a degree. I am Prex, a Commander with the Federation Guard Command based in the Orion Constellation."

"Who? What?"

"You heard me, and I'll not repeat it. I require restraint from you. At times, I require silence. Some information I provide will cause discomfort. Allow me to finish as we must consider the aged man sleeping beside the pool."

"Oh! That's Albert. I need to check on him."

"Unnecessary. He's within my view. I'll inform you if he has needs."

"He's in my charge. I'm responsible, and I'll check on him. now"

"No. Stay seated."

Quil's thoughts traveled inward. She knew she was frazzled and not performing well, but she resented being told what to do, especially when it came to the care of her elderly friend. She was willing to give some, but he needed to meet her halfway.

"No. Albert's my friend, and he's old. I'm the one to look after him. You have no right to take my responsibility or anything else without my consent." She climbed down the boulder and turned around. The alien blocked the path. Crossing her arms, a steady gaze sent the ultimatum. Again, minutes passed.

"I agree with you—this time. I should have gained consent to assume watch over your elder companion." With a brush of his hand, Prex motioned her toward Albert

Albert was sleeping with his head resting on her backpack.

"Do I now have consent to watch over the elder so we can continue our conversation?"

"Okay, sure."

He pointed to her boulder. She climbed.

Prex reflected on the human as she remounted the stone. *She challenged me. Who is this small creature? She seems intimidated by my appearance yet defied me. She wears courage well.*

"To continue, you know of the rogue force and the Procyon counter force on the planet. You heard of the Alliance that formed to observe humankind but later engaged in questionable testing. Many are displeased with the Alliance's actions. It may please you to know that there are those who believe a species should be allowed to develop naturally."

"Yes, I am glad to hear that." He ignored her comment and continued as if speaking from a script.

"Certain experimentation is allowable. Improving a species through DNA engineering is, at times, acceptable. Attempting to hybridize a new species using native DNA is rarely permitted."

Allowed experiments? Quil didn't like the turn this had taken.

"You know the Alliance study is ending, and the destruction of humanity appears imminent." He spoke without emotion and shrugged.

That shrug inasmuch said humanity's demise was of no concern to him. Lowering her head, she shielded her face with her hands. *Don't lose your temper. Stay in control.*

"Do not grieve. I haven't concluded the dissemination of information. I think it necessary you hear why the Assembly is leaning toward eradication. Will you listen?"

She bit her lip but nodded assent.

"Two major points were voiced; both have merit. First, your government chose to convert fissile materials to nuclear weapons. Many governments made the same decision. The Assembly believes it is a matter of time before humans destroy this planet and its inhabitants. Ending a civilization swiftly rather than allowing prolonged self-destruction is considered an act of compassion."

That did it! Her mouth was not staying shut.

"Act of compassion! So when through tormenting us, the panel of God pretenders do what—gently toss us in a warm, *compassionate* incinerator. No muss, no fuss. A tidy cleanup to a neat ending. How comforting. What other *acts of compassion* are you sharing with me today?"

"It seems I've provoked you to anger." He walked closer to Quil, staring at her face. "Let's walk." He offered a hand to assist her in descending. She refused it.

"I may disagree with statements I'm conveying. Do you understand?"

"Yes, but humanity deserves a chance. Do you understand?"

"We'll continue the talk here. The second concern of the Assembly is humans' propensity for war. I question such rationale as warring races exist, the Reptoids species being one. Still, some contend it would be a mistake to add another warring group to the already existing number. As many of your nations have nuclear capability, they are considered a threat to other worlds—especially as your leaders lack perceptive judgment. That raises a question. Can humans arrest their penchant for war?"

Is he expecting me to speak for every person, country, and government on the planet? I think I'm being tested. She breathed deep and, surprisingly, replied calmly.

"I'll be candid." Almost whispering, she spoke as softly as her voice allowed. "I'd like to make a case by telling you the primary concern of the human species is the caring for this planet, its environment, and its inhabitants. In other words, we stand united, and the welfare of all life is of utmost importance."

Prex moved closer, listened attentively.

"If I spoke those words, we both would know they were false. In truth, I don't know if the human species can be a non-warring tribe. There is now and always has been a struggle for power. Even our religions clash, creating tension leading to holy wars. But I have a question for you. Is there an answer to … are there options available to aid in solving our problems?"

Prex's eyebrows rose. "I believe the Procyon may have chosen correctly in selecting you as an emissary. It's wise to ask if solutions are possible rather than attempting to conceal or excuse faults and wrongs. It's also rare a black and white solution presents itself. Being open to options is prudent." Again, he waited.

"Well, can you help us? The Assembly's clock is ticking. Will they turn back the countdown clock or extend the deadline? I cannot address the question concerning the ending of war. Those in authority are the ones to make that happen—if it can happen at all. We need time to make contacts and meet with those with power. Gene—the Procyon said the rogue force must be terminated. We're running out of time."

"Follow me." He walked away. She hurriedly climbed from the stone, catching up to him at the mesa wall. "The sun is setting. Before the day ends, tell me what you see on this rock wall." It was the battle scene. She scanned it again.

"It's a war. It's difficult to know who's involved as ancients did the drawing. Rock drawings as this one captured an event as a way of passing history to future generations."

"What do you make these out to be?" He pointed to the strange shapes in the sky.

"Aerial vehicles. The strange figures could be warriors with weapons."

"And these?" He pointed to stick people.

"Humans, either being killed or trying to escape."

"Come with me," walking beyond the battle scene. She followed.

"Tell me what you see on this section of the wall."

She looked at the mesa wall, seeing nothing depicted. *What is it he wants me to see?*

"I don't see anything on this wall."

"Nothing's there. That's because the outcome of the battle you spoke of hasn't been determined. You noticed airships in the sky and unfamiliar beings involved in war. Yet that battle hasn't occurred. It's a forecast drawn on this wall by primal inhabitants of this planet."

"A prediction? How—no, wait? Maybe they could know. The indigenous people are intuitive, very close to nature and this planet. Those possessing inner sight may have seen this coming."

"Echoes of distant consciousness. Not unheard of. But there's more. The POX have a fleet approaching Earth. The armada is fierce with innumerable warship and superior weapons. Earth's militaries cannot stand against them."

"What can we do? Is help available?"

"Possibly. This planet is in its early stages of development. Advancing planets can receive assistance from the Provenance Guard. I came to evaluate the situation and provide a recommendation. Based on the Command's decision, help may be sent."

Quil sighed with relief.

"Pay heed. If the Command chooses to war with the POX, there will be destruction and death. The inhabitants of Earth will suffer battle fallout. In the end, it could mean the annihilation of humankind."

"I have no response to that. We seem doomed whatever action is taken."

Prex walked to the scene of battle again. "I was intrigued to see the Guard in battle as depicted on this age-old wall. I'll submit my recommendation in support of Earth. I'll assist until I receive an official decision from the Command. If they say we are not to defend this planet, you'll be alone."

"You say you'll help now? We need weapons and fighting power. How many of you are there?"

"One."

"They sent you alone, only one."

"There's only one planet."

She considered the star traveler's brag. Was that confidence or conceit? But then, she heard her named called.

"That's Albert. He's calling for me."

"It seems our meeting is ended. For now, we must know the site of the enemy base. You and your people help in locating it. Speak not of me." He hesitated, then grinned. "I'm pleased to see you're not the strong-willed, obstinate, argumentative creature you were made out to be."

"Good. I was hoping you'd see that."

"I've made my final comments. Do you have any??

"Just one. I'm curious if you're a replicant, a computerized machine without the ability to feel, or if you're a sentient being capable of feeling but choose not to?"

"I'm a warrior! We of the Command are sent to fight not coddle. If you want pampering, you seek assistance from the wrong faction. Which do you want?"

She gaped at the looming giant, feeling small, insignificant, and thoroughly intimidated—exactly what he intended. He knew how to put a person in their place alright, and that place was not at his level.

"Warriors, I want warriors. But I've one more comment before you go. You're plenty intimidating in your armored suit. I understood the point you made earlier about wrongfully judging others based on appearance; however, I recommend you keep your clothes on. The full body reveal was a jolt, as you meant it to be, but was it also an indication of a bloated ego?" She heard a low rumble coming from behind the mask. Rising swiftly, he disappeared beyond the mesa walls.

"Possibly, that could have gone unsaid."

Quil quizzed Albert on the way to the Jeep. "Albert, tell me about your vision?"

"In a dream, I met a big demon crow and took him to see the message on that wall we just left."

"A *demon* crow? Did you think him evil?"

"At first. Then I saw he was there to learn, and I was his guide. Now, I think he might be an angel. Do angels have black wings?"

"I don't know."

"You're troubled?"

"I am. I could have done better and wonder if I'll have another chance to talk with … the demon crow."

"I need to sit. I'm tired."

They rested on a downed piñon tree, and Quil pushed further. "What about another vision? Do you think you could see if there'll be another meeting?"

"Maybe yes, maybe no. I can try."

Removing a pack of papers and a pouch of tobacco from his pocket, he rolled a cigarette, sealing the ends with dampened fingertips. Smoke swirled about his face as he sent a veiled message to the spirit world. Staring into the mist with clouded eyes, he chanted, like a rustling of wind moving across the sand. With far-away vision, he studied the unknowable. The mystic leaned forward, listening to star spirits. A ghostly shaman had entered a realm of shadows. Enthralled, Quil wished she could be with him there.

"Nope." Albert abruptly stood and walked away.

Her eyes followed the old man trudging down the trail. "Maybe it *was* the peyote?"

As they neared Jim's ranch, Albert asked, "Your talk with the crow. Was it good?"

"I insulted him. More than once. It's my mouth. I lack control sometimes."

He patted her shoulder. As she was preparing to leave for Durango, Albert told her to wait before boarding the plane. Going to the house, he returned with a packet and an item gripped in the palm of a hand.

"I made this long ago, my Annie's design. She was good at design. The bluebird's eye turquoise is sacred. It was dug from the Cerbat Mountains in Arizona. It's ancient and has been passed from generation to generation 'til the one who's meant to have it arrived. You're that one. What's meant to happen is not always easy to understand. Two worlds can brush against each other without dwellers knowing the reason for the joining. Wear this. It will help you focus." He placed it around her neck and lowered the long silver chain.

"Albert, it's beautiful, but I can't take it. Your wife, Annie—"

"Take it. The white part of you is sometimes stupid. It'll help with your tongue. I don't want you to end up a pile of bleached bones in the sand."

"That's a vivid image. How can I thank you?"

Waving his hand like shooing at a fly near his face, he let her know nothing was expected, then handed her the packet.

"I wrapped this, but you find a better way." Inside a piece of brown paper torn from a grocery sack was an eagle feather. "Give this to the demon crow when you meet. Tell him we welcome him to our land, and we're glad he flies with eagles to watch over us. Tell him I shield him while he's with us."

"You sly old fox, you did have a vision. But it should be you who gives the gift so he can see the honor in your eyes."

"It's for you to do. Fly good, granddaughter."

In Durango, she had just enough time for a quick stop at the bookstore. The poets excitedly shared a list of posers uncovered from spy activity. Of great interest was the information on Ramona Rand and her red-haired partner.

"We have leads of upcoming events they might be attending. We're rearranging our schedules to attend those," said Inger.

"Has Ned or Cedric contacted you?" Gretchen asked, placing a slip of paper on the table.

"No, they haven't. What do you know?"

"Ned called asking us to browse the web for information on a list of names. He said most came from Wolf and Josiah. They're all military people. We got this information and called him back. I thought you might know more about what they're doing." Quil looked over the list.

"I don't know any more than you do, but it might be good news. They could be searching for military people they can trust. Let me know of other calls. This list is important."

"It'll stay in the safe."

She should have known Gretchen and Inger were in the thick of it. The spy game was a dangerous field, but it was exactly where they wanted to be.

twenty-four

Quil drove that evening with Emma Six as spotter. The road was a problem. Spring runoffs washed out backcountry roads, and keeping them maintained was challenging to justify to taxpayers. Slides blocked the way, causing reversals and re-maneuvering to get to the observation point.

"It'd be hard to get down fast if we were on the run." Six had eyes on a sheer drop-off that they barely skinned by, flinching each time rocks fell into the chasm.

The observations point was not good either. After consulting the map, they selected two separate paths that allowed a view of a sheep herd. A scarcity of trees and undergrowth made concealment difficult. The Widows chose a thicket nearer the valley floor. They didn't like it, but they settled in and waited.

Quil was positioned higher for a wider view. She listened to sounds of cricket beetles and night birds, thinking about the mistakes she'd made at the conference with the demon crow, wondering if a second meeting would happen. She wasn't looking forward to it, but it was a must.

"Eight?" whispered Seribeth over the headset.

"They're here. Everyone quiet," said Quil.

A sudden hush fell like a burial cloth settling over the dead. Scanning the sky, Quil searched for approaching crafts.

Consistent with the usual MO, the bell ship arrived, dropping sheep to a worship position. But within seconds, the white light moved to a thicket not far from the Window's location. *Have we been made?* But it wasn't them they were after. Two bodies rose and dropped to the valley floor. *No, not again!*

A second shock. Quil expected a delta ship to show—but not two. Both settled near two females on the ground. Her eyes moved back to the Wisps working steadily; they'd soon be ready to depart. Would they take the women with them or turn them over to the snakes? A storm raged in her mind. *We need to do something but what?*

A commotion erupted. A familiar scene, the same thing occurred before. While partners in a nasty bid for world dominion, the Wisps and Reptoids seemed consistently at odds over authority. Four serpents, two from each delta, instigated an argument with the two Wisps on the ground. Seeing two uniformed men leave deltas, Quil expected to see the snakes herded back to the crafts.

That didn't happen.

The men sauntered over to the captives. One pushed a female with his foot. Not getting a reaction, he kicked her hard in the ribs. A woman's scream sliced the stillness. Laughing, the men dropped to the ground, tearing at the women's clothing.

Rape!

Panicked breathing came through Quil's earpiece. *Stay calm. Stay down.* She debated options. Attack would mean certain death. They couldn't go up against that ship. The Wisps needed to leave. Did she chance a telepathic message to the Wisps on the ground? Maybe that was the only option. But then a startling thing happened. The Wisps opted out, rose to the ship, and departed, leaving reptoids and *traits* on the ground—alone.

"One," she whispered.

"With you," replied Seri.

Their rifle fire was concurrent. Both *traits* slammed to the ground, skulls split. The four reptoids bunched, trying to locate the shooters. Weapons drawn, they crept backward toward ships. One broke from the group and sprinted for a delta. *The radio!* The other three blindly fired at terrain, sending stones and debris skyward. *They're creating cover.*

"Take 'em down!" Quil dropped the one running toward the ship. The Spiders opened fire. It was fast. The snakes fell near the human traitors.

"Four, Six, get those women out of there! Tres, cover!"

The victims were screaming nonstop. Closer to the women, Four and Six called out, attempting to get them to run to cover. No luck. Thinking they might be Native American, Six yelled in Ute, followed by Tres shouting in Apache. The women stood, looking around, trying to find the source of the voices. Naked, surrounded by dead bodies, they shrieked at the top of their lungs—and still, they didn't move.

Leaving cover, Four ran into the field. Grabbing one woman by the arm, she slung her toward the thicket. She grabbed for the other one, but the woman fought. Her mind had crossed the line; she'd lost all awareness. Four slapped her hard twice, sending her to a stagger. Pushing her from behind, Four screamed, "Run!" The woman ran.

Four didn't.

A second—and it was done. Four lifted off the ground, hanging in space, head snapped back, legs bent at the knees. Slowly falling, she hit the ground facedown, bouncing only once before settling. Still, she lay so still.

Screaming and on a downhill slide, Quil fired at movement on the valley floor. A snake held a *trait*'s handgun. Tres was firing on the run. Six was running toward Four. Charging down the rocky slope, Quil stumbled and collided with Tres, who caught her arm keeping her upright, and they ran the rest of the way together. "Seri, stay there! Cover us!"

Six was talking to Four. Four wasn't responding.

"I saw the gun raise, but Four was in the way." Six was shaking badly. "I had no clean shot. No clean shot."

"I know. I saw. Is she alive?" She knelt beside Four.

"She moaned when I dragged her here."

"Let's get her to the Hummer." Six wrapped her arms around Four's chest. Quil grabbed her legs, and they climbed. Tres was trying to get the victims up the hill.

"Don't hurt us anymore," begged one woman.

"Move!" yelled Tres. "We're women! We're trying to help you! Move!"

"Tres, watch our rear," Quil rasped, short of breath.

Seri's unit repeatedly fired at those in the field; snake or human didn't matter. Bullets pumped into bodies caused jerky motions of limbs, making them seem alive. Tres turned before following and sprayed the field with her assault rifle. The Recluse unit remained on watch. When the Widows disappeared over a rise, they withdrew on a dead-out run.

"Let's lay her down here, so I can cut off her jacket. Shot in the back, bleeding bad." Quil checked for a pulse. "She's alive. Four, can you hear me? Where's Seri! Seri!"

"Get her inside!" Seri yelled as she ran. "I'll get the kit." They laid Four face down on the rear compartment floor. Seri squeezed in beside her, immediately applying pressure to the wound.

Hearing sobbing, Quil spun around, looking at the women. "My god, you're kids."

"What are you doing up here!" yelled Six. "Our friend got shot because of you!" Six was covered in Four's blood and shaking so bad, she swayed, trying to stay on her feet.

"Six, enough." Quil squeezed her shoulder. Taking off her jacket, she handed it to the smaller girl. "You're just a little bit of a thing. Here. Cover yourself." The girl tried to fasten the coat, but her hands shook so much, she couldn't do it. Quil fastened it for her. The girl flung herself into Quil's arms. "Oh! Okay, let's get you in the car." Six grabbed her arm and pushed her inside the vehicle.

Tres handed her jacket to the second girl. "Let's get outta here before they come back."

"They'll be back!" The girl gasped, stumbling backward.

"Probably. Everyone in the Hummer."

"I know—uh, I know a faster way out." The girl was wild-eyed and beginning to hyperventilate.

"Are you're sure? You thinkin' clearly?" said Quil.

"Back road. Shorter. Please, don't let 'em get us again."

"Sit up here with me and Six. What's your name?"

"Rebecca. Ruth's my sister, pointing over her shoulder." Quil listened to Rebecca's stammering directions as she steered the vehicle through undergrowth. "Our truck," she said, pointed a shaking hand toward a black pickup backed into trees.

"We're not stopping for it."

"Turn left ahead." Quil physically dodged, jostling both Rebecca and Six.

"Who are you?"

"Don't be concerned, pilgrim. I thought you could use some help. We have a better view from up here, and there's a faster way to get you out of there. Turn left now. Trust me."

"Gene! I'm listening."

Following his instructions, Quil hit the road fighting a spin but made the descent in less than half the time on the other trail.

"Seri, update?"

"The bleeding's slowed; bullet might've hit a bone. I sent Gracie a text telling her to get a doctor, and we're bringing guests.",

"Where're you taking us?" Rebecca looked concerned.

"With us."

"Where you from?" asked Seri.

"Bayfield. Can you take us home?"

"No. We have wounded needing attention."

Adam was waiting to carry Four inside. Gracie led the way to a back room. "Dr. Wilson's on the way. He's retired but good. I have hot water on the stove to clean the wound, but I'll wait until the doctor gets here before removing the bandage."

"I'll help him, Gracie." Seri set her medical kit beside the bed.

Back in the living room, Quil saw the two girls huddled in a corner. "Come over here and sit down. We need information so we can get you help."

"Our parents are going to kill us. We told 'em we were staying at a friend's house." Rebecca had Ruth by the hand, pulling her along.

"No, they won't kill you, but they'll be plenty pissed. What were you doing up there?" Quil asked, pointing to a sofa. When seated, she covered them with an throw.

"We heard about the alien hunters and wanted to see a UFO. We didn't hide good enough."

"Give me your parent's phone number. And tell me, would it be better to wait 'til morning or contact them now? It's goin' on three." The younger girl had never stopped sobbing. All eyes were on her.

"Ruthie can't help it. My sister's only thirteen." Rebecca wrapped an arm around the small girl. "We never imagined we'd, I mean, we've been kept safe. I don't, I don't know what to do."

A stony silence fell over the room; the sobs of the girls echoed off the walls. A squad member moved to the sofa and knelt before them.

"Listen, you two. Bad shit happens, but we live through it. You'll carry the emotional scars forever, but you'll live. You'll find strength you didn't know you had until it happens to you. Dig deep. You'll find it."

Having just entered the room, Gracie spoke quietly. "These children have been hurt?"

"Raped," said Six.

"We killed the bastards that did it," added Tres.

"Children, I'm so sorry this happened. Come here." Gracie wrapped her arms around the girls and walked toward the back. "You need to get mad; scream if you feel like it. I'm here to listen, and I'll always be here to listen, anytime night or day. One of you spiders draw baths, and someone look in the donation box for clothes that might fit." The girls in Gracie's able hands, Quil checked in with Seri.

"Has she come to at all?"

"Not yet. She's still bleeding. I wish the doctor would get here. She might need a transfusion, and we can't deal with that. Maybe we should get her to a hospital."

"Let's give it a little more time."

They heard loud talking, followed by the doctor entering the bedroom. He quickly assessed the wound. "Let's get that bullet out. I have a sedative to help her through this. Seri, you'll assist?"

"I'm right here, Dr. Wilson. She might need a transfusion."

"Do you know her blood type?" I can do a transfusion if we have a donor match."

"I know where our med records are kept. I'll be right back." Quil ran toward Gracie's office, returning with the squad's medical records. Two and Seven were close behind. "Type A positive. These two are matches, and there are others." Two and Seven were already out of jackets and rolling up shirt sleeves. The doctor pointed to Seven and told Two to standby.

"Call me if you need anything, Seri." Quil backed out and returned to the front room.

"The girls want their parents contacted right away," said Gracie. "I can make the call, but the girls need to talk to them. Do we wait, or do we call now?"

"Make the call." Informing the team what was to happen, she gave them options of going to Seribeth's trailer or staying while the parents collected the girls.

"We stay," said Five. "They need to hear from us."

Gracie called the parents and put Rebecca on the phone. But telling the parents about the assault was too difficult. Taking the phone, Gracie made it clear. "Your girls are in a parsonage and safe, but they've been hurt. They need you."

It was agonizing. Between crying and shouting, the parents finally came to understand the need not to involve law enforcement to protect the squad and mission.

Dr. Wilson came in, letting them know he had successfully removed the bullet. Four would be okay but required an extended recovery period. Learning of the girls' violation, he conferred with the parents, who agreed to an examination and recommendation for care.

Before the girls and parents left, Ruthie, the small one, stood before Six. "I'm sorry I caused your friend to get shot. I'll make it up somehow. I promise."

"No, that's okay," said Six. "I was scared that's all. I'm glad you're alright."

"I'll make it up. I promise." The way she spoke those words made Quil think she'd stand behind that pledge.

Sleeping bags stayed in the corner; they would not sleep. "What did we do wrong?" asked Quil. "We need to get it said."

"It's my fault," said Six, wringing her hands. "About the time we think we're on top of things, it all goes nuts. I did everything wrong. Everything."

"No, you didn't. Placed as you were, if you'd tried to get off a shot, you could have killed Four. You did it right."

"Our positioning was bad, and we knew it," said Tres. "We even talked about it before we snugged in. Poor concealment tactics—and I messed up big time. I let my focus slip. We let our training go—didn't we?"

"Those damn thickets. Too close, poor vision, couldn't maneuver. They strapped us down," said Five.

"I agree with everything you said. Thinking about that location now, what could we have done differently?" Quil pulled out a notepad and tossed it in the middle of the group. "One of you sketch the location, noting elevation differences as you can, add cover you can recall, and our placement, by number, so we know where each of us was. Then, we laying it out better."

Seven grabbed the notebook. "I'll do it. I've done nothing but think about that location since we left. I'm a landscape draftsman. I do layouts every day."

While Seven worked, Quil asked the question none wanted to hear. "Should we have left the girls to the enemy? They were in trouble because of their own doing. Would it have been smarter—thinking as military strategists now—to leave them be?"

"Maybe smarter from a military stand, but I couldn't have." Seri received nods of agreement from the others.

"I agree, but we need to consider that a day could come when sacrifices have to be made."

"No!" Tres's jaw clenched. "We don't allow anyone to be sacrificed. Not again."

Seri and Quil looked at each other and nodded. Never again.

"I'm ready," said Seven. They stayed with it, adding cover, changing elevations, unit member locations. It took a number of tries, but they were satisfied they could have done it right. They learned a hard lesson on concealment. The subject of allowing innocents to die stayed with Quil, and she hoped they'd never have to face it.

This is what I expect of you. I do not want you found.

"I hear you, Josiah, I hear ya," she whispered. Finally, in sleeping bags, they tossed for hours. About daybreak, Quil heard even breathing around the room and drift off.

Sleep time seemed short, but it was afternoon when they roused. Gracie made her way through the maze to the TV. The news was reporting on a fire on a mountain. They jumped out of their bags and huddled before the screen. After giving the location and attempts to contain the fire, the newscaster moved to another subject.

"We better stay low for a while," said Seri. "I'm scheduling knife training while we hunker down."

"Four's awake." Gracie motioned for them to follow. "She wants to see you. Don't jostle the bed." They rushed to Four's bedside, squeezing everyone into the small room.

"You look good, girl, considering." Relief flooded Tres's face.

Six held Four's hand and tried to speak but couldn't. So she stood there, bobbing her head, tears dripping off her chin.

"I lost my rifle," murmured Four.

"We have other rifles." Quil was thankful to see Four alert and talking.

"I just don't my pay docked for losin' it." She tried to laugh but sucked in her breath. "What's the doctor's opinion on use of this arm?"

"The bullet nicked a bone but no breaks," said Seri. "You're looking at mending time. You'll experience tightness in the shoulder muscle, but you're lucky. Any lower, it could've been the heart or a lung."

"At least it's my off arm. I can still brace a rifle and fire a sidearm. Quil, I need to say something. When we were getting positioned, I had a *direful* feeling grab me. It shook me hard. Our grounding wasn't good. That direful was a warning. Don't you think I'm right?"

"A *direful*? A good way to describe it. Yeah, the whole thing felt off from the start. From now on, we pay attention to our *spidey sense*. Trust your intuition; don't back off from it. Hereon, we go where we're needed but get set as we should. Thanks for bringing up the direful, Tilde, and I'm glad you're okay. Rejoin us as soon as you can."

"No worries there. I'll be back. Did anyone notice how young those girls were?"

"Yeah, very young. They were looking for UFO hunters. Anyone have ideas on how they learned about us?"

"I do," said Five. "I talked to Rebecca. She said there was a man in a fast-food place talking loud about it. He was telling anyone who'd listen about UFO hunters in the mountains."

"He had to be talking about the men's squad. They were recruiting everywhere," said Gracie.

"Per Rebecca, he said, *women* UFO hunters."

"Women! Could she describe the man?" Seri looked at Gracie.

"No, I asked her. He was a few booths away, and she didn't see his face."

"Gracie, we need to get on this. Our communication line has holes in it, and we need to find out where."

"We'll start right away."

"Another thing," said Four. "I blame myself for my predicament. I was right there and still didn't see it coming. This is my own fault."

"No. I carry blame or a good part of it," said Tres. "I didn't cover as I should. And I'm sorry.

"Oh, shut up. This is my spotlight."

"You get better, Tilde," Quil said. "We need you."

"Well, of course, you do. I'm the one with the boom box."

"You're right." laughed Quil. "We'll find your player and get it to you."

"Before we break, I'd like to add something," said Maria Seven. "Quil, we hear you talking in our minds. I don't know how you're doing it, but I, for one, appreciate you being there. I've never felt so totally alone as when I'm in scrub staring at alien enemies. It helps to hear your voice drifting through my mind." Others expressed the same sentiment.

"That means a great deal, especially coming from all of you."

A racket came from the hallway. Adam was trying to get their attention. "Hey, in there. The doctor's back and wants to check on Four." They left the room except Emma Six, who refused to let go of Tilde's hand. Deciding to take a break, they went separate ways, planning on regrouping for knife training the next day.

twenty-five

Quil headed for the house, having finishing two laps on the running path. Last night's foray weighed heavy on her mind. They almost lost Four. That was too close.

"I'll speak with you." It was Prex. She slid to a stop and whirled around, expecting to see him behind her.

"I wait in the wooded area. Do you remember?"

"Yes. I'll be there as quick as I can." She picked up speed and rushed inside. Exchanging running shoes for Wellington boots, she grabbed a heavier jacket and ran out the back gate. "I forgot." Running back inside, she tucked a silk scarf inside her jacket, zipping it to the neck.

She slowed her pace walking through darkening pines, turning every few steps to look over her shoulder. Shivering, she had a strong urge to turn back to the house. Was that a *direful*?

"Here." Prex stood in a small clearing before a rocky outcropping.

Rocks, of course. Right away, she chose one large enough to elevate her as much as possible. She wanted to avoid looking like a jackass again.

Prex silently watched the woman approach. An unusual being. I think one with veiled knowledge. Often makes things more difficult than necessary but doesn't hide behind falseness.

"We aren't remaining here. You were followed."

The *direful*. "No, I need to touch your body." Prex lowered his face armor, looking puzzled. "I mean, I can shield us from sight, but I need to touch you … like your hand. I want to see who it is."

He sat beside her, holding out a gloveless hand. She placed her hand in his, sensing a slight tingle as his fingers curled about hers.

She whispered, "Stay quiet now." A shadow moved behind a tree, then another and another. None revealed themselves. *They're closing in. I don't like this. They need to go.*

You see only trees and rocks. She's not here. Turn around and leave. From her side vision, she saw Prex eyeing her, but he said nothing. The three shadows turned and slipped away.

"They're gone. Shadow watchers. Only fringe frights, intending to cause concern but without power to do harm." Or so she hoped and wondered who was directing their actions? Another unknown.

"A noteworthy experience, but we're still leaving. I want no interruptions in our exchange. Hands around the neck, remember the wings." He wrapped an arm around her waist, bringing her close to his chest. "Hold on. I'm not equipped with a safety harness."

She had no chance to argue; they were rising. She grabbed on to his armor. The lift-off was straight up and fast. As they climbed, she watched the planet rapidly diminishing. *If we don't level off or descend soon, I could be in trouble.*

"We experience oxygen deprivation at about thirteen thousand feet. Do you know that?"

"I do now."

Moving into a descent, he orbited a mesa and landed. Quil felt her feet touch ground and quickly scouted the area, seeing nothing out-of-the-usual.

"I have items to discuss."

He seemed distracted, possibly avoiding saying something she might find upsetting. Quil worried the Guard had declined their request for help. Prex walked to the rim of the mesa and looked out over the vista. "You prefer this place called the high desert. Why?"

Tourist talk. He can't be serious. Where's he headed with this? But she responded, not wanting to appear argumentative and abrasive.

"It's wide and uncluttered. Space enough to find privacy and solitude. I like both."

"Solitude can be found many places. The desert is barren, lacks vegetation."

"It is a struggle to survive here. I admire the tenacity it takes to exist in such an unforgiving environment."

"You engaged the enemy to rescue two women, and a soldier was injured."

"That was an abrupt change of topic, or did I miss the segue?" He walked very close, staring into her face. *Is he meaning to intimidate me again?* She backed away. "We did engage the enemy. It was unavoidable. The one injured is recovering, as are the two female captives we took back with us."

"It was avoidable."

She then understood her reason for being there. He was questioning their decision to engage the reptoids.

"Unavoidable."

"Strong-willed and argumentative."

"Yep, that's me. Anything else?"

"The oxygen is adequate? You're warm enough?"

"I'm okay." She flipped up her collar and shoved her hands in pockets.

"That action could have meant death for the battle unit. Even if it was your decision to engage—or not—do you think it was a correct decision for your team?"

"This feels like a disciplinary hearing, and you don't have the authority to interrogate me. My squad thoroughly reviewed our actions last night and know changes to make."

"Answer the question."

"I believe it was the right decision based on what was occurring last night. In other circumstances, it might not have been. Sometimes, there may be adequate time to consider options before makin' a decision. But other times, there're only seconds. It's like standing on the rim of this mesa. You may not know what to do until you're standing on the edge of a decision. But you make the decision—you jump, or you don't jump—it may be right; it may be wrong."

"But do you think there's a need for levels in decision making, especially in a military sense? If you were a soldier in an organized arm and your commanding officer gave you an order, do you think you should comply with that order?" He leaned close, concentrating on her eyes. *Why is he doing that?*

"I've never been in that situation, but I don't hold with blindly following. Those leading armies have backgrounds in strategy and tactics, but they may not know an enemy's vulnerabilities. Or they've had noses so close to maps, they haven't stepped away to study patterns. I'd rather get information from troops who know the lay of the land. Plus, I've never read of a military commander incapable of making mistakes. Unless it's you. Are you perfect, Commander?" She stopped, knowing she was moving toward anger. She had to end this before it got out of hand. "Though I hear what you're saying. I'm being viewed as a loose cannon. Undisciplined and doing as I please. I guess that makes me a poor choice for an organized army."

"Only for some armies. And I'm far from perfect. I believe you called my attention to that in our prior meeting.

Oops? That sounded resentful. It was the snide remark about his ego.

"Why do you burn the locations where enemies have been killed? Why not confiscate weapons and aircraft for our use? You're not the only one who can question the actions of another."

"I have not done so, and I don't object to being questioned."

"Then the enemy is destroying those sites to conceal their presence in our society."

"Your friends see to it."

"Friends? You mean Gene and Jessie."

"Yes. They remove aircraft before destroying evidence that could expose their force. They have a small band and gather what weaponry they can as they await reinforcements from Procyon."

He moved closer, again staring at her. "Back to rescuing the *women* last night."

"So that's it? Don't tell me they should have been sacrificed because they were only female. Too many women on this planet still are told they have no value and are expendable. You disappoint me, Commander. I expected more from an advanced species."

"And they appear."

"Who appears?" looking around to see who he meant.

"The flames in your eyes. It happens when you become angry. But you must know that."

"No, I don't. I mean … yes, but only once before when I was a child." She flinched as small lights flickered before her face. "Oh, crap! I need this under control fast. Why does it only happen around you?"

"Perhaps I irritate you."

"Yes, you do, but you know that. Have you seen this before? The eyes, I mean? Anywhere?"

"I haven't, but I need to clarify a matter with you. Please sit." He sat across from her. "There are many matriarchal governed worlds. Women are equal and highly respected in mine, as they should be. I pressured you only to see if the eye sparking would reappear."

"You can stop all pressuring; I'll answer questions without it. And the matriarchal governing sounds good, but I'd wager female-governed worlds don't exist in this solar system."

"At a distant time, the fifth planet was matriarchally governed."

"The fifth? That would be Jupiter? That's not possible unless it was a moon of Jupiter."

"That now would be the inner belt."

"The asteroid belt? Then the destruction theory wins out. You know, many scientists dispute that theory believing the belt exists due to conflicting gravitation between Jupiter and Mars. But you're saying there was a Tiamat? I've always wanted it to exist."

"Have you now?" He was grinning. "It's been called by many names. Whatever one chooses to call it, it wasn't destroyed, not entirely. We're standing on it."

"We are? Does that mean … did humanity exist before Earth? If it did, that disputes gene-splicing to create humans."

"Bioengineering of humankind here doesn't conflict with humans existing elsewhere. Some citizens of Tiamat were hominin, some a blend of hominin and reptilian, and some crystalline. There was little warning to those on Tiamat before the planet's destruction. When the demolition occurred, citizens that were off-planet sought harbors on friendly worlds, at time cross-mixing with other species."

The wings. That explains how he got those. His ancestors must have crossbred with a winged race. "What about the crystalline? Do they live on other planets now?" She hoped for information on the glazen beings in her dreams.

"None have been seen since Tiamat's destruction. Many believe they were lost. But we dwell too long in ancient times. Back to strategy. You've explained the reason for engaging the enemy. Still, such actions could cause the enemy to halt activities in the open, making it more difficult to locate their base. Do not engage the enemy."

"It's not possible to stop engagements altogether. We have a squad fighting further north."

"I know of that squad and its loss of men. They're being baited. The enemy's plan is to involve them in impossible-to-win engagements in the north while the enemy continues subterfuge here."

"The northern squad has changed tactics to observation only, but they're dealing with attacks. I believe they've attempted to find organized military help. They must be cautious as some part of our military is supporting the enemy. We don't know the scale of that involvement, but for the enemy to have any government support puts us at a great disadvantage."

"Yes. The subversive group has achieved power by consent. Prominent people are behind their actions."

"The northern squad also has an infiltrator who's alerting the enemy of the squad's location."

"Have they made progress in identifying the plant?"

"Not yet, but they don't want to bring the squad back here as it would expose our base of operations."

"I see. Moving to observation is a correct decision as it preserves fighting power. Organization, however, is essential. A scattershot approach will not succeed. Until reinforcements arrive, we must pick our battles and make them count."

"Pick *our* battles? Meaning our resistance fighters will be involved?"

"I said it; I meant it."

"Then I have a question. How do we go up against the enemy's directed-energy weapons?"

"I just said you're not to engage the enemy? You seem to have a selective memory. And what is that you're doing to your eyes?" Quil was scrubbing at her eyes.

"I'm trying to make the flickering go away. Otherwise, I can't serve in the emissary role."

"The Procyon wouldn't expect that of you."

"Possibly, however, the humans involved would be a problem. I doubt you'd understand, but on this planet, those that are different are not accepted. People here are hurtful, condemning to the point of killing those who don't fit their narrowly defined codes of acceptability. I've had to hide things all my life because of it. I'll never be able to hide these eyes."

"There's no justifiable reason to hide abilities or differences. The eye phenomenon must have a purpose. I wonder if you're making too much of this. When you were small, how were they made to go away?"

"Cold. My guardian took me to play in the snow, and it cured my eyes—no, that's impossible. Snow can't heal. Either the cold or the diversion caused the sparks to stop." She suddenly felt heat from under her jacket. It was the turquoise stone. Albert said it would help her focus. He said nothing about it radiating heat. *Albert's gift. I forgot all about it.*

"I just remembered I have something to give you." She handed him the bundle, watching as he unfolded the scarf revealing the eagle feather. He was quiet as he appraised it.

"Is there significance?"

"It's from Albert, the elderly man at our first meeting. He asked me to tell you that we welcome you to our land, and he's glad you fly with the eagles to watch over us. I'm also to tell you that he shields you while you are here. He's a holy man. It has significance."

Prex looked thoughtful. Quil wondered if he was he questioning its worth? "You may not have a place to keep it. I can hold on to it for you."

"I have a place." He quickly concealed it in a side enclosure. "We'll leave now. Morning strategy sessions are held at the Cyon facility. Consider attending. I'll show you the location." On the way back, she wondered how she could lose the eye flaming. An ice bath might work.

"This looks suitable." He was looking below them.

"This isn't where I live. NOOO!"

Whump!" She splatted face first in a bank of fresh snow. Thrashing about, she got right side up and saw she was missing a boot. She found it packed in snow and jerked it back on.

"Has no one explained smooth transitioning from one topic to another! Where was the segue!" she yelled, but he ignored her, engrossed in panning their location.

"I don't find this place inviting either. You go from one extreme to another. The desert, with no moisture, to a glacier, with frozen moisture. How could one enjoy a place like this?"

"Lower your facial armor and breathe the air. It's quite invigorating. I'm sure you'll like it." Hurriedly rolling snowballs, she lined them along the top of a bank. He lowered his mask and inhaled. The first one caught him smack between the eyes.

"Now, that was an abrupt change—as in *no segue*."

She hurled balls, hitting him in the head and chest, but he made no effort to dodge them. His face was caked with ice and still, he refused to dodge. Until … *uh-oh*.

"An unexpected ploy, but one easily countered." He came at her with a massive armload of snow.

"Stop! That's not allowed. Snowballs are small like this." She held one up high.

"Why must they be small?"

"My game, my rules."

"Game? Rules? Who said you make the rules?"

"I did—didn't you just hear me?" She snickered as she gathered more snow. *THUD!* The packed snow hit her like a sledgehammer. He dragged her out of the bank and shook her like a rag doll, snow flying everywhere.

"War is not a game; there are no rules. Always be prepared to fight. Do you understand?"

"Yes." While no meaning to, she spit ice crystals in his face. He dropped her to the ground. "Stop throwing me around like a sack of chicken feed!"

"Others expect you to serve with distinction. Expect the same of yourself." His facial armor snapped over his head. "I'll return you now." He leaned over so she could grip around his neck, but she backed away, her arms crossed.

"Stop the childish behavior." Still, no movement. Colossal black wings spread to their fullest as his voice thundered. "I'm leaving! Are you leaving with me!"

"Oh!" She lunged, grabbing armor, but once secured, held herself as far away as possible.

"The suit emits heat. Lean on my chest; it'll warm you." She didn't, and he didn't offer again. "The Procyon facility is below."

She recognized the terrain, the moonlight allowing a view of a runway and facility. "I see it."

Quil held on tighter as they neared her neighborhood to avoid being dropped again, but instead, he roughly deposited her on the ground, growling an order.

"I require a response. You've defined humans as cruel and condemning, harming others who don't meet standards of some contrived model of acceptance. In effect, you've made a case for the destruction of humankind. How can you support saving humanity if, as you have asserted, humanity is unworthy of life?"

Dumbstruck, she slumped down on a rock. A glob of wet snow slid off her head, landing on her boot. *Slush snot. I'm thawing.* What if she simply refused to answer? The easiest thing to do would be to walk away, but she wouldn't do that.

Think. Removing the right Wellington, she dumped icy water. No sock. She was sure there was a sock on that foot when she left the house. Is he a guide she was to meet on her travels? She didn't see him as that. Guides whisper like wind or speak wisdom from smoke visions.

She emptied the other boot. There was a sock on that foot. Or is he driving home a point about correct military comportment, namely respecting a superior officer? *Enough! This self-haggling is getting me nowhere.* She yanked on the boot and stood facing the inquisitor.

"I was wrong to condemn others in retaliation for their condemnation of me. I reacted rather than letting my rational mind control. I'm experiencing disturbing physical changes, but that's my problem. Humanity has problems. I want to think they're capable of solving them. Perhaps they cannot, but I choose to believe they can." Her voice was flat and mechanical. His facial armor vanished; his head still showing traces of clumped ice.

"That sounded composed. A response you think I'd expect of you. You're now the one speaking as a computerized replicant. Can we stop testing the other? Just tell me why you believe humanity is worth saving."

"Because—I believe in chances, allowing mistakes, working together to fix them, granting time, doing right by others, and … life. I believe in life." She turned to walk away. A gentle hand on her arm turned her around to face him.

"And you're not the only one in the heavens who does."

She wiped slush out of her hair. "Well, that's good to hear. Is that for Albert?" He held a glistening black feather.

"If it would be appropriate."

"Very appropriate. Thank you." She accepted the gift and walked away, but stopped, glancing over her shoulder. "And you can take off your clothes … or not. It makes no never mind to me." As she climbed the steps of her deck, she heard the rush of wings and what sounded like laughter.

"That was an abrupt change of topic, or did I miss the segue?"

Prex was gone, and she was cold and alone. She looked around for shadow watchers, saw none, and went inside. Who had sicced the fringe frights on her? Someone who was trying to distract her or possibly wanted to scare her into leaving? She'd do her best to disappoint whoever it was. Stopping before the hall mirror, she was relieved to see no eye flaming.

After bathing and pulling on a long flannel gown and woolen knee socks, she looked through the window slats before jumping under the covers. In an instant, Shade was sitting on the side of the bed.

"Good evening, Quil. Only listen now. Do not despair the becoming. You are to be what you were meant to be. A disclosing has been made known. What lies ahead will be difficult. Do not delay decisions. The sword must fall. Your warm and safe, snow angel. Rest while I keep watch."

twenty-six

For the third time, Quil sat gaping at a windbreak of closely spaced junipers. She knew the Cyon facility was on the other side of that hedgerow. What she didn't know was how to get beyond it. "This is wasting time. I'll walk in."

The first limb she pushed against disappeared. "A hologram." Jogging back to the car, she drove through the tree belt and found the road where it should be.

It was shortly before five when she tapped on a side door. It opened a crack, and Jessie's large almond-shaped eyes peered at her a second before she opened the door. Quil quickly walked inside. Having anticipated a room filled with otherworldly folk, she wasn't disappointed.

Curiosity must be a universal trait. An intriguing array ogled the newcomer. Mainly Cyon, but a smattering of other stellars were present. She spotted a blue string bean of a man, looking in her direction, appearing underwhelmed that she was there. He motioned her forward.

Quil didn't know what she'd be facing with this group but resolved to deal with whatever came, realizing she had turned a corner, at least in one respect. No longer would another's appearance startle her, or so she thought at that moment. *Well, now, it looks like everyone's had some tampering going on in the gene closet.* Joking aside, she respected these strangers who had traveled so far to help save their planet. Except, what's with all the Lycra? Tight-fitting spandex had never been a cloth she favored, and it was hot. They lived in a desert. Hadn't these people heard of cotton?

"You're out early, little pilgrim."

"I thought you might be holding strategy meetings before work. I'm here to learn how humans fit into the battle plan."

Feeling eyes digging into her back, she figured the others were trying to determine who she was and whether she could be of value to their group. A quick look around revealed no other humans were present. Opening her mind-sifting system, she intercepted their thoughts. Challenges came right away. *Is that a human here? Who okayed that? Humans have knowledge limitations. It's dangerous to include them in strategy sessions. She doesn't look trustworthy.* One out loud. "Remove the human."

"There will be no action against the human."

She recognized that voice. Prex stood at the back of the room, waiting for the crowd to part. She gasped at his sight. He wore Lycra, black Lycra, and mercy, he make that spandex look good. Overhead lighting drew attention to his build, streamlined muscles as tight as watch springs. They rippled even as he stood still. He was a beautiful creation.

She turned away, not wanting him to see her gawking, and caught sight of his image in a large window at her end of the room. Still dark out, it served as a mirror displaying the winged warrior's movements. As he moved through the crowd, he stopped to talk to those wanting his attention. Clearly, he was highly respected. The timbre of his voice changed, seeming to fit each individual he greeted. She had heard the thunder in that voice, one commanding respect. Trim and lean, he moved like a wild stallion, proud, sure in his step, his wings held high on his shoulders resembled a flowing mane. *How could anyone be so… perfect?*

He paused, openly pleased to see another winged being, unlike himself—it was short, stout, old perhaps, but one who looked to carry prestige. Prex didn't hesitate to show respect as he bowed to acknowledge this friend of his, and Quil wondered who it was. Prex laughed at something said, a deep, rich laugh, and she trembled, becoming aware that her female internals twinkle-toed against her spine.

Losing his image, she leaned forward at the waist to keep him in view, suddenly realizing he was beside her. She dropped to the floor, retying the laces of a combat boot. Straightening, she neatened her field jacket before raising her eyes to his face. *You're stunningly handsome. How could you not know that? I could drift away in those eyes.* But as he looked at her, his expression became solemn, and her spirits nosedive.

"Let's sit here, Quil." Telepathically, he said, *"I heard you just then. Be aware that I and others also have extrasensory abilities? I generally choose not to use them as it interferes with the free exchange of data. You're new to the game, so to speak, but consider limiting your channeling to certain people, not everyone. And now, you're blushing. Don't be concerned. Probably no one else heard you. Probably no one will notice you're flushed. Probably."* He grinned.

"I'll stand, thank you," turning her back to him. *Is he teasing me? No, he doesn't know the meaning of the word.*

"But I do. Teasing is to make fun of or to provoke another in a playful manner— SLAM. That shut him out, but not the grumbling coming from others. No bones about it, she wasn't wanted here.

"Cyon, handle this discord. The session must proceed," ordered Prex, though he was smiling at her.

"She stays. This is Quil Doolin. Her people are already involved in battle, and they have knowledge we require. Or more accurately, they're seeking knowledge that could prove useful."

"I wish to speak."

Instantly, Gene made that odd strangling noise and scowled, but he motioned her before the crowd. Such a mix of off-worlders. How did she address these people? Best be to the point.

"I welcome you to planet Earth. My message is a simple one. It's better to connect, share ideas and strategies rather than working separately. If you do not yet agree humans should be involved, hopefully, you will come to do so." The dissonance continued. She plunged forward.

"Gene generally addressed our efforts to aid in Earth's defense. Specifically, we're hunting for the enemy's base of operations. I know you also search for that base. Going over territory you've already searched is a waste of time. We know of the cave entrance to the enemy base and the appearance of the cliff in which it's located. We somewhat know the interior layout, including the clifftop sky port. Still, this is a difficult country to search. We need to narrow the compass."

"Did she say she knows—" Whoever was speaking didn't finish?

"How can you profess to know that?" Gene's tone was demanding.

"Cyon, move aside." Prex placed himself squarely before Quil, blocking others in the room, however Gene hurriedly repositioned himself to observe. "Can you provide evidence of your claim?" He spoke low for only her to hear.

"I have photos. Would that be enough evidence?" Neither the tall winged nor the tall blue man spoke. The noise in the room dropped to nothing. She heard herself breathing.

"Would you consider sharing those images with us?" asked Prex.

"Certainly." She removed the photos from her backpack, handing them to Prex. After a quick review, he passed them to Gene.

"Make copies of these for everyone." Gene was noticeably pleased as he handed them to another Cyon

"Hey, I need those back, just so you know," said Quil.

A Cyon stepped forward. "We have a map of locations we've explored. We hunt at night, attempting to follow the enemy to their base. But our ships are inferior, and we haven't succeeded. We recently acquired two reptoid ships that should aid in finding the enemy facility."

"Yes, we did obtain reptoid ships," said Gene, "and Quil's team placed those in our hands, eliminating four reptoids and two human conspirators in that encounter." Gene suddenly was of a better frame of mind.

"I would like to look at your map." Quil followed the Cyon to a wall of charts where she captured locations on her camera. "Thanks for this. It helps. Have you noted these sites on an aeronautical chart?"

"Here." Quil turned toward a voice with a quietness about it. It was the winged friend of Prex. "I'm called Prioress."

Ah, a female cleric. Very knowledgeable, the Prioress shared activity-tracking studies and charts that indicated the enemy had expanded activities into neighboring states.

She took several steps backward to focus her camera on the charts, and while at it, took a good look at the mysterious Prioress. How unusual. Her head was as wide as her body, making her appear square, though she really wasn't. Her wings, a soft chestnut, had lost their sheen. She seemed quite old. Her beak-shaped mouth spread from one side of the head to the other, giving her an eternal smile. But it was the eyes that drew attention. They were unlike any Quil had ever seen. Short, stiff black bristles stuck out all around her eyes, accenting their yellow color. Sadly, one eye was damaged, being neither opened nor closed. Lid heavy, it sagged like that of a stroke victim but with a glint at the bottom. A high-level holy woman, Quil felt wisdom and sorrow emanating from her. Others like her, though younger, stood in a nearby corner, their eyes never leaving the Prioress. They were her protectors. Quil bowed her head to show respect for her station. "I like you, Prioress. Thank you for the help."

Unexpectedly, the Prioress raised a hand in a manner as would a guardian of a temple. "And I like you, Quil, and pray you have the strength to vanquish what would cause you harm." Quil noticed Pres watching the exchange between the two. He seemed pleased.

"What's interesting you?" Gene interrupted by peering over Quil's shoulder, looking at the flight chart.

"I don't know yet," Quil replied courteously. "I look for patterns, but it needs study. When I know more, I'll fill you in." Walking beside Gene, she asked, "Who are they?"

"The greatest designers and builders of spacecraft that exist. They're the masters of anything connected to flight. We're very fortunate to have Carians with us. They're considered a premier species, one of the earliest of people. Unfortunately, they lost their battle again tyranny and are now refugees."

"We must stop this cruelty, Gene. What will be the role of humans in coming engagements?"

"Ground support. We've noticed your fighters are somewhat adequate marksmen. Your weapons are primitive, but it's what you have."

"Our fighters are excellent marksmen. Excellent. But we need advanced weapons, which is another reason I'm here today. Provide us the weapons you use."

"No."

"Then aircraft. The pilots of the reptoid ships are human. Give us the training we need—"

"No."

"We haven't enough for our requirements now," said Jessie, joining them. "As soon as we receive the expected reinforcements, we'll provide you with both."

"I disagree," said Gene.

"That is your privilege," replied Jessie.

"Then give me the names of the human representatives on the Assembly."

"No," said Gene, "It's critical we maintain our link with those supporting us on the Assembly. The humans there are *talking heads,* speaking for unknowns at high levels. If anything happened to them now, our presence could be exposed."

"On that, I agree," said Jessie, "but you'll have that information when time is right. I'll make sure you do. We thank you, Quil, for sharing material data on the enemy command post." Extending a three-fingered hand, he offered acceptance. Quil placed her hand in his.

She had been accepted, but it was clear they'd disagree if they felt the need. "If there's nothing else, I have another meeting to make."

Prex was waiting at the door, watching as she approached. There was a different look to his eyes, warmer. In his hand was the scarf that had held Albert's eagle feather. He handed it to her on her way out. Neither said a word.

She left feeling a foot taller than when she went in. Smiling, she tossed the scarf on the seat, seeing something fall out. *My sock?* Did he go back to that icy mountain to find a sock? Why?

She rushed to the training site where targets were already set up for knife skills. Quil joined the squad, paying attention to Seribeth, who pulled a knife from each boot, passing one around. "The blade is ultra-sharp. Be careful in handling it. She held the second knife high for viewing.

"This is a throwing knife, not to be confused with a combat knife. They're used in knife-throwing contests, but I've honed the edges razor-sharp to use as weapons. I prefer the no-spin throwing technique. Admittedly, it's hard to learn. A no-spin throw means there's no rotation; the point always points to the target. Adam, a former Marine, is here today to demo a Ka-Bar combat knife. You'll notice it turns once or twice as it nears the target. Blades are close-in weapons. You'll not have success if there's too great a distance between you and an opponent. Now, we'll demonstrate how to make these work for you." They were working with knives when they saw a vehicle coming, traveling fast and kicking up dust. It was Gracie, and Four was in the passenger side.

"Gather around. This could be urgent. Calls came in about trucks, semis, vans, pickups, all leaving the ranch called the Compound north of Archuleta Mountain. From the sounds of it, they've high-tailed it out, movin' fast."

"We need to recon asap," said Quil. We're near the airport. I'll do a flyover and see what's happening on the ground."

"I'll go with you," said Four. "I can serve as spotter. I brought binoculars with me."

"While the two of you do that, the rest of us will get ready to go in," said Seri."

"We're close to the ranch." Four's head bobbed between the chart and out the window. Quil overflew the guard towers, the ranch headquarters and moved to canyons adjacent to the spread. Neither of them saw activity on the ground.

"What do you make of this, Four?"

"People don't cut and run for no reason. Wonder where they went in such an all-fired hurry?"

"We're getting too close to whatever it is they don't want revealed. Let Seri know to get ready. We're moving as quick as we get down. Did Gracie put out the word to report sightings of that convoy? We need an idea of what direction they're headed?"

"I'll send texts right now. I'm going with you."

"Only if you stay with the vehicle. You're in charge of communications. "

"Okay, but I'm bringing weapons in case uglies show."

Jessie was waiting at Quil's hangar, wanting to know why the hurried, unscheduled flight. After a quick briefing, he said he was going with them. Hurrying inside, he returned carrying a pack and talking into a wrist transceiver. Oddly, two small people ran out of the hangar with him, also carrying packs.

"They're coming, too."

"Who are they?"

"Others who have a special interest in seeing the common enemy destroyed. They lost their people. We don't know their home planet. One day, they showed up seeking asylum. We have no other information, not even names. And they only talk telepathically."

"So what do we call 'em?"

"*You* don't call them anything. They talk only through me." As he placed his pack in the back, he spotted Four. "Who are you?"

"Quil, tell him I only talk through you."

"She's just giving you sass. Her code name is Four, and she's handling communications for our squad."

"Are the short ones fighters?" Four asked me, and I looked at Jessie.

"Some of the best." Quil nodded at Four.

"Let's boogie then," said Four, grinning.

"Are all of you cursed with attitude?" said Jessie.

"Count on it," chuckling as she grinned at Four.

Back at the training site, their guests got a lot of looks, and Quil got a lot of questions. "They're allies coming with us. The tall one is Jessie. Don't be surprised if he turns a very nice shade of blue and gets a lot taller. The small ones don't talk."

Seri had a terrain map spread on a car hood. "There's good concealment getting to the ranch HQ. No worries there. What did it look like from above?"

"Abandoned. But let's go see for ourselves."

Tres volunteered her Jeep for the allies if she could be the driver. The rest of them went in the Hummer. It took less than an hour to get to the padlocked entrance to the Compound. They drove past the gate as if headed elsewhere and concealed the vehicles. Jessie, again, was talking on his wrist transceiver, looking skyward. Following his gaze, Quil noticed a blank span of sky with clouds disappearing behind it, which meant there was a cloaked airship above them. *Good, we have backup.*

The small aliens shocked them when they appeared in their natural form, brown-furred, mandrill-like beings with round faces, ears, and eyes, and, of course, wearing neat spandex uniforms. Resembling Tarsiers, minus the tail, their elongated hind limbs pointed to superior climbing and leaping ability. When they noticed the squad staring, they looked at Jessie.

"They said *let's boogie.*" Jessie smiled as Four laughed.

They followed a dry wash, and it wasn't long before they spotted one of the guard towers. The Tarsiers climbed the tower, giving hand signals to proceed. All guard towers were found empty. The ranch quarters lay straight ahead. Jessie pulled out a scanning apparatus, aimed it at the ranch house, and motioned them forward.

"Not yet." Quill's eyes were on the ground. She felt movement under her feet and placed a hand on a slab rock. The Tarsiers did the same. "Vibrations?" They Tarsiers nodded.

"Something's under us. Wait here." Scouting the area, she found tire tracks of large vehicles that gave the answer she needed. "The truck tracks go to the barn, not the ranch house."

Stalls were empty of floor straw, feed bins had never held oats, and there was no sign of tack anywhere. "This barn has never seen a horse."

Walking the aisle, Quil noticed one stall was overly wide and heavily reinforced. She felt vibrations again. "We need down below." The team scattered, looking for control boxes. Seven and Five went loft side.

"Here's an electrical box with switches," called Seven.

"There's no schematic of what switch does what," added Five. "We'll try one but take cover in case a swarm of snakes is on the other side." Five threw the switch, and flooring rolled away, revealing a staircase. Further along the aisle, a wall silently moved aside, exposing an industrial-sized elevator, which they decided against using to avoid noise on the ground level.

"Welcome to my trap said the fly to the spiders," muttered Quil. "I'll go in first."

"I can't let you do that," said Jessie. "Prex said you're a hard-headed little goat ramming anything in sight. I have a heat scanner. I'll see if any bodies are ahead before we move on."

"I have abilities too." Quil felt a sulk coming on.

"Prex mentioned your numinous abilities but made it clear you're to be monitored. And I'm not to let you get by with pouting tactics. Now, stand aside and let me do this." He held the scanner before him as he moved on, but Quil insisted on observing over his elbow. They saw no sign of movement.

"All gear on," ordered Quil. Instantly, night-vision goggles, ear comm units, and assault rifles were readied. "A dark passageway's ahead. Units to sidewall; no weapon lights."

"I got a *direful*." Two said. Others repeated those words.

"Yeah, me, too. Oxygen." Masks snapped in place. "Here we go."

"Here we go? An interesting *advance* command," said Jessie, "but it seems to work."

Quil moved to the far side of the tunnel as Seri and Jessie took the near. A Tarsier marched at her side, its enormous eyes combing the tunnel. No light came from front or rear, the dark swallowing everything. In places, the floor was littered with boxes fallen or thrown, papers strewn, glass flasks broken, liquids puddling.

"Don't step in this stuff," Jessie said, stepping wide over a patch of iridescent goo.

The channel widened and intersected with another. Their beams picked up rails of an underground tramway system, the source of the vibrations.

"We're about to be found out," said Quil as a low hum was heard, followed by the tracks vibrating. They crouched against walls, knowing they were hanging on low branches and ripe for picking.

Quickly mind traveling, Quil detected two souls bearing down on them, neither emitting danger signals. "All lights off," she whispered. Headlights were closing on them. Abruptly, Quil moved, standing spread-legged on the tracks. Switching on her rifle's white light, she pointed it directly at the approaching tram. Brakes screeched and steel wheels smoked as screams from two humans ricocheted off tunnel walls. Ghostly faces of two men in lab coats stared into the light.

"Hi there. Where ya headed?" Quil rested a foot on the tram's front bumper.

"Hands up!" Seri laid the muzzle of her rifle against the temple of one of the men.

"You're th, that bu, bunch of cr, crazy women," stammered one man.

"Ya, ya, yeah, that's us." Tres had a rifle at the second man's head. "Who's doing the talkin'?"

"Me, I will. On work duty. Lab's short-staffed. We need to get there," the driver mumbled.

"This car's pulling a wagon," said Six. "It might hold all of us."

"We wanna see that lab." Quil climbed behind the two lab jocks; Jessie and the Tarsiers joined her. Others in the team climbed into the back car.

"Touch only controls to move us. No talking except to answer questions." The men sat unmoving. "Drive now."

Like a great weaving snake, the tunnel twisted for miles. They passed sealed entryways, endless in number it seemed, finally stopping at a set of double doors.

"How many are inside?" Quil asked.

"Two, the ones we're relieving."

"Call them out." The team dispersed, taking positions behind the tram. Two lab-coated individuals came out, immediately raising their hands. They were quickly cuffed with mouths taped shut. Nerves at a high mark, they charged through the doors in a battle-ready crouch, expecting armed guards, evil scientists, lab tables, test tubes, and abominable fabricated beasts.

"Babies?" Quil whispered.

"Babies?" Seribeth echoed. Row after row of babies in pastel smocks nestled in cribs. "Beautiful little things, they look like flowers in a garden. What are they?"

"And what are they doing?" Six pointed to tubes running to each infant.

"Feeding," said Two. "Look around; older ones are in side rooms."

Children filled adjoining rooms, gaining in age as the squad progressed through the lab. The older ones seemed involved in study, exhibiting indifference at the appearance of humans, even those carrying weapons.

"It's a nursery," said Quil. "They're our replacements. Let's talk to those lab guys again." They returned to the lab entrance, finding Jessie at a computer screen.

"Limited information. The children are the result of gene manipulation, but I can't establish what species or blend they are. They're all female, which is odd." Brought inside, the lab men told what they knew.

"We're not scientists. All we know is these rooms hold the results of experiments."

"Would that be the deep-black experiments?"

"I've heard a lab called that, but scientists cleaned that one out and moved what they were working on. These kids here are sterile, not what the scientists wanted. Our job is to feed and watch over them 'til they can enter the outside world."

"Failed results? Where are the scientists? The tall ones with long fingers?"

"Like we said, we don't know. Those with the long fingers took what they had in their lab and disappeared. We just care for what's here and help out in the replicant factory?"

"Replicants?" Seri asked. "There's a factory?"

"Yeah, they make clones there. Those that look like humans but aren't," feeling it necessary to define the term. "Scientists in that lab are the green lizards, though."

"Reptoids? How many?"

"I never counted, but many."

"What about other entrances to the lab?" Jessie said.

"There's one in the ceiling for supply ships to unload, and they transports the more mature children somewhere else when the scientists are done with them here. The ceiling entrance is concealed from the outside. You can't see it."

"I'm notifying backup to come in topside while we counter from down here," said Jessie. "How do we engage the opening to the sky port?"

"We can show you where the control panel is, but we're not allowed to touch it."

"We're allowed," Quil said, "but why are you helping them?" It seemed a fair enough question to ask fellow humans.

"No choice. Our families were taken and held somewhere under threat of death if we don't do as told. Or maybe they were already killed. We thought of that, but we don't know. Maybe we've already turned our own kin into food for these cannibal babies."

"What did you say?" asked Tres. The room went morgue quiet.

"You'll see for yourself in the next lab," replied one of the men, turning his face away.

"Take us to that factory," said Quil. Back in rail cars, they hurried forward.

"Don't forget the sky entrance. We must get it opened," said Jessie.

"The control panel is in this passageway. The greens thought that was better than inside the main facility. We'll stop there first." And they did. The squad's computer geek, Suzi Two, joined Jessie in studying the panel layout, finally punching in what they hoped was the correct code. Jessie focused on his transceiver until he received the wanted response. On his signal, they prepared for a stormtrooper entrance, knowing they'd be outnumbered.

Outnumbered they were, but the first bunch they encountered were humans in oxygen masks who seemed almost thankful to see them. The white-coated reptoids scattered, running for side doors. The Cyon ship, hovering above, took most of those down. The squad held rifles on a couple of dozen backed against a wall, openly snarling and screaming insults.

Almost knocked over by the stench, some squad members groaned, backing away from tables littered with body parts. It was impossible to grasp the revulsion around them. Hundreds of glass vats contained animal specimens of every sort, including the human kind. On a wide altar-like shelf stood lines of vacant-eyed humanoid fabricants. Along outside walls were vats of roiling gray substance.

"We're in a death factory," Quil said.

"Gotta puke!" Seven rushed to a near wall.

"Slump," said Five. "They're turning us into a slump, like dog food."

"But liquified for tube feeding." A human in a lab coat responded, speaking like a tour guide there to overview the factory's workings.

Unexpectedly, Tres broke from the group, racing down aisles frantically searching, only to return with eyes gushing tears. Seri was beside her, an arm around her shoulders. "There's nothing to take back. Nothing's left of my brothers to bury. I hoped …."

Quil watched Jessie keying a message into his transceiver. Why couldn't people have been equipped with such a means for pain control? If the sense of loss became overwhelming, pushing the pause key could halt heartache. It's odd that the Earth was granted an electromagnetic shield that hurls itself between the planet and deadly rays from the sun, but the human heart was granted no such shield. And grief was a mean SOB. When it invades your sanity, it bashes without mercy, slamming you down time and time again. Quil pulled Tres aside and whispered in her ear; Tres wiped her eyes and nodded.

"This ends now, Jessie," Quil said, slipping a fresh clip into her rifle.

"We have methods of putting things back in order," said Jessie, his eyes on Tres. "I called it in just now. All human remains will be removed and given proper rites. Listen, all of you. Don't react in anger—as you have a right to do. You would be justified in destroying everything here, but we need to salvage this lab. In coming days, we'll need places to provide medical and hospital care for our wounded."

"I'll leave that to you," said Quil. "But what about these so-called scientists? Do you think they have anything useful to say?"

"Possibly, but I doubt they'll lower themselves to talk to humans. I meant no offense in saying that. Let me try as myself." In a wink, the Cyon Jessie appeared.

"I'll listen as you talk." Quil stood apart, her mind weaving among the reptoids to pull in subconscious thoughts. Jessie attempted to glean information about the Mantian scientists and the location of the lab that had been moved. The scientists denied knowing anything. Their thoughts confirmed they spoke the truth. And then Quil heard a term she understood quite well. *Mind wielder*. They had detected her.

"They know nothing. Tell me truthfully, Jessie. Can you argue a case for keeping these reptoids alive, scientists or not?" Jessie shook his head.

"Can you argue a case for keeping humans alive who abetted in unconscionable crimes?" asked Jessie. Quil shook her head.

Looking for Tres, Quil saw her slumped against a wall. She snapped to attention when she saw Quil giving her a nod.

Tres ran the line of reptoids, cursing as she fired. The snakes tried to scuttled, but there was no escape. Taking the cue, the Tarsiers ran the line of humans with weapons spitting fire. Unlike the reptoids, the humans didn't run; maybe they welcomed their end. They were already in hell; it could get no worse than this.

"Those who do not fight to live are unworthy of life," said one Tarsier in a deep rumbling voice that contradicted its physical makeup.

"Listen to that," said Jessie. "I wonder why they chose now to speak. Regardless, I need to get back to the facility. We can leave in our ship."

"We need to scope out what's down here and make another stop at that nursery."

"The children can be taken off-world and given an opportunity."

"An opportunity to do what? They're ghouls. They have to feed, and it doesn't matter what's on the menu. Anywhere they'd be put, the natives would end up blue plate specials at the local diner."

"Then, I'll stay with the Cyon ship to arrange cleanup of this lab."

"We're taking the rail cars," said Quil. "Divide up and choose one." Speaking silently to Jessie, the Tarsiers quickly claimed a tram car.

Their first stop was the door closest to the fabricant lab. A storage room lined with shelves of canned and prepackaged foodstuff suitable for surviving underground for an extended period. They continued, opening doors and walking into soundless spaces. All cavernous, some of the spaces were divided into personal quarters with dust-laden furnishings and archaic plumbing. Others were assembly halls bearing rows of long tables with chairs shoved underneath. People had inhabited this underground facility ages ago. Quil removed her mask and drew in a breath.

"The air's stale but breathable. These shelters protected people from danger above. Remnants of systems to bring in air and water must still exist."

"It'll take a lot of people exploring what's down here," said Seri, "but it's our next step. We need skilled people to update ventilation and water systems. Where do we start?"

"Through communications," said Quil. "We let people know what's coming, and they'll join us. Let's finish up down here."

The last stop came. They stood before the nursery's doors.

"Preacher woman, you probably shouldn't be involved in this. If any of you want out, just say so. I can deal with this alone." Abruptly, shrill noises dropped squad members to their knees. The Tarsiers were whistling like woodchucks and tapping their chests. "They've volunteered to take this assignment if we want out. It's up to you, but I'm going in." *Time to cull the tar*es, she thought, and quickly stepped through the door.

There may have been some who would have preferred to opt out, but none did. They made short work of it, moving as they usually did, just getting it done. They hadn't the time to do otherwise. Sparing no age group, they started with the oldest to prevent a possibility of signals being sent and ended with the babies in cribs. It would cause night screams, but the sword had to fall. The people eaters had to lose.

Locating the tunnel they'd first entered, they left the rail cars lined front-to-end on the tracks. Jessie and Four had cut the lock at the gate entrance at were waiting for them.

"Cleanup needed in the infants and children's aisle," said Tres as she passed Jessie and headed for the Jeep. There, she pulled a bottle from the car pocket and drank far too much in too little time.

"I'm driving your Jeep back," said Quil, taking the bottle. "We stay together now, at least 'til we line up crews to do what's needed in the tunnels. We'll operate out of the church." Holding her cell high, Seri motioned for Quil to take the call. It was Inger.

"What time? Okay, Seri and I'll leave from Ignacio. We'll be in my car." She turned to the squad.

"Seri and I have scouting to do, but it shouldn't take long. Lay out plans to get people involved. The word needs to get out. Locate people at TV or radio stations, the web, some way of broadcasting a steady stream of updates. If the media people won't cooperate, move them aside and find an ally who will." Team members grabbed cell phones, iPads, and notebooks. They were moving to the next crucial step in saving those they could.

As they drove back to the church, Quil replayed their actions below ground. It's possible there was another way to deal with the children, but, above all else, they had to think of humanity's survival. Would they come to regret their decision. Perhaps, but it was done now.

And another matter bother her. Why did Prex openly criticize her, calling her a destructive goat and a childish pouter? Possibly because she was? There were reasons she behaved as she did with him. Or was she making excuses? Again, maybe. Still, she was insulted by his doing that. Or was she hurt? *It's best to learn what others think of you early on, I guess.* She hadn't the time to deal with self-worth issues. The might be a point when she could sit with it to work it through, but she had bigger problems to deal with now.

twenty-seven

Quil hunted for a parking spot at the Farmington Museum while Seri looked for Gretchen and Inger, who had notified them of the serpent posers' attendance at an art ceremony.

"I see Gretchen car. They're already inside."

They wanted a good view of attendees and took seats at the back of the room. The poets sat with a knot of people closer to the podium. Inger was standing, looking around the room, and turned back toward the front after she spotted Quil and Seri.

"Ouch." Seri kicked her leg and nodded toward the front door. Ramona Rand squeezed the shoulder or stroked an arm of everyone she came near, making the usual posturing entrance. Her mimicry of a human was a distortion in motion. It was surprising people were fooled by it.

"What do we have here?" Quil whispered as Ramona Rand stepped aside, revealing a repulsive figure with rust-hued hair. "Look what slithered out of a snake hole, the Red Queen herself."

"The killer serpent," said Seri. The snakes moved toward the front, sitting in the same group as the poets. "I hope Inger and Gretchen hold it together."

"Are you carrying, or do you need to go to the car?"

"I'm good. Let's sit back and watch."

At the end of the program, the speaker encouraged attendees to view displayed art. Quil and Seri walked through the exhibit, trying to stay within sight of the poets.

"They're separating. I'll take Inger," said Seri.

Quil didn't see Gretchen. Turning down an aisle, looking for her, she noticed Ramona Rand nearby. Suddenly, a mop of red hair popped up—the serpent queen, ugly and in her face.

"Move." The snake hissed. It wasn't a request. "I'm walking this aisle."

Quil looked into a glowering face with narrow, constricted eyes. Contacts couldn't hide those viper slits. *I'm not budging, bitch.* If she could have, the serpent would have spewed toxin from her eyes. Snarling, she recognized that Quil would never give way to her, never. Suddenly, Ramona was beside Quil, stroking her arm in her disgusting fashion.

"I'm not edible, Duchess. Stop testing for tenderness."

"There are people you must meet." Mumbled Ramona, grabbing the queen's arm, pulling her away, but instead of leading her to others, they sped out the building.

Seri had watched the exchange from across the room and rushed over. "Tell me what just happened there."

"What's to tell? The Red Queen and I cannot both live. And we both know that. This is between us now."

"Do you think we can catch up to them? They were moving fast, getting out of here."

"Doubtful. We don't know their vehicle. But they weren't running out of fear of us; they didn't want their identity made known. They have more nastiness lined up and don't want interference with whatever that is. We missed our chance tonight. We can't botch the next time."

Following the poets back to Durango, they parked at the rear of the bookstore and went inside to share information.

"Inger struck up a conversation with the red-headed one," Gretchen was saying. "Tell them what you found out."

"They're going to the theatre in Creed this weekend. I told her I enjoyed the performances there and asked what route they were taking as I knew a shortcut."

"What was her reaction?" asked Seri.

"Who knows? They're a slithery pair and hard to read. Anyway, I told her about the road through the Jicarilla reservation that exits just before Wolf Creek Pass. I said nothing else."

"Could I borrow a map, Gretchen?" asked Quil.

"Certainly. I'll get one."

"Inger, I think you're right about them being slithery," said Quil. "I have doubts about them going to Creed. Let's see what options they'd have in turning off elsewhere."

They spent a good hour highlighting sideroads and trails on the way to Creed before reversing their thinking, noting the same information in the opposite direction.

"It'll be hard to figure out their true intentions. Their car? Did either of you see what they were driving?"

"I stood watch at the front door after the program ended and saw them leave," said Gretchen. "They were in an XLT with an odd color, like mustard orange."

"You're getting good at this spy game. We're short on time, Seri. Let's pull the Spiders together early to see what we can figure out."

Hours marched by them that evening as she and Seri brainstormed what to do with their unforeseen windfall. They decided laying out an imperfect strategy was better than none at all. Yes, they needed to track the serpents. No, they couldn't do it as a group in the Hummer. Yes, they needed to relay, handing off from one team member to another to keep the serpents in sight.

How to set up the relay was the thorny problem. Farmington had to be the start point as Inger had learned the snakes resided there. Appointing a watchdog to fire the starter pistol was next. That left the tail cars and where to place them. Okay, so they arrive at the destination. The end. What happens at the end? Problems, gaps, and unknowns existed, but they'd work it out.

Sleeping on Seribeth's couch, Quil rose to an elbow when wind rattled the windows. A hushed whisper came.

"Action without insight is wasteful and ultimately ineffective, but insight without action is equally futile. The mission is not without hazards making the success route slender. Think and think again. Plan and plan again."

Promptly at five, they placed the bones of a strategy on the table and asked for squad input. In hindsight, that might have been a mistake as it took precious time, but eventually, they calibrated their thinking into something that seemed workable.

The critical first step lay in the hands of a designated watchdog, and Two was given that post. Assigned to Farmington, she had to stalk the snakes, alerting the others to what direction, east or west, they were driving. It fell to the rest to get into position and stay ready to tag in.

Concerned she could be recognized in her car, Quil swapped vehicles with Tres. She drove Tres's Jeep a few miles to get the hang of it while Tres changed out the license plates on Quil's SUV and added self-adhering tourist stickers to help with the disguise. As a last step, Tres drove it through a creek and a plowed field.

"That should do it," said Tres. "Do you think they'll leave Friday night or Saturday morning?"

"If they're truly attending the theatre, probably Friday evening."

"I feel like my brain has been scrubbed with Drano," said Seri, "but with what we have, we should be able to keep them in view. But we can't miss a tag." She distributed copies of a map.

That Friday, Quil watched the sunset as she waited for Suzy Two to report in. She knew it was an iffy situation but tried to stay optimistic. She jumped when the phone hummed.

"We hunt, dogs," said Two. "Get those tails in high gear. The prey departed Farmington but not by the eastern route. They headed out on the west side and turned north. That means they can go west toward Cortez, north to Silverton, or turn back east to Creed. Watch for an orange XLT."

Damn! If it's Cortez, they could go directions they hadn't charted. Their odds of success were diminishing fast. Quil parked on Durango's west end, figuring she could see the XLT regardless of the direction it headed.

"Westward ho the wagons," said Two.

Cortez! Falling in behind westbound traffic, Quil spotted other team members doing the same. The plan wasn't complex. As they traveled, one would fall off and another move forward. Those falling off would rejoin at the tail of the line. She hoped traffic remained moderately heavy as cover was needed for the plan to work.

"They're not making for Cortez!" said Five. "They took the Delores turnoff. I'm going on straight as I'd have to burn rubber to make the turn. I'll rejoin in about ten. Next in line better pick up speed."

"I got it," said Seri. "Remember, in Delores they can go left to Dove Creek or points north. Stay alert."

Tres picked them up in Delores when the snakes stopped at a gas station. "Looks like this could be a long night, comrades. They're headed toward Telluride and tall country."

Nothing to do but drive. They were being led into territory with fourteen to seventeen thousand-foot peaks and plenty of places to hide a command post. On Highway 145, things seemed to be proceeding smoothly, but suddenly Seven jumped on the line. "Heads up! They took a side road off to the right. I think it heads to Ophir. I didn't see a highway marking. Somebody tag. I'll give this away if I turn."

"Six here, I've got it but stayin' back. I don't wanna jump on their bumper too quick."

"I'm behind you, Six," said Quil, seeing Six's lights about a half-mile ahead. Lights of the XLT weren't visible.

"What the—oh, no!" yelled Six. "They turned right onto 550, heading back to Durango. Have we been played?"

"I'll take it now, Six. Turn toward Silverton but rejoin. We're not quitting now." On 550, oncoming headlights pick up an orange vehicle ahead. Quil increased speed to keep it in view.

Then the plans hit a wall. The turnoff happened almost immediately. Making a sharp left at a sheer drop-off, the XLT took an unmarked dirt track into the Wiminuche Wilderness. Quil pulled onto the roadside to give it time to move ahead and called Six. No signal. She was in a dead spot. She turned off the headlights, not wanting her presence detected and moved to the drop-off. Did she wait? Did she go?

Who can know when fate will take a turn dealing the cards? And who can know the card to play if that hand was dealt? A decision was called for. On the edge of the drop-off, Quil stared into a night as black as a pool of tar. *Do it! Just do it!* Taking a deep breath, she nudged the gas pedal and rolled into the viper pit.

She was in heavy timber and switched on thee dims. The occasional sighting of headlights sweeping trees ahead helped keep direction. She turned off the phone. If she regained a signal, calls could give away her location. Edginess twitched in her belly like jumping beans. She switched off the dims. Dark drop on her with a thud. Moonlight sifting through the trees had to be enough now. But long shadows dogged her like menacing specters seeking the unaware. She moved a hand toward the light switch. *No, play the cards sharp.*

What's this? The headlights of the XLT muted out, leaving only a pale aura. Maybe it dropped into a canyon? But the faint glow completely disappeared. *The end of the road?* Taking the Jeep further was out of the question. She backed into heavy thicket, hurriedly cut saplings, and covered the glass. Smeared her face with sooty grease to prevent moon reflection, she grabbed the pack and rifle and set out. On a guess, she moved toward the place she'd last seen lights, noting markers for a return. After almost an hour, a faint glow outlined a ridgeline. *This could be it.*

Quil inched into thick cover and listened. The wind in the pines moaned—or was it the wind? She held her breath. *The faraway howl of a dog. A dog howling in the deep of night—death comes near!* She tried to push away the old superstition, but hill notions were a part of her. She breathed fitfully, eyes darting from shadow to shadow. *Death surrounds me here. I can reach out and touch it.* Her first impulse was to run but didn't.

Hands shaking, she forced an eye to the scope, spotting the orange vehicle in a wide ravine. It appeared to be empty, parked nose-in toward the face of a canyon wall. A peculiar glow came from the canyon face, but she couldn't detect the light's source. *Nothing, I see nothing.*

Damn! I've been tagged! Flattened to the ground, she was caught in the downthrust of a ship, hovering directly overhead. She laid on the rifle and clung to brush, trying not to be swept from her blind. A delta ship moved slowly ahead, making a ninety-degree turn before lowering to the canyon floor.

Through the rifle scope, two men in camouflaged military suits debarked. They stood waiting, but for what? A faint whirring sounded. Was that movement on the face of the cliff? No—the entire cliff moved—sideways!

There it was—the cave entrance to the enemy base. The Red Queen, accompanied by Duchess Ramona, walked out of the cave. The men in field suits slowly walked toward the serpents. One took off his hat, brushing a hand through his hair. *What was that?* Something on the hat flashed. He replacing the cap, and again, she saw a glint. The other man wore a kerchief on his head biker style. He nervously fiddled with the scarf.

Moles! They're the moles! The two stepped forward, receiving packets from the queen. A payoff. They came for blood money. Getting what they came for, the humans boarded the craft and departed the same way they came in, directly over her. The snake returned to their vehicle, heading back the way they'd come. *Time to go.*

But that didn't happen.

The aspens rustled a warning, and, again, she was in a downthrust. Not just another ship, a steady stream of black ships swarmed into the valley, humming like digger wasps. And something else popped up. A light on the top of the cliff came on, and a bell-shaped craft rose, flew overhead, and was gone. Like its shadow, a black ship followed. Off to do harm to docile sheep and anything else that got in the way.

Another racket. A conveyer wrenched arriving ships into the cave. *That's a lot of aircraft.* They're readying for a major offensive. The men's squad had to be a target and not the only one. She had to get out of there but didn't dare move. Stuck in the middle of a flightpath, she would be easily spotted if she tried. She chewed on her bottom lip, trying to scope out a means of escape. Hand spun on the time meter as she remained pinned. Deciding to focus on aircraft activity, she tallied the incoming. *There's a pattern here.* Then, it all stopped. The fake wall slid in place, concealing the cave, followed by the light at the top going out. *Now.*

Moving fast, she worked backward, scuttling down slopes. With no moon now, finding markers was impossible. It was taking too long. She should be at the Jeep by now. Breaking into a trot, she jumped over brush—into air! Falling, she grabbed at anything to break the downward motion. It was broken all right by her face skittering across gravel. *My rifle?* She backtracked up the gulch, finding it under brush. Crouched, she checked to see if it was still firing ready. It was. Her face was wet, and she tasted iron—a cut near an eye and a busted lip. A piece of undershirt stuffed inside the lip staunched the flow. She blinked her eyes to see if the fall altered her vision. No, eyes seemed okay.

Wait, wait! What is that! A spider's web? No, it can't be. No spider spins a thread that large. Plus, it's red? She inched closer, shifting her eyes back and forth across the gulch. *It's my eyes picking it up.* She walked alongside the strange web construction but suddenly stopped, training her rifle on … a dead man. A corpse in hunter gear. She kept moving, keeping eyes below the red netting. Bones and animal remains stretched ahead. An invisible death barrier killing anything coming in contact with it. *It's a security shield protecting the alien base.* Backing up several yards, she tried to see how high it extended but couldn't detect where it topped out.

If not for the plunge, she could've walked straight into it. Were more of these traps ahead? *Get out of here.* Following the gully, she stumbled onto the hunter's track she drove in on and found the Jeep undisturbed. Finally, she sighted the highway ahead and gratefully crawled out of the snake hole.

She headed to Silverton on Highway 550. A light appeared in the rearview mirror. Morning? She was gone all night. Seri would be pissed, questioning her going silent. The rest of the team would be angry—but Seri? The preacher woman had a temper. She stopped on the outskirts of Silverton to refuel and called her.

"I'm going to whip your butt, Quilty, and you know I can do it. I've been out of my mind with worry. Where are you, and why haven't you called me? We waited up all night for you to show."

"Seri, just listen. Locate the Shadow Squad. We must get to them right away. Contact Josiah. Tell him this is for his ears only. Tell him it's urgent they head back this way so we can meet up. Find out where and call me the location. Get lat and lon if you can. I'll use the GPS to get there. I'll be leaving from Silverton. We need to hurry. Please, Seri."

"Okay, okay. I'll get on this and call you back. But stay in touch with me. I mean it!" The phone slammed off.

"Whip my butt?" That's the last thing she needed to hear. She rummaged through the Jeep, found a first-aid kit, and quickly stuck Band-Aid to cuts. Seribeth could whip her butt. She had met Seri in a gym where she was a boxing instructor. The first time in the ring, she took one to the jaw and came to with Seri holding her. She'd been laid on the mat several times by Preacher Woman. That left of hers was deadly.

"I hate this waiting." Seri paced the floor. Gracie had stayed near Seribeth during the long night waiting for Quil. Having heard from Quil, they now waited for Josiah to call back.

Adam had installed a punching bag in the garage for staying in shape. Wolf had taught Seri to box when they were kids, and she'd become good enough to make the school's boxing team. Now, she punched the bag when she needed to work through issues. At it for hours, even wearing gloves, Seri's knuckles were raw and skinned to bleeding.

"There's the phone," said Gracie, but Seri already had it hand.

"Josiah. Okay. Give me the coordinates. When are you moving out? Okay, I'll let Quil know. She's leaving from Silverton. I don't know who'll get there first. Just be looking for us." She turned, seeing the squad in full gear waiting for the word. "Let's roll."

twenty-eight

Wending her way across western Colorado, Quil headed for Utah, figuring the meet-up location would be near its midsection. She pulled off the road when Seri's call came through. The Shadow Squad was making for a deserted farm in central Utah. Studying the map, she headed for Monticello and from there would let the GPS direct her in. With the Shadows traveling southeast and the Spiders northwest, they'd meet up in little to no time. According to the nav finder, she was close. Driving through the gate of the old homestead, she saw the squad ahead and parked the Jeep alongside the Hummer.

Seri met Quil as she got out of the car, scowling on seeing her face. "I'm okay," she said, pushing Seri's hand away and briefed her on why they were there.

"Take someone with you," said Seri. "The rest of us will do what's necessary."

Surprised registered on Wolf and Josiah's faces when they saw her, but Quil gave them an imperceptible shake of the head. Stopping, they looked confused, but after a glance at each other, released holster snaps.

Walking past the Hummer, she tossed Tres the keys to the Jeep. Quil smiled at team members, seeing Four with them, shoulder bandage partly hid under her field jacket. "We'll catch up later. There's a matter we have to take care of now." Giving slight nods, they knew something heavy was going down, and none questioned it.

"Walk with me, Tres."

Unhesitant, Tres fell in beside Quil, releasing her holster strap at the first step. They slowly walked toward the crowd of men. Between fifty to sixty in count, all in field dress, standing in a huddle. Several wore field hats. One had his off, running a hand through his hair. As he flipped the cap back on, Quil saw a glint. *Gotcha! Now, where's your buddy?*

"Hey! You any good with that gun, girlie?" The man with the giveaway hat couldn't resist challenging a woman.

"Define good." Quil kept walking.

None of them wore a kerchief. The men spread away from the center as she and Tres walked through. Occasionally, Quil felt Tres's shoulder brush hers, as close as her soul. She caught subtle movement from the corner of an eye. The Spiders silently dispersed, readying for whatever was to come. Having walked the full circle, she was again in front of the man with the glinty hat. She didn't have to say a word. He knew she was there for him.

"Don't do it, Bucky. I'll drop ya where you stand."

He did it; it cost him. Two to the chest and one to the head told him the girlie was pretty good with a gun.

"Turn with me, Tres. There's another one." Back to back, they checked the remaining men. One stepped away from the huddle. As he turned, Quil saw a kerchief in his back pocket. Firing, she took out a knee, dropping him to the ground. "Don't let him get to his back pocket—don't kill him!"

He went for the pocket. A mistake. Tres pinned his hand to the dirt with a Ka-Bar. Seri's throwing blade hummed through the air pinning the other.

"What's going on!" Yelling wasn't the only thing breaking out from the men. Some had weapons in hand; others were reaching.

"Wouldn't do that," yelled Seri. "You're ducks on a pond."

"Stand down! Hands away from weapons. If they're out, put 'em down!" Wolf and Josiah ran toward Quil and Tres. Some men raised hands above heads; others slowly lowered weapons to the ground.

"Quil?" Wolf's confusion was clear.

"They're the moles."

The anchored man, struggling to free his hands, begged for help—such a waste of effort. Quil pushed him over and yanked the kerchief from his back pocket. Walking to the dead man, she picked up his hat, examining the underside of the brim. Wolf was beside her, and his expression said he wanted an explanation.

"They wore these things; signaling mechanisms is my guess. When activated, they sent your location to the enemy base."

Taking both, he and Josiah examined them, so small, they were barely detectable. Seri, Ned, and Cedric joined them to see what held their interest.

"Can you feel that?" Josiah asked, handing them to Wolf. "They vibrate when you hold one to your skin."

"That might be the reason this one kept pulling his hat on and off."

"We'd better get rid of these," said Josiah. "It's possible they could be triggered from their command base. Speaking of that, let's see if the other one will give up that information."

"No need," said Quil. "I got that information. But maybe we can pull information from him on who else is involved. Or at least those he knows. They traveled in a delta ship to collect blood money. They were taxied in and out, is my guess." The man cringing on the ground loudly denied knowledge of others or a payoff.

"Like we're going to believe that," said Tres. "Let me see what I can do to loosen his memory."

"This lady is the sister of the Torres brothers we saw murdered on the mountain. I'm turning her loose on this one after we question him." Tres knelt before the condemned. She wanted him to look deep into the eyes of his executioner. Seri handed her a rope to secure the man's hands as she looped a second rope around his feet, leaving two ends free. Both sheathed their blades.

"Got any preferences on where we do this?" Tres looked around the area.

"A gully back of the barn should do," said Wolf, "but I want one of our men in on the questioning."

"I volunteer." Cedric reached in a pocket, pulling out a pack of cigarettes. "This could be interesting."

"Cedric will do. His background in police interrogation could help," said Seri.

Pulling ropes over their shoulders, Quil and Tres dragged the traitor to his final stop. He wasn't going quietly, but he was going.

Cedric knelt near the traitor's head and blew smoke in his face. 'This'll go easier for you if you cooperate. I was in the interrogation business, and I'll know if you lie. We want names of everyone involved, military or civilian. I can stop the pain these women have planned. It's up to you, but we need a response now." The man was coughing from the smoke. Placing a knee on the man's shoulder, Cedric held open an eyelid and lowered the lit cigarette. The man screamed.

Like a starter bell ringing in her ear, Tres yanked a boot off the man and began slitting the skin around his ankle. "Have you ever seen a person flayed, Quil?"

"You know, I missed that class. Is that your intent?"

"One of 'em. I could use help pulling his hide off. You willing?"

"Sure, I'm game."

"No! I can come up with names. Don't let 'em flay me. Please, stop 'em. Please, mister."

Removing a small notebook from his jacket, Cedric handed Quil a few pages. She motioned for Tres to hold off.

The traitor talked; Cedric and Quil wrote; Tres waited. When he stopped talking, Quil looked at Tres, still at his feet. "That doesn't seem to be enough. What do you think, Tres?"

"Not enough."

"No, no! Wait! I have more." He added a number of high-ranking officers to the list.

"That's all? Sure you can't think of any others?" Cedric flipped cigarette ash in his face.

"It's all I know. I'm telling the truth. Just get those bitches away from me." Cedric shrugged and backed away.

"He's yours, Tres," said Quil, leaving with Cedric.

As they walked away, they heard Tres talking. "My brother Ramon was twenty-three. He was in college to become a doctor. My brother Roberto ….” The man’s screams drowned out her voice.

Wolf and Josiah were waiting at the top of the gully. Seri and Ned joined them.

“Let’s get you cared for,” said Josiah, “then tell us the location of the base.”

“It’s okay; I don’t hurt.” She provided the base location but withheld information on the strange red web, not knowing how to explain the eyes. An optical augmentation she figured but wasn’t sure.

“We’re still without heave artillery or air support,” said Ned, “and we’ve seen what they can do. We can’t match their power.”

“Yeah, and that’s rough country,” said Josiah. “I’ve hunted elk in the Wiminuche. We can’t get in there without being spotted.”

“There might be options. We need time,” said Quil, thinking of how best to contact the Cyon force.

“Time is what we don’t have.” said Wolf. “Let me see that list, Cedric.”

“I better check on Tres.” Quil jogged toward the gully, meeting her coming up from the ditch. She held something in her hand. “Is it over?”

“Yeah, but tell me. Do you know how to cure a scalp? This is a first for me.”

“Uh, no, I don’t. Uh, but Google it. You can learn anything on Google.” Quil looked away from the bloody hank of hair, feeling churning in the pit of her stomach.

Wolf met them walking back to the barn. “Should we bury him?” asked Tres.

“Leave him as buzzard bait. I’m having the other one moved here, too. And we’re leaving the tracers to give their boss a little help in finding his boys.”

The men gathered at the barn, awaiting orders. “Load up. We’re setting up at Wolf’s ranch.” Relief shone on the men’s faces. No question about it, they were more than ready to head back. Josiah noticed a few of the men talking with members of the Spider Squad. "Hey, if any of you Spiders want to join the Shadow Squad, you'd be most welcome."

"No thank you, sir," replied Five. "We prefer our own squad." She turned to the group of men. "But if you work hard and improve your skills, we just might invite you to join us. You never know. It could happen."

Hearing laughter from both camps, a pleased Josiah walked over to Quil and Sari.

"It's a good day to walk proud. The Spiders are a top-notch squad."

"Come on, Quil, I'll clean you up. Your face is a pitiful mess." Walking away, they were grinning ear to ear.

twenty-nine

Quil rode in the back with Tres driving. Sophie Five was in the navigator seat. In convoy, they followed the Hummer trailing behind the Shadow Squad vehicles. Earth's resistance force was together at last. Stretched out in the back seat, she listened to Sophie and Tres./

"You're handy with that knife. Do you use one in your regular line of work?"

"No, but there were days when I felt like it," laughed Tres. "I'm just trying to be funny. I hold a Doctor of Psychology. Yeah, a shrink, believe it or not."

"Holy cow, I didn't see that coming," laughed Five. "But I bet you're a good one."

" I tried to be." Tres cleared her throat. "Please take this the right way, Sophie. Speaking up to the men back there was a good thing to do. You're overly shy, and I recommend you speak out more often."

"Now, you're talking like a shrink. Cut it out." Sophie, though, was smiling. "What're your plans for the scalp?"

"I'm not sure. I now have two, you know."

"Where did the second one come from?"

"From the dude Quil shot. I'm tanning it for her as a Christmas gift."

"Oh, hell no!" Quil yelled.

"I didn't think you were asleep." Tres and Sophie laughed. Quil joined them.

Exhausted, she closed her eyes, listening to the steady thrum of tires on the pavement. But her mind didn't sleep. It chugged along, keeping time with the rhythm of the road. *Thrum, thrum, thrum.*

I opened my eyes, staring at sinister, wind-twisted shapes resembling ghouls and monsters. The Bisti Badlands? "How did I get here? Where are the others?" A flurry of sand screeched around misshapen rocks, sounding like moans of lost souls. Shivering as I turned a circle, I saw my car half-hidden in the shadows of a sandstone column.

Scornful laughter sounded, echoing across the ravine. A figure stood on top of a high mesa; a man in a bright yellow shirt buttoned at the neck and wrists wearing a brimmed black hat low on his face. I couldn't make out his facial details. Abruptly, he dove off the cliff, coming straight for me, growing larger and larger. I sprinted toward the car.

Out of nowhere, yellow shirt was running beside me, his face a blank except for a jagged-toothed mouth, howling in laughter. Abruptly, he shapeshifted into a two-headed coyote, snarling and biting at my legs. Tripping, I fell to the ground with him looming over me, teeth bared, breath rancid. "Run, run, little spider. I like the chase."

A wailing wind churning up sand obscured him from view. Shielding my eyes, I jumped to my feet, screaming, "I don't run. I don't run."

Thrum, thrum, thrum sang the tires. Her mouth dry, Quil gasped for air as a sudden gust of wind shifted the car sideways out of its traffic lane.

"Wake now. Sand sifts through the hourglass. Time is escaping. Seek the larger circle. The sand runs, runs, runs."

"I know the sand runs! Why do you keep telling me that?" She sat up, staring at the two in the front. "Five, did you wake me?"

"No, not me. You woke yourself up, Quil?"

Out the windows, Quil scanned the sky, sensing the coyote still above her. Tres and Sophie looked out side windows.

"I don't see anything. Do you, Five?" asked Tres.

"I got nothing this side."

Sinking down on the backseat, Quil laid an arm across her face. The hellion had her in a cold sweat. A treacherous two-faced coyote. A trickster was playing games with her. And Gnat sent a message? *Seek the larger circle.*

"Change of plan," she said loudly. "What's our location, Tres?" Getting it, she called Seri and Josiah. They pulled off the road, seeing those ahead leaving vehicles with weapons drawn.

"What's up?" Wolf's eyes were on the sky. Members of the Shadow Squad turned in circles, scanning the terrain with assault rifles at shoulders.

"Lower your weapons. It's time you meet our allies. We can't make it through this without them. They're not human, but they'll fight alongside us. And they have a fleet coming with advanced weapons and a fighting force. Will you come with me?"

"A fighting force and advanced weapons? We're in," said Josiah. "Do you want all of us? The Shadow Squad too?"

"All of us go. Tres, I'll drive now. We'll take the lead. The rest of you keep up."

They pulled into a small clearing near the Cyon facility; clumps of junipers allowed concealment of vehicles. Everyone milled, waiting for Quil to speak.

"I'll be brief and leave it to squad leaders to address questions you may have." She pointed to the Cyon hangar. "I'll go in first 'cause they know me. The people inside are from other planets. Some resemble us; some don't. I want that to sink in quick as you'll be facing them in just minutes. Many have lost their worlds to the enemy we're now facing. But they've come to fight alongside us to try to save this one. Here's the point. We must treat them with respect. They deserve respect as they've come a long way to help save humanity. One last thing. Our allies need to know we're worth fighting for. When you walk into that room, show strength and courage. Don't falter in your step. This is the day we walk proud." She nodded at Josiah as she spoke those words.

"Seri, I'll contact you when ready. Enter quietly, full field gear, rifles out, barrels down. Look ready for action. Remember. Strength and courage."

Quil glanced at her watch; the meeting was underway. Not knocking this time, she slung the door wide and moved to the front of the room.

Yeah, that got attention. Dirty and blood-smeared, She looked like she'd tried to break up a dog fight with a cat tied to her head, but no matter. She wanted them to see a fighter, one who wasn't afraid to bleed. As she neared the front, she glimpsed the aeronautical chart on the wall. Pulling a knife from a boot, she sent it true, seeing it slice through the location of the enemy command post.

"It's time you met our soldiers. They've come to plan for battle. The enemy is revving up for something big. I've seen them, and we need to get ready."

Gene seemed unable to speak. Jessie touched his arm, and he regained composure. "Should we transform our appearance?"

"No, and don't worry. They won't fall on their butts."

"Bring them in." He motioned the Citizen force to one side of the room as they made space for humans of Earth.

Sending the signal, Quil watched the Spiders approach, followed closely by the Shadows, all in field gear and fully weaponed. The Spiders moved light, deadly stealth assassins. The Shadows moved from strength, weapons in offensive position ready to engage. She mentioned them to the side of the room across from the waiting allies.

Damn, but they looked good; an impressive entry by determined warriors. The Shadows stood behind the Spiders with all eyes focused across the room. Not a flinch in the bunch, steady and strong. Walking to the center of the room, she asked the squad leaders to stand with her.

"I'm proud to present Earth's Resistance Force."

Gene and Jessie walked forward, motioning others to join them. As introductions were made, not all allies could converse in English. Quil stepped into another role, that of emissary.

"Welcome, Earth Resistance Force," said Gene. "We're the Joint Citizens Counter Unit, and as you can see, we have many species represented. We've joined forces to fight an enemy intent on your destruction. That enemy is massive in number and closing on us. Offensive action must occur before they arrive. Quil, you marked the enemy command post. We need details."

"I'll provide that information, but starting now, we're to be included in plans to fight this enemy."

'Agreed." He turned to Jessie. "See that a closed sign is placed on the hangar at the airport. We'll be working here for many hours.

Shushing danced about the room as the sky port opened and Prex lowered to the floor. The Earth forces weren't prepared for the demon crow to make such an entrance, and for that matter, they weren't prepared for the demon crow at all. In full armor, Prex was menacing, and he knew it. A band of armored warriors descended with him.

Instantly, the squads took a battle stance. "No, don't!" Quil ran forward, standing in front of Prex. "I need to introduce another ally."

"I'm capable of introducing myself." Prex slowly walked the line of Earth warriors, making sure each had a good look at him. Intimidation, most certainly, but it was also a message that the Guard was strong, capable, and had come to fight. *Well, at least he kept on his clothes on,* she thought.

"It's time the human legation arrived. We're the Federation Guard. Those with me are a scouting unit observing the approach of the enemy. They'll remain for the briefing and resume post at the outer limits of the solar system."

At a signal from Prex, armor disappeared, revealing stately beings, some were winged Carian, but no other resembled Prex. Male and female were represented, and in Quil's eyes, the lot of them were perfect in their natural form.

She also noticed some attractive Guard females hovered near Prex. *Their legs are taller than I am. No wonder I'm thought a goat.*

As the combined forces studied the location of the enemy base, the logical focus was on an air attack at the two entrances to the cave. The Joint Citizen force would control the air; the Earth's force would be in charge of ground attack.

As Quil listened, her belly suddenly flopped. *I messed up. I didn't collect enough information.* A critical factor had been overlooked. There was only one way to correct that oversight. She had to return to the enemy territory, and she had to do it pronto. Traveling by air was the only way.

"Gene, I must interrupt. It's a mistake to continue with this line of strategy. We need additional information. To get that, I need one of your crafts to take me to the enemy base location." Gene was openly disturbed at her interruption.

"We must not take the chance of our plans being found out. We can't delay." Gene walked away. She dogged his steps.

"No, wait!" Seeing Jessie and the Prioress walking toward her, she turned to meet them. "Jessie. I need a ship."

"I'll take you," said Prex. The others of the Guard were behind him.

"No, I can see you're busy with your … uh, *tall* people, and Jessie will help me. Won't you, Jessie?"

"I'll send a Carian for a ship from another site," said the Prioress. "I sense an urgency in her request."

"But I'm here." Prex's brow furrowed as Quil turned away from him.

"Thank you, Prioress—

"I said I'm here! And don't walk away when I'm addressing you." Prex mentally barked the command. She turned to face him.

"I don't cringe when you bark orders! Remember—I'm that stubborn goat butting everything around me. What? Have I embarrassed you in front of your comrades, Commander?"

In one stride, he had an arm around her waist. In a blink, they we were up and out of the building.

"Without question, you're the most confounding creature I've ever encountered. Tell me where we're going. And no pouting. "

"I don't pout! Go that way!" They skimmed treetops as they neared the enemy ground.

"I don't want you in this fight, Quil."

"Why? Haven't we've done our job well?"

"Your soldiers have fought admirably and you've honored the agreement to locate the enemy base which now enables battle. But you're injured. Did you take on a battalion of reptoids alone?"

"You consider us inferior, thinking we'll be of no help or even a hindrance? Humans are a part of the Citizen force. Even with our count, we number too few. We must be involved."

"You look cold. Are you cold?"

"Cold? No, I'm okay."

"You could be in the communications center with the Prioress.

"I don't want hidden away."

"You do not understand what we face. They in control of a stronghold. We cannot avoid bloodshed and loss of life. Listen to me this time, Quil."

"I am listening. And I've been there. You haven't. Let's look now and talk later." Keeping low to the ground, they took the same route she had driven, stopping at an overlook a safe distance from the cave. "The aircraft always arrive on the same approach, halting briefly at the same location and making a ninety-degree turn before landing in the valley. They never waiver from that pattern."

"That's relevant."

"This is where I messed up. First, I found a security shield but couldn't define its height. We need to know its layout and boundaries. And I tailed two reptoids here in a ground vehicle. They parked the car in front of the cave, meaning they have a way of entering the ravine from the ground. Did they drive through a break in the shield or under or over it?"

"Show me the security barrier."

She easily saw the red interwoven lattice rising from the ground. "It's right in front of us. Can't *you* see it?"

"No. Tell me what *you* see."

Describing it in detail, she could tell he didn't see the red filament. Walking the line, she pointed to skeletons of animals that had died on encountering it. "I want an eagle-eye view of this death trap. Fly me above this area but follow my guidance to keep us away from the barrier.'

It rose higher than expected, but its design was evident. They returned to ground. "It's a tiered wedding cake." He looked puzzled. "A layered structure with platforms receding as it rises. A stepped pyramid. A ziggurat."

"Ziggurat, I know. Continue."

"It decreases in dimension as it gains height and secures the entire area except for one place. A single flight corridor allows aircraft to enter and depart. It's narrow and tricky to fly. Any Citizen ships getting through the death shield by that means would be clay pigeons for the enemy inside the fortress."

"I must see this barrier."

"Then you need to see through my eyes. Can you accomplish that?"

"No, but you can."

"I doubt I can." He didn't verbally speak, but his expression did. "And you call me stubborn. Okay, okay, let me try something." Mimicking a hypnotist, she commanded him to see through her eyes. "Well, that was a wretched failure."

"This isn't the time for playing games."

"I'm trying here, Prex. Maybe this requires a touching, like the laying on of hands? So I'll touch your face near the eyes, and when I do, lay your hands on my face." Rubbing palms together to warm them, she focused, clenched her teeth, and slapped her hands on his face.

The unexpected happened.

Electricity charged through every nerve. She looked at Prex. His eyes had gone white; he had no pupils. She shuddered violently as an apparition afire with blue flames left her, whipping about her head. It charged forward and entered Prex through his eyes. Again she shook as a second apparition, a ghostly vapor, left her body, floating on a long delicate cord. At a distance, it turned back, pointing to the sky. Something was wrong. The stars were going out one-by-one as a dark demon blackened out the heavens. The corded specter pointed again. A savage beast with a blood-red eye pushed through an opening in the dim expanse. Like a demonic wraith, the swollen beast lashed across her vision, streaming a comet tail of glowing eyes. Again, the specter pointed a trembling finger at the red-eyed beast and then back at her. *It hunts for me?* Abruptly, the apparition retracted, whisking back into her body.

Suddenly, Quil convulsed. Her feet tore from the ground. Heat seared her eyes as wind churned, and thunder echoed. A fiery arc between her body and that of Prex sent sparks crackling through the air. She knew not how long they were joined, but the electrifying circuit at last broke. The crystal-like spirit departed Prex leaving a trail of flames as it entered her burning eyes. She felt calm returning; hands fell to her side as heat in her eyes lessened. Physically drained, her feet regained ground.

Prex had eyes again but seemed unable to move or speak. Thoughts raced through her mind. *I feel bonded with him now. Would stepping away be an option? Ever?* Recovery came, but neither spoke of the joining.

"I see the shield." Prex's voice was gritty. "Wait here." He spread his wings but spoke as he lifted off. "It's time you advanced your abilities, Quil."

Feeling confused and strangely ... crowded, she wondered what the beings were that shared her body? Why were there two? And those in the sky? I hunt one; one hunts me.

"This is a problem." Prex landed beside her. "We must locate the ground entrance used by the reptoids. Show me the route they used to get here."

"We can start where I hid the Jeep." They moved along the red web but found no entrance. "I don't know how to find it."

"We'll hunt until we locate it." Suddenly pulling her under cover of trees, Prex pointed to approaching headlights. A vehicle approached. Plus, the wind through branches announced an incoming aircraft.

"A ship's coming. We need to hide." She headed for brushy growth at the base of aspen.

"No, come to me." Placing her in front of him, he concealed her with his wings. A delta ship landed, but no one emerged. Watching from high ground, they talked of the terrain and a ground force's ability to get into position. Bringing in artillery and heavy military equipment would be impossible. There were no roads or even suitable hunting tracks to aid getting in anything but foot soldiers.

"It's about time for top action," said Quil, pointing to the clifftop as a light came on, and a bell ship departed tailed by a black delta.

An orange vehicle rounded a bend, coming to a halt in a deep gully. Leaving the car, a passenger walked to a stone wall, threw a lever, and a slab moved aside, exposing an underground tunnel. They drove under the death barrier.

At the cave, two uniformed men left the delta pulling black bags behind them. The Red Queen and Duchess Ramona watched as the men waved their arms, pointing to the bags. *The scalped traitors they'd killed had been found.* The queen silently viewed the bodies. However, the duchess exhibited frenzied terror. *Interesting. Genuinely distraught.* The two serpents entered the cave, followed by the turncoats dragging the body bags.

"We'll go now."

On the flight back, Quil considered patterns. Thus far, the enemy hadn't varied from established procedure. How could they use that to their advantage?

Landing at the Cyon facility, they were encircled by people wanting information. "Project the images," said Prex. "The others must see the death shield and the implausibility of an air attack. Do not deny who you are. Show your abilities."

What others thought of her had shrunk to zip. Images of the death shield appeared on the wall.

"This puts us in an untenable position," said Gene. "All of our planning for an air attack was for naught."

Wolf Severo stepped forward. "We'll take it from here. Our attack must be from the ground, and we welcome those who would join us." Immediately, allies stepped forward.

"There are other things I can offer if you're of a mind to listen."

"Tell us what we need to hear," said Wolf.

First, the two reptoid females the Spiders have been monitoring appeared again tonight. Again, they met a delta ship flown by humans, this time with body bags bearing the traitors we left in Utah. It seems the reptoid females appear when *turncoats* appear. The female serpents are the connection between the traitors and the enemy. That connection can be disrupted."

"And, the Spiders can bring about that disruption," said Seri.

"They use a mechanized pulley system to open the cave entrance and tow aircraft inside. The top entrance must have a similar arrangement."

"We take out the mechanized system and jam the doors so aircraft can't leave," said Josiah.

"If we jam the doors, how do we get in," asked Tres.

"We make a hole. But we must get in quickly. The enemy will destroy aircraft before surrendering them to us. We need machines to break through those doors."

"I agree," said Prex. "The POX are inbound. They won't need the aircraft here."

"We go in both entrances simultaneously to prevent the destruction of ships," said Wolf. "How many would you say they have?"

"I counted seventy-two, but it could be twice that hidden inside. I have no count of the enemy soldiers there."

"I've delayed long enough in bringing this news." Prex moved to the front to address the collective. "The reptoids have other bases on the planet. Cyon allies are in those locales forming resistance forces. Those we know of are in Australia, the northern part of Asia known as Mongolia, and the mountains of Peru."

Cheering erupted. Earth's troops slapped each other on the back and smiles were on every face. Settling down, loud exhales of relief filled the room. They were not alone. People of Earth were responding to the need to fight for survival. It was time to cheer.

"Attention." Prex held up a hand. "I applaud the forward stance of the Earth force. Choosing to lead the charge is commendable. However, reptoids are ferrying ships from outlying posts to the wilderness fortress here, the central command post. I'd venture they're planning to take the moon base to open a gate for the incoming POX armada."

"The fortress must fall first, and then we take the moon," said Gene. "Quil, what else can you tell us?"

"Aircraft must guard the air corridor in case enemy craft attempt escape."

"We can handle that."

"The time the bell leaves each night is around eleven o'clock. Is it possible to jam the sky port using the departing bell ship as a wedge? That would take the bell ship out of the fight plus it would provide a means for our squad to enter from above. That enables assault from two locations."

"Wait!" Wolf said, a scowl on his face. "That might be possible, but are you proposing the Spiders lead the assault from the top?"

"That's what I'm sayin'. We're smaller and can rig a system to lower us into the shaft. Those with military experience should charge the cave entrance as that's where most of the battle will take place."

Wolf walked to Quil, speaking low. "You women are not to be in this fight. I thought you understood that."

Well, butt a stump! I'm so tired of arguing with thick-headed males. Before she could give a response, the two Tarsiers ran to her side noticeably excited.

"We'll go in from above with you. We're slight of frame and adept at rope maneuvering. And we have military training."

"Now that's great! Spiders, did you hear? The Tarsiers are joining us." Quil led the Spiders to a corner of the facility to discuss training. *Wolf won't keep us out of the fight now.*

thirty

"Speak up! There's a lot of noise here!" Quil couldn't hear over multiple groups hammering out role assignments. "What? You have what information?"

"Luck is with you, sister fey," shouted Inger. "The snake demons walk the Animas River path in Farmington three mornings a week. We don't know what days, and it's large with trails on both sides of the river."

"Great job. Thanks, we'll take it from here." After conferring with the squad, Seri went to her car for a map of the Farmington river walk. Quil remained with the Spiders in what now was considered their corner of the Cyon facility.

"Isn't it time we know your names?" Six was sitting beside the Tarsiers.

"According to Jessie, they don't have names," Quil said, dropping to the floor beside her.

"We've taken names now," said a Tarsier.

"Oh, good," said Two. "What are they?"

"I am called Bob. And we wish to express our gratitude for permitting us to join you in delivering death blows to the oppressors. We will strive not to disappoint."

"And I am Fitzwilliam," said the second.

"Is that Fitz, a first and William, a second?" asked Six.

"It's Fitzwilliam. Did I not say it clearly?"

"Fitzwilliam, it is." Quil said, winking at Six.

"Do you always speak so formally?" Four said. "I didn't mean that as a criticism, but you can loosen up around us." The Tarsiers seemed baffled.

"What Four means is we don't speak precise English," said Quil. "Our American English is much less formal." The two allies talked silently between themselves before responding.

"At present," said Bob, "I fear we do not know how to *loosen up;* however, we will carefully observe."

"How do we tell one from the other?" Five asked as other Spiders nodded agreement.

"Is it not evident that Bob is female and I, Fitzwilliam, am male?"

"No disrespect intended, but no, it isn't. Though I think I have something that might help." From a cosmetic bag, Five removed a burgundy-colored neck ribbon. "This is velvet with delicate pearls and sequins. If Bob wears it, it'll help in knowing who is who."

Bob allowed Five to fasten the ribbon around her neck. "It's quite lovely. Thank you." Bob stood, modeling the new neckwear for the team."

Seeing the Tarsiers armed with energy pistols, the squad requested a demonstration of the weapons, quickly recognizing their advantages.

"This fighting unit must possess enhanced weapons," said Bob. "We'll address this need directly with the Cyon force."

"Good luck with that. Those guns were denied me." Quil saw Seri hurrying back to the group.

"Now, to our next mission. " Seri passed around maps. "We hunt the red-haired queen snake and her duchess pal. The hunting ground is the Farmington walk path at the Animas River Park."

"Somehow fitting," said Tres. "Rio de las Animas Perdita. The river of lost souls."

"That park has a lot of trails," continued Seri, "and heavy growths of salt cedar and Russian Olives that could work in our favor. In groups of two or three, we'll cover as much as we can. We don't know their walk schedule, so let's hope for luck. We start tomorrow." Fitzwilliam raised a hand.

"We wish involvement. We will project as humans to prevent detection."

"Certainly, you're in," said Quil. "Tomorrow morning at eight o'clock in the parking lot. Study the map, decide who's with who, park in different locations, and bring packs with weapons, ropes, whatever you think essential. And disguise the reason you're there; carry art stuff, books, cameras, get creative." The squad moved to regroup except for Tres, who slouched against the wall, shoulders sagging. Quil sat beside her.

"I'll swap that flask you carry for this," handing her a small book.

"What is it?"

"A book of poetry by one of my favorite—"

Oh, for pity's sake, Quil. Reading pretty little posies is not what I need."

"Listen, Tres. This poet understood the hard life, including pain and loss. I have several of his books but start with this one, *"What Matters Most is How Well You Wal Through the Fire."* His name was Chuck Bukowski. You can spend time with it tomorrow. Now the bottle." Tres first raised her eyebrows in defiance but handed it over.

"I have more where that came from, you know?"

"Yeah, but you're leaving it where it is. See the Tarsiers sitting by themselves? They've lost everything. They may be the only two of their species left in the universe, but they're in this fight. We need you in it, too. Now, get your head straight as you're looking after Bob and Fitzwilliam tomorrow. Don't let anything bad happen to 'em."

They sat on the east bank of the Anima with art supplies scattered across a table. "We've been here two hours with no sign of 'em," said Seri. "Looks like we do a repeat tomorrow."

"Or not." Quil pointed down the path. Carrying a camera, Tres strolled between the Tarsiers. As they neared, Tres raised her sunglasses. Moseying behind were the posers deep in conversation. Tres and the Tarsiers hurried by, heading for tree cover.

Keeping faces concealed, Quil and Seri shoved art supplies in carryalls and fell in behind. In a heated debate, the serpents seemed unaware of their presence. As they approached the ambush zone, two thin lariats whipped out, slamming them to the ground. Fitzwilliam stunned them to silence as Quil and Seri grabbed lines, pulling them to cover. As Seri secured hands, Quil searched for tracers, finding them pinned to the underside of collars. Bob held out a small card that converted to an expandable case; Quil drop the tracers inside. The team waited for the snakes to regain consciousness. Tres was the first one the serpents saw when they revived.

"Welcome, demons, to the river of lost souls. Allow me to introduce myself. I'm the sister of the two men you tortured and murdered on the mountain. We'll leave it at that for now, but I'll be back."

Surrounded by Spiders, the serpent queen's eyes flashed pure hatred as she recognized Quil.

"Aw, you remember me. It's nice to see you, too." Quil focused on the Ramona poser, shivering uncontrollably.

"Hi, Ramona. Not to fret, we're just here for information, and if you cooperate, we'll let you go free. All we want are you're your plans to attack the moon base. Now, now, don't go shaking your head like that. This isn't the time to be denying who you are. The charade is over." Out of the corner of an eye, she saw Tres unloading a backpack filled with blades of various sorts.

"I know you saw the condition of the traitors we left in Utah." Fear instantly registered on the snake's face. Quil motioned Tres forward. "Show her what you used on those guys."

Tres laid out an array of blades with slow deliberation, running a finger along each, checking sharpness. Placing one under the chin of the duchess snake, she ran it lightly around the throat, watching a trickle of green ooze run from under her chin. The snake violently shuddered, but the queen serpent calmly swayed in a slow, rhythmic motion, keeping her eyes on Quil.

"Look at me , human," said the queen snake, "not that sniveling underling. Yes, that's right, look at me. How do I know you're telling the truth? If I tell you what you want to know, what assurances do I have you'll release me?" Speaking soothingly, the queen almost sighed the words she said.

"Assurances? No assurances," said Quil, turning again to Ramona, now making choking sounds as she watched Tres wielding a machete. Abruptly, she screamed.

"No knives! Three days—the attack's in three days from the fortress! I gave you what you wanted, now kill her," slinging her head toward the queen. "She forced me to help her. Release me, and I'll give you money and positions of authority. I know the overseer. He'll see you're rewarded."

"I can protect you," said Quil, "but protection does cost. The name of the one in charge is the price. But talk fast as queenie might decide to trump your card."

"Don't play me for a dupe. I'll tell you when I'm away from here. Then, I'll see your granted everything you want, everything."

"You're don't have the power you boast. The queen snake might, but not you."

"It's good you recognize authority when you see it," said the red queen. "I rule here, and it's me who can grant rewards. Join us, and I'll take care of you." The serpent queen had never stopped weaving side-to-side, her voice gentle and calming.

"Quil, pay attention," said Seri. "She's a viper."

"Don't listen to her," whispered the queen. "Listen to me. Lean close, and I'll tell you what you want to hear." The queen murmured under her breathe, sounds Quil couldn't untangle.

"Don't worry, Seri, I'm not getting close to those fangs. If you were as powerful as you claim, queen, you wouldn't be in this predicament. And as the *overseer* hasn't been named, I'd say you're bluffing."

"Perhaps I don't want you to know who he is, but the *magus,* our *overseer,* certainly knows who you are. Yes, he knows you, and the narcissist devil is looking forward to wrangling with you—*again*. The overseer intends to rule the universe with me at his side. Nor can you defeat the *genius malignus* and his beast. I and only I know their identities. Why do you struggle so, earthling? You're tired, human. You're weak. You don't want in this fight. You failed your mission.

You failed everyone. You need *me* to save you. Look into my eyes. You know I'm right."

Two identities? Quil whipped out the Glock, pointing it between the queen's eyes, but noticed her hand trembling. "No one needs you. Stop looking at me that way and give me names!"

"Quil, don't," said Tres, touching her arm.

Quil shook her head, trying to clear the cobwebs. She was worn down, feeling so tired she could hardly stand, but she needed to know a name. Quickly penetrating the queen's mind, she searched for the information the snake professed to know. *She's lying! She doesn't know the identity of the magus or the genius malignus.* Quil's hand shook as she holstered the gun.

"You're a liar. And your mind trickery failed. You've lost, queen. Did you hear me? *You* failed! Tres, I hand this to you. Who else wants in this?" Quil walked away, her temples throbbing.

"Four deserves payback," Seri was saying. "Tilde, this is yours if you want it."

"This belongs to Tres," said Four. "My payback is watching these two meet their fate head-on. Or heads off, I should say. Wait a minute. I brought a player to cover noise." She turned on the music and nodded at Tres.

"Think about what's coming," Tres spoke without emotion, no remorse for what she was about to do. Bound and helpless, both snakes quivered as if to shed worthless skins. "I'll take my time hacking parts from your sickening bodies. I want you to watch as the other is dismembered piece by piece. In the end, your heads will bounce, and no one will care. No one will mourn your dying. Think hard on the pain that's coming and show me how brave you are."

Squad members somberly watched the dismembering, a few tapping feet in cadence with the music. Quil, however, had moved into questioning mode. *We're justified in doing this, aren't we?* Or are we becoming as vicious as the enemy? No, this was justified. They needed information, and the snakes needed to die. A fair swap—

"Oh!"

She backed away as the queen's heads rolled at her feet. Tres walked past, kneeling at the river's edge, cleaning the machete.

"It's done, Mama," she whispered. "If the Lord mistakenly granted these demons souls, I hope they wander these brushy banks for all eternity."

"God's not stupid." Seri patted Tres on the shoulder. "Does anyone have ideas on what to do about this mess?" Fitzwilliam raised a hand.

"To find the carcasses could alert the enemy to our objective. Bob has concealed the tracer beacons. I'll now arrange carcass removal."

Quil's thoughts remained with the queen's words. Two dark forces. One was a narcissist, consumed with excessive self-love, demanding adoration. That sounded familiar. Something was trying to break free from her memory, but she couldn't bring it forward. Suddenly, Seri was beside her. The others were ready to leave, but she was content to stay, listening to the river's comforting murmur like the whispering voice of the serpent queen.

"Isn't this a pretty place to die, Seri?"

"Come on. Let's get away from this killing place."

thirty-one

Like pilgrims traveling by caravan, the squad made their way back to the Cyon facility. After leaving the bloodletting at the river, no one wanted to talk, needing to withdraw to process what had happened. Seri called Wolf to say they'd report on the mission at the evening meeting. Then miles passed silently.

Again, Quil's replayed the queen's words. Two adversaries now. Both had trademark designations but no names or faces. The *magus* would be a sorcerer. It seems she should know a face to put with that one. The *genius malignus* was an enigma? She could only recall that term from philosophy study, a reference to an evil demon or a deceiving god. That meant nothing to her.

Was the red queen lying? About some things, yes, but not about the demons. She'd snatched her thoughts to be sure. But what was that weird weaving and tongue whispering? Did she imagine that? Suddenly, a worse thought hit her. *Wait! Am I bait?* Why did the *magus* want to wrangle again? What happened the first time. Were they in a battle? Did she lose? Is that the reason she was here? Was she the worm on a hook drawing in the prize catch? Is this her punishment for failing? *Stop it! Stop the infernal questioning.* She focused on the road.

Rain fell. Not a monsoon deluge, just steady rain drumming on windows. Water running down the windshield distorted the road ahead. Her eyes followed blurry white centerlines that seemed to stretch forever. *It looks like a never-ending stretch of rail cars. Where are you taking me long white train? Where am I headed?*

As her mind drifted, she debated letting Prex know of the enemy's plan to attack the moon. She should let him know but didn't want to. Instead, she wanted to run from the madness that had found her, just drive and keep driving. *You're tired, human. You're weak. You don't want in this fight.*

"Let's leave, Seri," she blurted. "We're not needed now that the Federation Guard is here. Let's just keep driving."

"I knew it! You've been seized! That demon possessed you, clouding your mind."

"Don't be ridiculous. I'm fine. I'm thinking clearly for the first time in a long while. But if you don't want to go, that's okay. I'll drop you off and go alone. Alone would be better anyway."

"I'm not letting you leave, Quil."

"You can't stop me. Wh—" She swerved to avoid hitting Prex, winging ahead of the car. Pulling over, she lowered the window.

"Tell your comrade to continue in the vehicle. You'll accompany me to the meeting."

How did he know that—unless he entered my mind without consent? How dare he do that! Knowing something was up, the squad had piled out of vehicles, standing near her window.

"No, I'm not going anywhere with you. Never again. You're through running roughshod over me. I'm leaving. I don't want in this anymore.

"Leave?" Tres yelled. "You can't leave!"

"She's under strain, Prex," said Two. "We've had a mean couple of days. She's not leaving."

"The devil I'm not. Watch me!" Quickly, Seri yanked the keys out of the ignition and jumped from the car.

"She's been spelled, Prex," Seri said, holding the keys behind her back. "Spelled? Do you know what that means? We must get her help right away."

Climbing out of the car, Quil screamed, "Give me the keys, Seri."

"What's happening, Quil? This isn't you. Let us help you."

"Let me reason with her," said Prex, walking toward Quil. She felt him trying to enter her mind and threw up a block—too late.

"You can't run from this. You're wrapped in internal questioning and self-doubt and letting it frighten you. Here is where you're meant to be. If you allow yourself to think clearly, you'll see that. Come with me, Quil."

"No! Get away from me! Stay back! I'm warning you!"

Thunder rolled as the dark cloud of panic held her in its grip. Reason absent, madness ruled—and she attacked. Her hands thrust against his space, forcing him backward. His feet slid through the gravel as he fought to remain standing. Steadying, he came toward her again.

"I won't let you push me away. Push against whatever's causing you to question yourself."

"You're the *genius malignus!* The evil demon. I must destroy you!" Again, energy left her hands, hurling him backward. He slammed against a tree.

"How's she doing that?" yelled Seven. "Stop it, Quil. He's trying to help you."

"No, you're all deceiving me." The team moved toward her. "Stay back!"

WHUMP!

"Damn." Seri rubbed her left hand. "I might have hit her too hard. One of you check her pulse."

"She's breathing, but her heartbeat's erratic," said Tres. "Something bad has a hold on her. We need to move fast. Are you thinking what I'm thinking?"

"Pretty sure I am. See if Prex is alright? Where did she get that power?" Prex was keeping his distance, but his eyes never left Quil.

"Prex, we have to go now," said Seri. "We're getting her to a healing person. Can the Tarsiers go back with you?"

"We'll stay with the team," said Bob. "Perhaps we can be of help. Commander Prex, please leave. I believe it imperative we hurry."

Saying nothing, Prex rose and was soon lost from sight.

"That was a mistake threatening him like that," said Tres, "I hope he doesn't take off for good. One of you help me get her in the car."

Seri was on the phone when Quil came to. "We should be there in a half-hour, maybe less. Get ready. I doubt she'll be a willing participant."

Seeing Quil stirring, Seri climbed over the center console to the back seat. Wrapping arms around Quil, she slowly rocked back and forth.

Quil pushed on her chin, trying to get her jaw back in place. "Hurt," she mumbled.

"Oh, too bad. Your jaw dislocated. Let me help with … uhm, okay. It popped back in place. I didn't hit you that hard. It's just you have a glass jaw that you need to shield. I'll put a poultice on it later to draw out the soreness. But for now, you need to listen. Together, we'll beat this, sister. We need you, Quil. We know we need you. Let us know you need us. We're family, and we're here for each other." Qui heard singing, only sounds to her, not knowing the meaning of the words. Tres was also chanting. She wasn't sure if it was the humming or Seri's words that sounded so right. *That seems to make sense. They are family. I need family.*

"Go past the house and take the trail leading to the river," said Seri. "She'll be waiting." Tres pulled into a grove, braking to a stop, instantly surrounded by cars of team members.

"We'll be with you the entire time, and it'll be over before you know it," coaxed Seri. "It's a simple healing ceremony, a cleansing rite. It'll be easy. You'll sail right through it. Let's get out of the car now so you can meet the witch—healing woman. I meant to say, healing woman."

Quil heard low chanting again and saw a figure in a large circle of stones with a smaller round in the middle. Inside the grand ring were three clay bowls containing river pebbles. A woman in native dress stood with her back to them, humming while waving a muffled rattle. Without turning, she chanted expectations.

"She stands in the inner circle, the rest outside the greater."

Inside the inner ring, Quil watched the others space themselves around her, sitting on their knees. Abruptly, the witch turned toward her with face blackened, a crow-feathered headdress, and dark scorching eyes burning into hers. The image of the snake-headed Medusa popped into Quil's mind.

"Nope, not doing this. Leaving now. I can heal myself. I just need to find solitude somewhere—the desert or a cave around here would do. Thanks anyway."

"No talk," said the witch. "You can't leave until you free yourself of the demon that travels with you. You can do this—you will do this. We'll help you." Tossing a yellow powder in the air, Quil watched it float around her."

She tried to step out of the circle but couldn't. An invisible force bound her inside the small space.

"Seri, get me out of here!" The team was chanting, led by the witch. "All of you, shut up, and get me out of here now!"

They ignored her pleas. Quil watched as the witch placed tied bundles in the clay bowls, waiting for flames as she lit each one. At a certain point, with one swift swipe, she caught the flame, leaving long tendrils of smoke wafting toward Quil.

Sage. I like sage. This might be alright, she thought. Walking to each bowl, the witch fanned smoke over her from head to foot. Then turning, with an eagle feather, she fanned smoke toward Quil.

"The bowls represent water; the unlit herbs and ashes represent earth; the feather and the wind it creates represent air; the flames used to ignite the herbs and smoke represent fire. The four elements. White sage, a sacred herb, will drive out negative forces. Let it cleanse you. Let it enter your heart and mind. Ask the Devine to help you banish harmful energies. Say this out loud, so the Devine will hear your voice."

Quil tried to say the words, but they wouldn't leave her lips. Instead, she heard the tangled murmuring of the queen snake. Suddenly, she was choking. Something was tearing her apart, claws ripping at her heart and lungs. Drooling, she fought for air as a green haze filled her space.

Wings! I hear wings. Carians! The Prioress! The witch, hesitating not one second, beckoned the holy woman inside the great round. Seri entered with her. The Prioress stood before Quil, a glistening, black-feathered rod in her hand. With a sweep of the rod the unbearable pain eased, and she could breathe.

"Quil, hold out your hand," commanded the Prioress. "Take the hallowed raven stave. It's your strength to drive away the evil. Take it—take it now!"

The feathered stave came through the invisible barrier into Quil's hand. Walking to each of the three bowls, the Prioress tossed in a powder transforming the white smoke to red.

"Heal yourself with the hallowed smoke. See the evil with you. Say the words. 'I banish forces that cause me harm.' Fight against the demon. Tell it to leave you—now!"

Quil spoke the words; a scream deafened her as green miasma swirled about her. Instantly, the heel of a hand hit her between the eyes, sending her ass over elbows to the dirt. But she was outside the ring. She scrambled to her feet.

"Hit it with the rod," shouted the witch. "Send it to hell." The Prioress rapidly fanned smoke over the evil. Quil swung furiously, beating at the green fume within the center stones.

"Go to hell," she yelled.

Hearing horrifying shrieks, she flailed harder. Another scream and the evil dissipated, vanishing from sight. The healing smoke entered the inner ring, spinning in a funnel cloud. But Quil wasn't stopping. She flailed until the Prioress took her hands.

"Calm yourself now; gentle your breathing. You won the battle. Think well of yourself for defeating a most powerful evil." She brushed the back hair from over Quil's ears.

"Now, a preventative so it can't reach for you again," rubbing a soothing balm on each temple. "You did well." The

Prioress was smiling, which made Quil feel better until she remembered the Prioress was always smiling. "Keep the raven wand near. Do not unintentionally feed negativity into your soul and never compromise with evil."

"Thank you, Prioress. I'll help you any way I can."

"You're already helping." She and the other Carians lifted off. "Don't be late for the meeting."

"Thanks, everyone. Thank you." That sounded lame, but she didn't know what else to say. "Seri, what am I to do now?"

"Pay the witch. You can't leave until you pay for the healing."

"I pay for this? Well, okay, I have cash, or I can write a check. What do I owe you?"

"She's not after your money," said Tres. "She wants something of yours." The witch was pointing to Quil's wrist.

"This? But this is my almost new aviation watch. See, this is for pilots." The witch didn't look impressed. "It's a Takeoff Auto Chrono with a yellow highlighted directional countdown turning flange. They're made for Swiss mountain rescue pilots." Still, the witch had her hand out. "It cost eighteen hundred ninety-five plus tax."

"Give it to her, Quil," said Six. "If you irritate her, she might take back the healing. And be sure to thank her."

"Take back— Well, *pfft.*" She removed the watch and handed it to her. "Thank you, witch."

"You got off cheap. It could've been your car. What'll this bring on eBay?"

thirty-two

Late for the meeting, the squad took seats at the back. At the front, Prex was making an announcement.

"I've received word from the Federation Command. We're entering the fight to save Earth."

People went wild. Optimism rose like mercury in a heat gauge on a mid-August day. Quil smiled. *As it should be, he owns the spotlight. He's bringing in the best warriors in the universe.*

Calling for order, Gene asked Quil to report on the interrogation of the female reptoids. She didn't want to stand as she had a large poultice taped to one jaw and a good-sized purple welt between her eyes, but she was at the point of not caring about her appearance. She motioned for the Spider Squad to stand with her.

"The enemy plans to attack the moon base in three days from the mountain fortress." She spoke the words and sat down.

Jessie took the floor, informing the gathering of the Spider Squad's finding of an underground enemy facility and the securing of the hold by joint forces. He withheld details of what the Spiders had done with those inside. With reporting done, the collective split into target groups.

The Spiders moved to one end of the hangar to prepare for the entry of the clifftop entrance. True to their word, the Tarsiers provided lightweight energy weapons. Bob also passed out touch-activated credit card contraptions that formed boxes suitable for containment of such things as enemy tracers. Then they got busy. The Tarsiers instructed on the use of thin repel lines, tossing them up and over ceiling beams. Climbing to the top, they repelled down while having a weapon in hand, ready to battle.

"That looks easy," said Seri.

"It does, doesn't it?" agreed Quil.

Well, it wasn't. Repelling was not a skill requirement for many jobs. The fine, lightweight lines the Tarsiers used presented a unique set of problems. With a certain twist, the line flew into the air and encircled a solid mass. With different handling, the line retracted to the hand. The Spiders repeatedly failed to master the lines. Getting up wasn't an issue; the line carried them up, often crashing them into beams. Manipulating the sensitive line while gripping a weapon in a controlled descent was a different matter. Deciding bulky clothing partly the problem, they stripped down to undershirts, trousers, and socks. Still, they flat out could not do it.

"We're not impressing this crowd." Seri panted.

"Yeah, I envisioned this going better," Quil replied as they watched Tres trying to disentangle from another Spider, both in a twisted mess of lines, while the others ping-ponged between floor and ceiling. The Tarsiers ran back and forth, tutoring on the up and down of repelling, while faces around the room showed disappointment, especially Wolf's face. Calling a break, the Spiders sat against a wall to talk options.

"I'm going outside for fresh air." Quil rushed out a side door, not liking the expression on observers' faces. *We must gain control of this, or we'll lose this chance.* She sat under a tree to work it through. Concentrating, she waved a hand to brush away an insect but suddenly stopped. In front of her face, a small spider dangled on a silken thread, its bulging eyes staring straight at her.

"Show me how it's done, small spider."

Entranced, she watched the spider release a silken thread while swinging head down. *Uh-huh.* Head down seeing ahead, front legs handling the silk, back legs controlling the descent. *Well, I'll be switched. Can I make that work?*

Returning to the hangar, she climbed to a beam, secured her legs around the line, then lowering headfirst. She repelled downward, gripping a weapon while using leg pressure to regulator descent. Surprise registered on squad members' faces.

"I went about this the wrong way for me. Give it a try, but use any method that gets you down that line, armed, and in control. Make it happen!"

Standing by, she watched as Spiders perfected descents. They weren't the classiest trapeze artists on the swings, but they were swinging. Glancing around the room, others in the hangar smiled in support. From a corner, Prex watched and nodded. Wolf was missing, no longer in the facility.

Before breaking for the evening, Josiah spoke to the rebel force. "It's time to get right with those you care about. Don't bring regrets to the fight. Talk to family and friends."

"I'll be late for the morning meeting. I'm going to see Albert. I'll try to be back early." Josiah seemed okay with that.

Glad to be home, Quil rested on the sofa, pulling the raven stave from the backpack. The feather glistened like black glass. *Prex has feathers like this.* The rod was carved on all sides. Hieroglyphics? With a start, she remembered the hieroglyphic document Josiah photographed. Could they be they the same language? She'd check that out tomorrow.

The wand didn't look all that imposing. It was only feathers fixed to a carved stick. "Does this truly hold special power? Or is it merely a potency token used to instill confidence in a doubting soul?"

Holding her hands in front of her, they didn't seem impressive, either. But they hid raw force that could cause pain, injury, and possibly death. And she'd hurt Prex with these hands. How did that happen?

Glancing at the fireplace, still filled with cold ashes, she turned her palms toward them—and flinched. The cinders flared, and flames sent sparks flying. She jerked her hands down, watching the fire go out and ashes turn stone cold. But flames lingered at the tips of her fingers. Touching them, they were as cold as ice. Amazed, she watched as the ice fire tail off, except for a tiny flame bobbing about her. And she was walking with Shade.

"Greetings, Quil."

"I'm not up for talk, Shade, and I don't need you to judge me right or wrong in what I've done. Go back to wherever it is you go."

"You're the one who called me, not the other way round. You have issues nagging you. I can help with those, and while you may think it so, I'm not come to judge you."

"I called you? I didn't mean to and certainly wouldn't call you or anyone in to sit in judgment of me. I'm quite good at judging myself."

"For what do you judge yourself?"

"I killed today, and it presses on me."

"You're suffering doubt. But doubt is encountered in times of conflict. And as you said, you were culling the tares."

"You heard that? Okay, but they were children. And don't tell me killing may be the only option at times. I question if killing is ever justifiable? And while we're questioning, why does war exist at all? Now, that's the puzzle we need to solve."

"But war does exist. And tragedy travels with war, and loss travels with tragedy. Could there be something else? Could it be you fear loss?"

"Loss?" Quil sighed heavily. "Possibly, but there's an evil force driving this, and I should be directing my energies to discovering who that is?"

"True. Let's discuss that. Evil need not take dramatic form. Look closer at those around you. Is a professor of knowledge truly a professor of knowledge or one wearing a façade? Does a deceitful one come and go like the tide, first near and then afar? Your brow furrows. Is the puzzle coming together?"

"No, I can't say that it is. And, now ...."

"Now?"

"It's my hands. I hurt someone with them, one I'd never want to hurt."

"You're amid change and gathering power you'll soon need. And what appears as a door closing may be a door opening."

"Well, I heard a door slam shut today, and it sounded mighty damned permanent to me. I don't want to talk to you anymore."

"Ah, such a petulant lower lip is a sign of obstinance. Your emotions travel a twisting road. Are you afraid to address a matter of the heart? You do have a heart, Quil, but one you've built an ice wall around."

"Leave my heart out of this."

"And so I shall. Good night, Quil.

Shade was gone, which was okay with her. Feeling her lower lip, it wasn't petulant, only slightly pronounced. What did Shade say about identifying the poser? Consider someone close—one who comes and goes like the tide. So many are on the move now. She couldn't track everyone, so that didn't help. What else? A false professor of knowledge. That could be an expert in a job field or one having special information. Verifying people were who they said they were would take time she didn't have. So that's of no immediate help.

Twirling the rod again, she watched hieroglyphs spinning by. If the Prioress can read these hieroglyphs, maybe she can read the papers Josiah took photos of. I need to get them to her. They could provide the answer I'm looking for.

thirty-three

Off the runway at first light, Quil found Jim tossing feed to a pen of milling sheep.

"What's wrong with the Dopers?"

"They sense something coming. Every animal on the place is jittery. All the ranchers are keeping stock close in. What brings you out this way today?"

"Bringing new mostly. Jim, your people need to get to shelter. We have an underground facility near Ignacio, but you'll need to get them there."

"Yeah, I've received calls, and we're trying to piece together a plan. Grandfather insists an underground sanctuary exists near to where he went with you."

"The sacred pool? He did mention a sanctuary being around there."

"He talks of another up there, too, like an ark. If that's true, and I hope it is, we'll have a place for stock. But we need to find it first." They went inside, finding Albert agitated.

"We need to talk." He went outside, the screen door slamming behind him. Quil turned to follow but stopped, seeing small globes of flickering dust motes moving toward a territorial wall map. There, they aligned themselves in a pattern she recognized.

"What do you know about zodiac signs, Jim, particularly the one known as Aries?"

"Not a thing. Why?"

"Hear me out. Some say the measurement of time commenced when star people landed in ancient Mesopotamia. As the Aries Ram just happened to be the sign over the northern polar region, zodiacal time began with the Ram. Odd how that set time in motion for us. I sometimes wonder if the star travelers would have preferred a more impressive sign to take the lead." Jim turned toward her, looking confused.

"Aries is on your map. Watch." She traced the astrological sign with a finger. "Another accounting, I believe it was Persian, said it was the Aries Ram that served as a guide to a spring of water and a place of safety in the desert." Suddenly, Jim became more interested in the map.

"Aries has three bright stars. The brightest star, Hamal, is the Ram's head, and one of the Ram's horns holds two smaller stars."

"Do you spell that A-r-i-e-s?" asked Jim, pulling up a graphic of the sign on his laptop.

"Turn your computer for proper alignment. Yeah, that's better. Follow the route from where we are now, your ranch, to the Ram's head, which should be the location of the spring or sacred pool as we know it. From there, proceed to the horn holding the two stars. The Ram's horn could hold the sanctuary and ark. Do you see the way?" Jim nodded as he drew the route on the wall map.

Leaving Jim, she joined Albert at the sheep pen. "Albert, the demon crow appreciated your gift of the eagle feather and sent you a gift in return."

As Quil placed the scarf in his hands, a sad tenderness touched her heart. The old man's hands trembled. Unfolding the scarf, he turned away to shield his emotions. *This teacher needs to stay longer. Don't take him from me too soon.*

Unable to read his face, she intercepted his thoughts, her eyes brimming with tears. *"A gift from the star people—for this old man. They know I'm here."*

"It has meaning," he said, clearing his throat. "When you see the demon crow, tell him for me."

"I will, grandfather."

"Now, you need to fix what you broke."

"What did I break?"

"You created a dark space between you and the demon crow. You must remove it."

Her mouth dropped open. *How did he know that?*

"Close your mouth. You'll draw flies. Come here. You need a token." With a pocketknife, he cut a lock of hair from her head. "String?" Walking to a hay bale, he cut a piece of baling twine and tied it around the curl. Using the scarf that had held the feather, he wrapped the lock and handed it to Quil. "See the Crow gets this. Leave it at the sacred pool. I sense his presence there at times."

"I can't do that, Albert. We're preparing for battle, and I must get back. I know I caused a problem, but the Crow won't back out of helping us. He announced the Federation Guard regiments are on the way. It'll be alright."

"Make time for this. It's important."

"Thank you for your guidance, Albert. I'll be eternally grateful. But I won't go." She hugged him and walked away. As she departed, she saw Albert standing where she'd left him, a brightly colored scarf in his hand. What she didn't see was an elderly man climbing in an old Jeep and driving off into the desert.

The squad practiced repelling when Four appeared, announcing she was going with them.

"I can't allow that, Four," said Quil. "You could get hurt again."

"I'll limit my physical involvement. You can still use my eyes and ears. And my arm is better. I'm going with you, Quil."

"You must stop the arguing and take these," said Bob, shoving unknown items into their arms.

"What's this?"

"Bodywear. Strong and lightweight. It will assist in performance."

"Spandex? I'm not wearing spandex." Quil tossed it back.

"It offers protection, adjusts to temperature, and the jacket has means of attaching weapons."

"Is that right? Well, I need larger. This one's the size of a postage stamp."

"One size."

"In all my days, I never imagined I'd put something like this on my body," laughed Seri. "Where do we try on these things?"

In a storage room, they worked through garment fitting but found nothing to aid in carrying essentials. Quil waved the Tarsiers over. "Bring the jackets, and they better cover up a lot, or we're not wearing these." Boxes came through the door with vested jackets, boots, and hi-tech malleable headgear fancied up with enhanced night vision lens and communication earpieces.

"Let's give these a try on the ropes." Seri pointed to the beams.

With some adjustments, it seemed the suits were better than field suits. "Will these work for you?" Quil asked the team.

"Well, sometimes I have to pull it out of my parts," said Five. "It's my extra-long legs, but it'll work."

Suddenly, Two gasped, her posture slumping. "I really want one of those."

Following her stare, Quil watched as Prex slowly drifted from the sky port. Of course, he had to be wearing black Lycra.

"Oh, my! That suit doesn't leave much to the imagination, does it?" Four fanned her face.

Pulling Two back to an upright position, Tres muttered. "We've got to get this horny toad laid."

"That shouldn't be hard. We're in a bull barn," said Seven.

Prex walked directly to a group of Cyon officers who immediately closed rank. Shortly after that, Gene called the collective to attention.

"We've located a narrow riverbed to serve as a flight path, allowing transport of troops to the vehicle tunnel. Our number one priority is taking down the security net. Ensure people with system knowledge get inside fast. Coordinate your departure with the Carian communication unit."

"Wait a minute," Quil whispered. "Does that sound like we're going in now?" The Spiders looked at each other, the question hanging unanswered. "Seri, did you know we were going in tonight?"

"I didn't."

Neither Wolf nor Josiah had told either of them. Why? They watched Wolf supervising troop and equipment readiness. "He's excluding us. Let's find out what's going on."

Wolf saw Quil and Seri approaching and walked to meet us. "We have another team ready to go topside. Go home and wait where you'll be safe." Stern faced, he turned and rejoined his men.

No dissent allowed. No discussion allowed. Just an order. Go home, women, and wait. Not one word came from Quil's lips. She walked away with Seri close behind. Looking around the facility, Quil saw Jessie talking with the Tarsiers. They rushed over to talk to them, the squad quickly joining them. "We need a lift to the tunnel. Can you arrange it?"

"It's already arranged," said Jessie. "We had notice of certain plans you didn't have. You're going in the first ship. You should thank these two for getting you ready."

"Bob and Fitzwilliam! Yes, of course. Thank you for all you've done to help us. We'll look to you as team leaders tonight. Just get us there."

"We'll get you there, but we go not as team leaders. Exit the side door. Transport waits." With notice to no one, the Spiders quietly slipped away. As they lifted off, Quil requested an update from the Tarsiers.

"From the ground entrance, the Spiders will proceed to the clifftop. Prex will jam the mechanized door as it's engaged to allow the exit of the Mantian ship. Our hope is it will lodge the ship in the opening, leaving space for us to enter. This is as you recommended, Quil. If successful, Prex will join the others at the cave entrance, and we'll be on our own."

The transport ship skimmed the riverbed, staying below line of sight of the wilderness fortress.

The ground passageway was open. Quil figured Pres arranged that. Checking the time, it was close to ten. They had to move fast to reach the clifftop by eleven. First scanning the area, they stepped into the valley of the enemy and began the climb. Topside, they found Prex waiting for the Mantian bell ship.

Just short of eleven, Quil conferred with Seri. "Keep your unit here, and the Widows will move to the opposite side. If the ship is trapped, the opening to the shaft could appear at any place along the rim. Positioning at different locations should enable a quick entry."

They kept eyes on Prex at the edge of the opening. At eleven, they heard the groan of a motor. The ship was coming. He readied his weapon toward the chasm rim, and on seeing first light from the shaft, blasted the opening. The gears stopped, and they heard heavy metal scraping against concrete. Success! Without a word, Prex was gone. Quil drew in a deep breath. *It's on us now.*

"Four, we need a person on overwatch. Will you be okay up here without support?" They needed as many as possible inside, but she'd pull someone if Four wanted help.

"I'll handle topside. Just take care down there. I don't want direful feelings coming from that big hole in the ground." Quil watched as Tilde placing standby magazines within easy reach. Quil handed her a spare rifle and magazines from her pack. Four nodded confidently. *Yeah, she can handle this.*

The team secured anchors and attached repel ropes. They were ready. Quil peered into the chasm, checking for activity. The bell ship was tiled on its side snagged in pulley chains. Two Wisps were leaving the disabled ship. Hushed shots from her energy pistol toppled them into the dimly lit shaft.

"Go," she whispered, watching repel lines slip over the side while scanning for movement, footholds, and concealment zones. Assault rifles ready, Spiders streamed downward. Quil and Bob landed on the bell ship, sliding on bellies to the doorway and sneaking looks over the edge. No movement. Dropping inside, they separated to scout the ship. "Nothing here. Let's rejoin the squad."

The sound of muffled explosions rose from beneath them. "Engagement must be underway at the cave entrance. Let's get to the floor. We're exposed on this ledge."

Linking with the tunnel floor, they crouched low against slick rock walls. As eyes adjusted, they spotted moving shadows advancing on the right.

"Snakes! Fire at will!"

The enemy fell, and they edged further into the dim tunnel. "Tres, Six, take rearguard." They had caught the enemy unaware; the unforeseen entry worked in their favor. Steadily moved forward, Quil sensed the squad's confidence rising.

Intersecting another tunnel, they found rows of black and silver delta ships, lining both sides of the passageway. After a quick parley, the units separated, positioning on either side, using the ships as cover.

"Quiet. Everybody, listen!" said Quil. The sound of running feet grew louder. Abruptly, reptoids streamed through the center of the tunnel.

"They don't know we're here," Seri said through her comm piece.

"Crossfire." The enemy fell, but more kept coming, slowing only long enough to pull dead out of the way. Quil counted four charges before the surge stopped. Enemy troops lay dead on the tunnel floor; no others appeared.

"What do you think?" Seri whispered.

"They might be regrouping or trying to fake us out." They waited another quarter-hour. "Let's move out the direction they were running." Pushing on, they encountered yet another intersection.

"This place is a frickin' maze," said Tres.

"But this one doesn't look like the other tunnels." Quil studied the layout of the massive cavern or what she could make of it in the dimness.

"I can't see its parameters," said Six. "It's too dark in here."

Seri joined them for a confab. "Which way do we go now?"

"I don't know," said Quil. "We need lights. Look around. There must be a control box near this entrance." While checking for electrical panels, Quil felt a tug on her sleeve. It was Fitzwilliam.

"We should proceed cautiously." He pointed to the Recluse unit, walking deeper into the cavern. "They move too far away from safety."

"Seri, he's right. Let's wait back here for now."

"Oh, no." Seri gasped as she ran into the cavern, calling the unit back to the tunnel. Her unit turned, giving Seri thumbs-up signs.

Numbed, Quil couldn't speak. Then she screamed, "Thumbs up. Get back here! Run!"

"A bell! Another ship!" Six shouted, pointing toward an enemy ship.

"Seri, get out of there!" The Recluse unit was running toward them. "Back! Everyone back in the tunnel!" Quil pushed Six backward. Fitzwilliam had Tres by the arm, pulling her into the tunnel. Bob was running toward Seri's unit. Quil followed, but Bob reversed, waving Quil away. Chaos broke loose as rocks flew in every direction.

"They're caught! Cover fire! Now!"

Things went bad. The cannon on the ship's underbelly blasted rock walls, sending jagged projectiles helter-skelter. Debris dirtied the air, screening Seri and her unit from sight. Alive or dead—they didn't know. They could do little from where they were. A chance came, and Quil slipped into the cavern, finding a pillar to hide behind. Looking back toward her unit, muzzle flashes from all four came from the tunnel entrance. *What if*—"Tres, watch the rear."

"Copy."

"Shouts? In English." Faint shouts came from her right. Their troops were close. Of a sudden, a shrill scream pierced the air. She dropped flat. *TSCH TSCH TSCH.* Three fiery blasts hit the bell ship, sending it careening off walls. Its mortar stopped firing, but it was still alive. She strained to see the tunnel where her unit was but saw neither them nor reports from rifles. Unexpectedly, a door opened on the bell, and a lone Wisp jumped to the tunnel floor. A single shot took it down. The ship was out of control, pitching side-to-side. As it dipped low, she saw two Wisps through the open door at the control center. But the ship was leveling off. *If they regain control, they'll head for our troops.* Her eyes locked on the ship's open door; she had to risk it.

Now!

Running hard, she dove at the door, firing while skimming the surface on her knees. Both Wisps went down. In a crouch, she slipped to a sidewall, scanning the flight deck. A shadow moved. She fired. The shadow fell, but a blast above her head brought an avalanche crashing down.

And things went black.

Quil moved a hand into darkness, touching solid metal over her head. She tried to get up but couldn't. *Something's wrong with my legs.* Trying to pull them out from under whatever pinned them, a razor-sharp pain stabbed her in the ribs. *Damnit!* Falling back, she waited for the pain to slacken before running a hand down her side. *Trapped. Hurtin' like the dickens. Seems to be numbing. Maybe numbing is good.* She felt blood running down her face. A head cut but not bad.

Freeing her combat knife, she chipped away at rubble at her head. *Light!* She shoved, and the blockage gave way, sending a rush of air over her face. *That's Better.*

As she hacked at the debris, she thought back to the battle. *Everything went the wrong way.* Seri's unit cut off, rotating ray propelling rock missiles, chaos everywhere. Seri? The units? Did they make it through?

"Tres, do you copy?" trying to raise her on the radio. Nothing came back. "Six, report. Can anybody hear me?" She cupped a hand over the earpiece. Nothing.

Crap! And trapped in bloody crypt—but I'm not stayin'. She worked enlarging the hole, pushing debris out by pitifully small handfuls. *This'll take a month of Sundays, and the ribs are hurtin' bad. I can't keep this up. What if I try ...* Using the force of her hands, she pushed against space ahead of her; a wall of rubble fell away. *Well, it didn't bring the roof down.*

Now, to move what's on top of me out of the way. Large metal girders and support beams lay over her. Concentrating, she forcibly sent power from underneath; and a buttress rose. Rapidly shifting her hands toward an open space, she dropped it, or thought she dropped it, but it stayed in the air. *Wasn't expecting it to float, but as long as it's off me, I don't care.* Energized, she shifted pinnings holding her down. Most were floating, and she was running short of up-top space. She tried moving her legs. They stirred, but it was painful. She let her head fall back to rest her neck. *How can I be sweatin' like a stuck pig and freezin' at the same time?* A steady buzz in her ears was growing louder. *That can't be good.* She closed her eyes to let her breathing even—

And she heard it!

Something was coming, creating a lot of noise as it closed on her. She positioned her hands toward the clamor. If she could get it under the floating metal, maybe she could—

It's here!

She willed strength into her hands but suddenly threw them back over her head, sending the force behind her.

That's a wing!

"Prex! What're you doing here?" He tried to straighten, but the floating debris prevented it. "I mean, shouldn't you be in battle. Or is it over?"

"Not entirely over, but it soon will be. The better question is, what are you doing here?" In a crouch, his eyes shifted to what floated above him. "This is quite a mess you've made."

"A mess? Not really. I'm rearranging my quarters. It's a female thing."

"I see your attitude is intact. What's your condition otherwise?"

"Good. I'm good. But look at you. Shame, shame. You got dirt all over your pretty black wings. Thanks for making a hole outta here. You can go on back. I'll be right out."

"Stop deflecting and tell me your injuries. Or do I check you over myself?"

"Well, I am broken a bit. But feeling is coming back, so it can't be that bad." Bent at the waist with hands on his knees for support, he looked uncomfortable.

"You can help me, though. I need to put my stuff some other place. I was going to make a hole in that wall and push it through, but I don't know if people are on the other side." After a second, he grinned.

"A collaboration? A novel idea. I'll see what's there." He flicked keys on his wrist transceiver. "Looks good. Ready up. Brace." His weapon fired, sending the wall crashing to the cavern floor.

"Now for me," sending her debris collection through the opening.

"Is she alright?" Jessie's head came through the gap behind Prex.

"She probably could use a physician, Jessie. Are you available?" Jessie was already on the way to Quil.

"He's an aviation mechanic."

"I'm a physician and a scientist. Gene is an astrophysicist. The mechanics are the Carian."

"Oh, yeah? Because they can't transform, right?"

"That's right. Now be quiet, and let me examine you."

"You could have told me."

"I could have but chose not to. Here's other news. I'm female."

Now, that was a shocker, and Quil looked Jessie up and down, paying particular attention to where female attributes generally were found.

"You're being rude."

"I apologize. I won't ask why you pretended to be male as you must have had good reason."

"I pretended because it seemed the wiser thing to do. Good new. You're not in too bad a condition, leg bones shattered, ribs broken. We've got some fixing to do, but you'll sail right through it with no problem."

"Jessie, the last time someone told me that, I was hit square between the eyes and knocked to the dirt." She tried to sit up, but the pain hit, and she laid back down. "I haven't had time to deal with getting myself back together. I'm sure I can do it. I just need to think it through."

"Or you could leave something for the rest of us to do. Unfortunately, I don't have a way of putting you under just now. I'll relieve the pain as soon as I'm able, but it'll hurt when we move you. Though, I could hit you square between the eyes if you think it would help.”

"Permit me, Jessie,” said Prex. Kneeling beside Quil, he pushed tangled hair away from her eyes, looking at the head cut. “You seem to have a bent for head injuries.”

“It isn’t bad. My hair’s glopped to my head, is all. I need hosing down.”

“You need repaired, soldier. You did your job. Let the physician do hers. I’m putting you to sleep. You’ll feel pressure on your neck, but there’ll not be pain when you’re moved.”

“Wait! My team, what—”

thirty-four

Prex studied a skeletal diagram while waiting for the physician to return. Occasionally, he glanced at Quil, lying in a med pod. They were in the Cyon medical center, a typical sterile setting housing cubicle-sized rooms, exam alcoves, and patient treatment shells. Hearing hurried footsteps, Prex watched Jessie enter, balancing a tray of curative paraphernalia.

"I can see you're heavily scheduled, Jessie, but I'd appreciate an update on injuries and losses."

"Not a problem. We've had losses, but I choose not to dwell on numbers. Injuries? We're handling those with few problems. I will say I'm clashing with a few of the earthlings. I've never met such a bunch of obstinate individuals and so prideful."

"An understatement from my dealings with them. And Quil?"

"We repaired the damage, and with accelerated healing, she's close to release. Scarring is still to be removed. That's the reason I'm here. I do want to point out a couple of things before I begin that process. Give me a couple of minutes. I want her sedated a while longer."

Prex watched a robotic arm moved to the hollow of an elbow as a slender cylinder rested on a vein. A radiating light shifted from one damaged area to another.

"Look here," Jessie tapped a screen, "scarring from her very early years past."

As Prex viewed the monitor, Jessie pulled back the coverlet to expose Quil's legs. "What do you make of this?"

"A projectile wound—from a gunshot? Muscles were damaged when it was dug out with a blade of some type.

Primitive handling. It may account for the odd twist to that leg, impaired muscles, and possibly the reason for her unsteady movement at times."

"I agree. She couldn't have over four or five when she received that wound. The damaged leg muscles are responsible for the in-toeing condition you noted. And there are other scars. She experienced a great deal of physical trauma in her early years. I can remove old scarring, but she'll carry the damaged muscles for a lifetime. There's no question she can endure physical pain; emotional pain may be a different matter.

"Why do you say that?"

"I've quietly analyzed Quil since the first day we met. Many recognized that she was uncommon, but I sensed something … let's say unconventional, about her. She trusts few people, balks at closeness. The formative years could be the reason she spends too much of her time alone. I've seen a hunger in her eyes, like she's searching for something or someone, possibly her true identity or maybe the person she wants to be. But she's built a barrier around her, and that type suffers greatly from those they lose, although they'll hide it. That's my take. I must look in on other wounded now. The scar removal is in process. Stay if you like. She'll float in and out and might talk to you. Don't allow her to leave." Jessie hurried away.

"Do you hear me, Quil?" He received no response. "Your early years explain your combative tendencies. You've made yourself a warrior, by design or by necessity, and you're a good one. My take? I see a small, indomitable spirit trying to convince the world she's hard-edged and invincible. But under that hard shell, I sense a softness and a need. But I am puzzled by the preternatural power you've recently displayed."

Preternatural power? I wonder? His thoughts moved to an ancient myth concerning the origin of the first sentient beings. The Watchers, protectors of this universe. The legend tellers say only the strongest warriors are sent on certitude missions. Implanted in a womb to experience life in a troubled world, from birth, they learn the means of survival and ways of a warrior. In a measured awakening, they then come to know their purpose.

"Is it possible you're now in a gauged waking? That could account for the abilities recently unleashed. If that's the case, you've been placed here for a reason. It'll be interesting to see what that is, but whatever it is, it'll be consequential."

"What do you know, commander?" Quil's eyelids fluttered.

"You're on your way to recovery. We expect the Cyon force within days. The Guard is in the outer belt heading for Mars. Get better, soldier. Battles are ahead of us."

"I've been here too long."

"A day and a half at most. Not long."

"This bed could use a pillow."

"I'll pass on that recommendation."

"Do you know you trill your *r's?* It's very noticeable when you say a lot of words with a lot of *r's*. I like it. It's cute."

"Cute?" His laughter filled the room.

"Uh-hum. I want to get up now." She reached for his hand. His fingers curled around hers.

"I'm not to let you up. You need more time. Perhaps later today or tomorrow." But she didn't hear; she was sleeping again. "Your softness is not too deeply buried." He smiled, squeezing her hand.

In the hallway, he met Wolf charging toward Quil's room. "Have you approval to enter the medical chambers?"

"I don't need approval! I have injured in this facility."

"I'm not letting you in Quil's room with that anger you're carrying. She's not to blame for—"

"Yes, she is! I tried to keep them safe, but she'd have none of that. You're not free of fault either. I sent them home, but you put them in the middle of the fight."

"I did and would again. We can take this elsewhere if that's what you want, but the injured need time to recuperate."

"Some can't recuperate!"

"There'll be no yelling in my hospital," said Jessie. "You're not cleared to be here, Wolf. Leave now. I told you I'd let you know when—"

"You can't make me leave. These are my people."

"I'm Procyon, Wolf. I can toss you like a sack of lint. Don't test me."

"Stop the fighting. Please, not here." Gracie rushed toward them with Inger and Tilde close behind. "The doctor needs to care for the injured. Come with me now, and don't argue." Taking Wolf's arm, they left the center.

"Jessie, we're here to sit with Quit," said Tilde. "If it's okay with you."

"Good. She'll wake soon and demand answers. Prepare her as you can. I'll fill in the medical facts later."

"Hey, bright eyes," said Inger. "It's about time you stopped slacking off and rejoined us."

"I'm glad you're both here. What about the squad, Four?"

"Good and bad. Don't get up yet," seeing Quil swing a leg over the side of the pod.

"Where're my clothes?"

"I brought fresh clothes but lay back and let us catch you up on things."

"Listen to her," said Inger.

"I don't like the tone of that, but go on."

"As you've probably figured out, we took the wilderness fortress. Our people are converting the Compound tunnels to a med center and sheltering rooms. News of the invasion is being telecast worldwide, and thousands are working diligently to save what people they can."

"You say it's being broadcast internationally? How did that come about?"

"The young girls you saved on the mountain," said Inger. "Their team is transmitting twenty-four seven. Here, I'll show you, " removing a tablet from her shoulder bag and placing it in Quil's lap.

On screen was Ruth, talking non-stop. Quil's attention was drawn to military milling about and Rebecca and Adam standing nearby. "I want to talk to them. I need a cell." Inger handed her one.

"Rebecca, this is Quil. I see Ruth's broadcasting. How did you get on TV?"

"Hi, Quil. When we got word the public had to be alerted to the impending attack, I remembered we had placed a recorder high on the mountainside to get a video of aliens. Six and Gracie took us back up there, and we found it. We got all of it. Proof of the aliens and the military traitors' involvement. We aired it locally, and it spread like wildfire. Now, we're worldwide news. But the military has come apart. The regular troops are after the turncoats as well as top officials who betrayed us. We didn't figure on our own military fighting each other. Josiah and Adam are also broadcasting, trying to bring about order. Hang on, Ruthie wants to talk to you."

"Quil. It's me, Ruthie. Did we do things right? We didn't plan on this ballooning like it has. Our military established help centers, and we mainly tell people how to get to them."

"That's great. But go to shelter as soon as you get the alert. That looks like Adam on your left. If it is, I'd like to talk to him now."

"This is Adam. Things have gone ballistic, but I think we're effective in spreading the news."

"Great to hear. What's happening with the compound conversion?"

"All to the good. Military units have located thirteen stories of caverns just at that one location. Dozens of mechanical types are upgrading air, water, and sanitation, plus medical quarters are being prepped. People everywhere are bringing in supplies by the semi-loads. Troops are exploring caverns at the wilderness base to see how best it can be used. Underground bases and tunnels are being located worldwide."

"Talk to Josiah or Wolf. The military has over a hundred known underground bases that can be used for defense."

"We've done that, and those bases are being taken over." Quil heard him talking to someone else. "I have to go now. We'll see you back at the center."

"Everyone's running on fear. But I don't know how else people could have been told. We're out of time." Tilde and Inger's faces were solemn. "What haven't you told me?"

"Our side did have people hurt … and lost," replied Tilde. "We couldn't get to our stranded unit. There's no easy way to say this. Five and Seven were killed." Quil felt Inger's arm around her shoulders.

"It's my fault. I was given a sign and didn't heed it soon enough. I'm to blame."

"You're not to blame," said Tilde. "Soldiers are lost in war."

"What about Seri and Two?" Tilde turned her face away. "What about Seri—"

"Injured." Tilde blurted out the rest. "They're damaged. Two lost both legs below the knees. Seri … half her face was … but the Cyon doctors—"

"I need to see them. Now!" Climbing from the pod, Quil walked toward the door.

"Wait!" Inger said. "The doctors can help, but Seribeth's being difficult."

"What does that mean!" As she opened the door, she ran headlong into Jessie.

"Back inside." Jessie had an arm around Quil, pulling her back to the med pod. "What's going on here?"

"We told her about Seri and Two."

"Quil, both are undergoing reconstructive surgery now. We can give them back what they lost. Are you hearing me?"

"I want my clothes. I need to see for myself." As Jessie talked, Tilde handed Quil a satchel.

"I'll show the before pictures—which will horrify you—but when you see the after results, I damn well expect a thank you for my surgeons' efforts. Especially since I had to heavily sedate Seri to counter her demand she not be restored. Are you getting what I'm saying, Quil?"

"Why would Seri not want restored?" Getting dressed had left her mind. She needed to understand.

"I'll answer that," said Tilde. "She insists on carrying the blame for those that we lost and were injured. She believes God's punishing her for killing innocent children. She thinks she's meant to wear her shame for all to see."

"The nursery children!"

"I took that decision out of her hands," said Jessie. "Obstinate mules, all of you. Here are the before images." Pictures of Two and Seri appeared on the screen.

"My god!" Quil gagged. Long strands of ragged sinews hung from Two's legs, or where her lower legs would have been. Seribeth's beautiful face was a bloody pulp, a hole where an eyeball once was, one cheek, part of her mouth, and chin gone. "I have to be with them, Jessie."

"You will be but finish dressing. You're not going out exposed. I run a reputable hospital."

"Oh, right. I'll hurry," she said, pulling clothing from the satchel. "Tilde, did you bring only bring blue underpants, nothing else?"

"I brought what's there."

"We'll talk about this later." Quil hurriedly dressed.

They followed Jessie down a passage, hearing loud yells as they approached an end room. "Obstreperous humans," said Jessie. Throwing the door open, they stood gawking at Suzie Two, wearing fire-engine red panties, admiring her image in a mirror. Tilde softly laughed as she walked toward Suzie.

On the other side of the room, a tall figure with her back to them yelled as she pulled up underpants of moonglow yellow. "Is this my only choice? Four, I'll throttle you good when I catch up to you! Get dressed, Susie; we need to find the others." Flicking bands, she was pulling up at the waist and down on the legs trying to find more garment than was available. And there was no hiding the yellow butterfly on her posterior.

Seeing them, Two chirped, "Hey, guys. Look at me. I'm bionic," prancing around like a high-stepping pony.

Seribeth turned. Quil release a long breath. Seri's face was fully restored. Seri rushed toward Quil.

"I lost them," she said, grabbing at Quil like she was the proverbial straw in a wild and savage sea.

"No, sister, *we* lost them." They held each other as tears fell.

A shuffling of boots preceded several figures out of breath and covered with dirt. "Sorry we're late," said Tres. Beside her were Gretchen, Emma Six, and the Tarsiers. "Our sisters are at rest. We interred Sophie and Maria in my family's burial ground outside Dulce."

"It was a nice, personal service," said Six. "Tres and Gretchen read poetry. You would have liked it."

"I'm sure we would," said Quil.

Seri pulled Tres into her arms and held her a long time, and Tres didn't object. Tres seemed at peace; perhaps she'd finally gotten to acceptance. After a hard stretch of bad road, they were together again. Now, they had to move on.

"Would you two put on some clothes," quipped Tres. "Hey, Tilde. What colors do those butterfly bikinis come in? I'm partial to black."

"I don't see you with butterflies, Tres. You're more a black satin thong type."

"The day will never come when you get me in a thong."

"I accept that challenge. I promised you a lingerie party. If it's okay with everyone, we can do that now. Might this be the right time?"

"Let's do stay together tonight," said Two. "I'd like you all close now."

"Oh god, so do I," said Seri. "And I haven't been to a lingerie party since college days. Make this one to remember, Four."

Quil's concern lessened, seeing the team bantering with each other. Bob and Fitzwilliam had remained at the door, seeming unsure if they should join the group. Quil motioned them over to sit beside her.

"They need this time together now," said Fitzwilliam. They must be with others who understand their pain."

"Oh, pretty!" exclaimed Bob. "Are you attending the affair, Quil? Look at all the pretty's."

"I've been assessed. I'm blue serenity. You should go. Tilde would be happy if you did." Bob joined the affair, holding up various colors of lingerie for Fitzwilliam to see.

"She's such a cutie pie," said Fitzwilliam, "and it's good to see her smiling again. Losing her children in the war erased her smile for quite a long time."

"I didn't know, and I'm sorry. Are you together?"

"No, we were co-pilots on a warship in the fight against the POX. We saw our planet explode; no survivors. Though we've grown much closer. Have you noticed I'm speaking loosely now?"

"Yes, I have. Both of you cutie pies are a part of our family now." She squeezed his hand, grinning when he looked embarrassed.

News spread around the hospital and many medical staff came in, asking to join the party. Arriving late, Jessie eased into a chair beside Quil, stretching out her long legs.

"All is good?" she asked.

"Not entirely, but I think it will be," said Quil, feeling an odd sadness, tinged with joy. Sad for the sisters they'd lost; glad for the sisters still here. She turned toward Jessie, hearing her breathed a sigh of relief.

"Thank you, Jessie."

"You're welcome, Quil.

thirty-five

The following day, Quil stopped in to see Ned, recovering from injuries and confined to a med chamber. "These doctors can do unheard-of things in this place. I was broken up bad but look at me now. Good as new or even better. Quil, I heard about your squad. I'm saddened to hear of your loss and the injuries experiencedly

"Thank you. We'll be okay. What are your plans now?"

"I'm joining my family at the Compound. I figure I can fight there as well as anywhere. Did you hear we lost Cedric?"

"I hadn't. I'm sorry, Ned. I knew you had taken him under your wing. Was it at the wilderness fortress?"

"Yeah, I was injured by flying rocks. Cedric was right behind me. I turned to find him and saw the ceiling collapse. We lost several in that incident. He struggled alone for so long; I hated to lose him. And there's Seri. Did you know he was fond of her? I'm not sure Seri knew that. Would you let her know when you think the time is right?"

"I will, and I'm glad you're joining your family. What about Jon?"

"He's helping convert the Compound lab into a hospital center. Inger and Gretchen have been busy collecting computers and schooling materials to start classes when this is over. I'm glad for their optimism. My dog and your little Blackbird are with my grandkids there."

"Oh, thanks for letting me know. I wondered …. Any news of the Nighthawks and those out west?"

"Yeah. Jim said to tell you they located what they were looking for and are entrenched."

"I'm glad they found cover. You know, it's strange, but with all we've found, we still don't know where the Dorper ewes were taken."

"And we may never know."

Quil had been twirling the feathered stave as they talked and suddenly remembered the hieroglyphs. "Ned, I need to see the Prioress now. I'll look you up as soon as I can get back to the Compound."

Catching a ride to the Cyon facility, she found the Prioress waiting as if she was expecting Quil.

"I'm glad you've rejoined us."

"Thank you, Prioress. I've come to ask for a favor. Can someone set me up on a printer? I need to run a document I'm hoping you can decipher. It's hieroglyphs, much like those on the raven wand."

"I'll provide one." The Prioress ordered a laptop brought to her meeting room. Quil stood behind the Prioress while she reviewed the documents, but something pulled her concentration away.

"Where's that music coming from?"

"I don't hear music."

"It's faint, sounds like string instruments. Wait … is it possible?" She ran to the hangar door. "It's the Wisps." Turning to rejoin the Prioress, she saw Josiah walking toward her.

"Hey, Quil. Glad you're back. Were you looking at that strange lenticular cloud hanging over the Wiminuche? Looks like another blizzard moved in. I bet it's ice cold up there."

"Did you say *ice cold?*" Her memory jumped to the dying traitor's words, *cold, ice, cold.* Was that what he was trying to tell her? "Do you recall the elevation of that peak, Josiah?" seeing Josiah following her pointing hand.

"That'd be Pale Creek Mountain, and it's right at fourteen thousand feet. One of the highest …."

Quil ran back to the Prioress. *A place few would venture.* "I have to go, Prioress," grabbing her backpack.

"Where do you go, Quil?'

"I don't know."

With windows down, Quil followed the music. In the wilderness, deep snow on the back road she traveled forced a stop. Checking the rear hold, she removed cold-weather gear, hoping it'd be enough. No rifle. Hers had been buried under rubble, and she'd overlooked getting another. So be it; she had to move on. The snow came to her knees. The elevation wasn't granting needed oxygen either, forcing her to stop often.

GGGRRR! GGGRRR!

"Oh, no!" Struggling to get away from the roar, Quil stumbled toward a stand of pines, fell against a tree, and froze. The roar came from a gigantic ghost grizzly. Near the bear was an eagle, thrashing about, holding a snake in its talons. More were striking from below, their fangs glistening in the sun. *Snow snakes?* The great golden bear grabbed the snakes, whipping them against a tree trunk. The eagle flew to a branch, awkwardly landing with one wing drooping, then fell to the ground. Slinging the vipers aside, the bear started for her. *Oh, god! Lower your eyes, play dead.* Keeping her head down, she tried to see through lowered lashes.

Suddenly, the scene pixelated. Everything changed to tiny dots; the eagle, the snakes, and the giant bear faded away.

"What the devil was that about! A warning?" She quickly looked around, hoping not to see a bear. "I read ghost grizzlies had disappeared from the Wiminuche decades ago."

Then she saw them.

Tracks. Large bear tracks leading up the mountain. *There's at least one left up here.* The claw imprints measured three to four inches, and the stride would put it at about ten feet. On the plus side, it had packed down a track she could follow, one she hoped wouldn't lead straight into its claws.

The trail followed a river with banks both steep and muddy. She briefly stopped at a waterfall to scout for bears trolling for fish; she saw none and kept on. She was making good time but questioned why she didn't feel any wind from the cap cloud. "This isn't right. Winds gust over fifty knots in lenticular."

Ahead was the cloud, so thick her eyes couldn't pierce it. Pausing, she listened to an ominous wind moaning through the pines. *I've come this far, I can't stop now.* She stepped across the demarcation line into a different world. Nothing felt right. A haze, overly heavy, covered the sky like a blanket. It seemed unreal, simulated. *This is extreme dark sorcery. I don't think I should be here.* She reversed to go back down the mountain.

Crack, crack, crack. Massive ice swords cut into the crusted snow blocking the way out from under the veil.

"So I go on." Turning up her collar, she struggled against cutting winds and stinging ice pellets. In little time, the end of the trail came into view, a crevice in the mountainside. She was being led straight to it. *Be hibernating, big bear.*

Cautiously entering, the cave was smaller than expected. She saw no bear but heard rhythmic breathing coming from one end of the narrow chamber. But the Wisps harmonic sound was louder, coming from beyond a large granite boulder. *Now to attend the symphony. Let's see who's on the marque today and who's conducting.*

The boulder was wedged in from the other side. Quietly, she inched it away from her. Following it as it moved, she saw the bear cave had been cut down in size. Sadly, the great bear's mate was on the opposite side of the boulder; its skeletal remains against a wall of its prison.

Setting the boulder aside, she approached a steel door, opening it just enough to see what was ahead—a passageway. She wanted to know what lay at both ends, but she was at a decision point. Left, follow the music.

"Once, twice, thrice times done must be undone."

A cryptic utterance from the unknown. Quil waited, but it spoke no more. She edged on. The passageway ended at a moderately-sized cavern. Peered over a stone banister, instant rage boiled through her veins. Three rows of tables filled the lab, one holding human females, one with what could only be Dorper ewes, and one with hybrid females, older versions of the nursery children. All were connected to tubes and machines monitoring whatever required monitoring in this diabolical torture chamber.

At the far back wall stood scientists, insectoid Wisps, conferring before display screens, their long, feathery fingers continually sending out vibrating musical notes. *I've had my fill of that sound.* It was time to go vacant. She stepped into the chamber, seeing no sign of notice from the Wisps.

Walking every row, looking at every table, she wanted to cry. The wombs of Dorper ewes held life; she detected movement. *What are they carrying?* The essence of the human females had long since left their corporal bodies and now were kept usable through machine support. *We're more than this.* The hybrid females lay with vacant eyes staring at the ceiling or watching the scientists. *Why do you not protest? Can you not see your end?*

"Answers! I need answers!" Her scream echoed across the chamber. Panicked, the Wisps frantically searched for her. A few rushed toward an alarm panel with fingers of string reaching for levers.

"No, ya don't," she yelled. Pissed, she slammed them to the floor and against walls before shoving them into large glass vats; a mass of limbs struggling against each other.

"Who, who … are you an emissary of the master?" One meekly asked.

"I am an emissary." Not precisely a lie. "Tell me who you are and what you're doing to these females."

"Why, we're Mantian scientists involved in creating a new life form. We're highly-evolved; no other can match our abilities." Trying to right themselves in the vats, each fought to be at the top of the pile.

Roughly yanking one from a glass cask, she cemented it to a wall, knotting its fingers so it couldn't send signals, and clamped lids on the vats preventing others from doing the same.

"You on the wall, you do the talking. Tell me about this creation of a new life form."

"Yes, of course, you wish a report. We're on the very verge of success. It is true our past experiments failed; the hybrids did not possess reproductive organs. We still utilize human females, however they continue to reject the implanted fetus. We have made great gains using a lower life form to bear fertilized eggs—only to a certain point of maturity, you understand. We'll transplant the uterus containing the fetus to the hybrid females you see on the far tables. We're now ready to take that step and believe these impregnated hybrids will produce offspring. With that success, we will have mastered the creation of life."

"Rot! All of your esteemed brilliance, all of your grand scientific efforts, all the harm you've done to other species—for what purpose? You're imbeciles. You've created nothing more than idiot fabricants like the reptoid scientists—"

"We're superior to the reptoids! They make plastic models, manufacture rudimentary dolts, factory-made to mislead. Our life form will possess intellect and the ability to reason."

"A turnip is a turnip no matter what color dye you inject into it. Mixing genes is one thing; creating life is another. That's out of your hands. You can never create a sentient being. Look at your hybrid females. Look at what they never will possess, no matter how you apply your highly evolved scientific knowledge. Look at them!"

"I don't see …"

"Highly evolved! You're witless fools. Their eyes are vacant. They're without the light of a spirit. No matter how brilliant you may be or how hard you may try, you cannot create a soul."

The talking head turned to his cohorts encased in glass, raising his knotted fingers in an expression of hopelessness. They turned away from him. Resigned, he lowered his head.

He was the hanged man of the tarot deck. Upside down, hanging by one foot, he was entangled by his doing and unable to liberate himself. The scientists resorted to cruelty to retain life for themselves—few gamble with Fate and win.

"You think too highly of yourselves, but putting that aside, I don't believe you're contemptible enough to dream up this nightmare. Who ordered this?"

"The master. We must obey, or the master will send the changling beast to devour us."

"What beast did you say?"

"I dare say no more," refusing to look at her. Those in the vats did the same.

"Then what good are you." She moved back to the walkway, looking across the chamber. "What's the good in any of this?" With a flick of the wrist, all support measures fell away from what lay on the tables

The law of the Shield: Guide the innocent; protect the worthy; destroy the unrighteous."

"I know those words."

Of a sudden, a stillness settled over her. Closing her eyes, she felt an inner intensity swelling. Abruptly, her eyes snapped open, swamping the room with bolts of electricity. Blue fire flashed, flesh incinerated, finely powdered ash swirled into the air only to vanish. She fell back against the wall.

Burning brimstone turns all to ash."

"Brimstone?"

"This then is their portion of the cup."

"Portion of what cup? And who's that talking?"

Alarms! Lights flashing, sirens blaring! The burning brimstone had set them off. She ran through the passageway, feeling a tremor beneath her feet. Ahead was a door. She rushed inside only to see a sky port closing. A departing ship morphed into a glowing ball, then to a translucent vessel with dangling tentacles. The port sealed.

"Too late. I'm too late."

She leaned over the balcony. The place was empty. Unguarded was a battery of artillery emplacements, supercomputers, and communications equipment. *They bolted. Why?*

"Is this another fortress? But there's only one ship's bay. It's the lair of the *Genius Malignus*.

Again, vibrations. A double door on the passageway gave the answer. Sighting a panel, Quil hit a button, and the door spread wide, exposing a multi-channeled expressway.

"A zip-line transport system. The Cyon Force needs to know of this right away." Beside the door was a schematic of routes. Ripping it from the wall, she shoved it in her backpack.

thirty-six

In the cave of the bear, the massive creature lay beside the bones of his mate. It raised its head, its eyes following Quil's movements, but it did not contest her presence. "You're where you want to be." There was nothing keeping them apart now.

She hurried down the mountain. The sinister white cordon lay ahead. Would she be blocked from leaving again? "No, I'm getting out of here." As fast as the snow permitted, she loped across the demarcation line, not stopping to looking back. Continuing on, she mused about puzzle pieces. How do they fit together? The scientists' description of the master and its beast fit the *Genius Malignus*. Whoever it was had both the wisps and the reptoids under its control. Fear controlled the scientists, but the reptoids were not fearful types, however they would submit in exchange for power. The *Genius Malignus* had to be the red-robed figure on the mountain. *Why would it need to know the secret of creation?*

Umph! Slipping, she went down on a knee. *It was getting hot. Snow was melting.* Placing her gun in the backpack, she tied her jacket around her waist. Spying her standing still, vexsome crows decided to check her out. "Shoo! I have no food for you. Shoo!"

Back to the bizarre scientists? Did they genuinely think the elementary grafting of sheep organs into the hybrids would succeed? Not a chance of that happening, and they knew it. They were boiling the ocean, try anything to convince the master they'd succeeded. Buying time was what they were after. If their acts weren't so repulsive, they'd warrant pity. However, they had brought forward new information. What is a changling beast that devoured people?

274

A sorcerer could trance a person into thinking they were seeing the bizarre. But a projection that actually devoured? Not possible. It had to have been imagined, only mind trickery. Following that thinking, did flesh actually vaporize? Or was that a ruse, magic hocus-pocus to deceive her into thinking she burned flesh to ash? She couldn't or wouldn't have done that. She must have been spell struck. It didn't happen.

(Woeful sigh) "Are you wise, thinking like a fool, or a fool, thinking you're wise?"

That brought her to a standstill. "So you're back. Here's one for you, whoever you are. The truly *wise* rarely speaks. The fool talks too much. Take the hint." A spirited wind rustled through the pines as if laughing at her. "And now Drub, you're being a *wise* ass." *Drub? What's a Drub?* Hearing the waterfall in the distance, she broke into a jog.

"Shoo! Get outta here!" The nettlesome crows were back, swinging an arm to drive them away. *Uhhh!* She was sliding toward the river. *No, no, don't—* She lunged for a tree limb.

"Nooo! Let me go!" Trying to beat off whatever had grabbed her, she slid down the bank, dragging whatever held her down too.

"I have you, Quil! Stop fighting!"

"Prex!"

He had hold of the jacket tied at her waist. In the struggle, it gave way. She grabbed for him, snagging a leg, and wrapped around it.

"Turn loose! You're pulling me down!"

No way was I turning loose of that leg. I didn't like what I saw below. Downward momentum was increasing. His wings dug into the muddy bank, but they couldn't hold them. They were headed for rocks and rough rapids.

Shaking her off, Prex grabbed her backpack, pulling her face down through mud, tossing her in a snowbank at the top. Coughing in fits, she spit mud, blew it out her nose, and wiped it from her eyes which did little good as her hands were thick with it. All of her was thick with it.

"You startled me. I tripped," rubbing snow on her face to clear eyes and mouth.

"I saw you go over the edge but couldn't get to you soon enough."

He was mud-covered head to foot. All her fault, she reasoned. Felling an apology in order, she walked toward him at the exact moment he agitated his wings, throwing mud in her face like BB pellets. "Ow! That stung!"

"I didn't intend …" Seeing her with fistfuls of muck, he turned his face away, expecting a wad to the head. It didn't come. He chanced a glance, seeing her toss the mud to the ground.

She knew he didn't mean to do that, but he'd let her pelt him with mud like the snowballs—to a point. He'd shaken her 'til her teeth rattled when he'd had enough.

"I can attempt to retrieve your coat later; my immediate requirement is to remove the mud."

"Let the jacket go. I don't need it."

"Are you intact?"

"I am, but you don't seem to be. Your feathers are doing odd things."

"I only need a cleaning." Shifting his weight from one foot to the other, he seemed embarrassed by his condition, perhaps feeling a little vulnerable. She found that sweetly appealing.

"A waterfall's ahead. You can wash your wings there."

"A shower would help. You walk to the inland. I may not retrieve you if you fall again."

"Yes, you would." She said softly.

He crooked an eyebrow. That side glance and slight arch of the brow was his quiet language. She was learning to read him.

"So do you cruise around here often?"

"My first time this way. The Prioress mentioned you had been gone too long. Josiah told me of your talk about the cap cloud."

"It was good of the Prioress to worry about me, wasn't it?"

"I may have inquired of your absence." He grinned.

"And we're here, "motioning across the broad river, the roar of the falls drowning out conversation. The river spread across a rocky bluff created numerous cascades that dropped into a basin below.

"Yes, this will cure the problem. I'll take the large fall on the far side. You take a smaller one here."

He charged into surging current de-mudding his plated armor. Casting that aside, he stood naked as a jaybird enjoying the spray of a lawn sprinkler. The sheen of water on his back glistened in the afternoon sunlight—what an extraordinary being. *If there are others like him, I wonder why they haven't been seen?* Soon he would be back to his stunning self. On the other hand, she looked to be in the final stages of root rot.

Determined, she marched under the larger of two falls and staggered, the force of water near driving her to her knees. Duck walking out the other side, she sputtered. "Different tact called for."

The niche pleased her, a private space hidden behind foaming water. Leaves of nearby trees threw dappled shadows over smooth flat rocks. Peaceful, just what she needed. Sliding the backpack under a stream, she watched the mud roll off. Next, she beat her clothes on rocks to coax the mud out. That left her. She eagerly stood under a gentle cascade, cold as it was, to remove the grime. Done, she rifled through my pack, hoping to find socks, a t-shirt, anything dry but found nothing. Repacking items, she was about to replace the raven wand when she heard loud thrashing. Rushing from the alcove, she saw Prex flailing his wings, but it was what was on his arm that startled her

"My scarf?" She took a step toward him.

Hearing her voice, he saw her looking at the brightly colored favor he wore like a knight in a joust. And he saw her step toward him. It was all he needed.

He's coming for me. As he moved closer, he ran a hand through his hair, pushing it back from his face, sending water droplets down his chest. So held by his presence, she was unaware she still held the wand.

"I'm with you now." His hand rested on the stave.

"I knew they were yours." letting it go. His breath tickled her ear like a soft caress. Taking her hands, he kissed her fingers.

"Let me hold you, Quil."

"I want this. I want you." Heart racing, she eased into his arms. His head resting against hers; they simply breathed together. Hearts confessed, souls balanced, none other existed except them

"Time belongs to us now." Lifting her chin, his mouth, parting slightly, covered hers. She felt his hands caressing her breasts, move to her waist. Not waiting longer, he carried her to the private alcove, veiled by surging water falling to an accepting pool.

"Are you warm?" She lay on his shoulder, his wings draped over her. All was perfect, until ….

"What? Say again." Quil sat up, straining to hear over the noise of the waterfall.

"Forward must come. Look to the other side of tomorrow. Beware the vengeance of the bitter disgraced. Lies are not lies, truths are not truths. The deadly two seek to destroy."

"What is it, Quil?"

"Do you sometimes hear voices?"

"You speak of the mystical. No, but I have heard the Prioress talking to the unseen. Did you receive a message?"

"Yes. Many are confusing and take time to decipher. This one said. in brief, we need to move on."

"Return with me."

"I need my vehicle, but I'll hurry and meet you back at the Cyon base."

"Keep our line open. I want to know of your whereabouts at all times."

Bumping down a rutted road toward the highway, Quil thought about their time together. "That was about as perfect as perfect can get. Though a bit of chocolate would be good."

She swerved to miss a chughole. *What was that?* Braking, she backed up, trying to make out words on a faded sign thrown in the brush. *Double Down Mine, 2 miles* with an arrow pointing to the northeast.

"Isn't that the mine where Cedric met with the EPA reps on dumping in the river? But that road hasn't been serviced in a very long time. Why is the sign in the ditch? And, that's odd." Tree branches on either side of the trail had been broken as if struck by something heavy.

She pulled under cover of trees, grabbed binoculars, and jogged toward the mine. The main building and supporting structures were dilapidated, out of use for years, but a semi-truck was backed to a dock. She felt the ground quake where she stood. "It's a terminal. This is how they got the Mantian lab from the Compound to the lair of the *Genius Malignus.*"

She hurried back to the car. Are there two Double Down mines? Non-producing shafts are sometimes abandoned when a new vein is found elsewhere. Or, did she misunderstand where Cedric was meeting with the EPA? "None of which matters as Cedric is dead. Identifying the poser behind the destruction of planets is my priority.

thirty-seven

Main thoroughfares around Durango were packed with stalled vehicles. People were seeking safety. Quil wasn't moving. Seeing an escape route open, she left the highway, rammed a barbed wire fence, and cut across fields to uncongested back roads. Nearing the Cyon facility, she saw the reason for peoples' terror. Immense warships filled the sky. "It's either the Procyon fleet or the Guard Command."

Hurrying inside, she saw troops of both armadas milling with the Citizen force. Pushing her way through the crowd, she was met by Prex who had seen her enter."

"You experienced delays in route?"

"Gridlock on the highways. I'm sorry I missed the arrival of the Guard."

"The main force is near Mars, the primary point of defense. The Procyon fleet is holding there; however, they'll be shielding from the moon. The Earth forces will defend from the planet."

Gene, Jessie, and the Spider squad joined them. "We were worried, Quil. Where were you?" asked Seri.

"I located the genesis lab. I can show you on a map." Opening her backpack, the placard she'd taken from the lab corridor fell to the floor.

"What's this," asked Gene, picking up the placard.

"A train schedule. An underground zipline stops at all locations listed there."

"Genesis lab? You mean where the Dorper sheep were taken?" asked Seri.

"Yes, and that's not all they took there. I'll show you." On a nearby wall, she projected, the lab, Mantian scientists, and tables of victims. Moans came from the Spiders. Quil switched to the layout of the Malignus lair, focusing on the communications equipment, artillery, and the zipline entrance.

"Those scientists must be eliminated immediately," said Gene, openly incensed.

"They're gone now," said Quil, quickly changing the topic. "I also found an underground terminal at an abandoned mine. That's how they got the genesis lab from the Compound to the mountain lab."

"We need control of all station that feed that line," said Prex. "You'll be with me, Quil."

"Quil stays with me, said the Prioress, joining them. "Prex, you and the others go on. Quil and I will talk now."

"That mountain-top bunker is ours," said Seri. "It'll make an ideal com center for the forces here on Earth."

"I'll stay with the Prioress," said Quil, sensing it imperative she meet with the Prioress. "The Spiders will go with you, Jessie, if that's alright."

"Perfectly so. Let's move out." She waved the Spiders toward her spacecraft.

Quil and the Prioress sat in an anteroom, the Carian protectors just outside the door. "Prex said you receive messages from the unseen. I surmised that already. I know about you without knowing about you. Do you understand?"

"No, afraid not. Please speak plainly. Too often, the messages I receive must be puzzled over."

"Tell me of those messages, recent ones."

"One said a deceitful one moves like the tide, being near and then afar. That could be anyone of hundreds."

"Too general. I believe it would be helpful if I speak of antiquity and you allow your mind to travel with the unseen. I am of an ancient race. There is but one more ancient. The old kingdom. Do you know of it?"

"I know nothing of the old kingdom." Quil paused, the room had lost its edges, leaving them centered in shadows.

"Not surprising. Not many have recollections of the old realm. It was created with the first tick of time. Those of the kingdom were granted the ability to perform astonishing feats of magic. Known as the Crystalline, they could move between a state of dynamic crystal to a physical state of flesh and bone and back again."

"Shapeshifters then. Prex mentioned the Crystalline once walked the planet Tiamat but were thought destroyed when the planet erupted."

"They did walk Tiamat, but they weren't destroyed with the planet. They couldn't have been. They're the immortal."

"Immortal? If that's true, where are they? The Prioress held up a finger, pointing to the center of her eyes.

"Resume your wandering. Think of a person who moves like the tide. Were other words given in that message?"

"Yes. Something about a professor of knowledge being a façade. Again, that could be anyone, even you, Prioress. How do I determine the right one."

"Exclude no one in your search. Someone hides behind a truthless guise."

"There isn't enough time left in the hour glass to consider everyone."

"Make time work for you." The Prioress resumed speaking of Tiamat. Quil's mind drifted, envisioning her image walking the lost planet of Tiamat.

"Sadly, the perfect world was rent asunder and scattered throughout the heavens. She of the Shield, the relentless huntress, was sent to find *him*, the one who had turned dark."

"What was that about a huntress?"

"A fierce warrior known as A'albé, the protectress of the twelve."

"The twelve … that seems familiar ."

"It was he, the one who had veered from his calling, the magnificent magus, the most wise of the intercessors, who wreaked havoc—"

"Wait. The magus? The reptilian females used that term, but an intercessor's primary order is to serve as counselor." The Prioress's voice was entrancing pulling Quil into her mind, seeing as she did.

"Find him, she did. Captured, she cast him into a shadowed bay to reintegrate to wholeness—"

"That can't be right. It would fall to the Heraldry, the minders of the law to assign punishment."

"The Heraldry, of course. The wisdom council would make judgment."

"I remember another message. Beware the vengeance of the bitter disgraced. Lies are not lies; truths are not truths. The deadly two seek to destroy."

"Who are the deadly two?"

"The magus and the *genius malignus*, though I don't know their real identity. The bitter disgraced is one I feel I should know."

"Ah! And now perhaps, this will help" The Prioress placed the page of hieroglyphs on the table. "I can't decipher this for you, but you need no help." Quil looked at the paper.

"I've studied this before and don't understand …" But as Quil watched, the glyphs swirled in a twisting vortex. Spinning wildly, letters flew from the maelstrom like rags, slapping onto the paper and forming words.

"No, it can't be! Shoving her chair, it flew against the wall. "The Edit of Nefar-ex!"

"Nefar-ex!" The Prioress quickly stood, a hand at her throat. "The destroyer of Tiamat!" She quickly closed the door. The Carians tried to enter but were waived away. With faces pressed to the glass, they watched as the Prioress tossed handfuls of unassailable dust to the four corners of the room. "Speak softly now for fear of who might hear."

Quil scarcely heard her words, a confluence of memories flooding over her. There was a disturbance in the universe, agitation in the ebb and flow of the celestial sea. The stirrings seemed to convulse from the twelfth garden. She volunteered to go obscure and live among those of the garden world to learn the cause of the rumblings. The shadows between spheres trembled, and *I knew wo I was and why I was here*!

"I understand now, Prioress. Nefar, a Crystalline who'd forsaken his duty, decreed he would rule the perfect realm of Tiamat or else destroy it. The citizens of Tiamat refused his edict, and in an attempt to instill fear with an explosive, instead blew the planet asunder. What remained came to rest as the third planet of the Sol system, an oceanic world located at the tip of Orion's ninth arm. Earth was granted the honor of being the twelfth garden. Labeled an outcast, Nefar was banished from existence, his name to forever carry the disgraced 'ex' in the eternal records.

"You remember well."

"Nefar-ex is the magus, the overseer leading the POX force in the destruction of worlds using his explosive energy collectors. He intends to destroy what remains of Tiamat. Earth is the target."

"But why leave the Edict to be discovered?"

"Always a game player, he's gloating, wanting us to know he's back. I sense an increase in his power. Someone has strengthened him, likely the one known as *Genus Malignus*."

"He's among us now. I feel the death knot tightening. How could one person destroy a planet in the breadth of a second?"

"He could be anyone. I must leave.

"What am I to tell Prex of our talk this day?"

"Nothing at this time. I hunt alone now."

"Carve out time needed and take evasive action as you must to remain safe. Prex will not hear of our words from me, but he will know. Do you not recognize him as one of mystery and unnatural power?"

"What do you mean? He may be a mix of species, Carian genes explain the wings, but that doesn't make him a mystery."

"Carian? Not so. He's winged, yes, but he doesn't possess Carian genetic material. He came to us when our world was under attack. Little could be gleaned from him. He knew the story of Tiamat's destruction and once spoke of his search for someone. Perhaps you?"

"H'm, I see. Then say nothing to Prex."

"Huntress, I'm honored to stand with you."

"The honor is mine, Prioress. I must go." Taking the Edict, she hurried out.

tick the 3rd

Seek it with thimbles … seek it with care.

Do all that you know and try all that you don't;
not a chance must be wasted today!

—Lewis Carroll
The Hunting of the Snark

thirty-eight

How could he do that, the Prioress had asked! How could one person decimate a planet in the breadth of a second? By finding the correct equation, *that's how!* Think about it. A Mars dune buggy engineered to operate three months max still ambled along after fourteen years. Where does that power come from—the atmosphere, *that's where!*

Then think what could be done by harvesting that power, channeling it into easily accessible crystals—magnifying crystals, prismatic power collectors—and igniting that explosive power with a chain of photon bullets. Tiny photons freely darting about the cosmic sea, with little power singularly, but enhanced, they become a fast-moving directed-energy force—and what do you have? A planet destroyer—*that's what!*

From stardust we came; to stardust, we return. And the bloody bastard who figured it all out is back. Good night, sleep tight, don't let the bed bugs bite. *Pfft.* Signing off now with a Merry Christmas to all and to all a good night. The wheel turns; nothing is ever new. Power brings destruction; destruction brings power. BOOM! *This in-between time is coming to an abrupt end—permanently— unless I stop him.*

The pieces of the puzzle now had faces, too many faces. *A staccato beat pounded in my head. Go with the rhythm; work it down, work it down.* Consider a candidate of chaos, a deceitful causer of distrust and discord. Or, a wily coyote, hiding behind scrub, waiting for a chance to pounce on the guileless, the innocent. Or, a manipulator, the puller of puppet strings from behind a curtain, laughing at his brilliance as he duped the audience and exclaiming, *oh, what fun!*

Exclude no one the Prioress had said. Consider contradictions, missteps, acts … acts? Anyone who had performed acts of goodness, kindness, thoughtfulness then slung out hostility, causing mayhem. *I don't have time for this! Speed it up! Think!*

What about those near and far. *Scrap the far! Stay with the near.* Okay, there's Seribeth. A good heart, here to caretake this world, but she wouldn't dally around if she wanted to cause harm. She'd drop 'em to the mat. No, it can't be her. What about Tres? A hurting heart but a caring heart who laid to rest two of our sisters with respect and love. She's out to kill enemies, not those she stands with. Any of the Spider Squad? Tilde, an admitted witch, a caster of charm-spells, but only for good. Suzy Two, endowed with a hyperactive sex drive—that's ridiculous, she could hide anything. Emma Six, the student dedicated to carrying on the culture of her Ute people. Inconceivable to think it could be her. It's none of the Spiders. Hitting the garage opener, I pulled inside too fast, almost ramming the back wall. Grabbing the Edict off the seat, I ran inside.

Eliminate the dead, two of our squad and Cedric. Cedric, a tormented cynic. He'd be my first choice, but he's gone, buried in the tunnels. Ned, the preacher man, saw it happen. Preachers? Gracie and Adam? No, there's not a splinter of darkness between the two. Ned? What about Ned? A minister who teaches killing? Could it be him? Yet, I've seen him care for those in need, and Albert trusts him. Albert? What about him? A shaman guide who sees visions in smoke. Impossible. He's too honest and outspoken to be devious. But that ugly witch who took my aviation watch—no, forget her.

Of course, the military men. Yes, those specially trained to stalk, trap, kill. But they put themselves out on the fringe, becoming targets in a shooting gallery to protect those at home. It wouldn't be them.

Then who! Who have I missed? The off-worlders? They lost their home planets and journeyed here to try to save this one. No, can't see that. The blue Cyons? Gene, irritatingly arrogant but balanced by Jessie's calm counter side. No, they came here of their own accord to help. But the winged Carian who's not a Carian. The perfect man, totally disarming me with his very being. Could it possibly be him? He came to

Earth alone. Would that be a standard assignment? Would the Provenance Guard send a lone warrior to tackle a problem of such immensity? *Of course, they would. I'm sent out as a lone hunter, aren't I?* I refuse to believe it's Prex. We're bonded, our minds and … but what did the Prioress say about him being a mystery? No time for that now. Move on!

Pacing, I tried to cram puzzle pieces together. Of course—professors of knowledge—teachers, Inger and Gretchen! *Get a grip!* Gretchen, a bookish schoolmarm who mentors kids at a kitchen table? Jon, her sweetheart, an out-for-fun guy, coaching kids in outdoor activities. Plus, he saved Blackbird. What about Inger? A poet-philosopher who wears a bunny tail, karmic t-shirts, and receives danger alerts? Impossible. She's too busy contending with chickens, ducks, and all manner of fowl.

Where am I going with this!

Tone it down. Slow the chaotic energy swirling around me. The tick of the clock on the mantle served as a devilish reminder of time passing. *Carve out needed time.* With a snap of fingers, the clock stopped, the hands failed to move. Candles on the hearth flickered to life. Light is the symbol of knowledge. *See through the fire; the answer is in this room.*

Think back. What happened here? Deliberations, debates, arguments. Scenes floated out of the flames, my eyes leaping from one to another and another, always returning to one name, the most obvious name. *Cedric.* But Seribeth believed in him, and Cedric is dead. Ned saw him buried alive—although any sorcerer worth his salt could cast a muddle, a dummy scene.

Cedric? Is he the devious manipulator, a poser hiding behind a bearded mask, or is he the last survivor of a secret delegation searching for the deplorable, deep black project? Most certainly, he was a sneak, prowling my house in the dark—and fractious, demeaning, seeming to lead people astray. But he dispelled that distrust by sharing special knowledge of the joint alien/military operations. *Special knowledge! He's a professor of knowledge.* But they'd worked together pushing the Hummer to escape the mountain and stood together against the two enemies in the bookstore. Or were those ruses? No, he led the interrogation of the traitor in the Shadow Squad, even stuck cigarettes in his eyes. But did he also block words of the turncoat that could implicate him as the enemy? Still, he moved into my townhouse to protect us—or was it to keep an eye on me? He is the logical candidate. But I have to be sure. Hunches didn't count. Time can't be wasted chasing the wrong suspect. One piece of the puzzle, no matter how small, just one piece had to fit.

"I need to know." I checked the calendar and saw that Cedric was scheduled to be at the Double Down Mine. *But was he there?* The computer was slow, the world's information links going down, but finally, I found the EPA schedule showing a meeting at a Double Down Mine … which had been canceled. *H'm, Cedric didn't inform us of that cancellation.* Checking further, I found a Cedric O'Malley who had served in a low-ranking Air Force position and one who had been a middling law enforcement officer in Colorado. No commendations, achievements, nothing of significance noted for either post. The first rule of power—stay hidden, don't draw attention to yourself—until you're ready to take over. *Lies are not lies; truths are not truths.* Was his life a sham? Had he given shades of truth, fragments of lies?

Running out of the house toward Cedric's townhouse, a small spirit animal appeared beside me, first as sparkling crystal then in physical form. "Where have you been, little dog?" Entering Cedric's place, Bird instantly began checking dark corners, under furniture, and behind doors. A quick walkthrough revealed clothing strewn about, ashtrays filled with butts, and wine glasses cluttering tables. A desk in one room had been cleared of all items. I walked to the back deck. He had a clear view of my place, allowing the monitoring of my activities, including meeting with Prex … and when to send fringe frights to tail us.

"There has to be something." Back inside, I climbed the stairs to his bedroom. The bed mussed, nothing in a bureau, the closet holding only slacks, shirts, jackets—*no, wait!* Wait a minute. On the upper shelf was a black, wide-brimmed western hat. Cedric had never worn a hat. Shoving clothes aside, a bright yellow shirt buttoned to the neck glowed in its garish contradiction to everything else. "The Bisti skinwalker! A two-faced coyote."

It is him! The game player who wanted me to run as he enjoyed the chase. Cedric was Near-ex, the fallen Crystalline. He wanted me to find this outlandish shirt, an obvious clue leading to him. Why? So I would know he'd been laughing at me all along.

"Well, now I know, Nefar. And now, it's time to turn this game around. You become the quarry, and I the hunter. We'll see who laughs last."

Searching every room, I found nothing to give insight as to where he was. Even the pantry and refrigerator had only empty shelves. Jerking a calendar off the frig door, I quickly scanned it, found no entries on any page, and sailed it across the room. "Nothing. Where would he be?"

Yip, yip. On the way back to my place, I turned at Bird's bark, seeing her dragging the calendar. Dropping the papers, the dog laid her head down sideways, wanting me to look at something.

"Nothing's written on it, Blackbird, I've checked." The dog huffed in reply. "Okay, I'll take it, but nothing's there … or is there?" The spirit creature woofed and faded away.

In the living room, I studied the calendar month by month, week by week, day by day. "Nothing. But Bird saw something. Not written words, but something else. " Wiping the sheets clean, again, I scoured the pages. An astronomical calendar that showed moon cycles by month, times the sun rose and set, and the position of planets in the solar system. "It shows the movement of the planetary bodies throughout the year. What's the message that isn't written? Perhaps those?" Scattered around the solar system were minute-colored dots that changed location with each month. *It's a hidden code.*

"I'm coming in, Quil."

Prex charged through the door, gathering Quil in his arms. "You didn't keep the line open."

"Something came up."

He moved the hair away from her face. "No new head injuries, at least." Sitting with Quil in his arms, he placed his feet on the ottoman.

"Now we talk. Report. What do you know?"

"Must I remind you that I don't report to you?"

"But you will report, little goat." He spoke gruffly while grinning.

"Okay, a bad sort, Nefar-ex, posed as a human named Cedric. He was right here in this room, and I didn't detect him. Nefar-ex is an extremely adept dark sorcerer—no, he's a brilliant dark sorcerer who—"

"I know who Nefar-ex is. Have you settled on his whereabouts?"

"Not yet," wondering how he would know of Nefar-ex. "But take a look at this. The dots on this astronomical calendar are clues of some kind. What do you make them to be?"

They studied the pages, noting differences in alignment month by month. "Let me try something." Placing a finger on the month the dots first appeared, Quil chanted softly. "From first to last, reveal the course of your calling. Like diminutive bugs, the specks moved, intersecting, changing direction, until they arrived at a page where they came to a rest.

"It notes routes the POX will take to Earth," said Prex. "We anticipated they'd come from the Oort Cloud to Mars, the Moon, and then Earth. This indicates one arm of their armada has taken that route. But they've stationed regiments throughout the asteroid belt. They're already within the inner system. Earth is surrounded."

"Look beyond tomorrow. Words of the last message I received. They attack the day after tomorrow."

"And from every direction. Our forces must have these coordinates. We'll take the moon base at dawn to get the Procyon force in place. This is dark news. Our military will be spread thin." He sent a message to his troops.

They sat quietly, holding each other. Neither would tell the other to take care or say things lovers say on separating in a time of war. They'd been in endless battles and knew the outcome was not solely in their hands.

She didn't want him to go, but it had to be. A gentle gaze, a lingering kiss, and he was gone.

"If fate allows," I whispered.

thirty-nine

"Time to wake the dreamers." Quil closed her eyes, feeling energy emanating from within. A spiritous hum spread throughout the heavens.

"All are needed. Armor up! We fight!"

Someone approached. Turning, she saw Inger and Tilde walk through a wall, Inger pausing only long enough to maneuver her back into proper alignment to walk unfettered.

"He's back." Quil pointed to the Edict on the table. "Nefar-ex has been posing as Cedric."

"That scurrilous mongrel!" said Inger. "I thought he had a blinky milk stink about him."

"So the big bad is knocking on our door again," said Tilde. "Where do we start?"

"By getting as many as possible to safety. We'll try to do that through Ruth and Rebecca's worldwide broadcast. Then, it's war. Hopefully, we'll keep this planet." Snapping her fingers, the TV switched on. Rebecca was giving a news update.

> *. . . no reports on what the strange lights are in the sky. The military's tracking their movement by radar. The army informed us they will take defensive action if they're determined to be the enemy. We'll broadcast additional news as soon as we know more.*

Quil grabbed her phone and got Ruth on the line. "Ruthie, this is Quil. Can you hear me? The line's full of static. Tell me if you can hear me."

"You're weak, but I hear you. Do you see them, Quil? The angels in the sky? Do you see them?"

"Those are not angels, but they have come to help. It's time to tell people to go to safety."

"No, they're really angels. They're shiny with wings. Look out the window."

"Let me do this," said Inger. "Hi, Ruthie. This is Miss Inger. You were in my poetry class some time ago. Do you remember me?"

"Hi, Miss Inger. Can you speak louder, please?"

"Of course. Listen now. The shiny objects you see are magical beings who've come to help us slay the nasty dragons. Can you tell everyone that?"

"Magic beans? No, they're flying lights. I'm pretty sure they're not magic beans."

"The reception's bad," said Tilde. "Let me give it a go. Ruth, this is Tilde from the Spider Squad. Listen closely. What you see is the prismatic or reflective result of light on crystal that gives the impression of shiny wings, but they're not wings, and they're not angels. Do you understand?" Ruth didn't reply. On screen, she appeared to be staring vacant-eyed into space.

"Obviously not," said Tilde.

"Well, *pfft*, hand me the phone."

"Hi, Ruthie. It's Quil again. Just tell the soldiers not to shoot the frickin' angels. They've come to help. People must get to safety. Make that announcement. Now, put Emma Six on the phone."

"Six here, Quil. What's the word?"

"Get everyone underground. The enemy could be here within hours."

"I don't think Ruth hand Rebecca will go. They're determined to broadcast throughout the whole thing. I think they're carrying this too far, but I won't desert them. If they stay, I stay."

"Drag them underground if you must. Or set up the TV cameras in the tunnels and broadcast from the Compound stronghold."

"That could work." Six disconnected. Ruth was giving a broadcast.

*BREAKING NEWS! Do not shoot the frickin'
angels! They've come to help us. Spread the
word. It's time for everyone to get to shelter.
Go to safety now! And don't shoot the frickin'
angels!*

"Way to go," laughed Inger. "We'll be called before
the Heraldry for this."

"Wouldn't be the first time, and if they can do a better
job, let them get down here." They were laughing, but it was
a serious matter. They were immortal, yes, but immortals
could be hurt, put out of commission for a time, and everyone
able was needed in the fight.

"You two know the drill—half of the *Sachmet* forces
to the northern hemisphere, half to the south. I'm going for
Nefar-ex. I've found no clues to his whereabouts here, but
perhaps the all-knowing Assembly will lend a hand."

"How do you want to do this?," asked Tilde. "Flip for
it."

"You got a coin to call it?" said Inger.

"I have the first nickel I ever earned," said Quil,
taking it from her pack and giving it a spin. "Heads to the
north, tails south." she slapped the nickel on the back of a
hand.

"Heads," said Tilde, nodded on seeing what was
revealed.

"Let's get to it," said Quil. Instantly, the three
transformed into Crystalline, dressed in the standard gray
tunics, leggings and boots, light chest armor, and visored
battle helmets. The *Sachmet*, a fierce regiment of female
warriors allied with the Crystal Shield. Clasping arms, they
quietly voiced a solemn oath, *protect the worthy*. No other
words were necessary. They'd stood together like this all too
often. Quickly turning, Inger and Tilde disappeared through
the wall.

Alone, Quil quietly viewed a collection of items
scattered on the table, placed several box thingums the
Tarsiers had provided in a tunic pocket, and concealed two of
Seribeth's throwing blades in her boots. Waving a finger over

the raven wand, two glistening black feathers wrapped around her upper arms. Smiling, she whispered *thank you*, as she touched the faded photograph of Aunt and Uncle, placing the nickel beside the frame. On the hearth, the stone etching of Star People seemed to be calling to her. "I know. Here we are again."

"This has been one of the best havens I've had. I rather hate giving it up." She walked to a corner where a small, almost indiscernible, black speck was spinning a web. "Spin me a silken thread, small spider." A delicate filament wrapped around an outstretched finger. "I bequeath this haven to you."

On TV, crews reeled in electrical cords and rolled cameras toward vehicles. The screen went black. Hands of the clock speed forward to the present hour. Time moves but one direction; it cannot remain in the past. Neither could she. Giving one final glance around the room, she entered the night sky, pausing mid-air to listen. No night beetles chirped, no dogs barked in unison, no trees whispered in the wind; the unnatural silence a prelude to the coming thunder of war machines.

Above were fluttering lights, resembling fireflies released from a mason jar. The Crystal Sphere would respond to every soul; none would hesitate to answer the call. The *Heraldry*, proprietors of protocol; the *Bureau*, keepers of the eternal record; the *Intercessory*, givers of guidance; and the *Shield*, mighty spirit warriors of the mist who yielded to no other. Flying higher, she saw the world below also was lit. Highways had become rivers of headlights, streams of people on the move. She turned her focus to a glowing amber ball reclining in an ebony sky.

"Prex said he'd be on the moon at dawn. I'll be there before the cock crows."

It wasn't difficult to locate the Assembly's base on the far side of the moon. It was in full sun. The sometimes heard *dark side of the Moon* referred to what couldn't be seen from Earth, not that it was devoid of light. The surface blemished, immense craters could hide entire cities, but it couldn't hide what she was seeing. Ahead was an obelisk, rising at least twenty miles high and sporting a glass pyramidion apex. The grand-scaled spire, however, was seated amid a complex of ugly squat buildings. Certainly not the envisioned Olympus nestled above the clouds. Before descending, she flew a tight circle around the citadel, seeing no sign of activity. It looked deserted. Entering through a wall, she moved down a hallway toward a jumble of voices, expecting a chamber of marble and gold with the overlords decked out in royal finery and feasting on ambrosia and nectar collected, of course, from gardens of low-stature Earth dwellers. *My imaginings are not always on point.*

An assortment of species clad in dingy smocks milled around in a depressing room of sallow walls and tatty furnishings. Quite unimposing for the godheads they professed to be. Nor did their conduct rise to the stature of the divine, those responsible for decreeing death over life. Squabbling about actions they could or couldn't take to escape the inbound POX, they loudly placed the cause of the predicament on a pasty-faced Mantian scientist, musically lamenting the loss of the genesis lab. The only human present, a military officer, leaned against a wall with armed crossed at the chest, watching the others.

She moved next to him. "So, what's going on?

"They've been fighting for two days. The reptilians took all the ships, left none for this bunch—holy crap! Who are you! Where are you!"

The Assembly members stopped ranting to stare at the officer. "What did you say?"

"Someone just spoke with me, but no one's there." He waved his arms in empty air.

"Oh, I'm here," Quil said, becoming visible, "and needing answers. All of you grab a seat. That includes you, human." Not arguing now, they hurried to take chairs.

"Officer, you be the spokesman. I'm looking for someone who most probably appears human, possibly a politician or of the military. What can you tell me?"

"Listen, I'm just a flunky with no authority. The other officer is the lead representative for humans, not me. I just stay out of the way. I don't even know why I'm here."

"Calm down. You say there's another soldier that's from Earth. Tell me about him. What does he look like?"

"Him? He's uh, well, he's top brass, wears more braid and fancy medal than I've seen on anyone. Air force uniform, honors down his chest on both sides, most I don't recognize."

"What about his face?"

"A beard and mustache cut close. Large aviation glasses hide most of his face. Never takes them off. He wears a peaked cap that's the tallest I've seen covered with gold braid and an unknown insignia."

That described Nefar-ex, a narcist who would present himself in gilt and dazzling ornaments. "Do you know his whereabouts?" The soldier shook his head.

"What about the rest of you? Do you know where he is?"

Assemble members talked among themselves in hushed tones while pointing fingers at each other, a typical response of cowards. Allowing them time, Quil walked the walls filled with charts of planets and scientific data. Hearing someone clear a throat, she turned, seeing a raised hand.

"Go ahead. Speak."

"I don't know where he's gone, but he spent most of his time in the tower room at the top of the spire. We need to leave. Can you help us?"

"What? Have you suddenly lost interest in toying with the human species? You're a bit late with that decision, as you've failed miserably as guardians. Most sub-standard. But, yes, I can help you leave." The group seemed to relax, appearing relieved. Or was that smugness?

"I don't know a great deal about the different species represented here, but it seems the one thing you all have in common is the need for some measure of oxygen to survive." A sky port flew open above the council chamber. "Get off this moon!" Like projectiles, they shot out of the opening, clutching at throats. The portal slammed shut.

"Tower room, it is." The place resembled a lighthouse complete with a signal beacon and an impressive telescopic apparatus that clearly allowed the viewing of distant objects She peered through the eyepiece, curious to see on what it focused. "Interesting." A sudden shadow moved across the lens. Arriving spaceships. She returned to the Assembly chamber to await the Citizen force.

"Kin's coming," she said as gray mist filled the chamber. "Myka. Good to see you, brother. You're just in time to greet the envoys from Earth. I've only now obtained the first real lead to Nefar's whereabouts. I leave immediately."

"Wait a few minutes, A'albé," said the large, muscular warrior. "At least until introductions are made. Our appearance at times requires an explanation."

He spoke the truth. Myka, a commander with the Shield, was a mighty beast of a man and a ferocious fighter, as were the others with him, but their look was off-putting to most.

Myka had called her by her Crystalline name, A'albé, a name she'd hadn't heard in a long time. It was good to be with other Crystalline again. "I'll stay, but not long." While waiting, she studied a planetary chart she'd noticed earlier. Heating footsteps, loud and hurried, she stepped into the heavy mist.

Prex entered, hesitating only briefly when Myka stepped from the haze. "I'm Commander Prex with the Federation Guard, protector of Provenance worlds and presently assigned to Earth."

"Commander Prex. I'm Myka, a Prime of the Crystal Shield. We've come to offer our assistance in your battle against the POX—if you need our assistance, that is." Prex seemed openly pleased, however the Procyon and Carian with him appeared hesitant to walk among the colossus-sized warriors in strange helmets and breastplates, carrying unrecognized weaponry.

"We're honored you join us, Prime, very honored. But first, a question. On entry, I noticed cadavers floating around the Assemble center. Are you responsible?"

"Done before our arrival, a Prime of the Sachmet responsible."

"A Sachmet Prime?" Prex looked around the room. A'albé went invisible, thinking it best to avoid further delay.

"Come, Commander Prex, we must prepare for war," said Myka. "I wish to meet the members of your contingent."

With a swipe of his hand, Myka cleared a table and offered a chair to the Prioress. He was an intimidating titan but a diplomatic one. A'albé turned to slip quietly away, but her attention was drawn to long shadows of Prex and Myka cast on a far wall. Prex's wings were moving ever so slightly while Myka's hulking form appeared to tower over him. *The eagle and the bear!*

"Myka! Beware serpents beneath the eagle's wings." Myka pivoted toward Prex and nodded his understanding after only a second, needing no further explanation of the boding. However, Prex took several steps in her direction, seeming to look directly into her eyes. Unsure, she met his gaze. *He is looking into my eyes! He sees me!* Startled, no other had shown an ability to see her when invisible. *I cannot allow time for this, not now.*

Without a look back, she vaulted into the vastness of space, horizonless, extending without end. Or so it thought. Yet, as with all things, the great cosmic sea was bounded, its waves lapping the shores of the far reach. This was her realm, and she knew it like the palm of her hand. Moving freely, her objective appeared straight ahead. She began a carefully considered descent.

forty

Ceres, a child planet, had formed in the outer zone of the galaxy. But long ago, when Jupiter was beckoned by the Sun to clear debris from the inner system, the mighty planet pulled Ceres and other chunks of rock along with it. Upon completion of upkeep duties, Jupiter returned to the outer ward. Ceres, though, chose to stay closer in.

An oddity, the small rock was an ocean world, a frozen mantle above its hidden sea. And there was but one mountain on its entire surface, a fifteen thousand foot cryovolcano formed from spewing water and mud rather than fiery lava. Caught between the pull of Jupiter and Mars, Ceres was now just another floater in the asteroid belt.

A'albé touched down on the pockmarked surface. Extreme quiet caused uneasiness. The illumination was weak, much like that from low-watt bulbs, due to the play of light and shadow through ever-mowing asteroids. The landscape, too, appeared tired, a concrete-hued surface with patches of shimmering material. She picked up a handful; it felt grainy like Epson Salt. She tossed it down.

She was an intruder in this quiet land, but she wasn't the first to invade its silence. She knew Nefar was here; her skin prickled, vibrating from his presence. Narrowing her eyes, she scanned the ice fields, dull, dirty, revealing anything that would be alien to its surface. *Now, where would I stand to watch the show? The grand finale of the master magician who connived the destruction of Tiamat.* A nonsense question, of course, he'd be high on a pinnacle with a swelled chest full of medals and ribbons. No doubt, he wished for a looking glass, so he could watch himself as he pulled off his second masterful sleight of hand against the Universe.

304

The volcano. Would Nefar be so taken with himself that he wouldn't notice her approach? Perhaps, but she couldn't take chances now that she had him within reach.

There! He paraded in front of a spiny wall of jagged rock, a devil's backbone. How best to approach him, announced or silent? Still wearing the sham uniform boasting a medallioned chest, he acted the part of a supreme conqueror. His gaze on the vast Milky Way, he followed the shimmering arc of stars. But what's that? Something else shimmered, a crystal force field surrounding his platform. *Clever.*

"Soon, all of this will be mine!" Nefar's shout thundered through the silence. "No longer forced to mingle with the absurdity of humanity or be caught in the undertow of senseless officialdom from pompous espousers of justice. The universe doesn't need them—it needs strength and power. Me—my universe needs me! And I'm ready. The first to be destroyed after that easily forgotten garden will be the land of mist, the Crystal Sphere."

Stomping a foot, he disturbed the thin layer of salt, exposing an ice sheet, gleaming like pale green glass. "Why are they dallying? Stupid, uninspired reptoids! Speed it up so I can glory in the blaze when it goes up in flames. This time, Tiamat will be crushed under my boots completely!"

A'albé made her decision. He was a gibbering lunatic. No time to attempt reasoning; he'd never fall for that ploy. She had to go in silent and fast —but as a realist. Nefar was a magician of some force, and he might best her in a strict battle of magic. Better it be a mental battle, discern his weak spot, dig into his psyche. What would make him vulnerable? She'd need only seconds to do what she'd come to do.

Surveying his station, he had the advantage of high ground, but behind him, she'd be at an equal level. Carefully keeping concealment between them, she moved toward the back of the spiny ridge, seeking a bastion. A rocky outcropping, bearing a keyhole opening, allowed a view of his base. *But what are those?* Kicking his foot again, Nefar sent out a salt spray that outlined small disks. Warning buttons?

"Time for a test run," he bellowed. "Mars, let's see you dance when I pull your strings." A flash rose from the red planet. Nefar's loud cheers erupted in the gloomed light.

"Perfect! It'll work this time. A flawless plan designed with curbed circuitry, meticulously calculated eruptions will rip Earth and Mars asunder."

Now! Hurrying around the outcropping, her foot bumped a warning device—not a warning device! The bolt hit her head, throwing her into another button mine. A second powerful blow struck her leg. Going down hard, she acted on instinct and rolled to cover. But Nefar knew she was there.

"A'albé! You again! *Button, button, who's got the button.* I'm prepared for you this time. No sneak attacks from the rear. And did I hear breaking glass? Are you injured? Good! You caught me the last time we tangled, but this time, I have you. Come, sister, watch the destruction of your precious garden. I want to see your face as all you've worked for crumbles to dust. *Come out, come out, wherever you are.*"

Now he's singing ditties. His mind was totally offline. Dragging the injured leg, she made it back to the rock shelter and examined the damage. *Stupid, clumsy move!* The pain was paralyzing. It needed tending. Seeing the silk thread on her finger, she cast a sheathing spell. *Bind my leg delicate ribbon, wrap it tight to ease the pain.* While the silk worked, she felt her face. The oversized cheek protectors of the helmet saved her head. It was hurting but intact, and Nefar was still screaming.

"Where are you, A'albé? Or is it Quilty? Quilty— such an appropriate name for a silly goose of a poser. What a degrading mask. An ignorant hick, drawing attention to yourself rather than away. You must be the laughing stock of the Shield. An embarrassing show of inferiority from one who claims to be one of the Shield's finest. "

"Me, a weak, inferior poser. What of you, Nefar?" A'albé cast her voice from above, watching as Nefar swiveled, attempting to detect her presence. "You're nothing but a flawed character in a third-rate play; a pseudo-commander dressed out in gild and gaud, impressing no one but yourself." *Time, I need a little more time. The wound dressing was almost complete.* "Ned reached out to help you, accepted you as a friend, a brother—"

"Ned—a pawn! Humans are empty vessels. You can fill their heads with any nonsense, tell them anything, and they believe it."

Keep talking, braggart. She needed time. Maybe, just maybe …. Remembering a Chinese magician's trick, she snapped off a piece of the silken thread and halved it. It might work if she was fast enough. Working another spell, Seri's throwing blades rose from her boots, a silken line attaching to the handle of each. She cautiously positioned at the keyhole. *And I think I know what just might be the key for this to work.* Nefar was sinking deeper into madness. His face flaming, he ground his boots into the ice.

"You think me a pseudo-commander? I'll show you I'm not a hoaxer. Watch as your miserable, worm-ridden garden quakes under my power. Are you paying attention, A'albé?"

The talisman trembled over her heart. Shifting her position, she watched a red blaze struck Earth.

Now!

"Cedric, help me, please," cried Seribeth, or an image of Seribeth. Pleading before Nefar, she fell to her knees, reaching out for him. Beautiful Seribeth, the one person who had captured Cedric's affection.

"Seribeth!" Nefar stepped from his protected base, his force field falling away. Instantly, Seri's blades flew—stabbing his eyes, jerking them from their sockets. Retracting, the lines returned to where the card boxes floated with lids open. The eyes slammed into the boxes, the lids snapping shut, and returned to her pockets. *Blinded! Now's the time! Penetrating Nefar's mind, she quickly snatching his thoughts.*

Pushed beyond all reason, Nefar hurled flaming sabers, creating fire trenches, zigzagging away from his base. Resenting the fiery assault, Ceres sent water plumes shooting skyward, geysers from her hidden sea. The small world rapidly turned into an ocean of angry, boiling mud. Limping from concealment, A'albé leaned against a rock for balance and hit him with everything ounce of strength she had.

Lightning bolts struck him broadside as a firestorm raged from her hands, ripping at his shell, shattering crystal. So quickly he fell, only shards in puddles of boiling water. His crazed form, like his crazed mind, sifted down as ground glass. A'albé hobbled around his remains, viewing what could have been a Crystalline held in high esteem. But his scheming mind and irrational pursuit of power gained him only defeat and dishonor.

"I've tired of these engagements with you, Nefar. Let's see if the Heraldry can find a more permanent place to hold you this go-around." She cast a gossamer web over his residue with the silk thread and pulled the cord tight, confining him in a taut prison.

"Shield warriors, seize my thoughts now!" she commanded. "Nefar-ex has planted prismatic collectors on Earth and Mars. Removed them now!" Transmitting the coordinates she'd stolen from his mind, she watched pinpoints of light charging across the heavens, descending to each planet, then reversing, shearing away in all directions. And through the steam, brother Myka appeared with another figure, Rafe, a healer.

"How badly are you damaged, A'albé?" asked Myka.

"Not bad, and you both should be in battle. I can mend myself."

"Stand still so I can assess the damage," said Rafe. "Remove the wrapping, sister."

"What about the garden?" she asked as Rafe place a stone, yellow in color, on the worst damage. The stone immediately fragmented into nanobots, spreading soothing ointment.

"The war is underway. The combined POX force is the largest we've battled. We fight until we win, you know that, but we make no promise to save worlds. What do you intend to do with Nefar?"

"Me? It's up to the Heraldry to assign his punishment."

"They're in combat to help save the twelfth garden, at your bidding as I recall, and Nefar needs containing now. You're injured and unfit to fight. The responsibility for imprisoning him falls to you."

"I don't want …. Well, *pfft*. Where do I put him is the question?"

"You can choose to keep him with you. That way, you could keep an eye on him for all eternity."

"No! I won't take three steps and drag Nefar the balance of my existence."

"Well, until you decide what to do with him, it's three steps and drag, three steps and drag." Myka and Rafe disappeared into the mist.

Tying together the ends of the silk cords, she slung Nefar over her shoulder and rose above Ceres. The space around Mars was black; enemy ships, moving like a herd of tarantulas, covered it completely. Earth was now the center of battle. The bruised sky surrounding the once beautiful blue gem was a mix of red, yellow, and black as weapons battered away. Lacerated beyond recognition, blood-red, septic streaks spread to the moon and back again. They had not prevented the attack on the garden. Turning away from the disheartening sight, she heard the last grain of sand fall through the hourglass.

"What have you allowed into our existence, Nefar?" A'albé had returned him to his prior place of exile, a parallel universe. There was no missing the rent in the cosmic bubble; the flow of the sea was carrying her straight to it. Each swell of waves sloshed over the precipice. Through the gulf, she saw the other universe stripped of color and sloughing away like bark off a dead tree. The rift had destroyed the tubular portal between the two worlds, and from all appearance, the parallel world would soon be as nothing. A second banishment there would not be possible.

Clutching a side of the rent, she peered over the edge, noticing a narrow slit between the two universes. *Could I slide Nefar between the two realms?* What's down there that he could harm if, by chance, he puts himself back together? But she still had his eyes. That alone might curb his greed. What he can't see, he can't covet. In a roundabout way, she will have cured his hunger for power. One could even say she had done him a favor. *And that is a pile of dung.*

As she hoisted Nefar over her head, she wondered if there were appropriate words she should say in assigning punishment. The Heraldry certainly would do so. But she had said all she wanted to say to him and silently watched as he slipped into darkness.

Backstroking, she considered options for mending the tear. She could think of only one thing to do. Gathering handfuls of ether along the sides of the rip, she meshed it together and sent silver needles, threaded with fine, delicate silk, around the edges. Tugging and stitching, finally, she felt the surge of the sea washing around her rather than rushing toward the edge. The repair seemed to hold. She back away to survey the work.

"Puckered. I was never fond of needlework. Now, to the eyes now. One in the coldest of ice; one in the hottest of flame." That done, she dusted her hands together and turned toward the Milky Way.

As she neared the glowing dust and gases of the Orion Nebula, a sudden shudder … no, not a shudder … a pulsating force moved through her unlike anything felt before. A glint of red flashed on the right, then the left. She turned a circle, twice. Something was close, too close, and it felt deadly.

"*Jack and Jill* went up the hill to fetch a pail of water, but Jack fell down and broke his crown, and Jill pushed him over the edge of the deep, dark well filled with fearsome beasts with gnashing teeth. Now, the ravenous quiddities gnaw the bones of Nefar, your poor blind brother. Sad, so sad, Quilty."

"Who are you?" The rasping voice sounded strained, a rattle in its throat like it labored to draw breath.

"*Mary, Mary, quite contrary,* how does your garden grow? With silver bells and cockle shells and pretty maids all in a row. And pretty maids they were too, the flower children you savagely slew. My, my, Quilty, girl. How could you slaughter helpless babes as they lay in their cribs?”

“No, that’s not how it was!” she yelled. “There was good reason!” She couldn’t locate the voice. The vibration, getting stronger, seemed to dither within her, pulling at her strength. She struggled to follow the sound of the voice, turning, turning.

“*The itsy-bitsy spiders* ran up the water spout. Down came the rain and washed the spiders out. But the itsy spiders didn’t make it out, did they, Quil? You lead them into the cavernous spout where they suffered badly because of your need for glory. How easily you shrugged off the killing and maiming of your sisters. Pity, pity.”

“That’s enough, doubt caster! Taunts, only taunt! I’m leaving.” But she wasn’t. She was caught up in a quivering web!

“*Jack be nimble, Jack be quick,* Jack jumped over the candlestick. But poor Jack stumbled and fell into the deadly flames. Gone, gone he is, so perfect in form and manner—”

“No! Shut up!” Slicing at the web with fiery bolts from her hand, she wriggled further into the nebula’s thick dust and away from the gasping voice. *Don’t listen to him! It’s lies. Don’t listen.*

“Ah, protectress of genesis worlds, you cannot hide. Nefar led me to you, and now you belong to me. You’re the one to uncover the secret I need.”

“Secret? Genesis worlds?” moving further into the nebula’s swampy film, hoping she was concealed. “Tell me, *Genius Malignus*, or whoever you are, why is knowledge of creation so important to you? Do you suffer a lack of male fecundity, or is it more than that? I hate to be the bearer of bad news, but I don’t know the secret of creating an inner essence. Now that you’re clear on that, I’m leaving.”

“*NOOO!*” Something held her. Sea snakes slithered around her arms and legs, slapping at her face.

The devour beast! Shooting up like a bullet, she sent flaming projectiles without direction. She broke free but saw the bloated beast coming at her again; its mouth of needled fangs dripped slime as tentacled eyeballs swung wildly.

Uhhh! No! Magnetic pulses hit again, paralyzing her limbs as deafening wails assaulted her brain. Fatigue was draining her of strength. She shook her head, but the thundering booms jackhammered through her brain. *It's taking me over.*

"LEAVE ME!*"* Unleashing waves of brimstone, the beast retreated, vaulting over waves, its burning eyeballs popping like glass bulbs. She hit it again, driving it further away. Hissing, the demon beast plunged into the waves, becoming one with the sea. *I can't see it! Is it coming back!*

"You cannot hide, and you cannot run from me," came a hoarse whisper. "I release you now, but I'll be back, protectress of genesis worlds. I'll be back for you." The voice grew fainter, fading away.

"Why not now!" she screamed. "I'm not running! Let's get this done and over!" Of a sudden, there was a yank on the back of her armor.

"Now is not the time to swagger," said Myka. "Curb your brashness, A'albé."

"Myka! Announce yourself next time. The beast—you saw it?"

"We saw the beast and its cloaked master in the scarlet robe. We also felt a powerful pulsing. What do you know them to be?"

"What I know is near nothing. The master is called *Genius Malignus*, meaning evil demon or dark god. He uses magnetic pulses to drain his victims of strength and takes their life force."

"A fatigue attack weapon?"

"Yes, and he searches for one who can give him the ability to create souls. Why that is, I don't know. I believe they emerged from a dead universe."

"How would you know that?"

"I saw it through a rip in our fabric. It had to be dead. I sensed no particle waves moving through its sea, heard no music from its planetary spheres, felt no warmth from its stars. And its outer cloth was shedding away."

"An unknown killing force? Perhaps the winged holy woman will have heard of it. But you cannot travel alone now. He made it clear he's after you."

"His tentacled beast ran from me. I'm not afraid to travel alone."

"I'm sure you'll agree, Prime, the priority is to rid the universe of these demons. We did see the beast run, but it eluded us, and we know too little of its cloaked master." He paused, placing a hand on his chin as in deep thought. "But perhaps, you could be the lure drawing them into a trap."

"I can't believe that statement came from you, Myka. Don't you think the demon would figure out such an obvious ploy; me dawdling along with a troop of you nearby would not be difficult to see through."

"Not if the one you traveled with someone appearing physically in need of your protective care. You would be seen as easy prey. And as you are aware, we can appear in an instant and put an end to the pair."

He must mean the Prioress with the one eye, but she already travels with protectors. But it might draw *Malignus* in just close long to allow trapping.

"I'll consider that, Myka, but tell me. The twelfth garden? Did I survive?"

"The rock is still with us. You'll have to assess its needs. It bears scars of war."

"But it's still with us. And what of …."

"The Guard Commander?" Myka looked away as he spoke, his voice solemn. "He was an able fighter."

Jack be nimble fell into the deadly flames. Like a stone dropped in a deep well, she pitched over a jagged edge and slammed into brutal emptiness. *Gone? No, he couldn't be. I read the sign. I gave the warning. Fate, why would you take him?* "I need away from here." She turned toward Earth. "The garden must be seen to. Tares grow in an untended garden. They must be culled quickly, or the garden could be overwhelmed."

forty-one

The fresh evening breeze had a dusky softness about it, night velvet on the skin. The sun was setting, and ahead were towering mesas, turrets guarding against danger creeping in from the outland. She watched the fading light. Some say the sun travels away from us, allowing sleep in the night's quiet. But the light remains constant. It's the tumbling of the rock on which we stand that brings the dark. The light is always there; it will come back.

She traveled alone here, although comrades could have been close by. Not wanting others around, she didn't look for them. The inner system between Mars and Earth now bore a metal beltway, skeletal remains of warships. The butchering rampage of the POX ended at the gates of the blue-haloed Earth. The moon spread its pearly glow over expanded seas, the poles having lost much of their chill. If there were survivors, they would never know the world of their forebearers, the cities and monuments of humankind in ruin.

Dawn would come soon, and what remained then could be seen. She walked without direction. With the folding of the night coverlet, the day would bring with it work. She needed work. Aunt Rho once said that ants stay endlessly busy, never stopping their work, and some people try to avoid pain in that way. She intended to work; pain would not pierce her concentration.

A light breeze ruffled her hair as her nose detected a familiar scent. Following it, she knelt, digging at bare stubs of branches. She knew that fragrance, desert sage. A shoot flexed between her fingers, and she allowed a smile, the first since arriving.

She moved to high country, seeing tall pine trees bowed as if having stooped shoulders. It reminded her of the

Tunguska forests felled by air bursts of a passing comet. The ground was covered in brambles, smashed as if run over by a giant brayer. "The wild rose grows from brambles."

Brushing aside piles of chaff, she wanted to see greenery of any kind. With dawn, patches of green did appear in ravines and hollows. She breathed easier and walked, following the ticking call of a bird flying nearby. A common Dark-eyed Junco owl landed, hopping and running as it foraged for food. The black head feathers were distinctive, highlighting its bright yellow eyes.

"He's a handsome fellow, isn't he?"

Turning, she saw the Prioress standing nearby. "Very handsome. He reminds me of some I knew from a not-to-distant time." They embrace, as old friend do.

"Come, Huntress, there are people you need to see." Falling in step beside the Prioress, they make our way to a low valley "Don't be concerned about your appearance. Crystalline walk among us again, here on Earth, the new Tiamat. You're just in time for a congress. People of many lands have gathered to make plans for a future."

There were people. People of different countries on Earth and immigrants from faraway planets, varying in shade and physical form. Gathered at the place formerly known as the Compound, they moved freely among each other.

"Allow me to be your guide," said the Prioress. "The clusters you see have unique talents and work in focus groups to define needs. Less than a quarter of a percent of those on the planet survived, but those remaining understand the need for cooperative effort for this world to live again."

"Earth's caretakers got a do-over," said A'albé, thinking of Seribeth.

"The underground thoroughfare opened up great opportunities," continued the Prioress. "Cities are being erected underground or under glass domes using remnants of disabled warcraft. The underground affords protection of people while allowing reclamation of the planet."

"Both in need of mending and ..." She paused, looking around, thinking she'd felt a soft breath tickling her neck. But she saw nothing close. The Prioress looked at her with a questioning eye.

"I'm sorry for the loss of Prex. Myka said he fought bravely, taking on an entire regiment alone." Caught off guard by the mention of his name, A'albé looked away.

"I'm to tell you that Albert expects a visit. We sometimes show up at the same places. Huntress, I give words of caution now. Seek truth from the great cosmos. I've looked a great distance, and some may not be as they make out to be. It will test your perceptive skill." Puzzling over her words, A'albé wondered where they could be leading.

"The people know it was you who discovered the placement of the explosives meant to destroy the planet. They're grateful. Too, the Sachmet forces are the ones who determined the means of stopping the POX armada. Well placed blows by spirit warriors ignited the enemy's weapon magazines, causing them to explode. Maneuvering as closely as they did, blasts from within the enemy's ships brought them down.

"A cascading result. The warriors of the Crystal Sphere are without equal. I'm not surprised at their success."

Suddenly, they heard key tapping and a long drawn-out sigh. "I smell a faint odor of brimstone."

"Drub, what are you doing here?"

"I need information to finish up this record. Thus far, I have you throwing brimstone bolts at the dark Crystalline, turning him into lightning stones, blinding him, binding him in a woven bag, followed by ... what? Did you cast him into the River Styx, feed him to a three-headed dog, or what?"

"Prioress, this is Drub, a chief records clerk with the Bureau." Drub nodded at the Prioress while her fingers continued to move on keys. "For the record, I blinded him with flying daggers, no lightning stones, and performed only the usual shattering. I tossed him into alien space, and watched him fall."

"So the disgraced was flung into the bottomless pit of anguish, the dreaded deep of the never-ending vacuum of rejection. Do me a favor, A'albé, and vary your routine occasionally. Your existence seems boring." The tapping continued as she vanished, quickly appearing at the elbow of another Crystalline.

"Drub, an interesting moniker," said the Prioress.

"Yes, I mistakenly called her that long ago, and it stuck. *Drub* being the superlative of *drab*, you see. Though superlative is the highest point of quality, and she's unequaled at her job. But I would like to see her take a break from that infernal data entry."

"Perhaps I could invite her out for coffee and doughnuts? I'd like to ask her questions about the ancient eras." The Prioress jumped backward as Drub suddenly reappeared.

"We're given limited time for snacking, eating, that sort of thing, as we're not to be seen as frittering away our time. And absolutely no submitting of unnecessary filler into the records. The employee's union has made some gains in that regard, but still, no frittering. I can address your questions, Prioress, but do have them neat and in priority order, as I'm swamped."

"Oh, I see. Well, I'll take a sip of water before we talk, and my list will be pristine upon contacting you." Drub vanished again, but her exit was followed by the appearance of a heavy gray mist. Stepping from it was Myka, laughing.

"I see you met Drub. She has a good heart but she can become tiresome. Would you permit me time, Prioress?" He bowed gallantly before taking her arm. They walked away; A'albé figured it was to talk over the undercover assignment with her being a lure.

"Was that a—a rattle?" flinching when the feather-hooded healing witch appeared. Seeing her in a defensive stance, the witch laughed and shook her rattle again.

"This watch you paid me with isn't working properly. I'm returning it."

"It was working perfectly when I gave it to you."

"It isn't now. Its tick is too loud, reminding me of a second conscience, always making me feel I have emergencies to deal with. I've tried to stop the ticking but can't, and one conscience is enough to have to deal with." She dropped the watch in A'albé's tunic pocket.

"It shouldn't be ticking at all, and I have nothing else to give you."

"Nothing's need. I'm glad to be breathing air right now. That's plenty." Shaking her rattle, she wandered into the crowd. Seeing Inger and Tilde, A'albé ran to greet them.

"Fine work detecting the means to destroy the enemy fleet."

"They undid themselves," said Tilde. "Overconfident because of their numbers, they failed to attend to internal protection. Some turned tail and ran. The Procyon troops are pursuing the runners. What of Nefar? Is he truly gone now?"

"Only time will tell. I did steal his eyes and hid them in different places."

"What about the mysterious Crimson Robe?" asked Inger.

"The *Genius Malignus.* He's a boojum and is stalking me. He'll have to be dealt with."

"A boojum! Then stay alert front, back, and in between. A devious boojum can appear in any form and can make a person disappear in the blink of an eyelid."

"And give a jingle if you need us," said Tilde. "We're staying here awhile to help with the master planning."

"Good move. I'm not staying long. I have the other gardens to inspect, but I'm seeing Albert before I go."

Wandered the desert skies, she spotted a stooped man digging with a staff. "That can only be Albert," she said as she landed, transitioning to human form.

"Quil! You're just in time to help with the planting."

"Sure, I can make time for that. What are we planting?"

"Peyote."

She checked his expression to see if he was teasing. He wasn't. "Of all the things to save in a devastating catastrophe, why peyote?"

"How else am I to enter your dreams, granddaughter?" He ducked his head, but Quil saw the grin.

"You're working me, old man, but tell me what you need me to do."

"Find yourself a broken branch to use as a stob, dig a hole, and plant the seed. It's not a hard thing to do," handing her a dried peyote button. She dug a hole and tossed it in.

"Not the whole bud. The seeds are inside. You dig the holes. I'll plant the seed. Four inches deep. Work the soil so it's loose."

"I'm a gardener, Albert. I know how to prepare soil for seed." She worked ahead of him until he called a halt. At least it was arid here. Not a great chance of rain. No rain, no peyote cactus. "I'm returning the turquoise amulet to you, grandfather. The dark watcher who stalked me is gone now."

"Keep the talisman. You constantly walk in shadowed lands. It might be of help one day. You need to see the new rock art on the mesa wall. I helped with the etching, along with the bird lady. But before you go, I had a vision water was under that boulder up yonder. I want you to move it about two inches that way."

Walking to the boulder, Quil laughed. "A vision. Are you sure it wasn't tracks of animals digging here, trying to bring water to the surface, that called your attention to it?"

"Can you move the rock or not?"

"I'll try." She nudged the boulder aside, seeing water seeped from around its the edges.

"Another inch."

She gave it another shove, and a steady stream of water gushed downhill. Albert whooped, quickly channeling water to his peyote garden.

Chucking, Quil gazed at the elderly gentleman working his plot of earth. Beyond him, a flock of sheep fed on hay bales. The Dorper ewes had lambs at their sides. The seed falling from the bales would start grassy fields for them to feed on. As it should be. She felt at ease."

"Evil is after you, granddaughter," called Albert. "Be wary of those hiding behind masks. Keep your protections close. It won't be easy."

The *at ease* feeling crumbled to dust at her feet. Thrusting her chin up, she glowered into the deepness of the sky. "I know you hunt me, evil demon. Even here, I feel your foulness brushing against my space, but I'm readying for our next meeting. You may have enjoyed toying with the unimpressive being you perceive me to be, but no matter. For a day of reckoning is coming, and on that day, I will bring you down!"

"Don't forget the mesa," called Albert, pointing toward the bluff behind her.

Quil studied the first wall of people dancing with star beings, moved on to the battle scene, and on to what before was a blank wall that now showed people dancing again. No longer stick people, humans had gained form. Too, she was glad to see they were not running or hiding.

"I wonder if humans have seen enough of war to work for a peaceful existence?" She walked to a bare wall ahead, a blank slate. "Whether they dance together or self-destruct together, the future is for them to write."

Noticing a small drawing tucked in a protected corner, she climbed up to see what it was. A woman stood with a small dog at her feet and a black-winged figure beside her. The catch in her throat came suddenly. Reaching out to touch the image, she suddenly withdrew her hand, fearing she'd cause it to be erased.

"Will you sit with me?"

Did I imagine his voice? She turned, and he was there, sitting on a boulder, one wing hanging at an odd angle. "Are you dead, and I'm dreaming?"

"Neither."

"Feel free to expound on that." Climbing down, she strolled around him.

"I believe you have the ability to project images of yourself. Can you do that at some distance?"

"Yes, I can cast a muddle of myself. Are you a muddle?"

"Not presently."

"Again, elaboration would be helpful."

"I could go into greater detail, but time is flitting by, and others will be here soon. Thus, if you have a question or two, now would be the time."

"I find it curious how often the passing of time enters into conversation these days." Continuing to study his form, she considered his eyes, the timbre of his voice, the trilling of his '*r*'s'.

"Are you truly undergoing repair, Guard Commander, and chose to recoup in the desert, a place of your least liking? Also, I should think Jessie could help with your incapacitation."

"Anyone thinking I'm incapacitated would be making a fatal mistake." He cast her a sly side glance with a cocked brow. "You're testing me. I thought we'd progressed beyond that."

"Maybe I was, but your objection smacks of avoidance. Do you know of the Killdeer bird that feigns a broken wing to distract interlopers away from what it's protecting? That came to mind on seeing you with an injured wing. By the way, have you talked to Myka lately?"

"An intriguing comparison, but I haven't seen Myka since … It's true I'm undergoing repair, but I've not come to the desert to recuperate. I've come for you. I'm involved in an investigation and believe your skills in discerning patterns would be useful. However, there is the possibility of danger involved. That's little information, I know. Still, I'm hoping you'll *choose* to join me."

"I don't see that being possible. My current assignment demands my full attention. I'm circuit rider of the twelve gardens, responsible for ensuring their stability."

"Granted, that's an important post; however, I believe the one I spoke of is more so. I would go so far as to say your presence is essential."

"I'm fascinated. Exactly what would the assignment entail?"

"You'll accompany me in an omni-dynamical, dimension-faring ship that offers comfort and the very latest scientific and technological equipment. The assignment locations will vary, not only being in this universe."

"H'm, well, you know, that sounds confining, and I don't think I'd like it much. I'm used to open space, you see. And I'm admittedly ignorant of science and technical matters." She droned on, still trying to separate falseness from the truth. "Why, I even failed a cheese-making class because I couldn't get the enzymatic stuff to clot the milk to get it to a cheese wheel stage. That's a long-about way of saying your very latest equipment wouldn't impress me." Prex had calmly waited for the babbling to end.

"Not a problem. The wheels we'll be involved with are already formed, though some have suffered destruction."

"What wheels?"

"The spaces you call universes are called wheels in my dominion. There are many wheels, wheels within wheels, wheels stretching beyond wheels in every direction, all operating gyroscopically, preventing masses from pitching and rolling so as not to collide with each other. The full explanation could become overly technical, therefore I'll stop there. What's important is the wheels contain diverse worlds and communities of dwellers. Unfortunately, there is a sickness— a malignancy—destroying life forms within the wheels and the loss of the wheels themselves. *Malignus* is causing the perturbances that lead to loss of worlds."

"You came here to warn us?"

"Yes and no. Initially, I came to follow up on a lead. I heard Nefar-ex had convinced *Malignus* that the keeper of the genesis worlds here knew the secret of creation."

"Nefar was lying for his own gain. *Malignus* did contend that I possessed that knowledge, but I told him I hold no secret to soul creation—and I don't, so you understand. That being the case, I can't see that I'm needed."

"I do not doubt your veracity, but you are … needed. I haven't time to elaborate now. They're getting closer. I'm in pursuit of *Malignus* and his vehicle mount, a creature that can swiftly travel anywhere. *Malignus* triggers his decaying malady and jumps to another wheel. The closest I've come to him is here, where you are—however, presently, he's not in this universe."

"Now, I get it. Again, I'm the lure. This is getting old. I understand you need a solution to a problem, but I don't want to be the worm tied to the fishing line. That makes me nothing more than a useful idiot—which could help you but doesn't do much for me."

"Exactly. I can't promise there won't be problems as problems forever present themselves. I encountered a major, unanticipated one in coming here." He reached for her; she backed away. "Quilty, the problem is … you turned out to be you."

"I find I often turn out to be me." His words took her by surprise, and she plopped down on a rock—there was no place else to plop. Walking to where she sat, he raised the sleeves of her tunic, gazing at the glistening black feathers encircling her arms.

"I can return those."

Smiling, his hands slowly moved down her arms as he leaned close, gazing into her eyes. "I like where they are. I felt your sorrow when you thought I'd been killed, my lady. Know you need never grieve for me. And it has become quite clear that the way to keep you from harm is for you to be with me." She felt his breath on her ear.

She pushed away; though, in truth, she didn't want to as she wanted in his arms. But the forebodings of highly intuitive seers could not be ignored

"I'm sorry your wheel was destroyed, but I can't abandon my duty."

"My realm is not a wheel. It's more the hub of all wheels. Again, it would take time to explain—"

"The hub? Are you saying—what are you saying?"

"They're here."

And they were. Seribeth and Tres waved as they drove up the trail in an ATV. Myka and the Prioress came from above. Prex wasn't to be seen. She did a thorough look around to be sure, and he was gone.

As for her, she wished she was moss on a rock, simply existing in the cool breeze and mottled light. *What's wrong with just being? I could turn myself green and spread myself over this stone—like mayo spread on a bread slice. I rather like the idea of having nothing expected of me, just sitting on*

*my bread, listening to the watch ticking in my pocket. H'm.
Well, there is that.*

Seri and Tres talked at the same time. "Inger and
Tilde told us about the crimson-robed demon. Stay with us.
We have weapons and underground fortresses now. We'll
fight to protect you, and together we'll slay the monster."
Sincerity was in their eyes. Doubting them not at all, she
treasured them all the more.

"This is larger than one planet, especially a planet that
barely survived utter destruction," said Myka. "The universe
is under threat. Shield warriors are the ones to fight the dark
god and his beast." That, too, was a truth. The spirit warriors
would do all that was necessary, including their very
destruction, if it came to it.

"There is the option," Quil said, "of me proceeding
on my circuit. *Malignus* is no longer in this universe, but if he
should show up, I could signal for help."

"How do you know the demon is not here?" The
Prioress asked.

"Prex told me, just minutes ago." Silence, then
everyone decided she required counseling.

"Quil, you well know I understand how loss can mess
with a person's thinking," said Tres. "People sometimes can't
get to acceptance and see images of those they've lost."

"That's true," said the Prioress. "It's very difficult to
let go sometimes, and Prex was a very special individual."

"Sister, I carried him out of his ship myself. His last
breath was in my arms."

"We'll have a smudging ceremony," added Seri. "The
witch will do one for you."

"No, no! Nothing with the witch needed here." She
laid down on the rock.

"What are you doing, now?" Myka didn't hide his
frustration.

"Reclining on my bread. I need a pondering moment."

Prex re-appeared, sitting beside her, obviously unseen
by the others as if they could see him, they most certainly
would say so.

"Is there some way I can move this along? The clock is ticking."

"I'm considering how best to determine if you're alive or a ghost. I could vigorously attempt damage to your manly jewels—to check your reaction—though, I think that would be considered an overused theatrical act. And it could hurt like the dickens."

"I vote against an overused theatrical act," he chuckled, mostly to himself. *"Are you ready to leave?"*

"Just like that? Aren't you being presumptuous thinking I'd drop everything and sail off with you? And you did say it was up to me."

"IF that is what I said, little goat?"

Sitting in the lotus position, she considered those around her. There would be no gazing ball where answers floated, to tell her what to do next. She'd been handed a fistful of options, diverging paths to deliberate, and others who would stand with her in the fight. She could triangulate this six ways to Sunday and back again always ending up right where she started.

When all was said and done, it would get down to a one-on-one confrontation with the demon. Isn't that the way it always happens? Why should she expect otherwise in this case? And at the end, who truly knew who'd be left to brag? Although it could make for an interesting story to tell in a dimly lit den before glowing embers—or riveting reading on a dark and stormy night. Maybe, just maybe.

"Sachmet Prime, we're waiting," said Myka. "What are you going to do?"

"Yes, that is the question."

Tick, tick, tick, tic—

forty-two

It would be easy to lose oneself under this spellbinding sky. The darkness highlights the great silver river flowing above and brings a calming stillness.

The curious woman telling her story had stopped talking. I had been hired as a ghostwriter to assist in placing her story in print, a tale she said had come to her in a dream. She insisted we meet in this wilderness to experience the high desert, the setting of her saga. Thus, here we were under the blackest sky I'd ever seen with the great rift clearly visible, but I also noted we were well away from the populated world. However, I did find her compelling and listened intently as we walked through the night, sitting to rest in a grove of flowers. Because she had been silent for such a long period, I ventured a question.

"What did Quil do?"

"Oh, that was clear. What do you know of moonflowers?"

"Moonflowers? Nothing. But I didn't catch the ending."

"It wasn't the end. Moonflowers are nocturnal, beautiful creations bringing delicate magic to the night. The fragrance is quite intoxicating. Their magic is even more pronounced when a full moon bathes everything in its glow—such as this night. Strange though, the plant has the power to kill. It's deadly, you see. And when the sun rises, it takes the flower. Another replaces it that blooms the very next evening, and then it's gone too. Odd, isn't it? I liken it to people one meets as they journey. Did you enjoy the characters in my dream?"

"Why, yes, I did. A diverse group, some disturbingly demonic in character, but I did have difficulty accepting that some walk among us as … as what you termed *watchers*. What did you mean it wasn't the end? Will you continue the story tonight or perhaps another time?"

"Why would you not believe there are watchers that walk among us? They can manifest in a number of ways. Some come and go, popping in and out like will-o'-the-wisps, while others temporarily borrow a body of someone for a particular need. And, of course, there are those who take an emergent route, rather like pollywogs in a puddle. First buried in a mud bank as an egg, then morphing into tadpoles paddling around, and after getting legs under them, they leave in a finished state. Watchers mingle with us in everyday life. Never doubt this that I say. Eyes are on you. You're being watched. Everyone is."

"Um, pollywogs? Well, that's a grabber, but to be honest, it's hard to accept."

"When I say moonflowers are like people we meet as we journey, I mean the people who walk beside us seem to continually change. One minute here, the next gone. One replaces another, like these flowers, a stream of changing faces. We can learn much from that stream of faces, wouldn't you agree?"

"Certainly. And I'd like you to know I am interested in writing your story. Would you object if I placed it on paper and shared it with a few others just to garner their response? I can't say how people would receive it. Some would like it, some wouldn't, and some would think me a loony for putting it in print. That last part doesn't bother me—however I admit the persnickety types do annoy me. Persnickety meaning self-appointed critics who seek to find something they can belittle in the first few pages, refuse to read further, and then are generous with their censure. Okay, I was a bit critical there, so I'll rephrase that. I can see your story is important to you, and I wouldn't want you to experience hurt caused by fault-finders not giving it a chance or be disappointed in my telling of it."

"Why would I object to your placing it on paper? You would be the one having to address questions and explain matters, not me. If you have difficulty remembering the order of events, just sleep on it, and your dreams will lead you to the correct remembering. However, I do have a few requests. Strive for a balance between action and contemplation. After all, how can one act wisely without having given some thought to the consequences of an action? And be poetic in some instances—as a touch of embroidery adds a certain charm to a piece—while still inserting appropriate punctuation to emphasize boldness and action where needed. Oh, and please handle my characters respectfully, except for the demons, of course. You can stomp the snot out of them. As for snobbish fault-finders, simply declare them demons, and ..."

"Proceed to stomping. But why would you say I'd be the one responding to questions. Shouldn't it be you addressing those?" Again, there was a lengthy silence. Thinking she wanted time to get her thoughts together, I surveyed the sky, but too much time passed, and, again, I asked the question. But when I turned to look at her, she wasn't to be seen. I walked in circles to be sure she hadn't wandered off and fallen in a ditch, but she was actually missing.

"Well, that's a kick in the shin," I said to no one. "What do I do now?" Sitting back down, I felt it appropriate to wait for her return, my thoughts drifting to her tale. "Logically, I heard nothing that would come close to supporting what she said. Yet, a work of fiction doesn't need logic to support it." I yawned and considered leaving. It was quite a drive back to civilization, but I had charged the electric car I drove just before coming so that shouldn't be a concern.

"I might as well finish the night right here. It's almost dawn, and I can look for her again. I should do at least that much. And by then, I will have decided whether to report her missing, if she is missing. I have no personal information to provide the law, and I doubt she'd want me to do that anyhow." I remained sitting among moonflowers, thinking of how I would pen her story.

"She wants this to be about people, character-driven; I'd need to portray those as crystal clear as possible." I chuckled. "*Crystal* clear, a good one." I had a sudden fit of laughter. "Huh, I think I'm stoned on flower fumes." I walked the outskirts of the patch. "Do I write it or not? I could put it in draft form and see how it reads, and then, who knows."

Dawn came and still no dreamer. I gave up and left the moonflowers behind, noticing the night blossoms had fallen to the ground, and the plant had become jimson weed. Still suffering pangs of guilt for deserting her, I started the car, took one long, last look around, only then noticing something on top of the dash. "What …. a watch? With a yellow … How did …. Oh, my word—that was her!" I quickly scanned out the windows to see if she was around. But she wasn't.

Wondering what to do, I stared at the minute hand spinning round and round for an incredibly long time—two minutes forty-three seconds to be exact.

"That's long enough! Well, I'm off to a great start. A foreshadowing of what's to come, no doubt." I drove away feeling strange, as if things were shifting around in my head, turning heavy notions into those much lighter. Suddenly, a strange calmness settled over me, and words of poet Chuck Bukowski floated through my mind: *The centuries are sprinkled with rare magic with divine creatures ….*

H'm, so true. And so very well stated. Perhaps I can use that in the book."

(Woeful sigh) "Quotation marks should accompany insertion of a line of poetry within a sentence before and after with an appropriate notation as to the person having said it."

"That's okay, Drub. I've got this now."

Lowering the windows, a fresh morning breeze ruffled my hair. I breathed deep, smelling the scent of sage wafting through. It was a glorious day; the sun was bright, the sky wondrously clear. I glanced at the watch ticking on the seat next beside me and laughed. I don't know why; I just felt like it.

"I suppose it could be tricky to write. I'd most certainly need the right approach. An unbelievable storyline, settings, and characters. Toss in magic and moonbeams, dream light, sorcerers, shamans, feys, witches, watchers. What's not to believe? And without a doubt, I'd be judged certifiably insane for penning it."

"*Pfft*—I can live with insane."

"I'm not crazy.
My reality is just different than yours."
The Cheshire Cat

—Lewis Carroll
Alice's Adventures in Wonderland

*The centuries are sprinkled
with rare magic with divine creatures
who help us get past the common
and extraordinary ills that beset us.*

Charles Bukowski
The Pleasures of the Damned

Appreciation

To the people of Native American nations, all indigenous citizens of planet Earth, and our forebears, whoever they may be and from wherever they may hail, I extend my respect and gratitude.

References

Direct quotes are noted in the book. Comments of a general nature may refer to one or more writings either listed herein or known by way of wide-ranging knowledge.

Wroth, W. (ed.) Taylor Museum of Colorado Springs Fine Arts Center *(2000) Ute Indian Arts and Culture From Prehistory to the New Millennium*

Southern Ute Cultural Center and Museum, Ignacio, CO

Stone, J. (2016) Russel Box Sr.; *The Physical and Spiritual Journey of a Southern Ute Elder*

Valdez, Greg. (2013; Dulce Base; The Truth and Evidence From the Case Files of Gabe Valdez

Mezrich, Ben (2016); The 37th Parallel

Wikipedia: *Jicarilla Apache* [Web Page]. [First Accessed 01 January 2017];
URL https://en.wikipedia.org/wiki/Jicarilla_Apache

Wikipedia: *American McGee's Alice* [Web Page]. [First Accessed 29 June 2017];
https://en.wikipedia.org/wiki/American_McGee%27s_Alice#Reference

About Cas Raguel

When not writing, Cas Raguel delves into faded worlds, myths, and paths of spirituality. All contribute to a hybrid approach to writing, interlacing the ancient with the contemporary. The ancient appeals for a reason. When very young, a twice-removed great aunt told Cas she was born old, would know of matters others wouldn't, and, probably, animals would be the only ones that could tolerate her. Interesting betoken, but what did they mean?

Proceeding with life expectations, she obtained a degree in business administration and economics and held administrative posts in human resource and risk management. Still, the idea of being born old tickled her lobes, and the day arrived when she could no longer delay a journey into that which is not easily understood.

She holds a third-class pilot certificate and owned and operated a Piper Cherokee 180. Other interests include exploring ancient ruins, reading, gardening, and art, water media preferred. Seldom without an animal companion, dog or cat and sometimes both, she appreciates their non-judgmental attitude and willingness to traipse along on her journeys. (The third token could be more or less true.)

Cas has traveled much and now lives in the four corners region of the southwest, a land of ancient bones, haunting winds, and secrets waiting to be revealed.

Also by Caj

The 9ᵗʰ vault. The moon blinked off and on, or so it seemed, but that was an illusion. Blankets of rubble winging across its face like squadrons of witches interrupted its glow.

Below, a woman crossed the desert, trying to reach a vault, a sheltering place. Even at a late our, the desert boiled in white-hot fury, but the deviant temperatures weren't limited to this small patch of Earth. The planet was suffering heat exhaustion. For more than 800 years, Cajetanus Bradán had readied to speak the prophecy of ancient texts accepted as truth by The Initiative, a secret order preparing for the coming of a death star. "Men forget the days of the Destroyer. Only the wise know where it went and that it will return in the hour of its next coming. I say that hour is now!"

What were they willing to do to preserve humanity? Government officials, military strategists, and scientists debate whether to believe a 21ˢᵗ-century Druid shaman. "This should not be a matter of science versus supernatural. Both forces regularly occur together," argues a man of science but also one believing in the reality of shadowed realms. "If we act, humanity may survive. If not, this is where humanity will be buried."

A hot-tempered prophetess joins a beleaguered colony in an around-the-clock struggle to live, battling savage hostiles, assaults by natural forces, dark magic, and each other.

Dragons and witches and ghosts! Oh my! You can run, you can hide, but inevitably, the hour comes when you must face your worst fear.

www.ingramcontent.com/pod-product-compliance
Lightning Source LLC
Chambersburg PA
CBHW072203130726
47910CB00011B/1800